MW01077522

I greatly appreciate you taking the time to read my work.
This book was written for you and other runners.
Please consider leaving a review wherever you bought the book
and tell your friends about it, to help me spread the word.
Thank you for supporting my work.

FINISHING
KICK

a novel

PAUL DUFFAU

Finishing Kick

Published 2013 by Cruiser Publications
www.cruiserpublications.com

Cover art by Kit Foster
www.kitfosterdesign.com

Book design copyright © 2013
Cruiser Publications

ISBN 13- 978-0-9889479-1-7

Acknowledgements

A novel may be the creation of one person, but many people help and guide that person.

First, always, is my wife, Donna, who encouraged me to keep working even as I wanted to cower under the bed. For thirty years, Donna has been my biggest fan and greatest joy.

My daughters—Katie, Lyn and Sara—read the early drafts and let me know when I hit the mark-and, more importantly, when I missed.

Several young ladies that I coach volunteered to be beta-readers and shared with sisters. Thank you Maia, Carmen, Maria, Lucy, and Madeline.

A special thanks to Steve Cowdrey, running buddy and relay partner, for spending part of his summer reading and offering suggestions.

Christina MacDonald edited from start to finish with a gentle hand and keen insights, turning my words into a novel.

For all the winners that never had a chance to break the tape . . .

FINISHING
KICK

Chapter 1

As Callie crested the hill, the finish line appeared, lined with colorful flags—and then the line seemed to recede. The illusion shattered when another girl thundered past.

Callie chased her on a gentle downhill slope, three hundred meters of fairway to the finish line of the State Cross-Country Championship. Through eyes hazy with exhaustion and the remnants of a cold, she could see her twin teammates, Anna and Hanna, sprint past the finish marker in a dead tie.

Two hundred meters to go and Callie could hear the gasping breath of another runner closing on her. Five strides later, the girl was beside her. Callie pumped her arms harder, willing her legs to move faster. Legs that could carry her for miles were failing now, with the finish in sight.

Noise flooded both sides of the course and, penetrating over the clamor, someone shouting her name. The cheers of the fans and coaches slid past her as she fought for position.

She saw the red singlet and slashing white diagonal as the last of the Fairchild Academy runners eased by her. Swearing, Callie leaned forward to gain momentum, rising up into a full sprint, her calves already starting to cramp, the pain alternating with each foot strike, each spasm an opportunity to quit, to let the girl go.

Seventy meters and Callie still matched strides with the Fairchild girl.

At fifty meters, another girl caught both of them. She was a tiny runner from a small school up north, and her breath came in sobs.

The three of them closed on the flags at the top of the finishing chute. Callie felt the agony of each breath as it exploded from her lungs, too little air for starving muscles. The blood pounding in her head drowned out the runners beside her, and Callie's vision squeezed down to a small circle focused on the white line that marked the end. She could sense the presence of the runners next to her and drew on their struggling effort, seeking just a small advantage.

The sobbing girl finished one step ahead, the last sob a moan as she collapsed. Instinctively, Callie dodged the fallen runner as she lunged past the line, a half step ahead of the Fairchild runner.

Relief and exhaustion mingled with joy, but a small doubt blossomed.

Was it enough?

"You did okay."

Callie, huddling to avoid the chill, brisk breeze that snaked its way to her still-sweaty skin under the Cloverland High warm-ups, looked over to Mark. The wind had been worse out on the course, but there, movement generated heat. The twins, Anna and Hanna, were shivering under the blanket they were sharing, blond heads touching as they all waited for the results.

"Not good enough," she said, feeling the echo of the final kick, legs heavy with lactic acid overload, girls passing her on the long straightaway to the finish line.

Mark shifted to his other foot. "You don't know that yet." Sweat, bobbing on a curl of hair over his eyes, dripped off. Mark still had not put on sweats after running his own race, exposing his broad shoulders and legs to the wind. An inch over six feet, he towered over the girls on the team.

Callie kept her face impassive, looking toward the microphone stand, waiting to find out whether they had made it or not.

"I mean, with a cold and all . . ." Mark shifted uncomfortably back to his original foot. "You did great." He trailed off as Callie kept her eyes on the awards table. Lined up were the trophies for the top four teams and medals for the top eight finishers.

She was listening, but between the head cold and the gnawing sense she had let down the other girls, his words were just washing over her. Idly, she thought it was nice that he was trying to cheer her up. He was a little on the weird side but a nice guy. Feeling a sneeze coming, she searched her pockets and found a tissue.

There was activity up front and Callie's attention sharpened. She put the used tissue, folded, back into her pocket.

"Finally!" said Anna. They watched the announcer, a slightly overweight man, make his way to the microphone beside the podium. The podium, a broad white stand with a pyramid of steps numbered one to eight, was the goal. Callie and the rest of the team unconsciously closed ranks, pressing up to the rope that separated the crowd from the podium. The top four teams would get to the stand. Cloverland was close, closer than they had ever been.

The official photographer, camera resting at her hip, waited for the teams to be called up to the stand, one at a time, for their brief moment of recognition. Her job was to shoot the picture quickly so that the next team could file onto the stage, everything organized with impersonal precision. The winning team, the champion, was allowed to linger for a few extra moments. It was on the schedule.

"Thank you, athletes and parents, for your participation in the Washington Interscholastic Athletic Association's State Cross-country Meet. The individual results for the Division 1 Girls' Race are as follows . . ." He proceeded to read the names of the top eight finishers, with each runner taking her place on the stand as her name was called.

Jenessa, Callie's teammate, also a junior, had placed eleventh overall, easily the best finish ever for a Cloverland runner. The two seniors on the team were waiting at the rope, staring at the podium, praying for one last chance to stand there, a reward for the years of work they put in.

Two Fairchild runners were among the eight. One was a senior and she stood there on the third-place block. The other, Roxanne, a junior, placed seventh. She and Jenessa had run together for the first two and a half miles before she dusted Jenessa heading into the finish. Callie frowned when she saw Roxanne glaring at Jenessa. *Not a very good winner,* she thought.

They finished with the top runner, who had qualified on her own, then went out and outran the entire field. She was a junior too and had already accepted a spot at the West Regional at the Foot Locker Invitational next month. If she did well there, she'd be racing in San Diego in December. It was a select group, runners who had both the talent and the work ethic to excel. Callie wished she had the talent.

Watching the diminutive runner accept the first-place medal, Callie thought it had to be a lonely feeling, running as an independent, racing without a team. There was a bit of steel in that girl that was missing in most of the runners.

"And now for the team results . . ."

Callie felt light-headed and realized she was holding her breath as the pudgy man ran down through the results. The tension was growing for all of them. The seniors had their arms wrapped around each other's hips.

"In sixth place, with a score of 183, Winston . . ."

"In fifth place, with a score of 102, Cloverland . . ."

The team deflated. Little sighs combined into a collective groan as the girls realized that, once again, they were one step shy of getting onto the podium. Months of hard work had got them to State but it wasn't enough to get them into the top four.

One of the seniors wiped a tear away. There was no "next year" for them.

"In fourth place, with a score of 101, Asotin . . ." The Asotin fans cheered and the team made their way up onto the podium and had their picture taken, and then they were herded off.

One point! Callie thought. *Just one point.* She realized that the place she had given away to the sobbing girl at the end of the race was the difference between a fifth-place ribbon and the seniors standing on the podium.

The third-place team, followed by the second-place finishers, took their places in order but Callie wasn't paying attention anymore. A guilty mantra—*one point . . . one point*—echoed through her mind.

Finally, the winning team, Fairchild Academy, was announced. The Fairchild girls were strong runners and their team had not lost any meet—not even the big invitational in Oregon—in more than three years. It was their fifth consecutive championship.

The Fairchild team took to the podium, laughing as they climbed the steps. They goofed around getting settled while the photographer waited impatiently. As the camera came up, they struck a pose, five fingers of their left hands up, the forefinger of their other hand pointing toward the crowd as they laughed.

There was a murmur from the crowd and Callie felt the flush of anger. She looked to the seniors. They had both stiffened at the implied insult. Jenessa looked grim and even the twins were taken aback. It wasn't just Roxanne—the whole team was a bunch of poor winners.

Mark shook his head slightly. He was standing right next to Callie and he watched her flinch when the results were announced. She was busy blaming herself, he thought, even though she was still getting over a killer cold that had kept her from running for two weeks before the district meet.

Girls, he thought, *are aliens. Guys know that you have to go for it. If you win, you're the hero. If you don't, if you blow up, you're a hero returning on his shield. Winner either way. Girls don't get that . . .*

He watched the misbehavior of the Fairchild team and saw Callie's cheeks flush red, almost as red as the nose she kept wiping. He glanced down at her face, studying it—the auburn hair pulled back in a ponytail and the vivid green eyes—when another random thought bounced around, then out and surprised him: . . . *kind of a cute alien, though.*

Chapter 2

Doc climbed out of the van and stretched as he rounded the front bumper. *Time was*, he thought, *I'd drive double that far for a race, get there with ten minutes to spare, and be on the line ready to win.* A little shake of his head dismissed the memories and loosened up the muscles that had tensed at the back of his neck.

Doc had driven using the rumble strips along the edge of the road as a guide. He had slowed down after accidentally giving Mark a bloody nose and the rest of the team a bad scare. The boy's face had collided with the side window of the van when Doc swerved violently to avoid a big bull elk parked in the middle of the winding road. It was the sort of apocryphal story that received skeptical looks in Seattle but in the rural outreaches just got a nod. That sort of thing happened to everybody here at one time or another, the nods acknowledged.

"Come on, guys, grab your gear. Seniors, take charge—your folks are waiting." He looked around to make sure he hadn't just lied to anybody. About half the kids lived out of town on gravel forest roads that meandered back into Umatilla National Forest. There were times when he would pick up his athletes or drive them home but it looked like today it wouldn't be necessary.

Callie looked up from the fogged window, then began to unwind from the seat. Farther back, Jenessa started to yelp as a calf cramped. The others laughed and Hanna climbed over the bench seat and flopped next to her, reaching over to press her thumbs deep into the knot of muscle, giving it a fast massage.

"Ow, owwww . . . geez, Hanna!" Jenessa cried, but the muscle started to relax.

"Baby," Hanna said, amusement in her eyes.

The seniors began organizing the cleaning party, getting the van spotless inside. Only once had the van been returned dirty. When Doc got the phone call, he told the school secretary it wouldn't happen again—and it hadn't. The hill workout that followed that phone call was legendary.

Doc took a few minutes to talk to the waiting parents, chatting about the race. Soon, he was alone in the parking lot, watching the late fall wind swirl the multihued leaves this way, and then that. The end of the season wasn't official until the team dinner the next Thursday, but, standing alone on the asphalt, he knew the fun part was already done. The team dinner was always the hardest part of his season. He hated saying good-bye to his seniors.

"Hey Callie!" Hanna shouted over the heads of the teenagers milling in the hallway. "We're running before the team dinner. Want to come?"

Callie glanced over her left shoulder from her locker to Anna and Hanna, whose lockers were just down the long row from hers in the noisy hallway. They were both tall—over-tall really for runners, at five foot ten—and slender with almond-shaped blue eyes. Today, like every other day, they were dressed in matching jeans, blouses, shoes, and jackets.

"Nope," she said, turning back to her locker.

"Why not?" asked Hanna.

"We still have nice weather, won't last for much longer," added Anna.

"And besides, it's not like we're going anyplace else because. . ." started Hanna.

". . . we have to set up for the team banquet tonight for Doc," finished Anna.

"I'm still not recovered from the race so I'm taking it easy," said Callie, reflecting again on the fact that talking with the twins was like getting run over by a bulldozer. You could see it coming but there was no good way to get around it.

"Active recovery," Hanna said. "It's good for you."

"Rest," said Callie, "is good for me."

"Oh fiddlesticks!" said Anna. She stared at Callie, and her blue eyes got a little bigger.

"Fiddlesticks?" said Callie, pressing her lips together and desperately fighting back a laugh. She couldn't help it; she started to giggle.

Hanna stared at her sister, dumbfounded, and then she started to giggle, too. She looked past Anna to Callie. "So come on. Run with us." She looked at her sister and asked, "Fiddlesticks? Really?"

"Fiddlesticks is a fine word," protested Anna.

"Sure it is, for a grandma," replied Hanna. Anna was older by twelve minutes. To Callie, she said, "If you change your mind, we're doing an easy out and back on Weissmuller Road."

"That's okay. I'll see you at the banquet. I'll be there to help set up. You guys going home first to change?"

"Yep . . ." said Anna.

". . . or we're going to get a whole table to ourselves," added

Hanna. Together they turned and headed down the hall to their next class. Callie reached into her locker to take out her binder and book for precalculus and thought for the umpteenth time that the twins were just a little *different.*

"Okay, one more," said Callie.

Callie launched the tennis ball high into the cold afternoon air and watched as Sophie, the family's Chesapeake Bay retriever, charged after it, little tufts of turf flinging up from her paws in the damp yard. The ball landed thirty yards away, near the edge of the cleared lot. Sophie snagged the ball high off the bounce and sauntered back, tail wagging, to drop it at Callie's feet so she could fling it again.

"That's it, no more," she told the panting dog, picking the ball up with the Chuckit and walking back to the veranda of the big log home that her family had built. Sophie, blowing little clouds of vapor with each pant, looked up quizzically as if to say *Quitting already?* The Chessie turned to follow Callie inside.

It was weird to be home so early in the afternoon, the natural rhythm of the day upset. Following an arc of motion from chores in the morning, to school, to practice, to home and dinner, to homework, to reading, to bed, Callie always had full days. Now there was a yawning gap between activities and she wasn't quite sure what to do with the extra time. She filled ten minutes of the void by throwing balls for Sophie.

Their house sat in the middle of a cleared lot ringed with lodgepole pines and the occasional Western white pine, its green metal roof and river-rock chimney providing contrast to the logs that blended with the surroundings. A graveled driveway snaked east to the forest road then onto the highway that led to Clarkston and Lewiston, thirty minutes away in good weather. Three thousand feet of elevation made a difference; the weather up in the mountains was infinitely changeable, unlike the valley below, which thrived with the reputation of a "banana belt" nestled in the Pacific Northwest.

She knocked the dirt off her boots as she opened the back door, sliding sideways to let the exuberant dog through first, and walked into the bright kitchen. Callie felt her stomach rumble. Snack time. She got down and poked through the snack cabinet, spying a box of chocolate-chip granola bars in the back. Her mom walked in as Callie was extended halfway into the cabinet.

"What's wrong with the ones in front?" Sarah Reardon asked, addressing the backside of Callie's jeans.

"They have peanut butter," said Callie, backing out of the cabinet and clambering up from the floor.

"Okaaay . . . ?"

"I don't like peanut butter," offered Callie. "Jenifer likes the peanut butter ones," she added helpfully.

"Since when did you not like peanut butter? You used to take a PB and J to school every day," replied her mom as she organized the groceries that she had brought home earlier. A bit below medium height, Callie's mom still looked petite. Callie was slightly taller but the family resemblance was strong, reinforced by the warmth of their eyes.

Callie gave a small shrug and said, "Don't know. Just decided I don't like peanut butter." She ripped open the first granola bar and took a bite. Sophie hovered underneath, waiting for crumbs.

"Not going for a run today?" asked her mom.

"I'm taking some time off. Doc said we should take some recovery time."

"You normally don't listen when Doc tells you to take time off," said Sarah.

Callie shrugged again as she scrounged around in the refrigerator for something to drink. "I just need some time off."

Her mom watched her and a frown showed briefly. "Dinner is at six, right?" she asked, changing subjects.

"Yeah, six o'clock," said Callie.

"Do you have the taco meat cooked up yet?" The team dinner was always a potluck held in the school multipurpose room.

"Not yet," said Callie, heading back to the fridge. "We probably want to bring a couple of pounds. Jenessa's supposed to bring chili."

She plopped a large package of ground beef on the counter next to the stove and started to unwrap it. She glanced at the kitchen clock. She had an hour.

"Seniors first, then juniors, you guys know the drill," announced Doc. As usual, the team banquet, potluck really, was off to a late start as parents dribbled in from work and home, bringing with them the siblings and, sometimes, grandparents.

Callie took her place behind Mark and grabbed a paper plate. She watched as Mark proceeded to overload three shells with meat and cheese and jalapeños. He had a second plate with rice and beans balanced precariously in his other hand.

"That's going to burn," Callie told him, looking over the mound of peppers on top of the cheese.

"Yep," Mark agreed. "Love spicy stuff." He grinned. "These fresh ones are really hot."

Callie thought he was going to regret it, and loaded her own plate with an overstuffed flour tortilla, then added some Spanish rice and beans to go along with some fruit and cornbread. By the time she was done, she needed both hands to keep the plate from folding in the middle. She looked down the table. She'd need a second trip to get a drink and a bowl of chili.

Her mother, along with Jen, settled onto lunch benches next to Callie. The athletes segregated themselves off to one side, and the noise of multiple conversations bounced off the hard walls. Doc waited for everyone to get settled and then started his awards presentation.

"Glad to see everybody here. As you already know, your kids had a really successful season. The girls qualified for State for the first time as a team and, also for the first time, we had two boys at the meet. We're looking forward to the girls getting back next year and, if we can get a few more boys out for the team, hoping to get the whole team there next year."

Callie ate as Doc started with the freshmen. It was her third year, and each year he followed the same pattern. He found positives for every runner, hitting on their triumphs during the year or how well they had handled adversity. As he talked about them, Doc made them stand next to the portable podium with him. It was Nate's turn now, and he was standing, shuffling a bit under the unaccustomed attention.

While the coach talked, Mark surreptitiously took some of the peppers from his burrito and tucked them out of sight into Nate's tortilla. Callie saw the movement and started to say something to Mark but he held a finger to his lips and gave a little grin. Callie shook her head but smiled.

It was time for the twins.

"Anna and Hanna—I still have a hard time telling them apart—are just a joy to coach . . ."

As Doc spoke, he made eye contact with the audience, scanning across the room from one small group to another.

Callie saw his eyes narrow as Doc saw the expression on Mark's face. Just as he was about to continue, Nate erupted into paroxysms of coughing, his face flaming red. Nate reached for his glass but knocked it over in his haste, flinging water all over the table. Mark, trying to look innocent at Nate's sudden discomfort, reacted too slowly. The ice-cold water flooded his lap. He leaped up with a shout, caught his knees between the bench and the tabletop, and landed in an inelegant, slightly stunned heap on the floor.

The kids closest burst out laughing while everybody else tried to get a view of the commotion. Mark's pranks were fun but tended to go astray. Usually the wayward ones were the funniest.

"You two done dancing over there?" Doc asked rhetorically as the boys straightened themselves out. "As I was saying, the juniors did a great job all year. Jenessa was terrific, eleventh at State this year. . ."

As Callie got up to walk to the front with Jenessa, she locked eyes with Mark. *Serves him right,* thought Callie cheerfully. His eyes were twinkling—he had just as much fun when everything went haywire. Nate was still gulping water and glaring at Mark.

Doc reached the seniors and he choked up, and the seniors were a little misty-eyed, too.

Mark again won the top scholar-athlete ribbon when they got around to academic awards, his third consecutive. The teams together won a state ribbon based on GPA, and then it was nearly over, the season officially closing. Doc started to wrap up the meeting.

"One more thing for you guys that want to run over the winter. They've got a new race down in Lewiston—more like a fun run—on Thanksgiving Day. They're calling it the Rubber Chicken Relay and anybody can run it. Entries are a donation of food for the food bank, or three dollars, your choice. Find a partner if you think you want to burn some calories before stuffing yourselves with turkey."

As the team began to clean up the room, Jenifer bounded away from her mom and rushed up to Callie, who was helping to fold up a table.

"Hey, big sis! You want a partner for the race?" She looked up at Callie expectantly. Jen, a more natural runner than her sister, always looked for excuses to run. She was nearly as fast as Callie in the mile already, which Callie found mildly discouraging. Callie looked down at her sister, half a head shorter than her, startled. *Not really,* she thought.

"Sure, little sis," she said. "It'll be fun."

Callie flopped down into the beanbag chair in the corner of her room and frowned at the spikes next to her gear bag. It had been nearly a week since the state meet, and she still hadn't unpacked the bag. She kept running the last half mile of the race through her head, listening to first one runner, then another, catch her. There was anger in the memory, and a touch of self-recrimination.

She had worked hard before the season started to become a better runner. In a bit of a surprise, she discovered that there was something about the simple, clean action of putting one foot in front of the other that resonated in her and let her reach a place where she was happy. Happy, but not very fast, despite her form becoming silky smooth and efficient. She simply did not have the extra gear that Jenessa had.

Above the gear bag was her Prefontaine poster. Pre was sprinting for the finish line, elevated above the track in perfect form. The caption on the poster was one of the most famous running quotes ever made by the eminently quotable Pre: *To give anything less than your best is to sacrifice the gift.*

She wondered what it was like to be able to run like that, with that kind of speed and grace. What was it like to win the race, break the tape? A wave of bleakness settled over her as she stared up at the forever youthful Oregon runner.

Into the silence of her room and turbulence of her thoughts, she asked, "What if you don't have the gift, Pre? What do you do then?"

Chapter 3

I'm supposed to run with this thing? Callie thought. The rubber chicken sat heavy in her hand, squishy, limp, and cold, the red-painted legs and head flopping over the edges of her glove, jiggling in the air. *Ick.*

"Let me see!"

Callie turned toward Jenifer's voice as her sister's arm snaked around to reach the fake poultry.

"Very cool! Can I run the first leg?" asked Jenifer as she snagged the chicken from her sister. "It's naked!"

"I think you mean plucked."

"Nope, meant naked," said Jenifer with an impish grin, bouncing the chicken in front of her by a single leg pinched between her fingers. "See?"

Callie's lips twitched at the corners, and she turned away from Jen, who was jouncing over to show their parents. Across the road in the gravel parking lot, she saw the twins getting out of their minivan while at the other end of the lot Mark was parking his black Jeep. Turnout for the race was pretty good, with about sixty teams milling around, smiling as they recognized friends in the small crowd. Some runners were jogging up on the asphalt path of the levee, warming up. She watched

17

them, noting the difference between the serious runners and the seriously talented ones. The latter seemed to glide and were nearly silent as they went by, their feet flicking the ground and propelling them forward with no wasted effort.

"Hey, you," said Mark, coming up behind her.

"Hey back," Callie responded.

"How are you doing?" Mark glanced over to her sister. "You running with Jenifer?"

"Yep. She's been pestering me all week. She's running the first leg."

"You running the other three?" The race was set up with four legs, each two miles, with the runners taking turns as they finished each elongated lap.

Callie shook her head. "Nope, she wants to do both of hers."

"Wear her out early. Good idea." The junior high and high school teams intermingled on the track, and Jen had been a regular at the cross-country meets, cheering for Callie and the other girls. He started to say something else but stopped as a gust of wind buffeted them and sent the entry forms at the registration desk scattering.

"I hate wind," said Mark.

Callie stifled a grin. The day was clear and crisp but was already into the forties, which for Thanksgiving Day in the northern half of the country was downright balmy. The wind was a different matter, gusting to twenty miles per hour.

After a particularly windy mile the previous spring at a track meet in Oregon, Mark had searched and found the equations for wind resistance and running. Using them, he reengineered the results to show that, absent wind, he had won. It hadn't changed the race results, but he said it made him feel better. Nobody bothered to double-check his figures.

Callie didn't like the cold but didn't complain. Even with the warmer temperatures, she was wearing black wind pants and jacket along with her gloves, multicolored with stripes of pink, green, and navy blue, and a beanie to match. When it came time to run, she'd strip down to shorts and the wind jacket. Overheating sucked but until it was her turn she planned to stay warm.

Anna and Hanna jogged over. Today, they were wearing matching black running capris with red stripes, Cloverland sweatshirts, and ponytails. The sweatshirts had just their last name printed on the back. Each had on one blue sock and one green sock and Asics shoes. For as long as Callie had known the twins, they had worn the mismatched socks.

"Hey!" they said cheerily in unison, rosy cheeks setting off blue eyes and blond hair.

"Howdy," replied Mark.

"Great day for running—" said Anna.

"Warm, not too windy—" said Hanna, drawing a snort from Mark, who was busy scanning the several parking lots.

"Pretty good crowd," said Anna.

"Considering it's a holiday," agreed Hanna.

"Anybody know if Jenessa is coming?" asked Callie when Anna stopped to draw a breath.

"Jenessa isn't going to make it, out of town," said Anna.

"She's in Portland to visit her aunt or something for Thanksgiving," finished Hanna.

"Twins!" shouted Jenifer, flying over, a guided missile seeking hugs. Callie's little sister buried her face between them and wrapped them up, one in each arm. She adored Anna and Hanna. Laughing, the twins disentangled themselves and Jenifer peered up at Mark.

"Hiya, Mark. Who're you running with?" Jen's head was on a swivel, seeking his partner. "Or going solo?"

Mark looked a bit uncomfortable and replied without looking at Callie. "Mattie Rede," he said, shuffling his feet. His voice got defensive as he continued. "She missed a couple of basketball practices because of the flu and doesn't have her ten in to play"—the school district had a policy that athletes needed ten practices before their first game or event—"and her coach said she could run the relay and pick up an extra practice, and she asked me for a partner."

"Mattie's here?" asked Callie. It was her turn to sound defensive.

"Not yet," said Mark. "Her dad was driving her in but—"

"Yeah, she is," said Anna as the twins, scanning over the top of the crowd, spotted her.

"It's the redhead herself," stated Hanna, sticking her arm up and waving in short loops, trying to make eye contact with Mattie. Mattie saw the tall blonde, then Mark, and started walking over.

Partially hidden by her taller friends, Callie watched her cautiously. Despite playing on the basketball team, Mattie was slightly shorter than Callie and very lean—not just slender, but burned down to well-defined muscles and bone. She moved like a natural athlete, lithe and loose, but Mattie was also constantly aggressive, an image reinforced by her posture, body leaning forward, and her steps, quick and assertive.

She had a small hitch in her stride when she spotted Callie, and then plowed on. She greeted the group but avoided Callie's eyes.

"Hey, Mattie," said Mark. "Ready to run?"

"If I have to. How long until this thing starts?" she replied, looking at the small crowd that was gathering at the starting line next to the parking lot.

"About ten minutes, if it starts on time," Jenifer said, "but they never do."

Mattie grunted and Callie kept her mouth shut.

Mattie had moved into town about a decade ago, long enough that she wasn't the "new" kid but, in a community that measured in generations, still a newcomer. They had been friendly enough with each other, the way most little kids were, though they were never best friends. That changed when they ended up on the same basketball team in junior high, the last year that Callie had played ball.

Callie had been guarding Mattie, who was much quicker and fouled her, hard, on a drive to the basket. Mattie, always explosive, had bounced up from the floor to deliver a hard shove back at Callie. Callie pushed Mattie away, trying to open some space from her hotheaded teammate.

Before she had the chance to apologize, her left eye exploded in lightning bolts of pain from a well-aimed punch. Callie forgot about apologizing and, as the team looked on aghast, the two girls fought. Mattie had tackled Callie and was wrestling her to the floor when the coaches grabbed a girl each and dragged them upright. Mattie was dripping blood from a sorely damaged nose while Callie already showed signs of bruising around her eye.

Both were suspended from school for three days. It was the only time Callie had ever been in trouble, but it marked the start of trouble for Mattie. When Callie got back into class, she still sported a wicked black eye. She spent a week suffering through the embarrassing jokes, along with a suggestion from Mark that she learn to duck faster.

Later that week, the rumor mill exploded with the news that Mattie's mother had walked out on Mattie and her dad the night before the fight. Callie's efforts to reconcile with Mattie were rebuffed, and a watchful but unhappy truce had existed.

"What are you staring at?" accused Mattie. Conversation between the twins and Jenifer stopped. Mark, confused by the sudden animosity, looked from one to the other.

Callie realized with a start that she had been staring at the other girl while she drifted in memories. She sighed. She didn't mean to provoke another fight; she just wanted to be left alone. At Mattie's accusatory tone, though, she felt a prickling of annoyance build.

She was annoyed at Jenifer for talking her into running the race. Annoyed with the idea of running with the stupid rubber chicken. Annoyed at Mark for inviting Mattie. Annoyed because he was running with Mattie.

"Nothing," she said, her lips twitching downward in a quick little grimace. "Just . . . thinking." Mattie held her glare, jaw set, for a second longer, and then looked away to the sign-up table.

"I'm going to get signed up," she declared, and stalked over to join the rear of the line.

Callie watched her stride away, shoulders square and defiant. Jenifer jumped into the uncomfortable gap left hanging in the air by Mattie's departure.

"Can I run with you?" asked Jenifer, talking to Mark. "If you aren't racing?"

"Sure, piglet," he replied, but he was still looking from Callie to Mattie.

The relay started ten minutes late. For Doc, this was fortunate, since he was late to the start line. Sixty runners stood in waves behind the line, waiting for the starter to begin the race. Doc made his way toward the front of the pack.

There was always the evolution of runners from front to back of the pack. At the front were the diminutive runners, men and women, stripped all the way down to skimpy racing shorts and tank tops. The next wave were the serious runners, the ones that wanted to be in that first group but lacked something—speed or the lungs or the perfect mechanics—the fast pack had. Doc ran with the lead pack but, at sixty-two, had resigned himself to fate and age. Even with lungs and speed and mechanics, age eventually won. Most of the fast pack, including Doc, would be running the entire eight-mile race without a partner.

Mark and Jenifer, along with Hanna, settled in at the middle of the group. Mark wore a thin T-shirt with *It was fowl play!* handwritten in red on the back and a bright blue fleece hat. Callie, looking on from the side of the path, considered the combination and decided that Mark might be the least self-conscious person she had ever met. Like most of the joggers, Jen stayed bundled up with sweats and gloves. Callie was pretty sure most of them were going to get too hot once they got moving, including Jen.

"You set the pace, piglet," Callie overheard Mark saying to Jen. "I'm just running some miles, okie dokie?"

Jen, looking up, nodded.

"Don't forget we have two laps," he reminded her.

"Okie dokie, yourself," she replied, bouncing up on her toes. Shorter than everybody else, she couldn't see what was happening up front with the speedsters. Behind them were the slower folks, fitness runners, and, at the rear, the moms and dads with jogging strollers. Jen looked tiny in the crowd. Ahead and behind, the mass of people began to lean forward, and she took first a step, then two, then settled into a slowly accelerating jog as the race started and the pack accordioned out.

The race started up a gradual hill before following the top of the levee on the Lewiston side of the Clearwater River. Towering on the north side of the river were the basalt hills, covered in yellowed bunchgrass, rising two thousand feet from the valley floor. A mile farther downriver, opposite the direction the runners were traveling on the path, was the confluence with the Snake River that separated Idaho and Washington. The weather could drop below freezing but still there would be fishermen out on the water, floating in their small boats and heavy coats. It was a commonly held opinion that the fisherman were nuts. For their part, the fishermen shook their heads as the first wave of runners sped past them.

The first half mile was easy and both Jen and Mark warmed quickly, running with the wind. They passed a strategically located restroom but none of the runners needed to stop yet. Some would. Histories of the Boston Marathon recounted stories about the runners, mostly guys, urinating in the street. It was a little tougher for women.

At the first mile marker, Mark made a hairpin turn, Jen beside him, and dropped off the levee to the greenbelt trail that twisted through the trees and around the small ponds, connecting the parking lots that accessed the park. They were headed back into the wind and Mark felt his skin cool quickly, especially when they ran into the shade of the trees. Squirrels chittered at them as they went by while the geese by the pond moved en masse, honking their protests at the interruption, into the water where they would be safe. He could hear more geese up ahead complaining as the leaders went flying past.

"You okay?" Mark asked Jen, who was starting to pant.

"Just hot," she said, cheeks flushed.

"No problem," he said, glancing over. "Can you take off your sweatshirt while you're running? I can carry it for you," he offered.

"I suppose so." She started to pull the heavy fabric over her head. For a second she was running blind and she stumbled but Mark reached out, supporting her elbow, giving her a chance to regain her balance.

"Thanks," she said, handing over the sweatshirt. Mark weaved it around his spare hand and lower arm to keep it from flopping. His right hand held the rubber chicken.

They ran together comfortably. Jenifer was pushing a bit hard, thought Mark as they turned left onto the gravel access road that slipped between the top of the levee and the trail through the greenbelt. Four hundred meters from the exchange point and where the race had started, she picked up her pace. Mark matched her while he noted that Doc had already made the first turnaround and was headed out on his second lap already. Doc didn't have the spring that he must have had when he was younger but he could still move. Doc waved to them from the course above as he went past. Mark waved back but Jenifer was focused on the exchange point and didn't see the coach. Hanna had just received the chicken from Anna and was headed out, a smile on her face.

At the turn, he could see Callie and Mattie waiting. Callie wasn't smiling.

Chapter 4

Callie watched her sister and Mark approaching. Mark was running easily but Callie could see Jenifer working hard to keep up. Idly, she noted that her younger sister's feet were not tracking straight. *We can fix that....*

Mark and Jenifer hit the exchange point at the same time and Jenifer flipped the rubber bird into the air.

"Your turn," she said as Callie snagged it, already heading up the embankment. Mark handed off to Mattie, who took off in a near sprint ahead of Callie. *It's not a race,* thought Callie, running behind her, *and it's a hell of a lot longer than a four hundred even if it was.* Both girls were stripped down to running shorts but had kept on heavier tops. Mattie kept her gloves on—even in spring track when temperatures were much more comfortable, she complained that she could never keep her fingers warm.

Callie tried to figure out how to carry the chicken—the head was flopping all over, whacking the back of her hand. It was, she thought, annoying. Finally, she found a way to tuck the legs and head under the body. She kept it clenched in her fist and settled in to chase the other runners.

Mattie had slowed down at the top of the levee and was settling into a smooth stride, her feet nearly soundless. Callie, close behind, watched the movement. Mattie was just a natural runner. Her feet brushed the earth, light and quick, followed by a smooth powerful toe-off that covered ground surprisingly fast. She was almost as quick and light as Callie.

Callie had spent years trying to get fast. Mattie already had the speed plus that extra little bit of explosion in the stride that gave her a few extra inches' advantage with every step. Three inches multiplied by ten thousand steps added up in a hurry.

The headwind was getting stronger and beat at the runners as they made their turn back to the exchange point. Callie gained a few meters on Mattie as they dropped down the little grade that started the mile back to the exchange. The warmth she had built up running with the wind bled off quickly.

Up ahead, she could see Hanna, blond ponytail bouncing, winding in and out of the trees. She heard a "Yallooooo!" shouted down from the levee and smiled. She didn't know if Doc was shouting to her but it didn't matter. She kept running, feeling all the rustiness from her self-enforced layoff slide away, muscle memory taking over. Her stride got a little lighter, a touch quicker. Her heart was a steady, if quick, thump in her chest and her lungs poured air in and forced it back out.

At the exchange, Callie swung the chicken back to Jenifer, who went chasing after Mark. Callie heard her sister shout, "Dude!"

Mark ran in place, grinning, until the eight-grade girl caught up, and then the two of them loped away, Mark shortening his stride to keep Jen next to him.

Callie walked over to the mound of clothes and gear that she had brought and rummaged until she found a water bottle and took a fast swig. Little wisps of steam were gently lifting off her shoulders and her hair was tousled. She slung a jacket over her shoulders to avoid getting too chilled waiting for Jen to get back. Behind her at the line, volunteers were calling the bib numbers for each incoming runner so their partner would be ready to go.

Over by Hanna, there was a group of local runners being entertained by an older runner in his forties recounting an ultra-run he did that summer. Runner stories were popular, especially when they involved missed turns and minor disasters. Callie wandered over to listen, perched on the outside of the audience.

The man was waving his arms to punctuate his words. "Yeah, I saw that herd of elk,"—wild arm swing punctuated the direction of the herd—"man, it was great! And I was reaching for my camera when that tree root reached up and grabbed—"

"Number Sixty-two," said the volunteer at the line, "you're up." The volunteer scanned the crowd, looking for confirmation that the message had been received.

"—my right foot. Here I am, fifteen miles into this run and suddenly—"

"Number Sixty-two," announced the volunteer at the line again, still searching.

"I'm airborne sideways until I go *splat,*" he said, spreading his arms wide now, "on the trail and skidded—lucky for me, it was pretty soft—and the herd just bolts. I didn't even get a pic—"

"NUMBER SIXTY-TWO!" This time the volunteer was staring right at the storyteller. "BOB!" Her shout carried into the circle of runners, and the guy talking jumped.

"Shoot," said the man, "that's me!" He lunged off in mid-story while throwing an apologetic wave to the volunteer, who was also his wife.

The next wave of runners, the stroller brigade, showed up. Callie looked at her watch—Jen was eight minutes out, should be about halfway. All the volunteers were bundled up against the wind and cold but the runners were staying warm from the effort of battling the wind. Callie took few quick striders, just easy accelerations of twenty or so meters, more to stay loose than to stay warm. Any minute now . . .

Doc went flying by, grinning at the crowd as he headed out for the fourth lap. Behind him came Anna, handing off to her twin. Callie paced a short circuit, looping around the guardrail of the parking lot, looking for Jen each time she turned back to the line and the shouting volunteers. She looked at her watch again . . . thirteen minutes. Soon. A few feet away, Mattie continued her own prowl, head down, waiting for Mark.

Around the turn seventy-five meters from where Callie paced, Mark and Jen hit the last straightaway and were closing fast. Callie looked at her watch. They were running under seven-minute pace. Jen's head was starting to bob from side to side, a sure sign she was tiring, but Mark looked smooth and comfortable. As Jen kicked in the final meters, Mark again let her lead to the finish, staying a stride back and just off her right shoulder.

"Here!" Gasping, Jen shoved the chicken into Callie's hand. Callie grabbed it as she sped up the asphalt. Callie knew Mattie was right behind her. *It's not a race,* she reminded herself, but she could hear the *swish* of the other girl's clothes, the whisking sound of footsteps were right there, a few feet behind, just to the left. Ahead Hanna was already up to the bathrooms and Doc was out of sight.

The wind started to gust and swirl, knocking Callie slightly off-balance. Callie leaned in a bit and tucked her arms in, altering her stride to take advantage of the wind. She was breathing harder now, pushing a bit faster than the first lap. Behind her, she could hear that Mattie was starting to pant. *Good,* she thought, and increased turnover fractionally, just enough to start gaining some separation from the other girl. Another step ahead. Then two.

She couldn't hear Mattie's footsteps anymore as she continued to drag in air, still breathing heavily. Each inhalation came a touch deeper now, the extra effort to maintain pace taking its toll.

At the hairpin turn that led down to the lower path, Callie risked a quick look over her shoulder. Mattie was fifteen feet back. Deep memories of Mattie's kicking ability stirred; she was too close. *Break her now.*

Callie surged on the downhill for five quick strides and then settled back into a groove on the level ground, a little faster than before.

She focused on the path and each of the little bends, setting herself up with smooth lines through the curves. She was locked in, running gracefully. She could feel the ground, small pebbles from the dirt to the side underfoot, taste the air, feel the heat building up now that she was running despite running into the wind. Behind her, over the wind, she could hear Mattie. Geese honked at the girls, just as they had on the first lap, but Callie didn't hear them.

She could feel the acid buildup in her legs again, familiar, a chemical signpost that she was nearing her limit, and tightness was settling into her shoulders. Callie tried to hold her breathing steady but she could feel it getting heavier and more ragged. She made the turn from the asphalt path onto the gravel and as she did, she sped up again. *Not yet,* floated in her head. *Kick the last two hundred meters. Win it there.* Seconds later, she heard Mattie's feet crunch the gravel. Mattie was close.

Callie stayed focused on form, chin down a bit, arms pumping to help the legs turn over just a bit faster, keeping her shoulders squared, but her hands were clenching and it was getting harder to keep her chin down. She realized she could hear not just Mattie's feet and raspy breath but her clothes swishing. Callie kicked.

Forty seconds to the finish line. Callie had gained an extra step on Mattie by kicking first, but from the sound of the gravel, she could tell Mattie had kicked right behind her. There was no way to get enough air now and she didn't even try to control her gasping. Her shoulders began to wobble, and behind her, Mattie sounded like she was in pain but she was still closing in. *She won't quit, you'll have to beat her,* she knew.

Callie wasn't really thinking anymore. Any pretense she had that it wasn't a race was gone. The effort to force it to the end was all she could envision. The line was twenty meters ahead when Mattie drew even with Callie, then started inching ahead. The good-natured crowd—a mix of runners, volunteers, and assorted family members who braved the cool temperatures to support their particular runner—was cheering both girls to the finish.

Callie tried desperately to stay just ahead of Mattie. She hit the line in a full sprint.

It wasn't enough.

Chapter 5

Doc heard the crowd cheering and turned to see the last seconds of the battle between Callie and Mattie. His cheerful grin disappeared as he watched Callie losing ground ever so slowly to the other girl. His gaze sharpened, sharp artic-blue eyes set into a face that had spent many miles in weather, desert heat in the summer and frosted cold in winter. His face—permanently tanned skin, deep crow's-feet at the corners of the eyes, capped with an unruly mass of blond-white hair—showed no emotion as he dispassionately assessed the runners.

This was no fun run; both girls were running full out. Callie was running strong, Mattie aggressively. *You can see so much of a person by how they run,* thought Doc. Callie's posture—everything driving straight ahead, eyes a fiery green even from where Doc stood, locked on the finish—said more eloquently than her words ever could that you might beat her but she was never, ever going to quit. Mattie's aggression spoke to an inner anger, a rage that was taking itself out on the runner even as she pushed ahead of Callie.

He watched as Mattie won the duel by a foot. An idea

had been rattling around in his head since the state meet and, watching the end of the race, he made his decision.

"Nice race, Callie!" said an excited Jenifer, patting her sister on her back as she passed within arm's reach.

"*Ack . . .*" was all she said in reply.

Callie was staggering in little circles just past the finish line, her head shoved between her knees, lungs heaving from her kick.

"Wasn't . . . a . . . race . . ." she finally wheezed out.

"Yep, saw that," replied her little sister. "That's why you got your head stuffed between your knees."

The little wisps of steam after the first leg had been replaced by billowing clouds of fog as the excess heat from the race released into the cool air. Callie could see very clearly the grass between her feet and the little piece of a race tag that had fallen off of someone, the laces of her shoes, the damp marks on the material of the uppers. She tried to stand back up and things got dizzy again and a little bit black again, so she dropped her hands back down to her knees and kept sucking air.

A few feet away, she saw Mattie hanging on to her knees too, Mark by her side. "I think I'm going to be sick," Mattie said.

Good, thought Callie.

"Yeah, it's like that sometimes. Told you it was fun," Mark said.

Mattie glared up at him, her face flushed a brilliant red. "Someday I'm gonna hurt you!" she threatened weakly. She struggled up to a standing position and took a tentative step toward Mark.

He stepped back, laughing. "Gotta catch me first."

"Jerk."

Yeah, thought Callie, agreeing with her rival. Again she tried to get upright. This time there were no dizzy spells. She was still puffing a bit but already she was getting cold.

"Hey, Jen—where's my sweats?" she asked her sister, looking around. They weren't where she had left them.

"I put them with our stuff. I'll get them," offered her little sister, jogging off to the far side of the parking lot where their run gear was stashed.

Hanna held out a cup of water for Callie, who took it gratefully. Anna was doing the same for Mattie.

"Thanks," said Callie.

"Uh-huh. Nice finish. You and Mattie were really cooking at the end," observed Hanna.

"I heard footsteps."

"That'd do it," Hanna agreed. She added speculatively, "Mattie's faster than I thought over distance. I didn't think she could hang with you."

"It's my first run since State—I was taking some time off," Callie said, defending herself.

"Hey, no worries. Still, we could use another runner or we're going to be running just with five—and that counts Jen, if she runs. Anybody gets hurt and we got no team."

Callie looked over to Mattie. Mark was standing next to her and, as Callie watched, he reached out and jokingly jabbed her in the shoulder. Mattie smiled up at him and Callie suddenly realized how pretty Mattie really was when she wasn't scowling.

"She can run," Callie admitted, a touch of gloom settling into her eyes.

"Yep. Attitude kind of stinks, but if she hangs out with us, she'll change," said Hanna. She smiled and her voice took on a playful tone. "I think it's the endorphins."

"Makes us happy and dopey," agreed her sister, Anna, who joined the conversation midstream. Across the way, Mark and Mattie were packing up to leave. Mattie looked up, then gave a little head bob, a quick upturn, toward Callie, as if to say *Nice race*.

Callie, her eyes showing her puzzlement, returned the nod, a similarly quick motion. *You, too.*

"Who's happy and dopey?" Jen asked, back with Callie's sweats. "I know who Doc is." She shot a fast glance to her sister as she handed over the clothes. "Callie is Grumpy."

"Am not."

"Are too, you've been grumpy for a month," said Jen with a snort. "Can I be Sleazy?" she asked.

"Only if I can be Happy," said Anna.

"Sneezy," said an exasperated Callie, hopping on one foot while she tried to get the sweatpants over her running shoes.

Jenifer shook her head vigorously, her bangs flying side to side. "I want to be a lawyer," she reminded Callie. "Sleazy fits and it's more profitable."

Callie started to protest, pulling on her sweats while looking at her sister. The tip of her toe caught on the elastic of the cuff of the sweats and, off-balance, Callie staggered and took a final hop before falling sideways, landing with a solid thump on her left hip in the wet grass, one leg stuck in the air.

"Crap!"

"Where's my phone?" said Jen, patting the pockets of her sweatpants. "I need a picture!"

"Need a hand getting dressed?" Hanna made no effort to hide her grin. The twins reached down and offered Callie a hand, one on each side.

"Apparently," said Callie, her face flushed and her jaw set. She pulled herself up, a large wet spot on her side. She looked surreptitiously around to see who had noticed. Almost no one had except Mark, who was silently laughing, and Mattie, who looked on expressionlessly. Callie went from embarrassed to uncomfortable. Mattie looked away first and Callie finished putting on her pants, leaning on Jen's shoulder this time. *Naturally,* she thought glumly.

Doc was in his usual spot, just ahead of the finish line, encouraging the last of the runners. He looked over and saw the kids prepping to leave. He needed to talk to Callie.

"Callie, can I talk to you for a minute?" he asked. He looked at the rest of the kids. "Nice job, all of you."

"Sure, Coach," said Callie with a shrug. "What's up?"

"Why don't you come on over here with me," he said, walking a small distance away from the group.

Jen looked on, curious, and said, "What's going on?"

Callie looked back over her shoulder and shrugged again, eyebrows raised.

Out of earshot, Doc turned to Callie, his eyes appraising the changes from the gangly freshman he remembered—insecure, all knees and elbows—to the outwardly confident young lady in front of him. The years of training and physical maturity had turned her into a solid runner but it was the emotional maturity that surprised him. The elements of the woman she would become, the demeanor that spoke of steadfastness and compassion and pride, were already there. He was certain he was making a good choice.

"Coach?" Callie asked.

Dang, getting old and rambly, thought Doc.

"Sorry, Callie, got lost in my thoughts for a sec," he said. He paused and a small frown creased his forehead. "Normally,

I wait a little longer before making up my mind, but no matter."

Callie watched him, not comprehending, waiting for him to get to the point.

He gazed at her evenly. "Are you willing to be the captain of the cross-country team next year?"

Callie felt her eyes pop wide and her eyebrows lift.

"Me?" she stammered, her thoughts scattering as she tried to process the idea.

"Well, yeah." He looked around. "I didn't pull anyone else over to talk to."

He watched the confusion on her face. The captains on cross-country teams were usually the best runners, who were also usually the upperclassmen. Callie's confusion was a result of not considering herself one of the best runners, and, frankly, from the viewpoint of racing, she wasn't. That was not the relevant factor in Doc's mind.

"Why me? I thought that Jenessa was going to be captain."

"Jenessa is a heck of a runner," he agreed, "but I need a *team* captain more than I need a great runner. I think you can do the job—though, no fooling, it's more than a bit of work and no reward," Doc explained.

"I don't know how to be a captain," evaded Callie.

"Of course you don't!" Doc grunted. "If you knew how, I wouldn't have to ask—you'd just do it." He fixed his eyes on hers. "It's like running. You learn by doing."

"What about Jenessa? What about the other . . . ?"

"I don't run a democracy," the coach snapped. "I run a team, I teach you how to play by the rules, work hard, run hard, and compete, and on a really good day, think that you guys will figure out that it applies to everything else in life too." His eyes held hers. "Like now—are you willing to accept the responsibility of being the team captain next year?" He glared at her, waiting and demanding an answer.

Callie hesitated, then, steeling herself, stood a little bit taller. Matching his intensity, she responded with a simple but direct, "Yes."

"Good. That's settled. Before the season, we'll get together to go over some stuff and I'll send some things home for you to look at over the winter. Not really study stuff, thinking stuff," he said.

"Okay," responded Callie. "Homework that's not homework. Got it."

"You forgot about the job without pay part, but that sums it up pretty good for now," Doc agreed. He checked his watch. "Shoot, I'm going to be late home. I'll see you soon." He turned to leave.

"Coach?" Callie called after him.

Doc stopped and turned.

"What?"

"You can be a bit of a bully, you know," said Callie.

"I know." Doc grinned, the smile a rare occurrence and the tanned skin creasing as if unaccustomed to the action. "See, I told you you'd learn."

"What did Doc want? What did he say?" pestered Jen as Callie walked back to her sister. The twins had left but Mark and Mattie had joined Jen, gear bags thrown over their shoulders. Mark looked at her speculatively and waited while Mattie looked bored.

Callie focused on her sister.

"Coach asked me if I wanted to be team captain next year," explained Callie. Jen offered a small squeal of excitement.

Mark looked pleased and Mattie continued to look bored and avoided looking at Callie.

"You said yes," assumed Mark. "I told him you would."

Callie got very still.

"You knew?" she asked.

"Yeah, Coach asked me about it after the team dinner. I told him I thought you'd be a great captain," Mark replied. Callie was still staring at him, so he continued, "You work really hard, you know what you're talking about, and most of the girls like you." His eyes got a bit distant before he added, "You're also kind of bossy, which helps." He refocused on Callie's grim face. His smile started to fade.

"You knew and you didn't tell me?" Callie asked, her voice low and flat. "And I'm bossy?"

Mark fidgeted, looking as though he'd just realized that he was, somehow, yet again in trouble.

Jen looked at him. "I strongly advise taking the Fifth," she said.

"Uh . . ." Mark started, confusion growing on his face. He was turning red, high on the cheeks first and spreading to his ears. Next to him, Mattie's lips twitched at the corners as Mark struggled. She looked out over the river.

Callie leaned in, organizing her thoughts, preparing to blister Mark for holding back on her.

"Wow, just look at the time!" announced Jen, interrupting the moment while making a big show of checking her bare arm. "Time to go. Come on, Callie." She pulled on Callie's sleeve, a quick tug.

Callie pulled her arm free but Mark looked at Jen gratefully and nodded.

"Yeah, we should be going too," he said. "I told Mattie's dad I'd get her home early."

This elicited another frown from Callie. A brief grimace crossed Mattie's face at the same time.

Mark turned to Mattie. "Hey, let's go," he said, angling toward the Jeep to make a getaway. Mattie followed him, bag thrown over her shoulder, feet dragging a bit.

"Bye, happy Turkey Day," Jen shouted at the quickly retreating boy.

Mark stuck his arm up and waggled it back and forth a couple of times in acknowledgement but he didn't turn around.

"You let him off the hook," accused Callie, as Mark climbed into his vehicle.

"I did," admitted Jen. She stood there, not quite smirking. Or trying to cover up a smirk. Callie wasn't sure.

"You could mind your own business, you know."

"Nope, violates the rules of sisterhood. Younger sisters are required to stick their noses into older sisters' boyfriend issues. I looked it up in the manual," said Jen.

"There's no manual," said Callie. "You just like meddling." Callie's voice was getting heated.

"That, too," agreed Jen.

"Besides, he's not my boyfriend."

"Not my fault you're slow," said Jen, flummoxing her older sister. "Now come on. Turkey is calling, Captain Big Sis, and I got dibs on a drumstick."

Chapter 6

Mark carried the turkey over to the table while his uncle Bennie used a sharpening steel to take the rough edges off the carving knife, each snap of his wrist making a snicking sound. His uncle stopped after half a dozen turns on each side of the blade and squinted at the edge to see if there was any improvement.

"You can't see the change, you know," said Mark, setting the bird in the center of the table, careful not to spill the drippings.

"*Au contraire,* puppy, I have the eyes of an eagle," said his uncle, still inspecting the blade, thick glasses tucked away on top of his head.

Mark's mother, Paula, chuckled as she put the garlic mashed potatoes into a serving bowl, leaving the spoon standing tall.

"It's not fair," said Bennie, eyeing the mound of food on Mark's plate, the sliced turkey draped over the stuffing.

"Life's not fair," retorted Mark, "plus I ran this morning. Morning runs always make me hungry."

"I hadn't noticed a difference," said his mother, but the subtle humor was lost on Mark as he began to work his way around the edge of his plate.

"I don't run," said Uncle Bennie. "I worked entirely too

hard to reach this refined state of decrepitude. A body like this," he said, leaning back and pointing toward his midsection girth, "doesn't happen by accident." He bit the end off a gherkin and, using the uneaten stub, pointed it at Mark. "I'm old school. Mountain Dew and Cheetos—that's the diet of a champion."

Bennie's sister—Mark's mother—looked on reprovingly but Mark just laughed.

"More like the runner-up," said the youth. "Who kicked whose butt on the Xbox last night?"

His expression more comic than intimidating, Bennie scowled. "Wait until I roll out the new game, then we'll see."

Mark sat up straight, alert. "You brought a new game?" Mark's uncle was a leading programmer in the virtual reality field, lending his skills—usually at impressively exorbitant prices—to gaming companies, and Mark was an unofficial beta tester for his uncle. He demonstrated an unusual aptitude for doing the unexpected and, consequently, discovering programming bugs. While professional testers were paid for their work, Mark did it free for Bennie in exchange for new games. Implicit in the deal was that Mark wouldn't share or pirate the games and Bennie wouldn't run him over with a tractor.

"Later," said his mother, trying to change the subject. Once they got into a discussion on games, she might as well be a flower decorating the table.

"How did the race go?" she asked, changing the subject.

Mark glanced across the table to her. "It was all right. Wasn't really a race," he said. A fleeting expression flared and faded.

His mother saw the microexpression.

"But . . . ?" she asked as she used her fork to dam up the gravy spilling from her mashed potatoes.

"Mattie went nuts and ended up racing with Callie anyway," said Mark. Conflicting expressions flashed and disappeared this time.

His mom shook her head. "How is Mattie?"

"She's okay, I guess. Her dad seems okay with me driving her around," he said. "I think he's still trying to get me to help with some kind of project." He paused. "Callie's mad at me though."

Bennie's ears perked up. "Rede has a new project?"

"What did you do to Callie?"

Mark nodded to Bennie. "I don't know what it is. He's real secretive." To his mom, he said, "Nothing. Doc asked Callie to be captain for the girls' team." His mother waited and he continued. "Doc and I talked about it when he was making me boys' captain again and now Callie is mad because I knew but didn't tell her." His eyes narrowed. "It wasn't my job to tell her, that was up to Doc and his timing stinks, telling her after Mattie chased her down at the run."

Bennie's face became noncommittal as he considered what Mark had said.

"And you're in trouble, why?" asked his mother.

Mark looked flustered as he tried to keep track of both conversations. "What do you mean?"

"Dude, give it up. She's a mind reader." Bennie's grin was good-natured but knowing. "Moms are psychic. It's genetic." Changing subjects, he glanced to his sister. "Rede always thought he was smarter than he is." His voice was dismissive. "Remember when he came back from Tech?"

She raised an eyebrow and leaned in to say something to him but Bennie wasn't done.

"He acted like he was king of the hill when he got the job setting up the new computer systems for the mills. Showed off that pretty wife of his like she was a shiny new Christmas tree ornament. I don't get what she saw in him."

"I remember," his sister said. "I also remember you hacking his system and releasing a worm that wiped out a ton of his code."

Bennie looked startled. "Who told you that?"

"Andy was pretty sure it was you." She glowered at her brother. "It made a mess at the mill and took them a month to get straightened out."

"Well, he pissed me off."

Mark kept his mouth shut as they argued. He knew his dad, Andy, had been an engineer at the mill, working to upgrade it and save the jobs it represented. In a bit of irony, not funny in the least, his father had been killed in a crane accident when the last of the new boilers was being hoisted into position. His mom had talked often about his dad once she had gotten past the initial grief. Other parts of family history had been glossed over or avoided—especially parts involving her brother, Uncle Bennie.

"It was your own fault," Paula said, "and you know it even if you won't admit it."

Bennie leaned over and, in a stage whisper, said, "Never have accomplices."

"If you had told him why you wanted to cut up that car, Jake would never have let you and Mom wouldn't have had to bail you out." Her tone of voice made it sound as though this was a well-worn argument between the two of them.

"It was a joke," her brother protested.

It all clicked into focus for Mark. Bennie had, according to legend, apparently had an inspired moment in his senior year, as he passed a poster urging the students to study hard. It featured a picture of a library with a caption that read *On the Road to Learning.* He had gathered a gang of boys to help him with his plan.

When students showed up for the last week in school, they discovered the body of an old car welded around the center post at the doors of the library. *Road Scholar* was painted in a garish red on the trunk of the rusted-out wreck.

The school administration was not amused and, in the investigation that followed, managed to turn up a single name, the one that everybody expected to hear. Bennie's. The only proof had been a tip from the previous owner of the junker, who stated he saw several boys hauling away the pieces. Mark didn't know that it was Jake Rede, Mattie's dad, who'd told the authorities that Bennie asked permission to cut the old car down for scrap.

Bennie never gave up his friends and was the only one suspended.

It was effective. Most seniors were happy to trade a moment of potential glory for their diploma and a chance to get the heck away from high school.

They were buried in sodas and chips when Uncle Bennie propositioned Mark. He didn't look at Mark as he spoke, focused instead on figuring out how his protégé had managed to crash the game.

"So Rede has a gig for you?" Bennie had his laptop setting on the wide arm of the sofa and was trying to backtrack Mark's moves before the screen went a bright blue and faded to black.

"He says he does but won't tell me what it is."

Bennie grunted. "Show me again what you did."

Mark ran through the sequence again and Bennie grunted

again and made a note in the program file.

"When we get to the forced entry and flash-bang, don't do that again—it'll crash sure as shooting."

Mark fished some potato chips out of the nearest bowl and leaned back into the cushions with the controller. "No worries."

"You got plans for the summer?" Bennie asked, trying to keep his voice causal but sounding blunt. Bennie was terrible at feigning nonchalance.

Mark shot a startled glance at Bennie. He paused before answering, intrigued at the sudden inquiry.

"Not really. Get a job someplace and run my ass off. Why?"

"I got this project down in the Bay Area. Cool company, doing some interesting work with VR."

Mark was shaking his head. "I'm not going into coding, Bennie. Too many small rooms and staring at screens. I want to build gadgets that will do stuff, cool stuff, not push out lines of code that never end."

Bennie settled in, orange-tipped fingers holding his controller. "Won't even think it over?"

Mark watched his uncle and saw the pursed lips and crinkling laugh lines at his eyes. Bennie was pulling a fast one on him but he didn't see where.

"What's the job?

"Better than anything Rede has to offer."

"Just tell him," shouted Mark's mom from the kitchen.

Mark looked at Bennie, confused. "Mom knows?" He glanced at the kitchen door. "Since when?"

"A word of advice, puppy, don't play poker with your momma, she'll take you for everything you got," said Bennie. "I cleared it with her last night. The gig is at a robotics development firm and the software is to train the robots. You'd be interning on the machine side instead of hanging in the small, dark room with me." He paused. "Interested?"

"Heck yeah!" Mark dreamed of building robots, not clumsy industrial tools but sleek droids, nimble and useful, that could become as universal as a computer or microwave.

"Going to be any problems with your girl?"

"Mattie? She's not my girl. I just help her out because no one else will and she's a sweet kid."

Bennie started to laugh, the bowl of Cheetos on his belly bouncing. "Is he always this clueless?" he asked his sister, who had come to the doorway, wiping her hands on a dish towel, to listen to the conversation.

"Be nice, Bennie."

Mark felt like his head was on a swivel as he tried to keep up with them.

"Puppies are so cute at this age." His uncle was laughing harder now and the Cheetos were in jeopardy of bouncing off his stomach.

Aggrieved, Mark picked up his controller, restarted the game, and proceeded to blow holes in Uncle Bennie's code three more times that evening. It felt good.

Chapter 7

"You heard?" Jenessa asked Callie as they slipped into seats still slightly warm from the previous class. In front, the British Lit teacher, Mr. Swofford, was putting the assignment up on the board.

"Not all the details, but yeah," replied Callie, turning to face Jenessa, taking note of yet another pair of new boots, black with moderate heels. Jenessa was always the one who came to class with the new blouse or jacket, the latest jeans, or the newest phone. Callie had a hard time figuring out who the real Jenessa was—the girl who would sweat and spit and run for miles or the daddy's princess that she saw in class every day.

Jenessa leaned across the aisle between their desks. "Nobody on the team is talking about it. I tried to get some info from Vickie" —she nodded her head toward a tall blonde sitting in the front of the class—"but she said the coach said she would be running suicides forever if anybody on the team blabbed."

"Must have been pretty bad. I don't think you can get thrown off a team for anything but grades or getting busted for drugs," said Callie. She glanced up to the front of the room. Swofford, a newer teacher with a potbelly and a ponytail, was still getting organized. She looked back to Jenessa.

"Maybe she's doing something," said Jenessa, speculating. "I mean, have you seen her?"

Callie was shaking her head. "No way. She's not that dumb and she's not the party type."

"Well, who would want to invite her to a party?" Jenessa went to a lot of parties, though she was careful to make sure that there was no booze around—stay at a party that had booze and the minimum suspension was one game or event. And that was if you self-reported. Get caught actually drinking and you lost the season. Most of the kids knew where the safe parties were.

Jenessa's head was nearly touching Callie's. "I saw her walking to class but I didn't ask her what happened. She had like this hostile bubble around her, kind of like, 'Leave me the hell alone!' and looked super mad. Like, she was just stomping down the hall. Everybody was just getting out of her way."

"You kind of have to feel sorry for her," Callie said, voice soft.

"Oh no I don't!" said Jenessa disagreeably. "Remember when her mom blew up and left?"

Callie nodded but resisted the urge to reach up to her eye.

"Well, her dad and my dad"—Jenessa's father was the president of the local savings and loan—"got into this big fight. My dad said he was being irresponsible, just leaving the house they had here in town sitting empty while he moved him and Mattie out to some dump out by Mark." Jenessa's face was rigid with the memory. "She comes up to me and starts blaming me for having to live in a dump, like I had anything to do with it."

"If you ladies are quite done with your gossip hour, we can get started," Swofford interrupted. Callie jumped. She had gotten lost in the gossip and, looking around, realized the whole class had been watching her and Jenessa.

"Not that I want to hurry you, but I only have fifty-two minutes—make that fifty-one minutes—and Romeo and Juliet await," said the teacher.

"Sorry, Mr. Swofford," said Jenessa. Both girls turned forward toward the teacher.

"We could ask Mark," whispered Jenessa out of the side of her mouth as the two of them got their books open. "She usually tells him what's going on and then he can tell us."

"Let's not," snapped Callie, eyes flashing with annoyance. Up front, Swofford frowned in their direction.

While Jenessa sat upright, a little smirk on her face, Callie just slouched into the seat as the teacher began his droning monologue. She glanced to Jenessa, who was studiously taking notes; unlike Callie, Jenessa liked Shakespeare. They had studied together since freshman year, Callie helping Jenessa with math and science, Jenessa helped Callie survive English.

Up front, Swofford was quoting from the end of act 3, *". . . I'll to the friar, to know his remedy: If all else fail, myself have power to die."* Callie's mind was already wandering to her anatomy test next period.

And to Mark—she'd ask him later, when they went for their afternoon run, what Mattie had done this time to self-destruct.

The seasons had slid from Thanksgiving and the relay to Christmas, and then into dreary late January. They were in that dead time of winter where there were no more holidays to look to for a reprieve, and the gloom of winter seemed unrelenting and permanent. The mountains, draped in white shawls of snow, overlooked the valleys. Sunny days were brilliant with light as the sun reflected off the snow glistening on the tree limbs and house roofs, but they were rare. Today it was overcast and gloomy and depressing, a perfect match for the inside of school with the too-bright fluorescent lighting and cold institutional walls.

The school was older, built in sections in different decades as many rural schools were, and Callie had to walk almost a U-turn from her last class to the newer part that housed the gym and locker rooms. A direct line would have taken a third of the time, but there were brick walls in the way. She ducked outside long enough to dash to her car and grab run gear, ditching her backpack while she was out there.

Callie gave the door to the locker room a shove and the murmur of sound that had been leaking into the hallway transformed into a flood of noise: scraps of conversations, banging lockers, bits of laughter. In contrast, the basketball players, usually boisterous, were looking glumly at each other.

Callie started to unload her run gear: shorts, long pants, sports bra, long-sleeved shirt, short-sleeved shirt, jacket, gloves, hat, socks, and shoes. It made a largish pile on the bench. She ruefully looked at the stack and started to change out of her street clothes, thinking that summer was a lot easier. Shorts, shirt, shoes, and out the door. *Wintertime, not so much,* she thought, shivering as she pulled the cold long-sleeved shirt over her head. Leaving the clothes in the car meant that they assumed outside temperature—about twenty-eight degrees today—but she didn't have room in her school locker for the clothes and her books. With a little all-over wiggle, she gave herself a quick rub on the arms and shoulders to warm them up.

Around her, the conversation of the basketball players stayed muted. Callie looked over to Vickie, the same girl that Jenessa had tried to pump for information earlier, who was sitting on the bench a couple feet away.

"So what's the deal?" she asked the starting center for the team, her voice muffled by the second shirt she was slipping over her head.

"Not allowed to say," replied the player, avoiding Callie's gaze. Then, after a slight pause, "It was just Coach and Mattie." The bigger girl shifted uncomfortably on the bench. She was already dressed for practice, but like the other players, was sitting there looking at the door to the gym and at her teammates. None of them were making the first move to the door.

Callie made an "um" sound as she listened. Deftly, she tucked the shirt into the waistband of her windproof pants. Vickie was still staring at the door.

"We were counting on her to start at point guard," the big girl said, "and now we're shorthanded, all because she couldn't keep her frickin' mouth shut." She sat there, lips turned down in a grimace—and then her eyes snapped wide as she realized what she had said.

"Please don't tell anybody I said anything," she pleaded with Callie as she rapidly scanned the locker room to see if anyone had overheard. "I'll be in so much trouble . . ."

"No worries, Vickie. I can keep a secret." The truth was that Callie could, and had, and, instinctively, other girls had grown to value it.

The big girl sighed in relief, but the nervousness was still etched on her features and worry reflected from her wide eyes.

"Thanks." She abruptly stood up. "I've got to get to practice," she said with a grimace.

As the taller girl headed for the gym, Jenessa came up behind Callie, dressed for the run.

"Ready?" said Jenessa. She had swapped the new boots for beat-up Asics. Even in winter run gear—a white fleece top, chili-pepper-red hat and gloves, black capris—she was svelte. She was, Callie decided, one of those people that just looked fast. Callie, on the other hand, felt like the Michelin Man, she had so many layers on.

"Yeah, sure. Hold on while I yell at my kid sister." Callie scanned the locker room for Jen. She wasn't with the junior high kids anymore. Callie spotted her over by Vickie, who was glancing nervously toward the door to the gym.

"JEN!" Callie shouted over the intervening girls while making her way through the crowd. Jenifer looked over as the basketball player beat a hasty retreat.

"How are you getting home?" she asked, meeting Jen in an open spot between the rows of metal lockers. Around them, the last of the athletes were slamming doors and getting ready to hit the court. Jenessa stood impatiently a few feet away.

"Dad was going to pick me up after practice."

"So I don't need to give you a ride?" Callie confirmed.

"Right," said Jen, "and practice will probably run long anyhow. We don't have any matches soon. Coach always runs long between matches." She was talking fast and bobbing her head, which sent the pigtails bouncing side to side.

Callie looked at her sister and the retreating Vickie and a suspicion formed in her mind. "Were you grilling Vickie?" Callie asked, eyes narrowing.

"Define *grilling*," said Jenifer, doe-eyed and innocent.

"What you were just doing to Vickie," Callie said patiently. "Be nice, little sis. They don't need any more trouble right now."

"Sometimes you're no fun," said Jen with a fake pout, "but okay. Gotta go—see you at the house." She turned to the hallway door that would take her to the multipurpose room where the junior high volleyball team practiced. It was a small school and there wasn't enough gym room for the high school basketball teams and the junior high teams to practice at the same time, fortunately for Vickie.

Callie made her way outside. It took her twenty steps and three temperature changes—steamy locker room to hallway to winter—before she joined Jenessa, Anna, and Hanna. Mark was standing next to them in jeans and black ski jacket, the only real color on him the insanely bright orange knitted hat shoved down over his ears, brown curls of hair escaping at the bottom.

The winter light, diffused to an overcast glow by the clouds, was already fading toward sundown.

"Hey, not running?" she asked Mark.

"Nope, skipping today. Things to do," he replied. In the parking lot, she could see his Jeep belching exhaust behind it as it warmed. "Didn't want you to think I was just ditching you." Mark was a regular at the runs and, if he didn't let them know, they would wait, expecting him to show up. Callie hadn't missed a run since Thanksgiving. Neither had Mark.

"Let's go already, it's cold," said Jenessa, with puffs of vapor punctuating the words. She kept shifting her shoulders toward the gravel path. It hadn't snowed recently and the path was mostly clear from a recent warm spell where it had gotten above freezing for three whole days.

"Got to get this done," said Hanna.

"Lots of homework," said her sophomore sister.

"Plus we're freezing our butts off," said Hanna.

"And my nose is getting cold," added Anna.

Callie glanced at Mark. "Okay, we'll catch you next time when it's warmer, wimp."

Mark chuckled. A week earlier it had been two degrees out and, on a dare from the twins, he had run in just shorts, gloves, and a tank top.

"Later," he said. "I'll catch you guys tomorrow."

"How far do we want to go?" asked Jenessa.

"I was thinking an easy three-ish to the old mill," Callie said to the gang of girls.

"Sounds like a plan." Jenessa turned and started a slow jog toward the path, and the twins followed her.

Callie watched as Mark sauntered over to his Jeep before scurrying over to catch up to the bundled-up girls. Jenessa was on one side, brunette ponytail bouncing next to the pair of blond ponytails. Callie heard the door slam behind her as she caught up to the others.

"I forgot to ask him about Mattie," Callie said to the other runners as she settled in next to Jenessa.

"I didn't," said Jenessa. "But he won't say if he knew anything or not. He's a dork."

"He's not a dork," defended Callie. "He's more like oblivious to most things, but he's mostly an all right guy."

"He's a math geek who's going into engineering and wants to play with metal dolls. That's kind of the definition of a dork," snorted Jenessa.

The twins looked at Jenessa with some surprise but stayed quiet.

"He's not real good with people," Callie admitted, "and he's always talking about taking stuff apart, but that doesn't make him a dork."

"Have it your way." Jenessa's voice had a derisive edge to it, and she notched up the pace a bit. Callie stepped up to match her, but her legs were heavy and sluggish.

The twins accelerated in unison and matched them.

A horn sounded from the road they were paralleling. It was Mark in his Jeep, headed up into the hills toward home.

"I thought so," said Jenessa, and a tight grin of satisfaction flashed before she could get it completely hidden.

"Thought what?" said Hanna.

"Nothing important."

Callie looked at the Jeep as it drove out of sight.

"Well, obviously something," said Callie. Sometimes Jenessa left her exasperated.

"I guess he really did have something more important than running to do today." Jenessa smirked as she said it. Callie, running next to her, glanced over and found Jenessa staring right at her.

"Mattie's in the car with Mark."

A setup, Callie thought. *Jenessa knew Mattie was in the Jeep before we ever left the school. And she played me for an idiot.* Callie's face got tight and her eyes narrowed. She started to say something—she didn't know what to say, how to say it—and closed her mouth again. She could feel the heat rising in her face but was not going to show Jenessa that she had scored.

It was the quietest run of the year. Callie ran, grim and fuming, while the twins, embarrassed for Callie, were subdued. Only Jenessa seemed to enjoy the run, moving easily, apparently quite satisfied with herself. At the old mill, they all wordlessly turned around and retraced their steps. Callie was cold and miserable by the end of the run and was pretty sure she hated winter.

The next day, Mark was back as promised. He brought Mattie with him.

Chapter 8

Callie was waiting outside, shivering and chatting with the twins over the noise of the buses as they left, turning right and left onto the main road that the school sat on, belching a fog of exhaust, when Mark nonchalantly strolled up. A heavily bundled Mattie hid behind him, shuffling along with all the joy of a prisoner brought to face the hanging judge, her gaze fixed on the ground in front of her. For all the layers of clothes she was swaddled in, Mattie seemed small, her energy at ebb tide.

"So what's the plan?" asked Mark as he reached the girls, a plume of frost punctuating his words. "Where's Jenessa?" He looked puzzled. "Track starts in less than a month. I thought she'd be here too."

"Jenessa said she was busy," answered Anna.

"She only runs when the weather is nice," added Hanna, dressed to match her sister in black running pants and blue running jacket. All the runners were bundled up; the skies had cleared overnight, bringing a brilliant blue above, but with it, much colder temperatures. Dazzlingly white clouds sat over the evergreen trees, creating a chiaroscuro effect of glaring light and deep shadows. The high temperature for the day was predicted to be in the teens and Callie was sure that it wouldn't even get to the high teens. Behind her sunglasses, she was frozen and cranky and the run hadn't started yet.

Mattie, lagging behind Mark, joined them, briefly looking up. Her face was mostly hidden, a black ski cap pulled down below her ears and her collar turned up covering her mouth. Her amber eyes, normally blazing with electricity, were subdued, but Callie could see her jaw set in stubborn determination even under the clothing.

"I was thinking," suggested Mark, "we could do a short run. We don't need to beat ourselves up too much." He glanced to Mattie. There was a small silence, uncomfortable, and Mattie seemed to shrink a little bit more as eyes turned to her.

"Suits us," said Anna. "We've got a ton of homework anyway."

"You, too?" Hanna asked Mattie, an awkward attempt to involve the girl who hung a half step back from Mark's left shoulder, just outside the circle of the rest of the group.

Mattie looked up with a quick upturn of her head and muttered, "Yeah." She dropped her eyes back to the frozen earth.

"How about you, Callie?" checked Hanna.

"I'm okay on homework," Callie said, looking at her friend questioningly.

"No, the run," said Anna. "You said you wanted to bump up your miles . . . three miles enough?"

Callie shrugged, the movement muffled by the layers. "Yeah. I ran this morning."

Mark shot a surprised glance at her. "Double runs?" His voice rose, his tone matching the surprise on his face. "It was like seven degrees this morning."

The others were staring at her now, too.

"That's kind of—" started Hanna.

"—crazy," finished her sister.

Callie found her shoulders rising and pinching together in the back. She hadn't meant to tell anybody about the extra runs. "Just trying to get ready for the season," she said, her voice measured. "Just a couple of times a week." She paused and looked at Mark. "Besides, at least I wore clothes. Who was out here running in shorts when it was even colder?"

Mark leaned back and started to splutter. "But that, it was different . . . that was a dare."

Anna interrupted, rescuing her. "Hey, enough yakking. We need to get moving before we turn into run-sicles."

" 'Run-sicles' is not a word," protested Hanna.

"A technicality, but if we don't get running soon, I'm going inside. My nose is cold and I can't feel my toes."

Callie was nodding in agreement with the older twin and was grateful for the change of subject.

"How about the Forest Road loop? It's short enough and gets us away from the path. I'm tired of the path," Mark groused.

The group moved off together, crossing the main road that bordered the school. The Forest Road loop undulated up and over small hummocks to the base of the largest hill just past the outskirts of town before they turned back at the edge of the forest as it reached down between the scattered houses. It was usually a quiet route, only a few cars to worry about and fewer pedestrians.

Mark uncharacteristically pushed the pace and Callie soon found herself panting and, despite the bitter cold, sweating. The twins and Mattie matched him, keeping up a steady patter of conversation between them.

Listening, Callie gathered that they were studying World War I and were arguing over the Treaty of Versailles, which ended the war. Callie was surprised they would argue. *Not very twin-ish,* she thought. Meanwhile, she huffed along, slowly falling back from the rest of the group. She glanced her watch to check their pace and found she was slower than she thought. She was only about ten feet behind, but her legs were already heavy, and her feet were clunking into the frozen surface. She leaned in. The stride would fix itself once she got warmed up.

In front, Anna asked Mattie what she thought about the treaty. Mattie replied with a couple of words but her voice was too low for Callie to hear from behind. Hanna responded to both of them but directed her comment to Mattie. Callie watched as the twins gradually pulled Mattie into their discussion. Mark said something Callie couldn't hear and all three girls, even Mattie, laughed.

Callie dropped her eyes down to the road in front of her and continued her trudge. Still struggling for breath in the frigid air, she slowed down slightly, breaking contact with the rest of the group completely and running in a solitary bubble, the crackling sound of crushed gravel underfoot and the branches of the trees that lined either side of the road narrowing the sky.

As she eased off, her thoughts drifted inward. Deep inside something was . . . *aching?* . . . but she shied away from the answers as they drifted up. Another round of laughter ahead intruded and the ache intensified then faded as she tamped it down. Her eyes narrowed— she focused on running and losing herself in the motion. A quick glance ahead showed Mark, bracketed by the twins on one side and Mattie on the other, farther ahead than she expected. She realized she had slowed more than she intended, but, when she tried to speed up, all she did was pant more without going any quicker.

By the time they had reached the halfway point at a hard bend that veered left on the gravel road, Callie was a hundred meters behind. As they drifted away around the corner, Anna looked back, said something to the others, and then they were gone.

Chapter 9

Keep running, Callie told herself as they disappeared. *A mile and a half to go.* The urge to slow or even stop was strong, but Callie focused on her breathing. Steady in, steady out. It was a game she played with herself. When nothing else worked, she focused on one thing, made it as right as she could. It must be the frigid dry air, she thought, creating an explanation for her inability to maintain pace. She doggedly forced herself to put one foot in front of the other, listening to the thudding of her feet and trying to suck in more air, to find a good rhythm.

"You okay?"

Callie jumped, a small sideways deflection in her stride, startled by the voice. She was so focused on the ground at her feet and the sound of her gasping breath that she hadn't heard Mark running back to her. She gave him a curt nod. He pivoted and dropped into stride next to her, breathing easily.

"You're kind of dragging," he said, looking at her.

She didn't respond immediately. When she did finally answer, she said, "You can go on ahead." The cold air gave her normally mellow voice a harsh, scratchy sound.

It was his turn to avoid responding.

Mark gradually slowed the pace, so gradually that she didn't realize it until her breathing was nearly under control. Past the turn now, they could see the three girls still moving away from them. Mark stayed beside her, maintaining a companionable silence. They covered distance, not quickly but steadily, feet in the same sympathetic rhythm, hers heavier and noisier, his quieter, smoother. Another few minutes and they had moved into full sunshine with the bulk of the hill behind them. Ten minutes and they would be back at the school.

The twins had moved Mattie into the middle and, from the motion of the waving hands, it looked like they were still talking, though Callie and Mark were much too far away to hear what the conversation was about. Callie was usually the one between them. The silence was welcome, though; she wanted to think and sometimes the twins were overwhelming.

"You know, you don't have anything to prove."

"Like what?" Callie asked, shaking herself out of her thoughts.

"Like you're the . . . the . . ."

"Like the what?" she said, but there was no heat to her words. She was too tired to fight.

When he didn't answer, she glanced at Mark. His face was almost a bright red, far more vivid than running or the cold weather could explain, and she almost laughed. *Whatever he was about to say must have been a hoot,* she thought. *He looks embarrassed as heck.* He saw her looking at him and brightened even more.

"Like the what?" she asked again, staring straight ahead, playing with him.

He set his jaw and furrowed his eyebrows, refusing to answer, but he made an unhappy noise in the back of his throat.

Callie looked up at him. It was easy to forget how tall he really was. Unlike the rest of them, he was running without a hat, his longish hair unkempt and bouncing. His face was completely flushed. *Very smart guy in math,* she thought, *not so much with words.*

She finished the run next to him, accompanied by a comfortable silence. Less comfortable, Mark did not disturb the quiet again. He was, after all, a fast learner.

Idiot, idiot, idiot, thought Mark, lambasting himself. *Like what, she asks? How about, like you're smart.* Callie was one of the few people that didn't treat him like a freak.

Like you're gorgeous. No way could he tell her that.

And a girl, said a droll voice in the very back of his head, *a pretty girl.* He ignored the voice.

Callie, eyes forward, was running smoother now, a little grin on her face, the first time he had seen her smile in days.

Way to go, Marko, he thought with another "humph" under his breath. *Cheer her up by acting like an idiot. Yes sir, that's a talent you got there.*

Jen was waiting for them in front of the school when they finally made it back. Callie was her ride home, but Jen cheerfully past the time engaging in a gabfest with the twins while Mattie watched. There was a steady buzz of noise when Mark and Callie reached the other girls. Callie saw Mattie looking at her quizzically, the amber eyes having regained some fire during the run. The ski cap was stuffed into a pocket now, but she kept her chin buried in the collar of her jacket. The effect was to release a torrent of mussed red hair, falling in waves.

"Hey Callie, hiya Mark," greeted Jen. "Practice is over early so, *yay,* we can go home early. I'm hungry."

"You're always hungry," pointed out Callie, though she could feel the incipient rumbles of hunger grumbling, too.

"It's the running," said Anna.

"Along with all this cold," added Hanna.

"Burns lots of calories."

"We need some cookies," said Anna, and Callie felt the rumble grow.

"The best part of racing is the cookies at the end," said Hanna. Every cross-country race ended with cookies and Goldfish, preferably the extra-cheesy kind. The team all agreed that Mark's mom made the best chocolate-chip cookies. They took turns buying the Goldfish.

"Chocolate chips and nuts."

"Or oatmeal with some raisins."

"Would you two stop?" Callie's mouth was beginning to water and she was glad that she had on multiple layers—her stomach was making a racket, but the two shirts and the jacket were muffling it. For now, at least.

"So," started Mark, looking at Callie.

"So . . . ?" Callie looked at him, eyes sparkling and lips pursed. "What?" Mark held her eyes for a second, broke contact, then, sheepishly, he looked at her again.

"So," he restarted. "How many miles are you running? You said you ran this morning," he said. He was being nosy but she could see he was worrying. They had been running on the team long enough that some signals didn't need to be spoken.

Which made his goofiness on the run more interesting. She filed it away for future thought.

"Only about forty or fifty a week," she said. "But it's all mostly easy miles," she added hurriedly.

"So you're doing about eight a day. That's pretty good," Mark analyzed. "But that means that you're running almost every morning, because we haven't been doing anywhere near that in the afternoon. It doesn't add up," he said, staring at her as if daring her to challenge the numbers.

"I've been doing a long run on the weekends, too," she amended.

"She's been running every single morning," said Jen. "Tries to sneak out real quiet, but the dog goes with her and the tail thumping on the walls wakes me up."

The twins stared at Callie and she winced. She hadn't told anyone that she was running that much and hadn't realized that Jen had noticed. Her sister had a big mouth sometimes. Most of the time, she corrected herself.

"Every day?" Mark was shaking his head, his eyes questioning Callie.

"Yep," replied Jen. "Super-runner, that's what she's aiming for." Jen was grinning, but Mark winced.

Callie contemplated strangulation, but there were too many witnesses. She settled for glaring at her little sister instead. Jen just smiled wider.

Mark muttered something so low that Callie could barely hear it. Something like *You don't have to prove you're a super-runner* . . . She gave him a piercing look and he started to blush again.

Jen laughed and Callie watched the change come over her. You could see it, that second where Jen decided to stir things up. She was not trying to cause real trouble, not really, but just . . . And right before she was about to instigate, there was a change in her eyes, they took on a bright and mischievous glint, and there was always this momentary hesitation before impulse overrode common sense.

It only took an instant and Callie saw it coming and she couldn't stop her. Jen swung around to face Mattie, who had been hiding at the edge of the group listening to the banter.

"So 'fess up," she said to Mattie, talking fast, catching the other girl by surprise. "What happened? Did you bean the coach or knock over the water cooler, or"—she paused and her voice dropped to a hurried conspiratorial whisper—"did you fart in the layup line?"

Into the sudden void created by her sister's words, Callie thought, *Strangulation.* She looked at a wide-eyed and shocked Mattie. *Definitely strangulation. And Mattie can help. . . .*

Chapter 10

The moment of soundlessness grew, an elastic bubble of time stretching and enclosing all of them. The bubble was crushed in a babble of voices. Mattie retreated a half step from the onslaught of sound while the group of girls turned to match her movement, all of them gushing to reassure her, their words turning to frost on the cold air, except Jen, who simply waited.

"JEN!"

Her sister stared at her, head tilted to one side and a smirk as if to say *What?*

Anna and Hanna were hurriedly talked over each other, assuring Mattie that they didn't expect an answer.

"Whoa, hey, we don't—" said Anna.

"Sorry!" said Hanna.

"—need all—" said Anna.

"She didn't—" said Hanna.

"—the details," said Anna.

"—mean anything," said Hanna.

Mattie recovered quickly and in typical fashion, anger flushing her face red and the beginning of a snarl forming on her lips.

Quickly, Mark slid beside her. "No," he said quietly to her, "you might as well tell them. The story will get out anyway."

Callie watched Mark move in front of Mattie protectively and then looked at Mattie, who looked just as angry with Mark as she was with Jen. Mattie shrugged, a violent jerk in her shoulders, and countered, "Why should I? No one will believe me anyhow."

"You might give us a chance, you know," Callie offered, holding her voice low but straightforward, looking directly at Mattie.

Out of the corner of her eye, she saw Mark shoot her a grateful look. Mattie stared back at her and Callie watched as the other girl fought her anger, taking a couple of deep breaths to bring it under control. *Much better,* thought Callie, and let go a breath of her own.

The twins nodded agreement and Jen managed to look chagrined.

Mark fidgeted, looking from Callie to Mattie, waiting.

"I don't know what you want me to tell you. I got thrown off the team." Mattie paused, then mumbled, "I guess I deserved it."

Mark shook his head, looking frustrated. "You didn't deserve it. I keep telling you that and you're not listening."

"You weren't there," Mattie said. "I was the one that—"

"I don't have to be there. I know Boland and—" Mark interrupted, his voice getting loud, tinged with anger, so that he was talking over Mattie. Callie couldn't recall Mark ever really getting angry; usually he was the one defusing arguments.

"I was screaming at Coach Boland!" Her pitch was rising and Mattie began to animate her words with jabbing fingers, first a stabbing movement to her chest as she said, "Coach can't have that on the team, the disrespect." She aimed a forefinger toward Mark's nose. "And it's none of your business."

Mark looked at the finger in his face and then at Mattie, and Callie watched him go from angry to downright pissed. As he started to reply, she managed to catch his eye and froze him mid-word with a scowl. Startled, he shut his mouth. High red color burned on his cheekbones, but the red was from anger this time.

Callie turned to face Mattie, the rest of the girls arranged like a gallery, expecting and dreading more fireworks. Mattie shifted her target from Mark to Callie, leaning forward, chin down, hands clenched.

Callie struggled to keep her voice neutral and nonthreatening. "I guess I'm slow, Mattie. Why were you and Boland yelling?" Callie held herself still, her gaze fixed on Mattie, and waited.

Mattie folded in on herself as the rush of anger drained off. Her eyes, fierce toward Mark and Jen, softened and focused on Callie. Her shoulders slumped and her chin lowered halfway to her chest. Callie saw her shiver; the temperature, already biting cold, was dropping.

"I lost my cool," she said, shrugging halfheartedly.

"Well, duh, you said that," Callie agreed, "but why?"

Mattie hesitated, looking at the girls arrayed around her and Mark to the side, took a deep breath, and began. "We were finishing up practice. Boland was really running us hard—she was crazy mad that we got blown out the last game, that was Saturday night—and was just killing us in practice, kept screaming about effort, effort, effort." As she spoke, she was unconsciously shaking her head, little tiny arcs. "You know how she is."

"Uh-huh," said Callie with an understanding nod. "Everybody gets her for freshman PE."

"Anyway, Sandy—do you know Sandy, freshman, plays

post?—screwed up a bunch, and the more Coach yelled, the more she screwed up. So Sandy is freaking out and she's in tears because Coach is riding her butt and the more she freaks, the worse it gets and Coach isn't stopping." Mattie's voice was rising again, her hands jerking again, getting faster, in pace with her words.

"Breathe," Mark said softly from behind her. Callie watched as the younger girl took Mark's advice, a shuddering, deep breath calming her as she recounted the events at basketball practice. The twins looked at each other, mentally filing the moment away.

"So Sandy started it all?" Callie suggested.

"No way," Mattie retorted. "Everybody on the team is scared to death of Boland. Sandy's the same, but she was trying to, you know, keep Coach happy"—the words were gushing now—"and nothing was going right and Coach just kept ragging on her. Coach finally lost it and made Sandy do suicides, sprinting up and down the court nonstop. Every time Sandy would slow down, Coach would scream at her, call her a loser, a quitter." Another deep breath. "And everybody else was just watching, trying not to be the next one that Coach yelled at. I lost it," she said, her voice fading, her eyes dropping to her feet.

Jen, hiding behind the twins, looked small and young and suddenly miserable.

Callie felt tears forming in her eyes. "What did you say?" she asked in a soft voice, encouraging Mattie to finish the story. There was still more that needed to be said.

Mattie glanced up but would not meet Callie's eyes. She started to speak, stopped for another deep breath.

"I blew up. Sandy was falling, she was so fricking exhausted, and Coach kept yelling. I finally couldn't take it anymore, it wasn't right, and I started shouting at her. Yelled at her that she was killing Sandy, that Sandy was doing the best she could. Told her that only a crap coach would tell the girls they were losers. Told her the girls were winners and she was the loser.

"I don't remember everything I said, I was shouting and Coach was shouting. All I could see was her in front of me. I remember throwing a basketball and then Coach grabbed me and threw me at the door, told me never to come back."

She looked up at Callie, made eye contact this time. She shifted, chin rising and shoulders lifting.

"And I'm not going to," she finished, staring fixedly at Callie.

It was a day for silences, Callie thought, staring back at Mattie. She saw Mattie shiver again and suddenly she realized she was freezing too. Around her, the world came back into focus, the shocking blue sky now darkening with the approaching night, black shadows from the pines reaching toward them, and little noises, banging doors from the school and cars on the road, again audible.

She turned away from Mattie but stepped back at the same time, enlarging the circle of runners to include the other girl and Mark.

"I figure I'll do another run tomorrow. Anybody else going?" she asked them all.

Anna and Hanna looked at each other uncertainly.

"Sure," agreed Anna, following Callie's lead.

"We'll be here," volunteered Hanna.

Mattie looked from girl to girl, her forehead wrinkled in puzzlement.

"I have to skip again," said Mark. "I've got some submittals I need to get in for an internship."

Callie turned to Mattie. "You in?" she asked.

"You want me to come back?" Mattie asked.

"You're not playing ball, you might as well get ready for track," said Callie. "Plus, misery loves company and it's miserable cold out here," she asserted, a fresh shiver emphasizing her point for her. "If you want to."

"Um, okay. I guess," Mattie replied, lengthening out the words, making them sound more like questions. "Do we meet here again?" She looked to Mark, then back to Callie and the rest of them.

"Yep. We'll figure out where we're running once we meet up."

"We have to go," said Mark, looking at Mattie. She nodded and, with one more questioning look at the other runners, she joined him as he headed for the parking lot and his Jeep.

"It's snack time," Hanna suggested.

"It's always snack time," Anna assured her. Living in town, the twins were closer to snacks. Callie felt a rumble in her belly. She had forgotten she was hungry.

Callie turned to Jen. "Ready to go?"

Jen looked at her, and then at the receding couple. Callie's car, an old hand-me-down Subaru, was parked on the street in the opposite direction. Jen looked at her sister again and said, "Hold on a sec, I'll be right back."

She took off at a quick jog behind Mattie and Mark. Callie heard her shout to them. Both Mark and Mattie stopped and waited for the youngster. She caught up with them about halfway to the asphalt parking lot.

She started talking before she reached them—Callie couldn't hear what she was saying, but Jen was flailing her arms, which was a reliable indicator. Mark gave a quick grin and Callie could have sworn that Mattie's mouth formed the words, *"It's okay."* and then watched, shocked, as prickly Mattie moved forward and gave Jen a hug. *"It's okay."* Jen's head bobbed her acceptance into Mattie's shoulder, then pulled away, wiping a hand across her face. She stopped to flail some more words at Mattie before reversing her path to rejoin her big sister.

"What was that all about?" inquired Callie.

"None of your business," was the blunt reply.

"There's hope for you yet, little sis," Callie said, not looking at Jen, a smile showing briefly.

"Oh shut up."

Chapter 11

The fragrant aroma of a pot roast in the oven filled the kitchen. From the counter opposite the sink, Callie worked at butchering the carrots that would go with the potatoes, each *ker-chunk* of the ridiculously large chef's knife slamming into the cutting board sending another piece of carrot bouncing.

Attentive and expectant, the dog positioned herself in the middle of the tile floor. Sophie properly considered it her job to clean up any mess that hit the floor, and experience had taught her the best location. With the exception of celery, the dog would eat anything. Already two bouncing slices had hit the cutting board and rolled off, each lasting a second before being inhaled by the retriever.

Three colored teardrop lights—red, yellow, blue—hung down, their combined luminosity sending warmth to the maple cabinets and marble countertops. The ceiling, like the exterior walls, was formed from natural logs, giving the room an earthy, organic appeal. There was a center island and breakfast bar that divided the kitchen from the living room, the fireplace there adding its warmth to the otherwise dark room, flickers from the flames floating, mutating on the walls. The island opened to the dining room where Jen was doing homework.

It was a week before the start of spring track, but spring was still in hiding. Outside, the sky held the remnants of the hidden sun, translucent clouds radiating hues of baby blues and peaches through the flat upper layer of clouds while fluffy stratocumulus clouds draped themselves over the surrounding hills in a brilliant white shawl. It was a pleasant change from the weeks of gray monotony, snow flurries, and occasional sleet, but the sun had been missing for three weeks.

The brutal cold of January and early February was gone, fading to a consistently dreary, not-quite-above-freezing dampness that let the often-gray skies seep into the nooks and crannies outdoors and slither under the doors and through the chinks into the log house.

Another *ker-chunk,* another carrot slice on an escape trajectory. Sophie moved slightly to the left, a centerfielder tracking a fly ball, deftly catching the carrot before it hit the floor.

"It's a good thing she's on a diet anyway," said Callie's mom, Sarah, watching the dog expertly hunt the carrot. "Here, slice these up," she said as she walked over with a double handful of Yukon gold potatoes.

Looking at the carrots, some slivered as thin as a dime, others wide enough to plug a wine bottle, she said, "Probably want to try for some consistency if we're going to eat anytime soon. You're going to need to cut the fat ones down some more or they'll never cook." She deposited the potatoes next to Callie.

Callie glanced at her mother but didn't respond, turning back to the cutting board with the knife, the ten-inch blade dwarfing her feminine hand, and started reworking the bigger chunks of carrot. Behind her, Sarah frowned as Callie chopped.

Sarah studied her daughter. She would never be the chatterbox that Jen was. Callie was quiet where Jen was exuberant, stuck more inside her head. Callie ruminated and chased ideas in circles when things bothered her. Once she made up her mind, though, she acted. She was their "all or nothing" kid— Callie didn't do anything in half measures. It just took her time to make the decision.

She still had a hint of her summertime glow, the golden honey tan she acquired every year, highlighted by the abundant shoulder-length auburn hair. When she wasn't running, Callie allowed her hair to flow free, a casual wavy bounce that caught the light, revealing the highlights and bringing out the color in her eyes.

Sarah frowned. Callie had added a light touch of makeup. Not much, and Callie didn't need much. Callie hadn't asked her for advice on cosmetics. It hadn't been a subject that had interested her. That had obviously changed. She was getting advice from someone, probably a girlfriend.

Probably Jenessa, thought Sarah. A second thought struck her: *She looks tired.*

"You want to talk about it?" she offered to Callie, keeping her voice low, sympathy in her eyes. In the dining room, Jen's head lifted, and she looked into the kitchen.

"About what?" Callie replied, keeping her voice equally low, not looking up. Finished with the carrots, she reached for the potatoes, snagging one and splitting it cleanly in half.

"How small do you want these?" she asked her mother.

"About one-inch cubes will work," said Sarah, and she moved around to face her daughter. Callie rediscovered the ability to cut correctly, the first half of the potato pared down into nearly perfect matching cubes. Callie kept her eyes focused on the cutting board in front of her, finishing the first potato and proceeding to start on the next.

"Callie," Sarah said softly, and waited for her daughter to look up, to make eye contact. Callie kept chopping. Sarah watched, silent, as her eldest worked on the vegetables. Watched and waited, patiently. She and Callie had played this game before.

"I'm okay."

"Hmm," said Sarah . . . and waited some more.

"It's just . . ." Callie started, hesitated, and then continued, "I don't know what to do." She looked up from under the mass of hair. "Jenessa and Mattie are constantly bickering and it's bugging everybody."

From the dining room, Jen snorted and Callie looked over and glared briefly before turning back to her mom.

"Why do you have to do anything?" asked Callie's mom.

Callie looked at her mom, started to answer, and, realizing she didn't have one, looked back down and started to chop potatoes again.

"I don't, I guess," she said reluctantly. "It's just that it's really frustrating running behind the two of them and watching it all. Mattie doesn't back down to anything and gets mad when anybody says anything to her. Jenessa knows it and is constantly prodding her." She looked across the counter to her mother.

"The other day, we had headed out and Jenessa is talking about her new shoes and how much traction they had in the mud and *what a shame that Mattie didn't have some newer shoes*," Callie said, wrinkling her nose in imitation of the other girl. "So we're running and Mattie 'slips' in the mud and knocks Jenessa headfirst into a snow bank. She didn't slip—she did it on purpose, I was right behind them, but Mattie says she's sorry and makes a big deal out of not having better shoes."

From the dining room, Jen started to snicker.

"It's not funny!" stormed Callie, glaring down the kitchen island to Jen.

"Oh yeah it is," grinned Jen. "Can't you just see Jenessa, always just perfect, with snow clods in her hair?"

"Shush," said Sarah, turning to face her youngest daughter. Jen put on her fake pouty face, but her eyes were bright and she was having difficulty maintaining the look.

"It isn't. It used to be easy, me and Hanna and Anna and Mark—" Another snort from Jen, another warning look from her mom. "—would head out and get a run in. Jenessa sometimes jumped in. Now Mattie is there every day and everything is different. She's always pushing the pace and dragging everybody else with her." Her voice stretched higher, not whiny, just . . . frustrated.

"Aren't you team captain?" asked Sarah.

"Cross-country, not track," corrected Callie, finishing with the chopping and moving to the sink to wash the knife. Sarah came around to gather the spuds and carrots. The smell of the pot roast and spices wafted out of the oven as she added the vegetables to the meat. Callie met her mom's look. "Besides, it's between seasons; there are no captains."

"Is there any reason why you can't start now as the leader, even if you're not the captain?"

"How?" The frustration was evident in the scowl on Callie's face. "They don't listen to anybody. Except the twins, they listen to everybody, but then they just do what they're going to do anyway. Jenessa is Jenessa, always doing things her way. She's got so much talent it stinks, but she just doesn't want to work. And"—she pursed her mouth and her eyes narrowed—"the only one that Mattie will listen to is Mark."

"Hah!" sounded from the dining room.

"If I have to shush you one more time, Jen, I'm sending you to your room," said Sarah with a stern look directed at Jen. "Let Callie and I talk, please."

She turned back to Callie. "You know, Doc saw something in you that made him think that you would be a good captain. You might try trusting his judgment—and yourself—instead of acting like a drama queen and going into a funk."

"I'm not a drama queen."

"Wanna bet?" said Jen from the table. Callie turned angrily toward her sister but was a half a beat behind her mother.

"Take it to your room, Jen," she ordered. "Now."

"But—" Jen started protesting.

"Now." Sarah pointed to the stairs, staring at her youngest.

Jen rumbled the chair back along the wood floor, a long grinding skid, gathered her books up into a rough stack, papers catawampus, and glared at her mother.

"It's not fair!" she said, chin thrust forward, indignant.

"Too bad, take it up with the judge," shot back her mother. "Upstairs, move it."

Jen passed around the end of the table and headed for the stairs, feet clumping across the floor, the weight of the armload of books leaning her to the right. She looked up to her mother, who met her gaze and nodded toward the stairs. Jen sighed as she walked past her mother, then turned her head to stick out her tongue to her older sister.

Brat, thought Callie.

"Keep going," said Sarah, as Jen stomped each tread on the way to the second floor.

Callie, fascinated by the theatrics, watched the production that Jen was making and said incredulously to her mom, "She calls *me* the drama queen?"

"Uh-huh," said her mom.

From the stairwell, "I heard that."

"Keep moving!"

Jen's feet disappeared up the last set of treads with a last loud thump and Callie's mom turned to her oldest child and took a deep breath. "Okay, you haven't been *that* big a drama queen. Jen has a talent." She looked at her daughter with concern. "But you've been moping around here for two weeks, and it's not just running. I can't really help you with the running. Doc could, if you asked." Sarah saw the reluctance flit by on Callie's face. "But if there is something else, maybe I can . . ." Sarah left the question and offer unfinished.

"It's just running," mumbled Callie. She turned away from her mom and stepped around the dog, grabbing a dish towel, and began to wipe down the countertop. "I'll figure it out."

Silently, she cleaned up the kitchen while her mom watched. Above them, they could hear Jen moving around and muttering to herself. In the fireplace, a log popped, but otherwise the house was mostly quiet.

"Callie?" said Callie's mom soberly, trying to get the girl's attention.

"Yeah?" said Callie, turning from the sink to face back to her mom.

"Sweetie. You don't wear makeup for a run. You wear makeup because of boys."

Chapter 12

Callie froze.

"Boys?" she repeated.

"Boys," asserted her mom. "You know, the ones that aren't girls, the ones that are weird and do dumb things. Then, one day, we kind of notice some are kind of cute and funny, or good-looking and dangerous, then they don't notice us or they do but for the wrong reasons—and both kinds drive us nuts—and eventually we choose one and we get married." Her mom paused. "Don't be in too big a hurry for that last part."

"I'm not in too big a hurry for any part!" Callie protested, her face flushing red.

"I know, sweetie, but sometimes it doesn't matter if we think we're ready or not. Sometimes it just happens."

Callie avoided looking at her mom while desperately searching for some way to change the subject, but her thoughts were jumbled and random and confused. She shuffled her feet a bit, shifting first to the right foot, then left and back before peeking up to see her mom watching her with a little rueful smile. Quickly she averted her eyes again. *Dang it* was the only clear thought that penetrated through the maelstrom inside her head.

"We've already done the 'where babies come from' talk, Mom," Callie said, diverting the conversation away from uncomfortable ground.

"Yes, we have. But this isn't that talk." Callie's mom sat down at the breakfast bar and gathered herself a bit, then continued. "This is the other talk." She began to add something else but then closed her mouth and resumed waiting. Callie could feel her mom watching her but didn't see a path to freedom.

Other talk? What other talk? thought Callie. She fidgeted with the dish towel, her hands twisting and folding it over and over into different shapes, stretching it then balling it up again. The flush on her face seemed to be growing hotter with each passing moment and Callie could feel her breathing getting tight and shallow.

"What other talk?" she asked doubtfully.

"The one that talks about feelings and dreams and the future. The 'birds and bees' talk is basic biology. You and a boy do this—"

Callie flushed even more. *That* discussion when she was eleven was bad enough but at sixteen, it was so *awkward*.

"—and a baby arrives," her mom finished. "This talk is different. It's about how you choose to live your life and who you choose to live it with. You're going to meet a lot of boys and some are going to be jerks and most are going to be okay but nothing that sets your heart aflutter. One day, one will— and now you get to deal with all the feelings that go with that. And I wish I could say it's easy, but it isn't." A pause and her voice became gentle. "There aren't any guaranteed right answers but a whole lot of wrong ones, and only you can figure it all out and decide what you want and need and deserve," she finished.

Callie stole a glance at her mother, then blurted out, "I don't know what I want."

Sarah considered this for a moment, then said, "That's a bit of a fib. You know what you want or you wouldn't be all tangled up. The problem is that you either want two things at once or something is blocking you from what you want."

That's where Jen gets it from, thought Callie, looking at her mom. Jen was never afraid of calling bull on dumb statements. There was a hush while she considered that thought, the only sounds a creak from the stairs, the occasional pop of the logs in the fireplace, and the dog, gently snoring, who had determined that no more treats were forthcoming, and decided on napping. Disassociated thoughts moved in fits and starts through her mind, adding to the confusion. The dog had it easy.

"Mom, why did you quit working? I mean, as a lawyer," she added hastily.

Her mom considered the question before replying. "Well, for starters, I was never a lawyer, just a paralegal. The hours that you have to put in to be an attorney were too high and I wasn't willing to pay that price. Working as a paralegal, I did a lot of the things that the lawyers did without anywhere near the stress and without going to court. I had other plans for my life that included you girls. But I really never stopped working—I still do my volunteer work in the valley for the elderly."

"Jen wants to be a lawyer."

"And she'll probably be a good one. That's a choice that she gets to make, just as you're making a choice. And she may change her mind yet. That's okay, too."

Callie's plans were set and she didn't think she'd change her mind. Finish high school, then straight to college to become a nurse. Pick up a job and move out of the house and on her own by nineteen. Eighteen if possible.

Nowhere in her plan were boys. She focused on getting out of the house and into college, securing her independence. An alternative track, one with boys, hadn't really hit her. It messed up everything.

She was staying in the valley, going to the local college—it had a solid nursing program, one of the most respected in the Northwest—then once she had her degree, maybe getting out, heading someplace more interesting than Cloverland.

"He's going to California," she said reflectively into the air. She heard the words as they left her mouth, shocked to realize she had said it aloud. Her cheeks went from flushed to blanched. "I mean . . . I . . . uh . . . ."

Her mother nodded. She wasn't surprised. "Mark?"

"An internship," said Callie. She looked at her mom with big eyes. "Please don't tell anyone. Not yet."

"It's not my job to blab," said Sarah. "The makeup was for him?"

"It was Jenessa's idea. I wanted to try to get his attention but not, you know, uh, I wanted him to see me but like a girl."

"How else is he going to see you?"

"We're friends, running buddies. It's different."

Callie's mother smiled. "Somehow, I suspect that he is very much aware that you're a girl."

"Not hardly. We see each other at school a bit and we run together, but now he spends all his time with Mattie. . . ." She stumbled to a stop, the flush back again but tinged with some anger.

"So it's not that she's causing problems as a runner, her and Jenessa," said her mom. "Or that's only part of it. Does Mark know how you feel?"

"I don't know," Callie replied with a shrug, stringing out the last word, discouraged.

"Does Mattie?"

"I don't know." Again the long, drawn-out end word, plaintive now.

Her mom thought for a moment while Callie continued her fidgety little motions, wanting advice, wanting to run. Callie steadied her eyes on her mom and the extra little motions faded.

"So what do I do?" she asked.

Sarah took a deep breath. "You know that part where I said there are no guaranteed right answers?"

"Yeah."

"There are no right answers. But there're a lot of wrong ones."

"That doesn't help!"

"I know it doesn't. You've got some decisions to make and I'm probably going to repeat a bunch of things you already know, but bear with me. First, you don't have a problem with Mattie. You have a problem with you. You can't control what she does. So Jenessa and Mattie feuding on the run is not your problem. Mattie and Mark seeing each other—" She paused. "How do you know they are seeing each other?"

"They spend all their time together, Mom. Wherever Mark goes, Mattie is right there with him. He goes to lunch, she follows. They're always bumping into each other at school, he's handing her notes and stuff. He drives her home after we run. It's obvious," answered Callie.

Sarah hesitated, recalling Callie recounting Mark's tongue-tied-ness not long ago, a flash of understanding of her daughter's situation. "Don't they live on the same road? Off Hershmitter?" asked Sarah, tackling Callie's points in reverse order.

"Uh-huh."

"And they always bump into each other? In the hallway or where?" her mother pressed.

"Sometimes the hallways and then at lunch with everybody," responded Callie, the fidgeting, little twitches, starting up again. She was uncomfortable under her mom's cross-examination. Jenessa never questioned her, just tried to help her beat out Mattie for Mark.

"I thought the whole high school had lunch together. It's a pretty tiny school."

"Yeah, but she's always sitting with him at our table."

"*Your* table?"

"You know what I mean. All us runners sit at the same table. Well, most of us, anyway. Jenessa sits with some other girls." The dish towel was getting mauled again and Sarah could see the confusion spreading on Callie's face.

"Sweetie, I'm trying to help," her mom explained. "And the only way I can is if I understand some of what's going on. I'm not trying to minimize what you're going through, just understand it."

"I get it, Mom, but I know what I see."

"I think," her mom started slowly, "that you need to be a bit easier on yourself. And on Mark and Mattie." Callie started to protest, but her mother raised a finger, the universal mom gesture for *Wait*.

"You need to be a bit easier on yourself because you're getting tied up in knots over things you can't control. You can't make Jenessa and Mattie like each other, and if you try to play referee, you'll get run over. Those girls will have to work out their own problems. You're not the captain of the track team, so you don't have that responsibility, and Mattie doesn't run cross-country. Once track starts, Mattie won't be running with you anyway, since she's a sprinter."

"Middle distance, four hundred and eight hundred meters," Callie corrected.

"Okay, but the point stands. They're in different events.

"You also can't make Mark like you." Sarah held up her hand as Callie again tried to interject an objection. "You can't. He'll either be a friend—and from the sound of it, he is, and you want him to be more—or he won't. Mark will either like you in a boyfriend/girlfriend way or he won't. Getting in a big hurry isn't going to help. Trying to be someone else isn't going to work, and neither will flinging yourself at a boy."

"I'm not!" exploded Callie. "I wouldn't!"

"I didn't say you were, but I like that answer. The point is that you have two problems that you've given yourself. One isn't your problem—Mattie and Jenessa—and the other you can't do anything about except be patient. Give Mark a chance and see what happens."

Callie chewed on this while her mother watched. Doing nothing bothered her. As she thought, the dog at her feet stirred. Sophie always heard Callie's dad's truck first. It was about that time, she noticed. Her conversation with her mom had left her spent and made it hard to think clearly. The sun had fully set and the house, except for the fireplace and kitchen, was dark, everything silent, broken by the sound of a creak of the wood in the living room. Sophie got up from the kitchen floor, tail wagging, and Sarah slid off the bar stool at the island.

"Right on time," said Sarah, following behind the retriever and giving Callie some space to think.

A few seconds later, Callie heard the crunching of the gravel as her dad walked across the driveway and, just after, Hank Reardon entered the living room from the front door.

"Howdy!" he said. He looked up the stairs and stopped.

"Tell me you're not eavesdropping again, Jen," he said with a frown.

"Jenifer Ann! Downstairs, now!" ordered Callie's mom, taking fast strides to the bottom of the stairs. There was a scramble from the top of the steps as Jen got to her feet from where she had lain, hidden by the shadows.

Callie had dropped the towel and, with a jerk, bolted for the base of the stairs. She could feel her hands clenched into fists, the nails digging into her palms, and an image of Jen's neck flashed through her mind.

"You sneak!" she shouted at the stairs.

Her dad intercepted her halfway to the stairs, placing a hand on her shoulder.

"Let your mom deal with it, Cal," he said. On the staircase behind him, she saw a white running sock, then an ankle, then the leg descend slowly to the next-to-top step as Jenifer began slowly traversing the staircase to her mother.

"But—" Callie protested, trying to go around, but her dad cut her off with a shake of his head.

"Let the mom be the mom."

Callie stared at him sullenly but stopped trying to push past her dad. She watched as Jenifer, white-knuckled grip on the rough-hewn handrail, reached the landing, looking tiny next to her mother. She stood there, shoulders crunched forward and chin tucked. Callie felt absolutely no sympathy for her.

"Callie, could you go to your room for a few minutes?" her mom asked, her voice tight and controlled. "Your sister and I need to have a talk."

Callie nodded, glaring at Jenifer but not speaking as she made her way past her. While she climbed the stairs, she watched her mother take Jenifer by the shoulder and direct her to the dining room. At the top landing, she turned to her left and made her way to her room, clicking the light on the way in. Pre, still in full stride, looked at her from the poster across the room, but he was focused on his race and didn't really see her. Along one wall was her bookcase, the shelves overflowing, a mix of teenage novels featuring vampires and witches, the complete collection of Harry Potter books, a few crime thrillers, and a dozen or so running books.

Her anger at Jenifer was already fading, which annoyed her. *I want to stay mad,* she thought. Downstairs she could hear her mother berating Jenifer. Callie knew that voice, the so-reasonable, *we're so disappointed in you, you can be better than that* voice; it had been a while since she had earned it, and she was happy to avoid it. She'd much rather have her dad shout and yell than have her mom use that voice. The shouting and yelling from Dad were over in a few minutes but the feeling of guilt, of being a disappointment, stuck around and nagged. She also heard an occasional whine from Jen as she tried to defend herself against her mother. *Hah!* thought Callie, closing the door to her room. *You deserve every bit of it.*

She flopped down on her bed, half lying, half sitting, leaning against the pillows and stuffed animals. She started replaying the conversation with her mother over in her head, thinking about Mark and Mattie and Jenessa. Her mom was smart, but she was also wrong.

During track, Mattie was not her problem. In the fall, though, Mattie played volleyball. The basketball coach was also the volleyball coach. There was zero chance that Boland was going to let her play. So Mattie wouldn't be playing volleyball in the fall next year. That door was slammed shut permanently by Boland, which left cross-country as the only other sport that Mattie could do.

Mattie was too good a runner not to have her on the cross-country team. Doc would know it; so would Mark. They would both talk her into running on the team. Callie was going to have to deal with Mattie. And Mark. And Jenessa.

A hollowness opened up inside her. Mark had been a friend since she started running when she was Jen's age. He had been goofy then, awkward and ill at ease except when he was running. He managed to be almost normal when he was running. By the end of his freshman year, he had exceeded the school's ability to challenge him in math and science. His mom had gone to them and demanded they find courses for him, and the school responded with an innovative approach using free courseware from MIT.

Callie and Mark, at least until recently, had always been able to talk, but something had changed. Callie was pretty sure it was Mattie. Now when she saw Mark he was tongue-tied and looked . . . well . . . guilty. Not guilty, scared. Something. Something wasn't right, she thought.

Enough, she thought with a quiet little growl, squashing her feelings and reaching a decision. *Mark's not my problem. Mattie is my problem. Mattie and Jenessa.* She looked at her alarm clock. 5:20 p.m. He might be home. Downstairs the voices were tailing off; if she was going to make a call, it needed to be quick, before dinner. He didn't check his phone after dinner.

She dug her cell out of her back pocket and hit speed dial. Cell coverage up in the hills was pretty inconsistent, but she had one bar. It would be enough. She dialed the number and listened as it went straight through to voice mail. Either he wasn't home or he was out of range. After the beep, she started talking.

"Hi, Doc. Hey, I was thinking about coming down the hill and running in the valley tomorrow. Would you run with me?" She paused to take a breath. "Let me know, Coach, and thanks."

Chapter 13

Seven miles away—unless you were driving, in which case it was more like seventeen miles—Mark was sitting at his house, staring. His mouth was relaxed while his mind sprinted through sequences, occasionally slowing down to wander a labyrinth of ideas. His book, a history of animatronic systems, was forgotten.

He'd tried to explain it to Callie once, that when he was thinking, all the threads of ideas glowed and tied together and untied and rearranged themselves into new patterns, shifting and weaving until they made sense. Callie had looked at him like he was whacked, the village idiot out for a stroll.

Which, in a way, he was.

When the book finally slipped from his hand, hitting the floor with a solid thump, Mark convulsively reached and stretched, his eyes refocusing as he stood up.

"I got an idea," he announced. His mother's cat, a large orange tabby named Fizz, lounging on the back of the couch, looked at him, largely unimpressed.

Mark looked around the small room. He needed paper. He could see the bones of it, but he wanted to draw it up, build a schematic to make sure that it would work. He found some on the counter in the kitchen and quickly started sketching the components. In between jotting notes, he would pace, striding the length of the kitchen and back. He'd need at least one motor, maybe two. As he drew, he also started to list parts that he was going to need. In addition to the motor, some form of explosive gas.

He looked at his notes. He'd have to stash them someplace safe before his mother came home. Paula Johnson was a tax specialist, working late again now that tax season was here. She had started part time shortly after she had lost her husband, and had quickly lost herself in the intricacies of the tax code.

As Mark got older—and got past the troubled stage when he truly understood that his energetic and chronically cheerful dad wasn't coming home—she spent more time at work, adding to her clientele until she was turning away business. When Mark did get into trouble, she forced him to step up and accept responsibility for himself. She was the one who had forced him into running. He discovered that when he ran, the noise inside his head would quiet for a little while.

Gas cartridge? . . . Maybe . . . would a servo or pulley system work better?

He quickly sketched a rough schematic of the mechanism. Now, what to do with it all . . . he started to laugh. He knew.

. . . gotta be a zombie.

Rough sketch complete, he looked over the list of parts and realized that he was going to need some help. Some of the gear that he needed simply wasn't available here. If he ordered it in, it would leave a trail that led right to him. He remembered Uncle Bennie's story. He needed a way to cover his tracks.

He also needed an accomplice—one he could trust.

Mark's grin got huge. Yeah, Uncle Bennie would help. This

was going to be the best senior prank since . . . never. It was going to be awesome. And the best part would be pulling it a year early. The seniors would get blamed, not him.

Mark briefly thought about telling his mom and decided against it. She thought her brother was a poor influence on Mark. Mark disagreed. Uncle Bennie was very, very cool . . . when he wasn't being a jerk.

He fired up his laptop and started to draft an e-mail outlining his plan to his uncle, and then decided against it. He grabbed his phone instead and hit the button for Bennie. He got Bennie's voice mail.

"Hey—Uncle Bennie. Got an idea and need some help." He quickly outlined the plan, adding a warning not to mention it to his mom. Uncle Bennie probably already knew that, but better to be cautious.

After he hung up, he rewrote the list of the pieces he would need and how the whole thing fit together. For good measure, he wrote down his plan for evading detection. He'd mail them to Bennie if his uncle agreed to help. Snail mail was slower but safer. Online was forever, but you could burn paper.

"This is going to be great," he exclaimed to the rotund tabby that had followed him into the kitchen, expecting more food.

Fizz yawned. It wasn't food; therefore, by definition, it wasn't great.

Twenty minutes later, he got a reply by text.

Dude! Great idea! Busy now, call me tomorrow.

Uncle Bennie was in.

Chapter 14

Callie had to wait two days before driving down to the valley to run with Doc. He had been busy with work, trying to get ahead as much as possible before the start of track season, now just a weekend away. Like most cross-country coaches, he had a full-time job and juggled the time off he needed with the task of earning a living.

Callie met Doc on the Washington side of the river. The greenbelt was dotted with small grassy parks filled with mature trees, maples and cherries and chestnuts. A ribbon of asphalt wound next to the river for seven miles, passing next to boat launches and picnic tables, connecting the parks. The trail on the other side, the Idaho side, was longer and more exposed, nearly a dozen miles starting at the Indian casino on the opposite bank before crossing the main bridge and wrapping around the town of Lewiston, ending up at Hell's Gate State Park. Callie preferred the greener Washington side.

Doc was early for a change, waiting when she pulled up. She was careful getting out of the car; her Subaru, grimy from the dirt roads and deicing chemicals, left black oily smudges on her anytime she touched it.

"Hey, hey," said Doc by way of greeting as he strolled

over to her, dressed in washed-out blue shorts and a dark blue long-sleeved shirt advertising the Portland Marathon, sleeves pushed up on his bony forearms.

"I wasn't expecting it to be this warm." Callie stripped off her fleece jacket. She was down to long sleeves and capris. "It's been a while since I went for a run and didn't feel like the abominable snowman." She reached behind her head and used a scrunchie to wrap her thick hair into a sloppy ponytail.

"Ready," she said. Doc nodded.

Together they began jogging through the parking lot and eased out on the trail. Next to her, she could hear Doc's feet pitter-pattering, his stride quick and efficient. She sounded like she was running in clown shoes by comparison. Her own feet were slapping the ground. Her posture was out of whack too. She was leaning too far forward. Callie gathered herself, forcing her back straighter and pulling her shoulders up, trying to run taller. Her form smoothed out.

She looked over to Doc, trying to figure out how to start the conversation about Mattie and Jenessa. He saw the glance and looked back at her, his grin lopsided to the left. "Not yet. We'll talk later. Just run."

"Yeah, but—"

"Just run," he said, and looked away.

Anna and Hanna could keep up a nonstop dialogue for miles, and the other girls joined in, a rolling gabfest on easy days. At first, she was uncomfortable with the silence, but she felt the relaxation inside as the steady effort loosened and warmed her.

They settled into the run and followed the trail, dodging around the overgrown blackberry brambles that reached out over the path waiting to snag the unwary. Callie let Doc take the lead and followed him as he turned right off the trail at the boat launch to run on the wet grass, staying close to the river. Through the trees, Callie caught glimpses of the small boats out on the river—a lake really, man-made as a result of a series of dams built by the Army Corps of Engineers. The fishermen, she knew, would be out there every day in anything less than a blizzard. It made her cold just to think of sitting in the thin-skinned aluminum boats in near-freezing conditions, wind whipping spray over the gunwales.

At least I'm moving, she thought. Doc was keeping the pace slow, really slow for him, and Callie felt grateful. She hadn't felt right in a while running. She couldn't point to any one thing that was wrong, just that it wasn't . . . flowing. She heard Doc's stride change, so she slid sideways, separating a bit, so she could see his feet. Doc always ran up on his forefoot; now he was heel-striking, a little more stiff-legged.

"Just practicing," he said. They came around the edge of the grass, rejoining the trail, and Doc reverted back when they hit asphalt again. They picked up a bit of speed with the better footing and Callie relaxed into the steady rhythm of putting one foot in front of the other, the steady easy intake of air with the shorter, more forceful push on the exhalation. Beside her, Doc was in the same easy rhythm and their measured strides matched, each footfall in sync with the other.

They ran like this for another mile and a half before turning around at the confluence of the rivers, the Snake and the larger Clearwater, and retracing their path back to the cars. The greenery was a welcome change for Callie after spending the winter running in shades of white: the brilliant white of new snow in sunlight; the blue-white in cloudy weather; the dirty white of refrozen slush and snow near the roads; the spotted white of the woods with pine cones and fallen moss marring the surface. Even with the trees still bare, the green of the grass forecasted winter's end here. Soon it would move up the valley, reaching into the hills and mountains.

They stayed on the trail all the way back to the cars, no more diversions onto the grass. They reached the parking lot and slow fogged to their cars. Callie's breathing quickly subsided to normal, but she felt light-headed and lighthearted. She put her hands on her slender hips and turned her face to the sky, eyes closed, taking deep satisfying breaths. The sun broke through the scattered clouds, and Callie felt it warm her face. Next to her, Doc was stretching, rustles of clothing as he changed positions. And she could hear boiling water.

She opened her eyes, puzzled, and looked around.

Between the trail and the river was a flock of wood ducks, dozens of them, probing into the saturated ground, their black-and-white beaks vibrating in the mud, looking for grubs and worms. The sound of each vibration, combined with all the others, blended into a bubbling rolling boil of a sound. Callie watched as they fed. The males invited attention, more vivid greens and browns standing out on their bodies. The females, less colorful, were just as striking.

"Now we can talk," said Doc, quietly breaking her reverie.

It took Callie a second to remember. Mattie and Jenessa. That's why she had asked Doc to run with her. She needed help in dealing with the two of them. She was assuming that Mattie would be on the cross-country team. The thought of Mattie on the team set off a disquieting grumble.

"Yeah, well, I uh . . ." Now that she was talking to Doc, she was uncertain how to start, to broach the subject. Doc waited patiently while she sorted out her thoughts.

"Cross-country," she began again. "I think Mattie Rede, you know her, she runs the four hundred and eight hundred?"

Doc inclined his head.

"She plays volleyball, but I think she'll be doing something else this fall." She didn't go into her reason on why Mattie would be doing something else.

"I know," said Doc.

"How . . . ?" Callie started to ask, then finished almost to herself, "Mark."

Doc nodded again. Callie had a sudden vision of Doc as a bobblehead doll, always nodding. It was disconcerting.

"Right. Anyhow, Mattie can run, maybe as fast as the twins, so she'd be good on the team." The words were coming in a rush, and Callie tried to slow them down.

Doc nodded again. "Doesn't sound like a problem so far."

"It's not. Or her running isn't." Callie thought about how she wanted to phrase it. "It's that she and Jenessa don't get along, they're always picking at each other. Jenessa will get all up in Mattie's face and then Mattie will get pissed off and go back at her and it just keeps building," Callie explained. "Shoot, Mattie planted Jenessa into a snow bank last week. It's getting bad."

He turned, tapping her forearm. "Walk with me. I'll tighten up if I just stand around," he said as he slowly began moving.

"Anybody else on the team complain about it?" asked Doc.

"No," she said, glad herself to be moving. "But they're always doing it. Even the twins notice—they're giving each other that look."

"You've figured out the twins' looks?" asked Doc, mildly interested. "That whole silent communication thing they do is kind of spooky sometimes."

"What are we going to do about Mattie and Jenessa?" Callie asked, trying to get Doc back on track.

"Why should we do anything?" responded Doc, stopping and turning to face the young girl. "Why not leave well enough alone until they either work it out themselves or we have to do something?"

Callie stared at him, flummoxed.

Doc continued, "You've got two girls that maybe don't like each other. In high school. Not much of a surprise there. Lots of things going on with kids in high school, and it takes some time to sort out. Most of the time, they get it done themselves." He fixed Callie with an intense stare. "Every once in a while 'something must be done' to fix the situation." He embellished his words by using the first two fingers on each hand to insert scare quotes. "But not often." He paused. "What did you think we could or should do?"

Callie kept staring at him, but she could feel two bright spots of heat on her cheeks. Doc was not much of a help. "If I knew what I wanted to do, I wouldn't be asking for advice," Callie shot back. "I just want them to get along."

"Then patience, Callie," suggested Doc. "Give them some time to figure it out and, if they need a nudge later, we can decide what kind of nudge. But right now, you're buying trouble before you need to. Cross-country is still six months out. First, we have track starting Monday, then summer, then . . . get the idea?"

Callie hesitated and then nodded. "Okay."

"Good," said her coach. He changed the subject. "So, you getting much running in?"

Callie's eyes narrowed. She had told him that she had been running, just not how much. Which made his question . . . *odd*.

"Some," she replied. "Most every day a little bit at least."

The lopsided grin was back. "Some, huh?" said Doc. "I heard that maybe you were overdoing it, double runs, long runs, no rest."

Mark! It had to be Mark, thought Callie. He had been keeping track of her training since he found out she was doing extra runs. She stifled the anger, working to keep her face mostly blank, a little wide-eyed with a *Who me?* look.

"I'm okay," she said, but, even to herself, her voice sounded strained and tight. She held herself still but she could feel little twitches in her upper arms; she wanted to rant and flail, but not at Doc.

"So you're okay. How many miles are you turning a week?" he asked.

A pause. "Average? About fifty," she answered, turning her head to look at the ducks, avoiding looking at her coach.

"About fifty," he repeated, eyes narrowing. "Average, huh?"

She nodded, still looking over at the ducks, watching a larger male push another duck to the side. A dog barked farther up the trail and all sound temporarily ceased as the ducks searched for the source of the threat.

"How many last week?"

She turned back to face him, looking up from under her bangs. "Seventy-two."

Doc let out a noisy breath. "Oh boy. Okay." Another breath. "I don't suppose you've taken any time off?"

Callie shook her head and avoided his face. "Not much."

"Define 'not much.' When was your last day off?" he demanded.

Callie shuffled her feet. "Um . . . the day before Thanksgiving?" she said meekly, wincing a little at the admission.

"Boy, oh boy oh boy," said Doc, looking at her.

Callie stood facing him, waiting for him to blow up. Doc brought his runners along slowly, adding mileage only when the young bodies had adapted to the current regimen of runs. He didn't have much say in the off-seasons; in the summer, he maintained a group workout schedule and would help the kids with training schedules, but injury prevention was always the first priority.

"Most other runners would be broken trying that stunt," he said. "That's a pretty aggressive ramp-up on your mileage."

Callie looked up at his face, surprised. "You're not mad?"

"Well, I would have preferred it if you had asked me for advice," he replied. "But mad? No."

"Oh."

"But you are right on the edge of overtraining. You were struggling a bit while we were running and Mark says—"

I knew it! Callie thought.

"—you've been getting slower and slower, having a hard time pushing to keep up with the group. Mark also said you've been kind of snappy, and the twins said the same thing when I asked them. To me, you looked heavy-legged, not nearly as quick and light as usual." He looked to her for confirmation and she nodded. "You've got great form and I know that you really work at it, but you need to learn too much is too much.

"See, this is part of being the captain," Doc continued. "It's not just being the best runner or just leading by example. It's communicating with the others on the team, making sure they know what they're supposed to do and when, what time practice is, all the boring stuff." He took a breath. "But it's also keeping an eye out on the new runners, like Jen next year, to see how they're managing. You also need to keep an eye out for girls that are tweaking something but won't say." He stared at her. "Or, someone like you, working too hard. Got it?"

"Yeah, but what do I do if I see something?"

"That's where it gets tricky," explained Doc. "You've got to make a choice. Is it something that you can handle or do you bring it to me? Mark decided to punt on this one and I was going to wait until practice on Monday, but this was too good a chance, plus there's nobody here but us chickens."

"Ducks," corrected Callie, almost smiling. He wasn't yelling at her.

"Whatever," growled Doc. "So here's your training schedule for the weekend. No running. None. Sit on the couch and eat chocolate or pretzels or something. Kick it back, take it easy, and get ready for Monday. Okay?"

"Uh-huh," said Callie.

The light was starting to fade but the days were already getting noticeably longer and she was glad she wouldn't have to make the drive up into the hills in the dark. She looked around at the bushes and grass; it would be a couple of months before Cloverland started to green up.

"Callie?" Doc called over as she was climbing into her car.

"Yeah?" she said. One leg was already in her car. She stood on one foot, leaning on the door, to look over the roof at him.

"It's supposed to be fun, you know."

She nodded. "Right, Coach."

Inside her car, she snatched at her purse and dug out her phone. She quickly tapped out a text, thumbs flying on the little keyboard, then hit Send, waited a moment, and hit the power button.

Tattletale! glowed on the screen as the phone shut down.

Chapter 15

"Well, this sucks," said Hanna as hail lashed the canopies while the runners hid beneath them.

Her sister mumbled something from inside her blanket, huddling against the sudden storm that had delayed the meet. For a few minutes at a time, it was spring in the inland Northwest. The sun would dazzle them briefly, only to be replaced by angry clouds. The hail was a new touch, and the team watched it build up on the track. With any luck, more than a couple of them muttered, the meet would get canceled and they could get back on the bus.

The whole team was sequestered under a pair of blue canopies that had been staked to the ground. When the winds had picked up, they dropped the covers to the lowest setting to avoid having them taken and broken by the gusting winds. They were little enough protection when the wind drove the rain sideways.

"It's April," said Nate. He was hunkered down and looking unhappy.

"Doesn't matter," came a muffled voice from under another blanket. Callie thought it was Mattie but with all the bodies wrapped in blankets and sleeping bags—runners and throwers and jumpers, laid in next to each other like a sardine can full of mummies—it was hard to be sure. Mark had picked a good day to have the flu, she thought, shivering.

Still, Callie wasn't unhappy. She had one more race, the thirty-two hundred meters, which was the next-to-last race of the day. She had already run her first race and, despite wind and lousy weather, had just set an eight-second PR in the mile and placed third overall, her best finish ever. Jenessa had won. There weren't many runners in the state at this level that could match Jenessa, and those ran on the west side, in the areas around Seattle, in real springtime weather. They didn't often make the long drive to inland.

Callie watched as a brilliant blue patch of sky approached. When the sun finally broke through again, the track lit up, each color vivid in the sudden intensity, the sky washed clean. The remote hills, each coniferous tree sharply defined and individual, appeared to be almost in reach in the crystal-clear air.

"Second call, girls' four hundred meters," the speakers announced, tinny and flat. The meet was on.

At the announcement, a groan came from one of the mummies, the one that Callie had thought was Mattie. Mattie had also run a race already, the two-hundred-meter relay, and still had two more: the four hundred, up next, and the four-hundred-meter relay, always the last event. She was skipping the eight hundred today because the sprint coach wanted her to focus on the relays and didn't want her worn out for the last race.

"High jumpers, please report to the pit. Throwers, please report to the discus circle."

There was more grumbling from various blankets as athletes began to rise and restart their events. To the left of Callie, the grumbling led to a mop of red hair gradually withdrawing from the cocoon. The rest of Mattie followed, one lanky limb at a time. Callie watched her as she stood up, arms crossed in front of her, trying to trap heat. Mattie had a parka on over her warm-ups but still managed to look waifish. She had been lean and rangy; now, well into the track season, she was being distilled down into bare essences. She looked around her blanket, found her shoes, and flopped back down to put them on. Then she took off to warm up, a slow jog away from the track.

Usually Mark warmed up with Mattie in between his events. Callie left them alone, unsure and unwilling to intrude. She and Mark ran the same events so they got prepped for the races together, too. Once, Callie had started to ask Mark about Mattie but chickened out at the last second and changed the subject. Callie watched the other girl go off alone and felt a sudden surge of sympathy for the lonely figure.

"Hey, you want some company?" Callie yelled over to the other girl. Mattie kept jogging away, not looking back.

"Mattie!" Callie yelled again.

The other girl stopped and turned, looking back toward the group.

"You want some company?" repeated Callie.

Mattie looked at her suspiciously, then simultaneously shrugged and nodded. "Sure," she said.

Callie scrambled to get her shoes on, digging in her own blanket, where the left shoe had disappeared. As she fumbled with the laces, the body next to her stirred.

"I don't know why you bother," Jenessa said in a snide voice from inside her down sleeping bag.

Callie looked at her but didn't answer. Jenessa had been agitating for her to confront Mattie. It dawned on Callie that Jenessa really didn't care about Callie and Mark so much as she wanted to cause Mattie aggravation. Unable to get Callie to go along, Jenessa resorted to little jibes at Mattie when the coaches weren't around.

Callie got to her feet and, stiff-legged, made her way over to Mattie, and they turned toward the small town that bordered the school.

"I don't talk much," Mattie said, looking at Callie as they started off, headed to the streets of town.

"Yeah, no worries. Just good to stretch things out," responded Callie, and the two girls fell into stride, starting slowly and, as they warmed, accelerating a bit. Seven minutes later, Mattie guided them back to the track in time to hear the third call for the four hundred meters. She nodded at Callie and headed to the start line, grabbing her spikes on the way. Callie, comfortable now, especially with the sun warming her shoulders and back, followed behind to watch the race.

Off to the side, she saw one of the twins—*Must be Anna,* she thought—getting ready for the three-hundred-meter hurdles. The twins didn't race each other. Even in cross-country, they always finished at the same time. Their first race in cross-country, they had almost been disqualified for holding hands at the finish. Fortunately, it was a small district meet and the race director, a fellow coach, had been forgiving. Doc explained to the distressed girls that the state association cared only for winners, losers, and none of their rules were broken. It was strictly a business, and it had no sense of humor.

Mattie was assigned lane three, two runners on the inside lanes behind her, four more outside in the staggered start, the reigning district champion in lane five. She set her blocks, and then stripped to racing singlet and shorts. One of the throwers hunkered down behind to brace the blocks. Mattie was bouncing on her toes, waiting for the starter. The starter, a large and avuncular man who had been volunteering at local events for four decades, gave them their instructions.

"Okay, ladies. You've done this before but let's go over it. I'm going to give you two commands, then the gun. The first, 'To your marks,' is when you get set in your blocks if you're using them. Next, 'Set.' Make sure you hold that. I have to see you all in position before I can start the race. So hold it until the gun. If someone leaves early, you'll hear a second shot. Stop and return to the start line. Remember, this is a single disqualifier, so if you jump, you're done.

"Everybody understand?" he finished, making eye contact with each girl. They all nodded back to him, little twitchy motions.

"To your marks."

The girls settled in, fingers splayed along the white line on the track that marked their takeoff point. The girl in lane one, running without blocks, toed the line. The starter swept his left arm across the arc of runners while extending his right hand up, the pistol pointed skyward.

"Set."

The runners lifted up, backs straight, coiled, looking at the track just in front of them, tension held in their thighs, potential energy waiting for instant release.

The flat bang from the starter pistol echoed off the bleachers and the girls hurled themselves forward, driving their arms as they leaned into the first turn, the *thock* of their spikes on the red rubberized surface drowned in the sudden cheering from teammates alongside the track.

Callie watched the quarter-milers sweep out of the first turn. Mattie had already made up ground on the girls in the outer lanes. Callie squinted, trying to measure the distances.

The single-lap race was heavily staggered at the start and the runners on the interior lanes would be making up ground on the turns where they had shorter lengths to cover. Both the girls in the inside lanes had fallen away from the other runners, their gap growing, not getting smaller.

Mattie settled into the rear straightaway and, even from across the track and intervening football field, Callie could see the muscles in the girl's legs, the straight back, the chin slightly down, the nearly perfect arm carriage. Mattie had been working on her form. She kept closing on the leading runners, passing another two along the backstretch, heading for the final turn.

As she hit the turn, the stride changed, got more explosive as Mattie attacked aggressively, leaning in to hold a tight line on the inside of her lane. "Predatory" was the word that floated into Callie's mind as she watched Mattie whip herself out of the turn onto the finishing hundred meters, only the district champ in lane five still ahead of her.

The other runner fought Mattie for eighty meters, the struggle to hold the brutal sprint as plain on her face as the fierce determination on Mattie's. The cheering from the teams rose as the girls passed in front of the grandstands. The fans shouted encouragements that the runners were too focused to hear except as noise. Twenty meters to the finish, the other girl broke, faltered for a half step, tried to recover, and lost the race. Mattie broke the tape three meters ahead of the other girl.

The runner in lane five had her hands on her knees and was swarmed by her teammates while Mattie walked off to find her sweats. Impulsively, Callie crossed the track, dodging the crew that was pulling out the hurdles for the next event.

Nate beat her there.

Callie could hear the freshman miler gushing his praise while Mattie stuck a leg into the sweats, focused on getting warm. She wobbled on one ankle and Nate reached out and steadied her on the shoulder. Mattie looked up, startled, and a brilliant smile transformed her face, softening it.

"Thanks." Her warm contralto carried her smile.

"No problem, Mattie," Nate replied, his voice rising and a touch squeaky when he got to her name. "That really was a great race," he continued on gamely.

"It was," Callie interjected as she joined the two. "Awesome kick."

The smile disappeared as quickly as it had shone and Mattie looked guardedly from Callie to Nate. Without replying, the sophomore steadied herself and slipped on the other leg of her sweats, looking up at both of them as she did.

"Thanks." The earlier warmth was replaced with careful disinterest. The sudden change caught Nate by surprise.

She gave them a long look each and turned away, back to camp.

Callie watched her walking away and said, as she turned to face Nate, "It's me, not you."

Nate wasn't paying attention. He was busy watching Mattie walking away, and Callie watched his gaze dropping the length of the other girl's body.

"Eyes," she warned, her voice light and teasing. "You're ogling."

Nate looked away, flushing a bright red.

"umm . . ." he fumbled, trying and failing to make contact with her stare. Callie gave an amused snort, eyes sparkling at the boy's discomfort, and walked to the edge of the track as the gun sounded to start the hurdles. As she did, she noticed that Nate's gaze drifted back to the copper-headed girl now on the other side of the track.

Boys, she thought.

Chapter 16

The better hurdlers looked so smooth. This was one race that Callie had never had any desire to attempt. Her hurdling efforts in junior high had ended with shocking abruptness as she planted her face and shoulder into the track.

The twins, on the other hand, were built for it, their extra height and leg length an asset and their happy-go-lucky fearlessness working to mitigate the occasional disasters that every hurdler experienced. It was Anna's turn to run the three-hundred-meter intermediate hurdles.

Callie watched Anna attack the hurdles, gracefully alternating lead legs as she went over each barrier. She could see first a blue sock in pink spikes, then a yellow in pink flashing as she cleared the hurdle. She was having a really clean race, thought Callie. It was a technical event, more like jumping than running, with each step measured, arms precisely positioned to drive on takeoff, the shift of the weight back into forward propulsion on landing.

One by one, the girls cleared the final hurdle and sprinted the final ten meters to the finish. Anna finished second. Callie went to talk to her but the tall blonde grabbed her gear and quickly traipsed across the track just before the start of the boys' eight hundred meters.

Nate was running the next event and, as they swept around onto the far straight, Callie caught sight of Mattie, standing on the far edge of the track, cheering him on. Twice around the track they looped and Nate finished a distant third, close by the second-place runner. The winner, a senior, already had partial offers for college. College runners were lucky to get partial offers—unlike the more popular football and basketball athletes, they didn't participate in a "money" sport.

Next up was Hanna, running the girls' eight hundred. She and Anna were alternating the races—after convincing the head track coach they would quit if they were put in the same events all the time. It was harder to tie in track.

Callie watched her settle into the crowd of a dozen runners. The blonde was inches taller than her competitors. The meet was using a waterfall start, a green curved line from the inside lane arcing forward and out to the last lane. The older man talked through the race directions again, brought them to the ready, and started the race.

The girls surged out, the pack separating quickly, and Hanna settled into third place. The eight hundred meters was a tough race, starting too fast to ever get comfortable and lasting too long to make the misery seem bearable. Callie much preferred her longer races, the mile and two mile. The eight hundred was a race that Mattie excelled at, her toughness gritting out wins. Today, she was an unhappy spectator.

Callie cheered as Hanna came down the track, completing the first turn. Her form looked good and, as she went past, Callie watched her foot strike. Solid as always—

She stared. *Blue sock. Yellow sock. Left foot. Right foot.* Anna and Hanna always wore the same colors but on different feet. Blue. Yellow. The same pattern as Anna in the hurdles. Callie looked over to the camp. There was a bundle still on the ground where Anna had been lying.

As the girls circled back around to the finish, Callie found herself staring at the Cloverland runner racing down the track. It looked like Hanna, she thought. As the taller girl faded to the finish, getting passed by two other girls, Callie pushed through the press of people.

"Good job!" she said. It was Hanna.

"Ugh," said Hanna. "Lousy finish."

Callie studied the girl. "No worries, Anna," she said.

"I'm Hanna," the twin said reflexively, staring at her intently.

"Sorry about that," apologized Callie. "Sometimes I still get you two mixed up."

"We're used to it," said Hanna, but she looked nervous.

Callie looked at her, then over to the camp. Hanna followed her eyes and grew more tense.

"Need some clothes on before I freeze," she explained abruptly to Callie, and turned away to get her clothes.

Callie gazed at Hanna's back. "Sure," she said. She left her but could feel the other girl's stare on her as she made her way across the track toward the camp.

She hurried across the damp grass as new clouds piled against the sun. The warmth disappeared and the temperature felt as though it dropped five degrees in a few seconds. She really did need to bundle up again, she thought. She minced her way around the few bodies left in the camp along with the bags and gear that was strewn all over the ground tarp and made her way to her stuff. She looked at the mummy at her feet. Earlier, she thought it was Anna next to her. Hanna had been sitting up. Callie was sure of it.

Callie could see Hanna scurrying across the grass, following Callie's tracks, worry oozing from her. Without thinking, Callie bent down and pulled the blanket from the mummy's feet. *Yellow sock. Blue sock. Left foot. Right foot.* The opposite pattern, like it should be.

A muffled, croaking "Hey" was emitted from the other end of the mummy and Anna emerged. "What the heck are you doing?" she demanded, her voice raspy, then seeing Callie holding the edge of the blanket and her sister hustling into the camp, looked back to Callie and winced.

"We can explain."

Anna struggled to her feet as Hanna squirmed. Callie watched the two of them, so nearly identical.

"Come on," she ordered, directing them away from the camp with a quick jerk of her head toward the end of the empty bleachers behind them. The twins dutifully fell in line behind her, Anna still wrapped in her blanket.

"You look like hell," Callie said, once they were out of earshot. They stood there, a closely bound triangle, Callie with her back to the camp.

"I feel like it, too," responded Anna, "but thanks for pointing it out." The taller girl was bleached out, with a runny nose and dark circles forming around her eyes. Small beads of sweat lined up at the top of her forehead where the hair was pulled back into a tight ponytail.

"Why'd you even come?" Callie asked. "If you were sick, you should have stayed home and—"

"I wasn't sick. That is, not when I got on the bus," retorted Anna. "I'm not dumb."

"I didn't say—"

"You were implying it," Hanna said in defense of her twin.

Callie looked from one girl to the other and took a second to retrench. She didn't want to fight the twins but Hanna running both races was cheating.

"Okay. Sorry. I wasn't trying to say you were dumb. Just, you got to be miserable," she temporized.

"Mostly," said Anna.

A strong gust of frigid wind surged around them and Callie shivered; both twins did, too, Anna clenching her teeth to keep them from rattling. She looked down to Callie's eyes, then to her sister.

"I told you Callie would be the one to bust us," she said to Hanna, obliquely engaging Callie.

"Me? Why me? And why didn't you just scratch? Hanna didn't have to run for you. Nobody would have said anything," Callie responded.

"You were right," replied Hanna to her sister, talking past Callie.

"Why didn't you scratch?" Callie was nearly pleading to get an answer that made sense.

The twins considered her, then looked at each other for agreement.

"Because that wouldn't—" started Anna.

"—be any fun!" finished Hanna.

Both twins calmly held their eyes on Callie and waited. "You've done this before?" accused Callie.

"Might have," suggested Anna.

"Maybe in junior high," Hanna offered.

"Everything has to be just right."

"And not too many people that know us good."

"But I was the one that said you'd catch us someday," Anna said in an unsteady voice, diverting the conversation.

"You said that. Why me?" questioned Callie.

"You look at people's feet," said Anna.

"What?" Callie's forehead wrinkled; the twins weren't making sense, or rather, were making less sense than normal.

"Like, last year in cross-country," began Hanna.

"We're running on the trail," joined Anna.

"And we're like, hey, that guy is totally cute."

"And you were zoning on the run and you're like, 'Wha—which guy?' "

"So we point him out," said Hanna, gesturing with her arm.

"And you're like, 'Oh, the guy that pronates.' "

The twins looked at Callie.

"You're a little—" the older twin started.

"—weird," finished the younger.

"In a nice way, though," Anna hurriedly assured Callie.

Callie stood there trying to decide if she should be offended or not. Having the twins call her weird was a bit like Jen calling her a drama queen. It was a matter of degrees.

"The socks," she guessed. "Nobody else noticed the socks."

"Uh-huh," said Anna, coughing, a hard barking sound from deep in her chest. She huddled more tightly into her blanket against the snapping wind. The sun was gone and the clouds were looking angrier by the moment, scudding across the sky, chasing the blue skies to Montana.

"What's the deal with the socks?" Callie asked. She felt sorry for Anna but her curiosity was aroused and she didn't think she'd get a second chance to ask.

Hanna looked at her older sister. "I got it," she said. She looked at Callie.

"The socks are something our folks did when we were babies. Dad had a hard time telling us apart so Mom would put our socks on to help him."

Callie looked at her uncomprehendingly.

"The socks are code. Anna was eldest so her socks were in alphabetical order. I came second so mine are the opposite."

"I still don't get it," said Callie.

"Blue, yellow. Read it left to right. Anna has the blue sock—b—on her right with the yellow—y—on her left. Alphabetical. Just like you were reading."

"Oh," Callie said, as the pattern became clear. "But why do you still do it? You're not babies anymore."

"Because we're still sisters, twins," explained Anna quietly. "Exactly alike."

"Except, not," said Hanna.

"We're just a little bit different," said Anna.

They looked at each other and then to Callie.

"So," Hanna ventured, "are you going to tell?"

Both twins were tense, waiting for her answer, but she didn't know how to respond. She wasn't sure that she even knew what the right answer was. She was wrestling with the question when Hanna looked over her shoulder and her eyes got big.

"Uh-oh," she said. "That can't be good."

Callie turned and traced the young twins' eyes back to camp. Mattie and Jenessa were standing nose-to-nose, inches from each other, practically quivering. Even from the bleachers and over the wind, Callie could hear the shouting, even if she couldn't make out the words.

Twins forgotten, she sprinted for camp.

Chapter 17

Callie dodged around the canopies, skidding on the wet grass and almost falling, to get to Mattie and Jenessa. All the mummies were wide-awake and wide-eyed. The small group of the other Cloverland athletes still under the cover gathered around the two antagonists.

Callie grabbed Nate by the arm.

"Go get Doc!" she ordered. "And tell him to hurry." She gave him a small shove.

Nate took off at a run. Doc was on the far side of the track at the two-hundred-meter start, trying to keep the mass of runners organized as they worked through the multiple heats of boys and girls.

Callie turned her attention to the belligerents. Fragments of words broke over her as both girls screeched in each other's face.

"—you're a spoiled bitch and—" Mattie was shouting, her face red, tawny eyes feral.

"—living in that dump of a cheap trailer and—" Jenessa was shouting back, back straight while her lips curled with contempt, leaning into Mattie.

"—you don't give a crap about anybody else!" Mattie yelled.

"—at least my mother didn't walk out on me!" Jenessa yelled back.

Callie reached them as Mattie, her face gone as dark as the clouds, reached out to grab the brown-haired girl. Callie squeezed between them, almost knocking heads with both of them, they were so close. She stood facing Mattie, felt the heat and pressure on her skin from both sides as the girls pressed against her, trying to get to each other.

"Mattie," Callie said, looking directly in the ferocious eyes.

Mattie's eyes flashed from Jenessa to Callie.

"Get out of my way!"

"Nope, not going to," said Callie.

On her rear, she felt the pressure ease as Jenessa stopped leaning in.

"Move!"

"Nope, still not going to," Callie repeated.

"Good thing she's here," sneered Jenessa.

"Shut up, Jenessa," Callie said over her shoulder without breaking eye contact with Mattie.

Jenessa spluttered behind her but Callie kept her eyes on Mattie. Jenessa was almost certainly the instigator but Mattie was the one that would escalate it. Callie stood there, willing Mattie to step back. Long seconds ticked by. The angry golden fire faded, replaced by hurt in the girl's eyes. She focused on Callie and the stiffness left her posture. She nodded and silently retreated a step.

Callie hadn't realized she was holding her breath until she felt it whoosh out, the immediate threat over. Callie, still tense, backed away from both girls so she could see them both at the same time while watching cautiously in case she needed to jump back between them. She faced Jenessa.

"What the hell was that all about?" she demanded of her teammate, her face tight.

"She started it!" Jenessa whined.

Behind her, Mattie started to protest and Callie shook her head, interrupting both of them.

"What, we're three? Seriously?" she said in disbelief.

Neither girl answered. Jenessa looked sullen while Mattie had put her mask back on, face inscrutable. Across the track, Callie could see that Nate had reached Doc. He was talking to the coach, waving his arms urgently toward the camp.

Come on, Doc, she thought. Doc looked over to the camp, then said something to Nate. Nate shrugged and started back to the camp at a slow jog. Doc turned back to the runners at the two-hundred-meter start. *Thanks for nothing, Doc!* Callie thought.

Jenessa saw the same thing she did. No help was coming. And Jenessa smiled, a little, mean-spirited smile.

"It doesn't matter now," said Jenessa dismissively. "I've got to start warming up for my race." She turned away, then back to look directly at Mattie. "It's a real race, the kind that takes guts to run, not just going out stupid fast and you're done." There was a low shocked murmur from the group around them, swelled by runners from other schools attracted by the shouting. Above was the rumble of thunder.

Callie stepped toward Jenessa and in front of Mattie before the redhead could reply.

"Pretty cheap, Jenessa."

"Well, at least you try, Callie," Jenessa said, but stretching out the word "try." "She just sprints."

"She at least runs like she cares," Mattie said angrily from behind her. Callie was shocked that Mattie was defending her. And a little pissed at Jenessa for the disrespect.

Jenessa's eyes narrowed and Callie could feel the embers getting stoked back to flame. Callie, heart thumping, took a deep, calming breath.

"Jenessa, why don't you go warm up?" suggested Callie. "You've got a race to run." Mattie snorted behind her, a derisive sound carrying more contempt than Jenessa managed with words. Callie glared at her. Mattie looked impassively back.

"What, you think you could do better?" Jenessa taunted.

Mattie looked at her and Callie felt a chill. The feral heat when they were fighting was gone but instead was a cold look, the huntress eyeing the prey. Mattie was scarier when she kept control of her anger.

"In the eight hundred I could kick your ass. You don't have the guts to hang," she said. Someone in the crowd said "whoa" and there was an undercurrent of ghoulish excitement mixed with trepidation.

Jenessa gaped at her, stunned. She mouthed words but nothing came out, then all sorts of spluttering sounds burst forth but no words.

"You're challenging *me*!" she exclaimed once she regained control. "I don't have any guts! Why you—"

"Jenessa, go warm up," urged Callie, while to Mattie she said, "That's enough. Let it go."

"Like hell," said Jenessa. "You want to challenge me, fine. We'll do a mile. Then we'll see who has guts." Her whole body was leaning into the other girl again and Callie nearly groaned. At least they weren't nose-to-nose anymore. Overhead, there was more rumbling but it wasn't raining or sleeting or hailing.

"Too funny, you want to race at your best distance," Mattie said bitingly. "Why don't we split the difference. Twelve hundred meters and I'll still kick your ass."

"The mile," insisted Jenessa. "What, you can't hang?" she taunted, rocking her head side to side as she spoke.

Mattie stared at her, eyes aflame again. The crowd continued to grow as word made its way to the other schools at the meet. *Doc has to see the crowd,* thought Callie, *he's got to know something is up. Where the heck is he?*

"Okay," declared Mattie. "We'll do the mile."

Jenessa fell back an uncertain step. *She's scared,* Callie realized. Callie looked from Jenessa to Mattie.

"Fine," Jenessa said, her voice filled with forced conviction.

Mattie just stared and the other girl turned to gather her gear to go, the crowd reluctantly opening a gap to allow passage. Lightning crackled above and the first heavy drops of bone-chillingly cold rain hit the runners.

How Shakespearian, thought Callie. *"When shall we three meet again, In thunder, lightning, or in rain?"*

Chapter 18

The first shattering forks of lightning signaled the end of the meet. The teams were already packing when the race officials gave up and canceled the final events. Rain soaked the athletes as everyone hurried to get gear on the bus.

In a very few minutes, the gear was stowed and the runners were on the bus. Ahead, Callie watched Doc clamber onto the top step behind the head coach of the track team—during track season, Doc was the assistant and only coached distance events. His white hair was plastered down onto his skull like a painted hat that had dripped onto his forehead. The head coach—a tall, lean man and former collegiate sprinter—was partially blocking the aisle, counting heads to make sure everyone was on board. Five minutes later, the seats began to vibrate with the rumble of the big diesel engine as the driver slipped the transmission into first and pulled out onto the road.

Callie sat by herself. The bus lurched around another turn and Callie's head rocked. With a sigh, she sat up and reached back to her hairbands, working them down her ponytail until they were out and gave her head a little shake.

"Whoa," came Hanna's voice from behind. Callie pivoted in her seat to face backward.

"What?" she asked.

"Your hair. It's . . ." Hanna said, making big round motions with her hands.

"It went *bumpf*?"

"Uh-hunh." She looked at her sister, who was trying to sleep. "We don't get that. Our hair is pretty well behaved most of the time," commented the hurdler. "It's kind of straight, not . . ." Again with the wavy hands.

"Callie," Doc's voice called, cutting through the din. "Come on up here for a sec."

The buzz of noise dropped off to quiet mutters.

"What did you do?" said Nate *sotto voce* from the bench seat in front of her.

Callie shrugged as she got up and staggered forward, trying to compensate for the motion of the bus, to where Doc was sitting with the other coaches. Her right hip banged into the side of a seat as she reached Doc. He waved her into the seat next to him while the other coaches continued on with their own conversation. Doc watched her as she slid into the bench next to him. The back of the bus seemed suddenly quiet. She willed herself not to squirm in the seat, but she was having no success at fighting the sinking feeling in her chest.

"Hey Doc," she said when he didn't say anything.

He bobbed his head. The thick white hair wasn't plastered down anymore; instead, it had dried and stood up in little spikes from his scalp, pointing in odd directions.

"Would you relax," he said, his voice gruff and hoarse from cheering and coaching his runners, "you're not in trouble." He sat there gazing at her.

"I'm not?" she replied.

"Of course not. You did good."

"I did?" Callie racked her brain. In all the hullaballoo with Jenessa and Mattie, she had forgotten about her race. She brightened. "Oh, the race. Yeah, it was pretty awesome. I'm really feeling stronger now at the end. All that mileage—and rest," she added hastily, "has really helped."

"Yep, you had a nice race, but I wasn't talking about that," Doc said.

The sinking feeling came back. He was talking about Jenessa and Mattie.

"Doc, I—" she started to explain.

"Why don't you let me say my piece instead of jumping to where you think I'm going," said Doc. "You did just fine. Nate told me that you sent him over to get help handling Mattie and Jenessa." His gaze sharpened. "Good move, letting me know. But you had it handled."

"But they were yelling and fighting and then Jenessa and Mattie—" Callie interjected.

"Did they slap each other silly?" He waited for an answer. "No, they didn't," he said when she didn't respond. "And with Mattie, that's a possibility. Touchy, like old dynamite. She's going to be a heck of a runner if we can get her to settle down a bit. All fire and heart but she lives up to that red hair."

Callie squirmed a bit more in the seat. Doc was giving her credit for doing nothing. The challenge race, if they went through with it, violated team rules. Doc was firm about saving races for meets. "But they—"

"No buts, you did fine. Now get back to the others," Doc said, "and try to look unhappy. Don't want you besmirching my reputation and telling people I'm a nice guy."

Callie stared at him. "Doc," she said, "you're a little weird."

Doc stared back and the little crooked grin broke through. "I'm not weird. I'm a character. There's a difference. Now git."

Callie got. As she swayed back to her seat, banging her hip again on a sudden lurch—*The same hip, dangit,* she thought—she saw the faces of the other kids looking at her. Most, seeing her look back, averted their eyes. But Mattie, sitting right in front of Nate, didn't. She watched Callie all the way past her, head rotating with Callie's progress down the aisle.

Jenessa watched her too, from her little clutch of friends at the back of the bus. Where Mattie had been impassive, Jenessa was openly hostile, glaring at her as if she were responsible for the fight. As Callie sat heavily into her seat, Jenessa turned away to plot with her girlfriends.

Callie fished around in her bag, shifting clothes, shoes, and all the little miscellaneous stuff that accumulates at the bottom until she found her cell phone. Quickly she tapped out a message.

We got trouble.

Minutes later, the screen glowed and she felt the phone vibrate in her hand. She looked down and emitted a small growl.

Who is this "we" you speak of?

"Need water?" Mark offered over the hood of the Jeep.

"I'm good," she replied.

Mark had parked his Jeep next to the skate park. The clacking of the boards on the concrete jumps, along with the shouts of the boys, provided a steady backdrop of noise. Several girls were there, though most were watching the boys, scrawny and shirtless, show off. Callie winced as she watched one youngster attempt a flip, miss the landing, and sprawl with a clatter across the bottom of the jump. He lay there for a second while his friends ragged on him, then popped back up. Laughing and rubbing his hip, he headed to the top of the ramp to try again.

Callie fiddled with her sunglasses while Mark made final adjustments to his shoelaces, loosening them on the toe box, cinching tight at the ankle. The greenbelt along the river was ten degrees warmer than home. New flowers decorated the fronts of houses on the way into town and the dogwoods lining the streets were in bloom, pink clouds floating just above the ground. Both of them wore shorts and T-shirts.

"Let's get going," said Mark. The only thing that they had agreed on was that they would run to the casino and back and that it was really nice to run in shorts. The conversation about Jenessa and Mattie had rotated through a frustrating series of loops, Callie insisting that the race shouldn't happen, Mark stubbornly disagreeing. Mark looked better than he had in the middle of the week but still didn't look completely healthy.

They dodged through the trees and past the little play area, populated with a dozen small children gaily swarming around the equipment while the moms sat on the nearby benches to chat, little snatches of conversation, disjointed, hanging on the air. She saw a small child slip off one of the multicolored hand-holds on the short climbing wall and land with a thump on her rear. The toddler reviewed this unfortunate turn for a moment then wailed for her mother.

Callie could feel the cold air under the trees prickling at her skin, but before long, they burst back into sunlight, heading east. Her back soaked up the heat and she felt buoyant in the bright spring day. Since it was a long run, they kept the pace down.

"I still think we should tell Doc," Callie said.

"And I still think we should leave well enough alone. Yeah, Doc doesn't want us racing in practice. But this isn't practice. This is a grudge match."

"Which is the problem." *He can be so frustrating,* Callie thought, *and arguing with him can be hazardous to your sanity.* Mark ran quietly and she could see he was thinking.

"Why do you care?" he asked, taking a different tack. "It's not like you have to race. You're not putting anything on the line. It's just them figuring things out for themselves. *Mano a mano,* so to speak," he finished, cheered by his own bad joke.

That stumped her. She had already decided that she wasn't going to say anything about Anna and Hanna—*if they didn't do it again!*—so it wasn't the rule-breaking.

Mark pointed to the right, to a short stretch of single track that snaked around one of the ponds. She took the cue and crossed the parking lot, leading the way onto the trail, Mark running a few feet behind her. Ahead, a small rabbit froze looking at them, then noisily darted back to the protection of the overgrown blackberries that were just starting to get leaves. They reached the end of the single track and arced over to the paved path. Callie guided them left onto the asphalt then right onto the gravel road that paralleled the old railroad bed.

"It's dumb when boys do stuff like this, and dumber when girls do."

"Oh yes, because girls are *soooo* much more refined. I've heard Jenessa and her friends in the hallways," Mark said. He started mincing his steps and talking in a high-pitched melodramatic voice. 'Ooh, Bobby thinks this, and Dorothy, the little weirdo, was hanging out with Munchkins—what was she ever thinking—' " He was waving his arms and Callie opened a bit of space between them. " '—and isn't the new quarterback just *hawt.*' " He finished, running sideways, batting his eyes at Callie.

An older couple on the top edge of the levee had stopped, staring stupefied at the show Mark was putting on. Seeing the disapproving looks on their faces, Mark waved to them. "Yoo-hoo," he yelled up sweetly.

"Stop that!" Callie ordered, trying to look grim and disapproving. "You're scaring them." It was getting hard to run.

"No way. They'll have the best ever guess-what-happened-to-us-today stories at the old folks' home. I'm providing a community service, entertaining the seniors, improv style."

"You're crazy," she declared.

"That is the other possibility," he acknowledged. He hesitated. "I usually ignore that answer."

Callie ground to a stop, making a hacking sound, hunched over and holding her waist. Mark skidded to a stop and jogged back.

"You okay?" he asked.

Callie waved with one arm, still hacking. Mark stood there watching. She didn't look okay. Her whole body was racking with spasms and her face was bright red.

"Callie?" he asked.

She started to stand up, took a deep breath looking at him, and convulsed into another series of fits.

"Do you need something?" he asked, voice getting urgent. They weren't that far away from local businesses—less than a quarter mile—but on a Sunday most would be closed. Maybe he could get help from the Dodge dealership. . . .

"Stop," Callie said weakly.

"What?"

"You're killing me. Running and laughing don't go together," she said as she regained some composure.

"That was laughing?" Mark asked, his eyebrows reaching to the bottom of his scalp.

"I think I inhaled some spit trying not to laugh."

"You do this often?" Mark asked, and instantly looked chagrined as he heard the words.

"No, you big jerk," retorted Callie, "just on Sundays." She stood all the way up and still only came just above his shoulder. "Come on." She turned and headed back up the gravel stretch. Mark watched her running away for a couple of seconds, then chased her down.

"Look, I'm sorry," he said. He sounded sorry but also like he wasn't exactly sure what he was sorry for.

Callie kept running. Without looking at him, she said, "It was just so funny, and those old folks staring." She saw from the corner of her eyes his shoulders relax and his hands loosen. Beside them, a black-tailed prairie dog chittered admonishments at them and scurried into his hole.

"Jenessa and her little clique aren't always the nicest people," suggested Mark, bringing them back on topic. "They're not as dumb as I made them seem, but still. And Jenessa has really been after Mattie."

"Well, racing isn't going to make it any better. Jenessa is going to kill Mattie in the mile, which will make Mattie madder. And you know that Jenessa will bring it up every time they see each other."

"I wouldn't be so sure of that," Mark asserted.

"I know Jenessa. Trust me, it will come up. Constantly," Callie promised.

"I wasn't talking about after the race. Mattie might surprise people in the race."

"What do you mean, 'surprise people'?" she quoted back at him. "Surprise how?"

Mark did not answer right away. He ran quietly as they closed in on the railroad tracks, one set of rails shiny from use, the others rusting and unneeded, three sets in total. The smell of the creosote was strong and, the closer to the mill they got, the more they could smell the acrid odor it belched skyward, too.

"You know that Mattie and I are, uh . . ." Mark started. Callie stumbled slightly crossing onto the railroad ties and regained her balance.

"You okay?" he asked.

"I'm fine," she said in a clipped voice.

He looked at her and then continued with his story. "Anyway, she's been running, not just at practice. I see her coming past my place every morning, and every morning she goes out nice and steady and she's hauling when she comes back. I mean, really moving." He high-stepped over the first pair of rails. Past the bridge, she could see locomotives and boxcars lined up. He angled toward a break in some pine trees that edged the rear of Locomotive Park, which sat at the entrance of town, near the foot of the bridge they needed to cross to get to the casino. "Jenessa will beat her, yeah, but I think she's going to have to work at it." He repeated the motion over the next set of tracks.

Callie high-stepped behind him and, feeling the rhythm, hit the next two sets in quick order, passing Mark as she did so. *Everybody has their demons, even if we don't admit it, but sometimes, for a little while, we can outrun them. Yeah, it makes sense*, she thought, reminded of her morning runs.

She quick-footed her way down the railbed and beat Mark to the trees. Mark's words earlier rolled around in her mind: *You know that Mattie and I are, uh . . .*

A low, deep voice by her leg growled up at her, "You know, I'd appreciate it, pretty little lady, if you'd not be steppin' on me."

Callie shrieked.

Chapter 19

Callie shrieked and jumped sideways and back, colliding with the branches of a scraggly pine. Her heart skipped a beat, maybe two, then raced off and she found herself suddenly breathless. She felt the little pricks of the needles piercing her thin T-shirt, scratching her arms and unprotected thighs. The boughs bent behind her, ready to spring her toward the voice. She braced herself against the tension in the branches and stared at the intimidating old man.

He was clothed in dark colors, boots black, heavy-weight pants of an indeterminate gray, his sweatshirt the same non-color. The hood obscured his face. Even his worn knapsack was a dark brown, streaked with dirt and dust and looking well traveled. His eyes were the only bright thing on him, alert and knowing.

Before she could decide to respond to the old man or run away, her view of him was blocked by Mark.

"Leave her alone!" Mark growled, hackles up. He stood with his arms pulled halfway up, hands almost closed.

"Nary a thought of bothering her, young pup." The man smiled. "Just too fine a day to be stomped." He glanced around Mark to Callie. "Even by a pretty girl, mind you."

"Callie, start up the hill," Mark said. He didn't look at her. "I'll keep an eye on the bum and join you at the road."

"Now, young pup, that is perhaps the meanest thing you could say to the Kid," the old man said, "but, this being a fine day and me in no mind to fight, I'll attribute it to your fundamental ignorance."

Mark bristled.

Callie disentangled herself from the tree and stepped around Mark, peering at the man. Even this close, under the shadow of the tree he was hard to actually focus on, his clothes blended into the surroundings like camouflage.

"Sorry, mister," she apologized, backing away. Her voice was shaky but her heart slowed its thumping. "You scared me."

"Not meaning to do that to you," responded the man. He looked at Mark. "You're pretty girl is safe, young pup. We done?"

Mark gave a sharp, aggressive nod. He backed away, still facing the man as he eased his way toward Callie.

Callie stopped about ten feet away, waiting for Mark. She stared at the man lounging under the tree. Now that the shock was over, he didn't seem nearly so threatening. His odd speech aroused her curiosity.

"What did you mean by saying we were ignorant?" Callie asked.

"I didn't say you were," said the Kid to the girl standing up the hill above him. "Young pup is, though. He called the Kid a bum. He uses words without thinking about what they mean."

"I know exactly what the word means," asserted Mark.

"Ah, that makes all the difference." The man's eyes locked onto Mark's and his tone became sarcastic. "You know the meaning of the word and still use it incorrectly, haphazardly. Yes, I see the difference."

Mark stopped walking, squaring his wiry shoulders. His feet slipped a little on the damp grass as he stared angrily at the bum.

"Come on, Mark," urged Callie.

"Hold on," he said to her. To the Kid, he said, "How did I use it wrong? You're camping under a tree, you look like you're wearing all the stuff you own and," Mark sniffed the air, "you smell."

A trace of annoyance flashed in the man's eyes. "I apologize for the odor, young pup. I—"

"I'm not a 'young pup'!"

"Then we had best introduce ourselves or young pup and bum we shall be," suggested the other man. He gracefully rose to his feet in a smooth languid motion that belied his apparent years.

"I am," he said with a flourish as he pulled the hood from his head, "the Kemosabe Kid. A hobo, I am, an itinerant worker and inveterate wanderer. A traveling man seeking work wherever he can, be it with a shovel or spade, hammer or saw, any honest work at all. In return, I ask only a few dollars and a warm meal—which I will most gladly repay, as you please, with rousing renditions of Chaucer, Shakespeare, and Yeats." He bowed and looked at the youth in front of him. "And you, sir?"

"Uh, Mark." Mark looked completely befuddled by the theatrics of the old man.

The Kid looked at him and said, in mock sorrow, "We need to work on your delivery. No one will remember *uh Mark* in a month."

She couldn't help it; Callie giggled. Mark looked up at her with a pained expression. The Kid, with his hood off, was completely unthreatening. On a lark, she called down to the Ke-mosabe Kid.

"Start of the third act, *Romeo and Juliet.*"

"A test the pretty little lady offers. A fair proposition. A romance she requests, a romance we shall recite." He paused for a moment. His bag wasn't large, just a knapsack, but if he had an e-reader . . .

He cleared his voice and, without moving from where he stood, began, in clear and melodious tones:

> *I pray thee, good Mercutio, let's retire:*
> *The day is hot, the Capulets abroad,*
> *And, if we meet, we shall not scape a brawl;*
> *For now, these hot days, is the mad blood stirring.*

He paused again and smiled up to her. "Does that satisfy the test or shall I continue?"

Mark snorted and the older man turned to him and smiled. Maintaining eye contact with Mark, who was only six feet away, he stuck out his right hand in invitation.

Startled, Mark stared at the hand and then to the eyes of the man. They were steady and projected warmth. With a shrug, Mark stepped forward. The Kid stepped ahead one pace and they shook. Callie was surprised to see Mark tower over the other man. He couldn't have been much taller than she was, she thought. His presence was outsized compared to his compact body.

"Thank you, Mark," said the Kid. He stepped back and looked at both of them. He sniffed delicately. "And now we must part. I've interrupted your day and onward you shall proceed. As for me, as Mark kindly mentioned, a shower. I am, for lack of a better phrase, a bit whiff."

They watched him weigh his pack, before he hoisted it to a shoulder. With a jaunty wave, he ducked under the branches of the trees and headed up the hill past them, headed toward the commercial district.

By unspoken consensus, the two of them turned, not to the bridge to continue the run, but back the way they came. They ran quietly, drifting in their own thoughts. When they reached the Jeep, Mark let her into her side and walked around to drive them home. They were almost back to Callie's house when Callie spoke.

"He was interesting."

Mark grunted. He had been driving on automatic, not really paying attention, relying on familiarity with the road to guide him while he was thinking. He was sometimes an erratic driver, mostly when he seemed lost in thought, his attention scattered.

"Yeah," he conceded. "He kind of blew me away quoting like that. You hear stories of people that memorize the Bible or stuff, but I've never met anyone that could actually do it."

"Me neither," said Callie. "I think he had it right but I'm going to check."

Mark grunted again and they lapsed back into silence. Clearly, he was now replaying the whole conversation with the Kemosabe Kid in his head.

"I'm not a young pup," Mark said under his breath.

"Okay," said Callie.

Mark steered smoothly into a turn. "How come you didn't introduce yourself to him?" Marked blurted out, diverting his eyes from the road for a second.

Callie dimpled. "I liked *pretty little lady*."

"Oh."

The roof peak and the top of the chimney of Callie's house swung into view over the tops of the trees and Mark shifted down through the gears, decelerating to make the turn onto the gravel, rolling to a stop in front of the veranda.

She unbuckled and opened her door. She swiveled her legs out and looked back at him, leaning slightly in his direction.

"Thank you, Mark," Callie said.

He looked over, surprised. "For what?" he said.

"Just . . . thank you," she said, leaving him perplexed. He nodded. He really was clueless, she thought.

As she watched the Jeep leave the driveway to backtrack to Mark's house, she thought, *Thank you for trying to protect me, you goof.*

The taillights blinked red and then disappeared onto the highway and Callie turned to go inside.

When Mark got home, he had a surprise waiting.

Uncle Bennie was there. He'd brought the stuff, all of it untraceable, he assured Mark. He had paid cash for it and shopped in different cities. They pulled it out of Bennie's SUV and laid the parts out. Mark went to get his schematic and started comparing the actual parts to the diagram. It was like Christmas for them. Some assembly required, but that was part of the fun.

Uncle Bennie had scored the explosive cartridges they needed. They were smaller than Mark had expected. He looked at the timing device—it seemed straightforward enough.

"Electronic?" he asked Bennie. He had planned on a mechanical timer.

Bennie laughed. "Better. Programmable. I can set it up to wipe memory when it completes its cycle. Not even the bozos at the FBI could get anything off it when I'm done."

Mark gave Bennie a high five. Bennie wanted to start right away but Mark's mom was due home. Carefully, they wiped all the components, placing them into a large duffel bag.

They hid everything in the barn.

Chapter 20

Race Day dragged on, interminable. Callie discovered that the momentum of the challenge between Mattie and Jenessa was more than she could stop. Callie had watched both of them get more irritable and twitchy as the days passed. It wasn't just at the track, though. Word of the race had spread through Cloverland High. She kept waiting for Doc or the other coaches to step in.

A note, hastily written in red felt pen, was pinned on the doors to both locker rooms when Callie got there. Callie squinted at the note suspiciously. Track practice had been changed. Doc and the sprint coach wouldn't be at practice. They were supposed to do an easy day on their own.

The handwriting on the notes was atrocious, which meant that Doc had probably written it himself. *Mighty convenient,* she thought, and pushed through the door to get changed.

There was a steady buzz inside the locker room. Softball players were taping up wrists and ankles and getting on sliding shorts, much more boisterous than the runners.

The tension at practice during the days leading up to the race had been palpable, growing more intense each day. Practice had been light for everyone all week, but both Mattie and Jenessa loafed through the workouts, saving energy.

It was hot in the locker room and Callie stripped down and redressed in shorts, sports bra, and a T-shirt. She padded out to the lobby carrying her shoes and socks. The twins were already out there, wearing their multicolored socks—red and white, noted Callie, matching socks and faces. Anna was on the left. They were in shorts and tees, sitting cross-legged with sweatshirts in their laps, heads touching while they shared a book.

Callie flopped down next to Anna, back to the wall. "Anybody know what the plan is?"

"Nope," Anna said, looking up. She looked fully recovered from the flu bug.

"Mattie hasn't been a Chatty Cathy," said Hanna, talking across her sister.

"Like Jenessa has?" asked Anna.

"She hasn't said two words to me all week," said Callie. She slipped on her socks, adjusting the seams at the toes so they wouldn't rub. They all sat quietly considering the upcoming race. Shouts echoed down the lobby from the commons, the junior high runners burning off excess energy. One of the voices sounded like Jen's.

"So who do you want to win?" asked Hanna, sitting forward and looking at Callie.

Callie thought for a second. "Doesn't matter. Jenessa is going to win."

"Yeah, but who do you *want* to win?" pressed Anna.

"Seriously?" said Callie. "Neither."

The twins frowned. It was an odd look for them.

"We were thinking—" began Anna.

"—that it might be nice to see—" offered Hanna.

"—Mattie win."

Callie shook her head. "It's not going to happen. Jenessa is a good miler. A really good miler, and you guys know it. Mattie's never even raced that distance."

The twins swapped looks. "That's kind of what we thought, too," said Anna.

"That's too bad," said Hanna, "because Mattie can be awfully nice."

"Mattie can be nice?" Callie retorted, her eyebrows raising. "Since when?"

Anna and Hanna stared at her.

"She's always nice to us," said Anna, daring Callie to disagree. "She's in a couple of our classes."

"Not like Jenessa," said Hanna. "She's kind of . . . snobby."

"Persnickety," agreed Anna.

Callie didn't have a response. She had a lot of words that she could use for Jenessa, but "persnickety" had never occurred to her. She rolled it around her head and decided it was a fine word for Jenessa. As long as you didn't say it to her face, thought Callie. That would be . . . bad.

Callie changed the subject. "What are you doing for a workout?" She gave the twins a rueful smile. "I don't want to go on a run away from the track and miss the race."

"We're going to do form work on hurdles," Anna said, smiling.

"We'll be right there whenever they go at it," Hanna said.

"I guess I'll figure out something." Callie slipped on her left shoe, tightening the laces and double-knotting them. "Maybe short intervals. Doc's been awfully easy on us this week."

"Good for Mattie and Jenessa," observed Anna.

"Yeah," Callie said. She could feel the discomfort, a sour

feeling in her stomach, as she finished with the other shoe, cinching it tight. Doc had to know. Coming down the hallway was the noisy gaggle of junior high runners, one coach in front, one in back, herding them to the track. Jen saw her sitting under the lockers.

"Hi, sis!" she shouted over the clamor of her teammates echoing from the walls. "Who are you cheering for?"

Callie grimaced.

They waited for the group to straggle past, and then worked themselves onto their feet. Hanna stretched languidly. They headed out the far door of the lobby, into the sunshine.

The track was located across the street, an odd arrangement that had sprung from the town adding the football field and track well after the school was built. The original school had sat on prime building sites for new houses. The developer had donated the land for the new school to get the old school grounds, taking the write-off for the donation and lowering his costs for infrastructure. Since then, the school had been added to twice, creating the current rabbit warren of hallways.

The fields followed later when the town had more money. The school had passed the bond to build the field and track, adding lights and bleachers that the old field lacked. The Cloverland kids marveled at the new schools they visited in cities like Spokane, with their newness, the cleanliness and size of the locker rooms, the manicured facilities for football and baseball, the huge gyms for basketball. Mostly they noted how organized everything was—and how impersonal.

Down on the field, they could see the jumpers manhandling the red pit pads into position, the pads dwarfing the slender athletes. The grass of the football field, healing from the previous season, was greening with the warmer weather, faint marks from the chalk lines still visible. A chain-link fence surrounded the field, channeling pedestrians into the crosswalks on the street side and keeping deer off the field on the forested side. It was more successful with the people.

They jogged across the street during a gap between cars and walked down to the edge of the track. On the far side, Callie could see Mattie, warming up. With her were Mark and Nate.

There was no sign of Jenessa yet. The twins broke off and started walking counterclockwise around the track to go set up the hurdles. Callie walked in the opposite direction and flung her bag onto the first boardwalk of the bleachers. About thirty kids, none of them runners, were scattered in the bleachers.

She watched the seventh and eighth graders circling around the red oval. As they got to Mattie, Jen separated herself and went over to say something.

"Can I warm up with you guys?" Callie asked the junior high coach as the gaggle made its way around the first lap.

"Sure," said the head coach. "Jump on in, the more the merrier. How you been?" He had been Callie's coach years ago. A teacher at the school, he brought great enthusiasm to the job, along with almost inhuman patience. Jen saw her sister swing in with the shorter runners and started to work her way up the pack.

"Pretty good, Mr. Stevens. I ran a lot over the winter and Doc has been working with me on using the extra strength. PR'd last week in the mile."

"Good for you," he said.

"Doc has me kicking earlier—grinding, he calls it. Make the folks with speed suffer longer and try to outlast them."

Stevens laughed. "Yeah, I know how that works. Just like I used to tell you and as I keep telling these twerps." He nodded his head at Jen as she slid in next to Callie. "You can beat talent if you're willing to work and they're not." He laughed again. "If they're willing to work, all you can do is watch and enjoy. You ain't going to catch them."

"You running with us?" Jen interjected.

"Just warming up," replied her sister. "Practice got blown up today. Coaches aren't here so we're on our own. Thought I'd hang down on the track and work on six hundreds, pushing pace."

Jen made a face and Stevens laughed.

"This one will be good if you can get her to stop talking and run," he said.

"Good luck with that, Coach," laughed Callie. "She even talks in her sleep."

"I do not."

"How do you know?"

Stevens chuckled and steered his charges onto the infield to go through the team drills. The assistant coach, running behind, directed the lagging kids onto the grass. Callie kept going, needing to get another couple of laps in to get everything loose. The younger kids started striders, picking up speed as they ran the length of the infield. Callie jogged over to Jen on the next lap.

"Jen," she said, "focus on your feet. You're kicking your heels out."

"I am?"

"Uh-huh. Try to bring your heel right back into the middle of your hamstring." Callie saw her sister tipping her head to the side, trying to picture what she was supposed to do.

"Okay, I think," Jen said.

Callie jogged back to the edge of the track, onto the back straightway, and resumed her warm-up. She kept her eyes fixed forward as she passed Mattie. As she cleared the corner, she heard another runner join her. She looked over.

"Hi," she said to Mark. She looked closer.

"You okay? You look like you still have the flu," she said. She glanced back to Mattie and got a glare in return. *He joined me, girl,* she thought resentfully. From the infield she could hear Stevens shouting encouragement—"Light and quick, light and quick"—as the kids went through the skip drill.

"I'm okay, just tired. Late night," he replied.

"You going to do a workout today or just watch the race?" she asked.

"I did a workout this morning. No worries if everything goes whacked for the rest of the day," he said. "Plus I have some stuff to do after practice."

He stopped talking and Callie could see a faraway look come into his eyes. His pace quickened and he started to leave Callie behind.

"Hey!" she shouted to him. The shot-putters, large, solid-looking boys who played the line in football, looked over. Mark didn't hear her over the noise in his head. She sped up to nearly race pace to catch him, poking him in the ribs when she did. Mark snapped his head back, arching his side away from the offending finger, and looked at her.

"Got lost again," he apologized, slowing back down to match Callie's speed.

"No kidding," she said. "What this time?"

He had made the same apology to Doc a couple of times after running away from the rest of the team. When he ran into a problem that didn't seem to have a solution, he explained to Doc, he would go for a run, get into a zone, and the whole process to the answer would pop into his head.

"Something Kemosabe said," he commented. Mark glanced over to her, indecision on his face. She was staring at him while they kept running. "What did you think of him?"

"I've been thinking of him," she admitted. "He was a little . . . um . . . unusual. Why?"

"I hired him to help out at the house," he said.

"With what money?"

"Uh-huh. That's what my mom said, too."

"I bet. Why?"

"I needed some help fixing a fence and Uncle Bennie is really lousy at stuff like that."

"Your uncle Bennie's in town, too?"

"Uh-huh. He's visiting for a week or so."

Callie frowned. Mark's uncle was famous—no, notorious, she corrected herself—for getting expelled his senior year. Everybody knew the story. She glanced at Mark and a disquieting feeling started worrying her stomach. He was looking innocent, the same look he'd had when he put the peppers into Nate's food or bubble-wrapped the van. "Just a precaution," he had said to Doc. *Innocently.*

They finished the lap at the bleachers and Callie slowed to a halt, Mark staying with her. She squinted at Mark as she grasped the wood platform and started her leg swings. She could feel the tension dropping from her hips as the swings went higher.

"You're not going to do something stupid, right?" she asked, pinning him with an intense gaze.

"No, Kemosabe's cool," he said, evading her question and avoiding her eyes. He leaned against the edge of the wood with his ribs, resting his shoulder on the metal stanchion that supported the railing, watching the bottom of her shoe swing by like a metronome. "Do you know why he was so offended at being called a bum? Bums don't work, they panhandle or steal.

Hobos work, it's part of their code of ethics." He paused for a beat and began to quote. "Always try to find work, even if temporary, and always seek out jobs nobody wants." He was talking fast, changing the subject. "That's what Kemosabe meant about doing honest work."

"Hobos have a code of ethics?" Callie struggled to get her mind around the idea. Nomads with codes seemed a bit of an oxymoron.

"Yeah," he said. "I looked them up last night. They've got their own language and signs too," he added. "Plus, Kemosabe and I talked until like three o'clock in the morning. He's an interesting dude, been all over the country, has all sorts of stories, getting on and off freight trains and the hobo jungles—they're mostly gone now, he says—"

"He's staying at your house?" Callie questioned. "What about your mom?"

"We got that little guest house in the back, he slept there. Uncle Bennie had the spare room inside," Mark said. "Mom was a little worried at first but she's cool with it now."

With a start, Called narrowed her eyes. He had done it to her again. They had been talking about Uncle Bennie and Mark had managed to bamboozle her into a different topic. He might as well have waved a flag announcing "teenage boy about to commit "felony dumb."

Behind her came a buzz of noise and she glanced back to see Jenessa jogging down to the track, scowl on her face, racing flats in her hand. She was coated in a fine sheen of sweat from her warm-up.

Mark saw her at the same time. He pushed off the metal stanchion and turned toward Mattie. She was staring at Jenessa, expressionless. He started toward her but Callie grabbed his forearm, a gentle grip. He looked down to her face, framed by the pink hair band. She knew he could see worry in her eyes.

"Don't do anything dumb, okay?" Callie said in a soft voice. "Don't be Uncle Bennie."

He gaped at her in surprise, and then at her small hand on his arm, and nodded.

As he walked back to Mattie, Callie could feel the tingle in her fingertips. She jammed them under her opposite arm, trying to dampen down the feeling as she watched Mark rejoin Mattie and Nate. Callie looked to the starting line where Jenessa was adjusting her spikes and sighed.

It was time to race.

Chapter 21

"You ready for this?" Callie probed.

Jenessa looked up. "Any reason I shouldn't be?" she retorted, face in a scowl.

"No, it's just this doesn't have to happen," said Callie, trying one more time.

"Screw it." A half-second pause. "Screw her," spat Jenessa. "She thinks she can get in my face and call me a bitch. Screw her."

What had Mark called it? Callie thought back. *A grudge match.* That's exactly what this was. The brunette in front of her looked like Jenessa, decked out in a stylish name-brand pair of shorts and matching top, every hair perfect, and expensive stud earrings. The attitude was foreign, though. Jenessa was a soft runner, incredibly talented but driving poor Doc to distraction by doing just the minimum necessary practice, then frustrating him with races that she should have won. Callie, usually well behind, could see her falter fractionally, her head drop the tiniest little bit as she conceded. On the cusp of winning, she would back down to other, more determined runners.

This anger, the rage, was something else entirely. She watched as Jenessa laced the racing shoes, tweaking and adjusting the tongue, making sure the laces laid flat, each motion sharp and aggressive. Jenessa was muttering to herself, short little explosions of sound, almost indecipherable but angry.

". . . can't call me gutless. . ."

With a shock, Callie realized she was seeing a truer Jenessa, stripped of the fancy things purchased by doting parents, stripped of her pretensions and cool fabrications. None of that counted on the track. There, you got what you brought: talent and sweat and the long, long miles of preparation. What Jenessa had done on the track, no one had given her. She had earned it. Mattie was wrong, Callie thought. Jenessa cared, more than she had ever shown.

They met at the start line. There was none of the usual pre-race ritual, no joking around, no wishing each other luck. They didn't touch hands. They both toed the line, Jenessa on the inside. They were evenly matched in height but Jenessa was more powerfully built. Mark was the starter.

"You two ready?" he asked. They both nodded.

"Okay, just a ready and go when you're set." He walked out about ten feet from them, standing on the infield edge of the track.

"Ready . . ." The girls tensed. Around the track, the noise fell away. The jumpers in the pit on the first turn stopped while the throwers on the far turn gathered shot and discs, staring down to the start line. Runners who had been pretending to do a workout while keeping one eye on the racers drifted to a stop and stepped away from the inside lanes.

"Go!" Mark said, dropping the arm he held in the air.

Jenessa and Mattie surged forward and Callie started her watch. One-on-one it didn't really matter but she noted that Mark did the same thing. As the girls rounded the turn, there was scattered encouragement, a "Good job, Mattie" and "Way to go, Jenessa" mixed in with the ubiquitous "You got this, ladies."

Mattie eased into the lead on the back straight and pushed the pace. *Mistake,* thought Callie. A fast early race favored Jenessa while a slow race would give Mattie the advantage on the final kick. She could feel her heart thumping. *This is stupid,* she thought, *I'm not even the one racing.*

When they came past the start line, finishing the first lap, Callie looked at her watch. She looked at Mark and shrugged her shoulders. Mark nodded. It was fast, very fast for an opening lap on the mile for these girls. Both girls looked like they were straining but under control. They circled the track again, Mattie still in the lead and Jenessa sitting just off her shoulder. Jen and her teammates were cheering, thin reedy voices of the younger kids drowned out by the louder voices of the teenagers. Despite that, Callie knew, the two girls were running in a bubble of their own sound, strained breathing and the pocking sound of the spikes.

They came through the second lap and started the third, both girls breathing hard. Their pace was faster than Callie's PR for the eight hundred meters. She did a quick calculation in her head. They were about seven seconds off of Jenessa's school record. *She has more speed to spare for the last two laps.* And, as Callie thought it, she watched Jenessa surge past Mattie.

Lap one was always a shock to the system, the first hundred meters effortless before burning off the initial excitement and energy, the shock at the pace catching up with the miler.

Lap two was a chance to settle into the race as the lungs and legs accepted the brutal pace. Lap two was about maintaining contact, making sure that you were in position to take advantage of the other runners in laps three and four.

Lap three of the mile was always the hardest. Lap three was when doubt crept in, when breathing became a struggle, the lungs unable to grab enough air; the legs started getting a hint of the tightness that was coming. And, as much as lap three hurt, there was still one more lap.

Mattie was struggling now. Jenessa quickened again as they went past the high jump pit, trying to break Mattie. Mattie fell back a step, then two, but no farther. Grimly, she held on, her head starting a little rocking motion side to side, her gasping reaching across the track. *Come on,* thought Callie, *you can do this.* She could feel her fingernails gouging into her palms and consciously relaxed her hands, but couldn't draw a deep breath with the tightness in her chest. She watched as Jenessa's hands pulled higher and higher up on her torso and realized that she was struggling too.

They completed the third lap faster than either of the previous laps. They were now three seconds off of record pace. No wonder Jenessa was struggling too. She still had a two-step lead on Mattie. Both girls' faces were contorted in pain, both were gasping now. Jenessa's pain was flavored with anger, as she used it to drive herself down the track, fighting the usurper. Mattie's eyes were rigidly locked on the miler's back, chasing her into the fourth lap.

Little cheers erupted from the team as, coming off the next-to-last turn, Mattie launched her counterattack. She used the force of the turn to swing out one lane, accelerating to catch Jenessa. Slowly she inched up on the other girl as they made their way down the backstretch. Her head was wobbling from the effort but she caught up to Jenessa with two hundred and fifty meters to go. She pressed her advantage and gained a half step going past the two-hundred-meter mark. Callie watched Jenessa's shoulder drop a fraction of an inch. *No,* she groaned to herself.

And Jenessa kicked, kicked away from Mattie, a convulsive movement that Mattie tried to match and couldn't.

"Go with her, you can catch her." The shot-putters on the last turn were shouting now.

Callie watched Mattie try, reaching down to find that final burst of energy, but it wasn't there. She staggered down the end final straight, form falling apart, while Jenessa came across the line. Race over.

In the woods, Doc put down his binoculars and looked at his stopwatch. He gave out a low whistle. Jenessa was one second off her record; Mattie had just unofficially run the fifth-fastest mile in school history. Both girls were totally spent. He was glad that he had kept practice easy. They were going to need some recovery time before the meet on Saturday. He shook his head. That was the best race of the season for Jenessa.

He put the binoculars up to his eyes again and saw Mark staring into the woods. He wasn't surprised that Mark spotted him. Doc grinned. *Good kid,* he thought, *just needs things to do or he gets himself into trouble.*

He waited until the crowd dispersed. The team was gathered around Jenessa and Mattie as they headed back to the school. The jumpers were putting away the pits when he pushed off the rough bark of the tree he was leaning on and started to pick his way through the overgrown brush back to his truck.

Out on the track, as everybody else left, there was a solitary figure. He watched as the slim girl set herself up and took off on the first interval, starting her watch as she did so. He didn't need binoculars to know it was Callie.

Three days later, in a meet in Spokane, in nearly perfect conditions, Jenessa shattered her own mile record by four seconds while destroying the nearest runner by nearly sixty meters. An hour and a half later, Mattie savaged the school record for the eight hundred meters, breaking the old record by 1.9 seconds.

Chapter 22

"Ready?" he asked. Excitement made his voice crack a bit.

"What's to get ready?" his partner replied. "I'm not the one committing a breaking-and-entering felony tonight."

"Accessory before and after, and yes, I will rat you out. I'm a minor. They'll take pity on me," retorted the younger man.

"Would you just get going, smartass. We're not going to get caught."

The younger man flashed a smile and, as he slipped out of the car, slipped a black mask over his head and a backpack over his shoulder. They were parked a block and a half away from the school. The neighborhood was older, with a mix of turn-of-the-century Victorians and kit homes from Sears—literally homes that had been shipped in pieces by railroad in the early 1900s to be put together at the home site, each piece numbered—along with some newer 1940s houses.

The sidewalk here was buckled and uneven, the old concrete heaved by the trees lining the street. The trees were one reason they had picked this street—they blocked the streetlights. The boy walked carefully, avoiding the light, a black shadow slipping into black shadows. Inside one of the houses, he heard a small dog yapping, but the front lights on the houses stayed black.

He reached the corner and looked left, down the street to the school. Clear. Looked right. Clear. The next part of the approach would be more exposed. Not as exposed as crossing the street to the back side of the school, though. He turned left and, as casually as he could with a heart that was rapidly trying to thump its way out of his chest, sauntered down the sidewalk.

He thought about lifting the mask but didn't want to take a chance on getting recognized. Belatedly, it occurred to him that anyone looking out the window would be more alarmed by a figure all dressed in black—black shoes, black pants, black sweatshirt, black gloves, even the backpack was black—sporting a black mask than they would be by a teenager loitering along the street at ten o'clock at night. Besides, one of the reasons to wear all this had been to make sure no forensic evidence was left behind—or at least so little that it wouldn't be a help.

He also hadn't counted on how hot the outfit would be. He could feel sweat starting to run down his ribs, and the arms of the shirt were sticking to his skin.

He reached the end of the side street and looked across the main street to the school. The exterior was lit by fluorescent bulbs over each of the entrances—there were three of them, two emergency exits for the gym and one that let out to the mechanical yard where all the compressors, blowers, and high-voltage transformers were located. It was this last door that he focused on. He had scouted the school a half-dozen times over the last two weeks and every time, this door was propped open by the janitor when he was taking trash out to the dumpsters.

He stared hard across the street. The door was nearly opposite him and he could see the slim line of light seeping past the edge of the door, creating a wedge spread on the ground, beckoning him. He looked both ways for traffic and more closely for pedestrians. *Old people,* he thought, *walk their dogs at all sorts of odd hours.* It was quiet, though; the occasional night bird called and he could hear the hum of the transformers. He looked again, scouring the night for any threat.

Satisfied, he hurried to his next hiding place, the deep shadows created by the fence enclosing all the equipment. Solid wood and painted a rustic brown, it ate light and, more importantly for him, had a large pile of pallets stacked several feet away. Quickly he slipped between the pallets and the fence, slipping the backpack in ahead of him. The stack was tall enough that with just a slight bend in his knees, his whole body was hidden behind them. Then he settled in to wait.

His timing, a result of his meticulous scouting, was good. Less than five minutes later he could hear the squeak of the wheels as the janitor rolled his trash cart toward the door. He was an older man, inclined to mutter to himself through the evening hours as he cleaned up the school for the next day. With an extra-loud grunt, he shoved the cart with his ample midsection and banged the door open, navigating the cart through the opening. With a sigh, he gave it a push and caught the swinging door with his left hand. The janitor checked to make sure that the wood block was in to keep the door from fully shutting, and shuffled into the little courtyard formed by the school and mechanical pen.

The youth stayed hidden behind his barricade, every muscle tense. The cart ended up just a few feet from him. The youth watched as, with another sigh, the janitor reached into his breast pocket and pulled out a packet of cheap cigarettes, tapped one out, lighting it with an equally cheap disposable lighter. The janitor took a deep drag on the cigarette, the glow adding to the already too-abundant light. The boy tried to shrink back farther but there was no place else to retreat to. Beside him, the smell of the day's refuse, rotting food, the sickly sweet smell of fruit juices combining in trash bags into a putrid mess, assaulted him.

The janitor smoked his cigarette down to the filter, and then carefully bent down to put it out before tossing the butt onto the stack of garbage. With a little more muttering, he retrieved his cart and squeaked off to the dumpsters.

The youth waited until the man had turned the corner around the edge of the pen before extricating himself from concealment. *Last chance to chicken out,* he thought, and shook his head. A glance over his shoulder toward the racket of the bags getting dumped. Clear. He strode to the door, opened it just wide enough for him to slither in. As carefully as the janitor had, he silently set the block. He was in.

Quickly he raced down the hallways. He had scouted his path inside and knew precisely how far to go. Fortunately, the school was too small to have security cameras inside. With the only janitor occupied, he worried more about speed instead of stealth. He needed to be in position before the man came back inside. The sound of his running echoed a bit off the institutional walls. Turning the last corner, he slid to a halt by the offices.

This part of the school was less than ten years old, built when the state coffers were flush with money. Attached to the original school, it resembled it on the exterior but inside was completely different. The new building, housing the gym and locker rooms, administrative offices, a band room, and science labs, had gypsum board walls and drop ceilings instead of the old plaster in the original. It also, the youth knew, had partition walls to separate the spaces. The wall he was looking at, to the offices, ended just above the drop ceiling, with a two-foot height between it and the bottom of the metal joists, another three feet to the deck that supported the roof. *Plenty of room to work,* he thought.

He nimbly jumped onto the counter for the office, then to the top of the trophy case. At the top of the case, he eased up one of the acoustic panels, guiding it past concealed wiring. He looked around one more time, and then pressed himself onto the narrow top of the partition wall, swinging his rear around to balance on it, backpack pulling him backward. From his sweatshirt pocket, he took a cheap headlamp and, turning it onto the red "night light" setting, reached up to grasp the bottom of the metal joist for balance. He swung his legs up and, with his other arm, he slid the tile almost back into place.

He looked across the semi-open space. Tendrils of light from the overhead fluorescents filtered through gaps in the fixtures, adding to his headlamp. There was a bewildering array of cable and conduit, snaking this way and that, some of it lying flat on the tiles, others looped above the metal tie wire used to support the drop ceiling. Fat tubes of insulation, wrinkled and dusty, ductwork enclosed, delivered heat to the ceiling registers. The dust tickled his nostrils and he fought the urge to sneeze.

Across from him, he could see the opposite wall of the lobby below. He used that and measured three tiles over. That was where he needed to plant the timer and charge. He eyed the joist. When he had been planning, he had been sure he could wiggle his way out onto the joist to set the charge. Now he looked at it doubtfully. It was skinnier than he thought.

He sighed and started to climb onto the truss, the metal cutting into his thighs. He pushed forward and snagged, unable to move to the next panel. The backpack was catching on the webbing, the diagonal pieces that formed the triangles between the top and bottom plates. He backed up to the top of the wall and wiped the sweat out of his eyes with a shirtsleeve. He flipped the backpack to the front—He should have done this first, he thought, chastising himself. How else would he get the stuff out when he got out on the span?—and moved out onto the truss again. He wormed his way out until he was over the tile he needed, and softly swore. He needed one hand just to hang on.

He unhooked the backpack and took the waist belt, latching it to the truss. A bit of string hung down and, one-handed, he awkwardly tied that to the top of the bag. At least now, he didn't have to handle the weight of the bag. He unzipped the bag and pulled out the first item. Everything was arranged so that each piece got put in place in sequence. He set the two small charges first, one on either corner of the panel. Each piece attached to the next until he had only the timer left. He activated the timer preset and balanced it on the lower plate of the truss. He reached below him to attach the wires from the timer to the primary cartridge. He cursed again; with the gloves on, he could barely feel the wires and, one-handed, couldn't operate the clips that the wires snapped under.

He fidgeted around until he freed his other arm, precariously balanced with the webbing clamped between his legs. Almost immediately, they began to cramp from the unaccustomed squeezing effort. Sweat was soaking his mask and he was beginning to pant. Reaching with both hands, one on each side of the truss, he guided the wires under the clips. He leaned to his left slightly to make sure the cartridge was perfectly set. If it failed, everything failed. As he did so, he bumped the timer with his shoulder.

It skittered sideways on the truss, and in front of the horrified eyes of the boy, hit a wire, sliding sideways down a blue computer wire like a skateboarder on a handrail, teetering as it went, to land with a thump and a beep. He froze, waiting for some sign that the janitor had heard. Waited. Silence. Waited some more. Still silence. He let go his pent-up breath in a long hiss.

He looked at the timer and did the math. It was out of reach. No angle that he took could get him close enough to grab it and put it closer. Maybe if he pulled it by the wires? He gave an experimental pull, gently putting tension on the wire. He felt more than saw the slippage as the wire slid a fraction of an inch out of the clip. *No go, not gonna happen,* he thought. Maybe if he could get out of the crawlway, down to the floor, up . . . bound to get caught and he didn't have a ladder to climb up anyway.

He let go another breath. It would have to do, he thought, and, freeing the backpack, started to back his way over to the partition wall. Once he regained the relative security of the wall, he eased the panel back and, holding the joist tightly, leaned down to peek down the hallway.

Clear.

Quickly he reversed himself, lowering his feet down to the trophy case. He slid the tile back until it fell onto the metal tabs of the drop ceiling. He retraced his steps down the hallway, moving much slower—he had no idea where the janitor would be now. There was no way for him to have reconnoitered the inside of the school at night. He listened as he moved, but all he could hear was the blood thudding through his ears and his panting, and maybe an echo off the walls from the banging that his heart was doing.

He crept to the back door. It was shut. He pulled up his sleeve and was shocked to see that he had been gone an hour. The janitor should have left thirty minutes ago if he held to his schedule. He breathed, peering out the peephole in the door. Nothing. He cracked it open and immediately froze, overcome by the stench of cigarette smoke.

He waited, straining to hear muttering. His forearm muscles started to cramp from the grip that he had on the door handle. How long had he waited? He didn't know. How long should he wait? One more minute, he decided, starting a slow steady count in his head. One, one thousand, two, one thousand, the whole childhood litany to sixty . . .

He eased the door open enough to slip out, right shoulder first, head poking behind the door and sweeping around the perimeter. Nobody home. The pent-up tension flooded away from his body. False alarm. He completed his escape from the school and softly latched the door, testing the handle, and slipped back across the main road.

Once into the semi-dark of the residential street, he burst into a fast jog, covering ground. He turned right, reversing his path from earlier, and looked for the car. He couldn't see it in the dark. Still moving fast, he made his way down the street, not making any efforts to conceal himself, searching the darkness for the car.

There! He breathed a sigh of relief and dropped out into the street. He slowed to a walk as he came beside the car, then popped the door open and slid in under the dim glow of the overhead light. The driver came alert from the half sleep he had fallen into and looked at his younger accomplice.

"How'd it go?"

"Just fine," the teenager said, gulping lungfuls of air.

"Yeah, that's why you're shaking like a leaf," teased the driver. "Everything set to go boom?"

"Yeah, a week from Friday, one o'clock. I'll be in Cheney."

"Assuming you make it."

The young man reached for his mask, breathing a sigh of relief to get it off. "I'll make it," he asserted. "Just shut up and drive, would you, Uncle Bennie," he said. "I want to get out of here."

"I wish I had thought of this." Laughing, Uncle Bennie started the car and eased away from the curb, not turning on the lights until he turned at the end of the block.

Mark stripped off the black jacket and felt the cool air hit his sweat-drenched torso. For all his bravado, Mark was worried.

The timer had beeped.

Chapter 23

"You have the wrong color socks on."

"And the shoes don't match either," teased Hanna above the cheerful buzz of teenagers. Down the hallway came laughter.

Callie looked over at the beaming twins standing by their lockers, the bright yellow doors open, different pictures taped inside. Like her, they were wearing sweatshirts emblazoned with STATE CHAMPIONSHIPS across the front, along with the year. Both were dressed in blue jeans and wore running shoes. Callie matched with the jeans and the same brand of shoes, but wore a different model—lower to the ground—and a different color—what used to be a bright-orange-and-white upper before hundreds of miles of winter running had turned the upper gray and the orange had faded in the onslaught.

"I think the hair might be wrong too," she replied with a grin, looking at the long straight blond hair the twins sported that hung well past their shoulders. Like them, she was wearing her hair down, but it was shorter and bouncier.

"We're jealous of the hair," laughed Anna.

"And the tan," from Hanna. "We don't tan that fast."

All three of them had made it to the state meet the previous weekend, Callie qualifying in the two mile, the twins tying in a frantic finish that got them both to the meet a fraction ahead of the fourth-place hurdler. Callie's race, earlier in the morning, had gone well, as she came within a second of tying her personal record. The afternoon temperatures in Cheney, where the state meet was held every year, had been in the low eighties, unusual for the area, and none of the athletes were acclimated to it. Between races and cheering on the other runners, the girls had soaked in the sun. Memorial Day followed and the good weather persisted. Callie was quickly turning a honey brown, getting a jump on summer. Graduation was in two days; school was out in six. Hooray!

"You got finals today?" Callie asked them as she pulled books from her locker.

Hanna grimaced. "Yeah, Algebra Two and history."

"I'm lucky. I'm done," Callie said. She saw Mark shambling along the hallway. From the opposite side of the hallway, she could see Mattie watching him too and frowning. Mark had dark circles around his eyes and had been getting increasingly anxious all week. He had worn his sweatshirt a couple of times, but he barely mentioned state, even after a strong finishes in both the mile and the thirty-two hundred. She knew he was excited about some internship, but every time she brought it up, he changed the subject.

"Hey," she said, right hand still buried in the locker, trying to get his attention as he passed by. Mark walked right past her, never even looking over. She watched him nimbly sidestep two boys roughhousing in the middle of the passageway without looking up. *At least he's not totally oblivious,* she thought with a mental frown.

"Has he told you what's wrong?"

Callie jumped. She hadn't heard Mattie cross over to her. The redhead had white marks on her face where her sunglasses had set while she was at the meet. Her few freckles, usually subdued, were more pronounced with the mild sunburn she had gotten despite obsessively putting on sunscreen.

Callie shrugged and replied cautiously. "Nope." Mattie gazed at her as if expecting more, and Callie paused. "Why would he say anything to me?"

Mattie watched with Callie as Mark moved around the far corner. "I just thought he might." She met Callie's eyes. "Something's not right," she said, hefting her book bag. She walked away without saying anything else. Callie, shaking her head, grabbed her own bag. She was convinced she would never figure Mattie out.

Mattie cornered Mark at the end of lunch. With the sun out, most of the students had wandered outside to eat in the courtyard attached to the student commons. Mark had meandered out as well but was sitting well off to the side, isolated from everyone by a gloomy bubble that the other teenagers shied away from. Callie watched Mattie go over to him and say something but Mark just nervously fidgeted, trying to deflect her. She gave up and strode away, looking peeved. You might not know what Mattie was thinking most of the time, Callie reflected, but you could always tell when the girl was mad.

Callie sat with the twins, joined by another small group of athletes, softball and baseball players, and talked about their plans for the summer. Callie's family wasn't traveling, which was fine with her. She had already arranged to volunteer at the hospital in Lewiston and was glad not to have to rearrange her schedule. The volunteer time would work with graduation requirements for job shadowing and would look good on the applications she submitted for college.

The twins were chatting excitedly. They were taking a two-week trip to Alaska to visit relatives in Kenai. It was their first time to the state. The girls were swapping ideas for staying in touch while the guys rolled their eyes. The boys planned on playing ball all summer. Just before the bell rang for sixth hour, Callie unobtrusively eased away from the table.

Mark saw her coming, marking her progress with his eyes. His narrow face looked harrowed and pinched. He swung his head from side to side as though a hiding place would miraculously appear where he could disappear. Abruptly, he stood, wiping imaginary crumbs from his shirt front in sharp flicks, a glance flitting to the door to the commons.

"Mark, wait," she called to him. She watched him hesitate, check his watch, weighing the option of fleeing.

The bell rang. Mark flinched and looked at his watch again. She hurried toward him, willing him to stay put. When she reached him, she reached out, nearly but not quite touching his chest.

"What's wrong?" she asked. "And don't tell me nothing."

Inside the school, the timer started its countdown, the electronic brain inexorably ticking off seconds . . .

Mark looked at Callie, then at his watch again. "No worries," he said snappishly. "I'm fine."

Callie watched him check the watch, listened to his voice, saw him relax. Below the level of thought, in the instinctive place where intuition resided, suspicion started to stir. *He wasn't just acting worried,* she thought, *he's acting guilty.*

Her eyes narrowed and she stepped in a little closer. Across the courtyard, all the twins could see was Callie snugging up to Mark, and they laughed at his discomfort.

"What are you up to?" she pressed, the concern fading fast, nearly certain she didn't really want to know.

. . . reaching zero. At zero, it sent an impulse down the first set of wires . . .

Mark looked at her, startled at the sudden change in Callie. She seemed a lot bigger, this close, and he could feel the heat of her body. His eyes darted to the side, toward the door and protection. He looked at Callie and said, eyes still darting nervously, "I—"

. . . connected to the first two charges, blowing them, before sending the next impulse down to the main charge . . .

The sound of the charges, nearly on top of each other they were so closely synchronized, brought instant silence to the courtyard, every head turning toward the offices. The silence lasted a short second, to be broken by a scream of abject terror from inside the school.

Callie never looked at the school. At the first muffled explosion, she had watched Mark's body go completely rigid. From a distance of less than eight inches, he stared back at her. *I can see white all the way around his eyes,* a dispassionate voice inside said. Then another voice, louder, much more passionate: *What the hell have you done, Mark?*

Chapter 24

"Principal Haster will be with you shortly," apologized the secretary. "Would you care to have a seat? It really won't be long."

"No, thank you," Ms. Edith Mendolsohn said. "I prefer to stand." The oval-shaped woman, a representative from the State Board of Education, lumbered out into the hallway, peevish at waiting. She sniffed as she passed the small reception area, eyeing the standard-sized chairs with apprehension, correctly measuring the space between the armrests and finding a substantial lack of clearance for her ample hips.

The hallway was filled with presentation cases and low brochure holders and was nearly deserted. Light bled in here and there from open doorways, overwhelming the overhead lighting, casting bright, sharp-edged patterns on the vinyl floor. She stopped in front of the trophy case, shifting her head to avoid the glare off the glass. It had the usual athletic awards. A waste of resources, she thought.

The state board had sent her here to evaluate recordkeeping for the school's gifted and talented programs. There were some oddities regarding the coursework for a student who appeared to be taking virtual classes. This was, in the opinion of the board, a clear threat to providing consistent education to all students. She glanced at her watch and frowned. Haster was two minutes late. Tardiness was not acceptable.

"Ms. Mendolsohn," Jonathan Haster said as the dapper principal stepped into the hallway behind her, "my apologies. I had a conference call run a bit long."

Edith Mendolsohn turned, shifting with her stout legs, to face Haster. As she did, the first charges went off. She watched as a ceiling tile exploded up into the cavity above the ceiling, leaving a gaping hole.

This provoked a small "eek" from Ms. Mendolsohn.

The movement of the tile also pulled a small ripcord attached to the bundle that Mark had arranged, layering it so that it unfolded properly. No longer constrained, the material began to unfurl, pulled by small weights when the second, bigger gas canister, normally used for airbags in cars, went off. The material immediately filled and snapped taut.

She had no air for even a small eek. Her eyes were huge and color was draining from her face. Mr. Haster started toward her, horror on his face.

Two feet from the representative's shocked face, a menacingly tall zombie, green and moldy, exploded into view. The zombie swung to a halt, a thick rope around its neck digging in and pinching down on the fabric. The fabric ripped and the weighted head popped off, bouncing erratically on the floor and rolling to halt against her leg, broken teeth grinning up.

That's when she screamed and her body began to sag backward. Mr. Haster tried to catch her, crushing under her weight as he broke her fall. Undulating above him at the end of the rope was the headless body of the zombie.

Free My People dripped in bloodred letters across the chest.

In the courtyard, there was a sudden crush of sound and bodies moving toward the doors as the students talked over each other. An impromptu stampede broke out, moving in the direction of the school doors to find the source of the mystery. Only two students weren't moving.

"What did you do?" Callie kept her voice down but it was angry and intense. She had Mark, knees pinned against the low brick wall that bordered the courtyard, leaning almost backward.

"It's just a joke."

"It wasn't just a joke!" He was leaning even farther away, hands raised as though to hold her back. "Jokes don't go boom and make people scream. Jokes make people laugh." She gave a violent shake of her head. "I don't know who you scared the crap out of in there but somebody's going to be looking to find the idiot that set the bomb."

"It wasn't a bomb," Mark countered. "It was a—"

"I don't care what it was," Callie snapped. "It was a dumb idea and you're suspect number one."

"It wasn't a dumb idea!" shot back Mark. "It took—"

"It's not a dumb idea?" Callie interrupted again, poking him in the chest with a forefinger. Her face was flushed. "Really? Is there anybody else here smart enough"—she scowled—"or dumb enough, to set off a bomb when half the country is waiting for another terrorist attack? You're six days from getting out of here, going to one of the coolest companies in the country for an internship. How is this not a bad idea?"

Mark scowled. Recoiling from Callie's prodding finger, he tried to push her away by turning his shoulders, creating space and sliding sideways away from the wall.

"It's not a bad idea because I won't get caught," he replied angrily.

"You won't get caught," she mimicked. Her voice was biting and sharp. "That's a great way to look at it."

"It's a senior prank," he said. "How else are they going to look at it?" He glared at her. "They'll be looking at them. It's always the seniors causing trouble at graduation," he said, adding acerbically, "Not that most people have any sense of humor. Whatever it was," he said with a slim, angry smile, "I'll bet it was epic."

"Real epic, super funny joke." Callie's chest was tight. "What about the people in there? Did you ever think of them, or is it just, *I'm Mark and I think it's funny*," she said, eyes accusatory. She carried on, mocking him. "Sorry if it scared you half to death but, geez, get a sense of humor, why don't you."

"That's not fair. I—" He stopped abruptly, shifting his attention from Callie to a point over her shoulder, and his face blanched.

She looked back. Storming across the courtyard at a near run in his patent leather loafers was Principal Haster. He was headed right at Mark.

"Think they'll make him do a perp walk?" Jen said from her elbow. The eighth-grade girl was vibrating from all the activity and rumors that were flying through the clumps of students. *They found more bombs. Two people died. Mark did it.* Nothing this exciting ever happened at Cloverland. . . .

"I don't . . . who does the perp walk?" Callie corrected. She was still fuming.

"Mark," Jen said, her head tipped sideways. "Everybody knows he did it."

"It's not what they know, it's what they can prove," Callie responded reflexively. *Great,* she thought. *I'm sounding like Jen.*

Jen nodded sagely. "Think they'll try him someplace close? I want to go and watch. Maybe they'll try him as an adult, he's seventeen and—"

"Would you stop?" Callie said with exasperation.

Jen sized her up; the anger on Callie's face was plain. "Well, you're no fun," she said, then, spotting a friend, shouted, "Hey Sandy!" and sped off, a brown-haired rumor incubator.

School was canceled for the rest of the day. The volunteer fire department arrived within three minutes. They summed up the situation to Haster. The entire school would need to be swept for bombs and they weren't equipped for it.

That evening, a special unit from Spokane arrived and scoured the building. It was a painstaking process to lift tiles in each section of the school to make sure there was nothing hidden above the ceiling. Their bomb dogs sniffed and snuffled through the hallways and rooms. They gave the building the all clear just after midnight.

Long after all the other students departed—in a mad scramble of frantic parents caught up in bomb rumors and school lockdowns mixed with the opportunistic kids who took advantage of the chaos to slip away from campus—Mark left, in the firm grip of his mother. Principal Haster wanted him to leave with the cops, in the firm grip of handcuffs, but, as they explained, there was no evidence that Mark was involved—at this time, anyway, they added, sounding hopeful.

Privately, the police agreed with Haster. They were quite sure that the forensics teams from Spokane would perform their little miracles and they would be back to collect Mark. They were wrong.

Mark and Uncle Bennie had been careful, very careful, in assembling the prank. No fingerprints, hairs, or skin tissue infected their work. The one piece of fiber investigators found—in the attic space—was from a school-sponsored sweatshirt that half the kids and a goodly number of parents wore. The zombie was traced to a store in Oregon, the gas cartridges to California. Neither had been shipped to any nearby towns. The timer, a modified lawn irrigation clock, had been purchased from a Home Depot in Utah. The forensics technicians thought it was a very nice piece of work, quite professional, especially for a teenager, but not the evidence they needed to prosecute.

Five days later, the day after school let out for the summer, Callie's world got turned upside down, courtesy of Mark.

Chapter 25

"I hope I'm not intruding," Paula Johnson said when Callie, alone in the house except for the dog, answered the chime of the doorbell. She stood there holding a white envelope while the warm sunlight streamed around her into the open doorway.

"Um, no," said Callie to Mark's mother. She looked over her shoulder. "My folks aren't home, though."

"Actually, I was hoping to speak with you."

"Me? Why?"

"Mark took off this morning with his uncle Bennie for the Bay Area."

"I thought he was leaving next week," Callie said. A hollowness built in her stomach.

"He changed his plans. Bennie rolled into town last night and talked him into leaving early," Mrs. Johnson said.

Callie grew aware that she was squeezing the doorknob. "I'm sorry," she said, "I'm being rude. Would you like to come in?" She opened the door wider and stepped back to the side. Paula Johnson walked in, and together, they moved to the sofa in the living room. Mrs. Johnson sat on the far end, facing Callie, letter held in her hands in her lap.

"He left early? Because of what happened at school?" Callie asked, searching the woman's eyes. "I didn't . . . it didn't end good."

"It wasn't school or the zombie," she said, "and it wasn't because you yelled at him." Callie twitched and Mrs. Johnson clarified. "He told me about getting chewed out by you. It upset him—he doesn't have many people he considers friends. I'm glad he heard it from someone other than me. Moms don't get listened to like pretty little ladies."

Callie stared at her. "Kemosabe called me that."

"I know. Mark was jealous he hadn't thought of it." She paused. "English was always a second language for him. I think he thinks in math. Bill—Kemosabe—made quite an impression on Mark."

"Bill?"

Mrs. Johnson smiled. "Kemosabe is not really a hobo." She hesitated and then rephrased her statement. "He is a hobo, he's just not a full-time hobo."

"How can you be a part-time hobo?"

"When you're a full-time English professor at a university in Iowa."

"He's a professor?" Too many new ideas were coming at Callie and she was struggling to get them organized. Mark gone. Kemosabe was a guy named Bill. An English professor. She remembered her Shakespeare challenge and blushed.

"He was on sabbatical and studying hobo literature and language before the last of them fade away," Mrs. Johnson said. "How do people put it now? He was . . . living large."

Callie sat there, a little stunned, trying to process the new information.

"Mark asked me to give this to you." Mrs. Johnson was holding out the white envelope and Callie saw her name written in blue pen in Mark's sloppy handwriting. She took it from Mark's mom and, fumbling, opened it to find several handwritten pages.

She looked up to the woman.

"I don't understand," she said.

Mrs. Johnson sighed. "I'm not sure I do either, Callie.

"If you like," offered Mrs. Johnson, pointing to the pages in Callie's hand, "I can wait while you read it. I think you might have some questions."

Callie, nodding dumbly, said, "Please," and finished removing the letter, then unfolded the paper. Sophie followed them from the door to the sofa and curled up at Callie's feet, her head heavy on Callie's arches.

> *Hi Callie,*
>
> *I figure you're probably mad at me still and this won't help much but still, I thought maybe I could explain some of it. I hope you understand.*
>
> *I guess I kind of don't really know where to start. The last week of school didn't turn out the way it was supposed to and I know that people are saying, "oh, that's Mark" even if nobody can prove it and they're laughing. I guess I'd rather they laughed than ignored me but still. You were one of the few people that never laughed AT me and you don't know how much that means.*
>
> *People will be saying the same stupid things while I'm gone with Bennie because they won't understand.*

"Have you read the letter?" Callie asked.

Mrs. Johnson shook her head. "No."

"He talks about leaving with Bennie."

"I'm pretty sure that Mark was the one that dropped the zombie, and that my brother helped."

"You think he did it?"

"I think it's very, very possible, but he hasn't admitted it to me."

Callie kept reading.

I thought about skipping the internship and hopping a ride on a freight. It's a big world out there and I need to see it all or as much of it as I can. There's something special out there, I know it even if we never hear about it, only hear about the bad news and the trouble. It's out there. I just need to look for it.

Callie's head snapped up. "He wouldn't? No way, he wouldn't be that stupid." She stared hard at Mark's mom. "He went with Bennie, right? Because he's talking about riding trains like Kemosabe."

"No, he left with Bennie," Mrs. Johnson said. "It doesn't surprise me about him wanting to be like Kemosabe. It wasn't just his charming way with words. He and Mark talked a lot the couple of days they worked out at the house." She looked at Callie with amusement. "Mark ordered a book on hopping freight trains."

"They have books on that?" Callie asked with a pained expression.

Callie looked at the woman planted at the other end of the sofa, then back to the pages in her hand.

We've got a big year coming up. I didn't think my senior year would be a big deal until it got here and suddenly it got real. The team captain thing last year with Doc was a big learning experience. Makes you look at things differently. For a crotchety old dude, Doc is pretty sharp and he really cares about all the kids, not just us fast ones. I don't think it's a team thing for him, it's a family thing. I think that's why he made you captain this year. You'll be great, know it.

The school part is easy and running was always easy too. It's the getting my head wrapped around the idea that it's getting time to move on, move out that's hard, like I've always lived here, soon I won't. Scary. Not sure I have it figured out yet but sometimes you just fake it and jump first and try to figure out where you're going to land . . . like I said, scary. Exciting. Both.

But I didn't want to leave without saying good-bye—not goodbye, never see you again—more like Kemosabe's fare thee well—to you. Like I said, you never laughed at me and, if nobody else could understand me, you tried. Probably hurt your head but you tried. You really don't know how much that means to me. I'm excited as hell to get out on this gig with the robotics dudes but sad. I'm going to miss seeing you and running with you. I'm bringing my phone with me so I'll be able to text and stuff. I promised Mom I would stay in touch so she wouldn't worry too much. If you're not still too mad, we can keep in touch, too?

Well, I got to get going—I have one more letter to write. Most of my stuff is packed. Bennie's here and

I've got to hit the road. Big changes, hey.
    Take care of yourself.
    Mark
    p.s. Tickle Jen for me—she deserves it

Her eyes moist, Callie looked up at Mrs. Johnson. Mark's mom was watching her and Callie saw, mirrored in her eyes, the sorrow and worry and fear. There was also pride there, which confused the young girl.

"He's left already?" Callie asked, confirming what she already knew.

She had met Mrs. Johnson at meets and school events. That was a different person. She looked anew at the woman sitting tall on the couch beside her, with her hands clasped in front of her on her lap, the tiny lines that spoke of personal tragedy at the corners of her eyes.

"Mark is a lot like his dad. Headstrong, always sure he's right. Most of the time, he is. He is an amazing young man." Mrs. Johnson hesitated a beat. "When his dad died, Mark was devastated. Any eleven-year-old would be. But Mark didn't show it by acting out or getting into trouble. At least, not till later," she amended. "He decided that he needed to be the man of the family. Picture it, little Mark, coming to me and, very solemnly, telling me that he'd take care of me." Memories floated in the older woman's eyes.

"His dad had always insisted that every little boy wants to be a hero. Not to grow up to be a hero, just be a hero. Said it was hard-wired into the genes, and encouraged Mark to aim for the stars." Mrs. Johnson's voice was catching. "You can't do that staying home safe on the couch. His father would have told him to go for it, give the world a whirl, swing the tiger by the tail." Another pause. "Bennie challenges him, and as much as I want to strangle my brother, it's good for Mark. Same with Kemosabe." She stared at Callie. "You do, too."

"Me?"

"You. A girl would, at some point."

Callie felt a hot blush blossom. "We're friends," she muttered.

Mrs. Johnson gave her an appraising look. "Okay. But he listens to you." Seeing Callie getting ready to protest, she added. "Not that he would admit it."

Callie closed the door behind Mrs. Johnson, the snick of the lock loud in the empty house. Her right hand hurt. She stared at the crumpled paper clenched there and consciously relaxed her fingers.

Beside her, Sophie whined, and Callie reopened the door to let her out, following her out onto the veranda. As the dog dashed down the steps, Callie unfolded the pages to reread them. As she did, the initial shock of Mark's disappearing act faded, as did the worry.

Callie watched Sophie get distracted chasing a squirrel up one of the nearby pines. The squirrel sat on a branch, angrily chittering, simultaneously warning the other squirrels while mocking the dog below. The dog would be preoccupied for hours clearing the lot of the noisy rodents, chasing from tree to tree and barking at the squirrels as they moved to their nests without setting foot on the ground.

I challenge Mark? she thought. *How? And who cares?*

Callie turned to go back into the house. The snick of the lock was inaudible as the door slammed into the frame, rattling the front of the house and momentarily quieting the dog and the squirrels.

Chapter 26

With a fling of her right arm, Callie slapped the alarm off and rolled over, away from the window where glimmers of summer light were already brightening her curtains. She pulled the sheets tight against her shoulders and drifted into a comfortable half sleep. In her half-dozing state, she was mildly surprised as Mark came up beside her. She didn't know he was back in town, and she was vaguely aware that she was supposed to be mad at him.

She could hear the movement beside her, feel him lean on the edge of the bed. She even thought she could smell him, an earthy scent. Eyes closed, she smiled. She felt his warm breath on her cheek as he came close to kiss her and—

—he licked her face.

She jerked away violently to the far edge of the bed. Fully awake, she looked to see Sophie, standing beside the bed, the leash at her feet, a hopeful tail swishing the air when she saw Callie's eyes open. Grumbling to herself and feeling foolish, Callie stared at the ceiling. Beside her, Sophie made a little peep, not quite a whine, waiting for Callie to take her on their morning run. Callie forced her body into a sitting position.

"Hang on, Miss Pushy." She swung her tanned legs over

the edge of the bed and quickly exchanged her sleep clothes for shorts and a T-shirt. Snagging her shoes and socks, she trailed the dog down the hall. She banged on Jen's door and poked her head in through the door.

"Hey, you coming?"

The bundle on the bed twitched, groaned, and the unruly hair disappeared under the blankets.

"G-way!"

Callie shut the door, leaving her sister. Jen kept promising to get up and run with her in the morning. Half past five came early and Callie usually ran with just Sophie. Since Mark had left, she had been doing two runs a day, a double shot of endorphins. They worked for about thirty minutes, until the high from the run faded.

The coffeepot was starting to drip as she stopped in the kitchen. *After my run,* she thought, inhaling the enticing aroma filling the air. Barefoot, she went to the sink and got a glass of water. She drank it as she finished dressing. Dad would be getting ready for work. Mom always got up with him.

"Come on." She gathered the leash up from the floor where the dog had dropped it. Sophie wiggled through the door before Callie had it fully open. Callie followed, rolling her shoulders and twisting through the hips. At low speed, she began to jog along the driveway while Sophie darted from side to side, sniffing the bushes and grasses, occasionally snorting when something caught her nose.

When they reached the paved road, Callie stopped to put the leash on Sophie and stretched a bit more. The two followed the road up to a disused logging trail that cut uphill through the trees away from the pavement. Out of sight of the road, Callie let Sophie off the leash and the two settled into the run.

Sophie continued coursing across the overgrown track, always staying within sight of the young girl. Callie was running easily now that she was warmed up. Like Sophie, she was becoming addicted to the morning runs. The sunrise kissed the few clouds with gold and rich oranges. The tops of the trees, capturing the light, glowed green while darker greens and rough bark browns prevailed at the forest floor. Later, when the temperatures would be in the nineties, the colors would be bleached out by the sun.

A little more than an hour later, Callie, a bit breathless and sweating, led the dog, now panting, into the kitchen. The smell of bacon frying triggered a pleasant grumble from her stomach.

Both her parents were up, her mom cooking breakfast while her dad checked e-mail. Her mom looked up from the stove where the bacon was sizzling and popping.

"Hungry?"

"Always," said Hank without looking up from the laptop.

"I wasn't asking you, hon."

"Who said I was answering for me? I thought feeding daughters would be easier than boys."

"Funny, Dad," said Callie. "Any coffee left?" she asked as she crossed the kitchen to make breakfast for the dog while Sophie slurped noisily at the water bowl.

"We saved you some," said her dad.

"I saved you some. Your dad was going to drink all of it."

Callie dug into the dog food bag, getting two scoops of kibble out. "I'm going to bump up Sophie's food. She's starting to look skinny."

"Look who's talking." Jen had come downstairs, still holding her teddy bear, looking groggy. "I smell bacon." She stumbled toward the plate that had the crisp slices. "Are you joining us at the river?" Jen looked at her sister as one hand snaked out to swipe a piece of bacon.

Her mother, without looking, rapped her fingers with the edge of a fork. "Wait for everybody else."

Callie ran hot water onto the dog food. "Can't. I'm job-shadowing at the hospital today, then I'm going to the track for some speed work. Nate's meeting me there."

"A boy?" said Hank, looking up from the computer.

"Relax, Dad. He's not *the* boy," said Jen, still eyeing the bacon.

"It's speed work, Doc is going to be there, too." Callie tried scowling at Jen to shut her up but Jen looked at her innocently. Callie walked over to the door to let the dog back out after Sophie had wolfed down the bowlful of food.

"There's a 'the' boy?" Hank was looking suspiciously at his elder daughter.

"Scrambled eggs work for everybody?" asked Sarah. "And yes, hon, there's a 'the' boy. Mark. You know him."

"Mom!"

Hank relaxed. "Mark Johnson? Smart kid, genius with equipment, hard worker. He took a summer job in the engineering department last summer. Did well."

"You approve of him?" asked Jen, surprised.

"Is he a boy?"

"Yes."

"No."

"It doesn't matter," said Callie, joining her mom at the counter, reaching for the bread with one hand while she pulled the toaster out with the other.

Jen sneaked a look at Callie. "Right. That's why Callie's been such a cranky cuss since he left."

"I'm not cranky." Callie slammed down on the lever to drop the first two slices of bread into the toaster.

"Wanna bet?"

"Why don't you butt out. I'm *not* cranky," she insisted, emphasizing her words with a jab of the butter knife she held. Callie took a deep breath and tried counting to ten, gave it up. "Mom, do I have time for a shower?"

Her mother looked at the eggs stiffening in the pan. "If you hurry. Five minutes."

Callie glared at Jen and headed upstairs.

Callie saw Jen disguising a satisfied smirk, and she stopped to yell at her.

"If you two were boys I'd give you boxing gloves," said Callie's dad before she had the chance to say anything, looking right at Jen as if he knew exactly what she was thinking. Callie expelled a quiet sound of disgust and walked to the stairs as her dad and Jen continued talking.

"I'd win." Jen tried to meet his eyes with confidence, and, failing, went to work buttering the first two pieces of toast.

"Want to bet, munchkin?" he said, his voice steady.

Jen looked up the stairs, then at him. "No, sir," she said. "I don't think I do."

Surprised, Callie looked back from the stairs. Then she started to worry. Jen was studying her and she had that look. . . .

Callie undressed and turned the water temperature up as high as she could stand, climbing in when the steam started to rise from the top of the tile enclosure. She soaped quickly and rinsed. She turned, putting her back to the showerhead, and wet her hair. It didn't need washing. It would do for the day with a little blow-drying and some hairpins to keep it out of the way.

The spikey heat of the shower beat into her back, turning the tan red. She leaned forward, resting her head against the cool tiles at the back of the shower, and closed her eyes. The turbulence inside subsided, the heat from the shower penetrating tight muscles, the white noise of the shower insulating her from the outside world.

I'm not cranky, she thought. *And he's not "the" boy.*

Chapter 27

Callie's dad and the dog heard it first.

"Someone's here," Hank said without looking up from the marinade for the pork ribs he would grill for dinner. Sophie barked.

Jen jumped up from the table and ran to the front windows.

Callie, bleary-eyed from a Friday night swing shift that had run late, looked up from her cup of coffee. She had finally pulled up to the house just after one in the morning and had collapsed into bed, exhausted. She had spent ten hours hustling, fetching supplies, answering phones, whatever she could to help the nurses. The stories from the ER always seemed to start with "It seemed like a good idea at the time . . ." or "We'd drunk about a six-pack each . . ." and always involved guys.

"It's Anna and Hanna," Jen said, sounding bright and happy.

"What do they want?" Callie said from the table in a sour voice. Nobody showed up out here without checking first—it was too far out of the way. In town, a neighbor might be thirty yards away. Out here it might be three miles to the next house.

Jen popped open the door without answering her sister.

"Hi," the twins said in unison, beaming at Jen as they stepped inside. They looked across the living room into the kitchen. Taking in Callie's unkempt hair and pajamas, they exchanged glances.

"Are we early?" asked Anna. They were dressed for a run, pink shorts and white tops, each carrying a buff-colored fanny pack with a water bottle.

"Early for what?" replied Callie as she stood up from the breakfast bar and walked toward the two girls. The twins swapped another glance while Jen eased out of Callie's way.

"For the run."

"What run?"

The twins swapped another glance and looked worried.

"You asked us if we wanted to go on a trail run with you today," explained Anna.

"And we said yes," Hanna confirmed.

"And you said, great—"

"—be here at ten o'clock."

"So here we are," Anna said.

"I'm confused." Callie looked at her mug. Empty. She needed more coffee if she was going to deal with the twins. "When did I ask you?"

"Last night—"

"—online—"

"—about eight." The twins were unhappily fussing with their fanny packs.

She stared at them as a slow realization hit her. "I was working last night." She heard a squeak from the stairway and whirled to find Jen retreating up the top step.

"JEN!"

The twins flinched at Callie's shriek.

A muffled reply floated down, something ending with ". . . in the shower."

"Dad!"

Her father looked up and sighed.

"Jenifer. Front and center, pronto!" His voice boomed up the steps.

He looked at Callie, standing grim-faced next to the twins. "Don't kill her, I still need the tax deduction." The twins shuffled their feet and ripstop fabric of the packs was being tested.

Jen appeared, slowly traversing the steps until she was at the landing.

"You hacked my computer!"

Jen stared into Callie's angry eyes, lower lip sticking out at a pouty angle.

"Allegedly."

"Allegedly, my butt. You hacked it and drug the twins over here."

The twins were shuffling, uncomfortable at the confrontation between Callie and Jen. Callie struggled against the urge to shout.

"Dragged, not drug," corrected her sister. "Allegedly dragged," she modified, correcting herself this time.

"It doesn't matter. You invited them under false pretenses and told them I was going for a trail run."

"Well, you were," said Jen, quickly clamping her mouth shut as a guilty look filled her eyes.

She *had* planned a trail run today, penciled it into her training schedule before she found out she was working the swing shift. Callie stared at her younger sister. . . .

"You hacked my training log!"

"Allegedly."

"Why don't you just read my diary while you're at it!" Callie shouted, surrendering to the internal pressure. The twins flinched again and their faces were scrunched.

"It's locked," said Jen, quickly adding, "allegedly."

From the kitchen, their dad snorted. Callie turned her glare on him.

Anna, looking stricken, said to Callie, "We didn't mean to be trouble."

Hanna: "We can go home—"

Anna: "—except we'll need a ride."

Hanna: "Mom is headed to the valley—"

Anna: "—and you said you'd give us a ride home."

The two girls stood, shoulders drooping, big brown eyes on Callie.

"I said I'd give you a ride home, too?" asked Callie.

They bobbed their heads, cheeks flushed with embarrassment.

From the kitchen, Hank Reardon said, "Callie, why don't you go. Jen and I can have a little discussion on how to stay out of jail as a juvenile."

Callie shook her head and looked at the twins. "Give me ten minutes?"

They nodded. "We can wait," said Anna, relief evident in her voice.

"—rained the whole time we were there," said Anna from in front as the three of them loped along the single track, the pine needles softening the sound of their feet. The air was filled with the scent of the pines and the small wildflowers that sprouted beside the path. Around them, the forest twittered and tweeted and crackled.

"Well, no worries of that here," Callie replied as she ducked under a leafy branch snapping back after Anna had let go of it.

Callie was short enough to duck under most of the over-hanging limbs but both twins would snag the branches with a hand just long enough to slip by, before sending them whipping back to the next runner.

"It never got over seventy. And it wasn't just the weather that was crud. Alaska is boring," Hanna said, continuing with the story of their Alaskan adventure. "You see the commercials and the nature channel and they show bears and bald eagles and stuff."

"Nothing. Real pretty mountains but didn't see a single bear," complained Anna.

"Maybe they weren't hungry," Callie said as the runners entered an open meadow and started ascending a middling-sized hill. The trail had a series of uphills before cresting to a long rocky descent leading back into the forest and the trailhead.

"We did get to hike a glacier. That was pretty cool." Hanna eased up next to her. "When you look in the crevices, it gets this really spooky blue."

"And you can feel it move. This kind of low rumble every once in a while."

The pair kept talking nonstop to the top of the hill, climbing with a graceful ease while Callie sloughed behind them. Anna and her sister slowed at the plateau before the next hill to wait for Callie. She wasn't far behind. To their left, at the edge where the hill plunged into a deep canyon, cows and calves fed on the wild grasses. The upper meadows were still used for livestock and Callie and the twins had already passed through several of the gates that limited the herd's range, careful to follow the unwritten rule: leave it as you find it. The cows, alert to threats, mooed, two of them moving in front of their calves to face the girls.

They tackled the next uphill, plateaued again, the twins not waiting this time. Together they hit the last uphill, the steepest, digging in, taking turns leading the other as they navigated the rutted trail. Dropping back, Callie continued her march up, on the balls of her feet as she efficiently drove each knee forward in turn, adjusting to the rocks and roots as she did. A minute after the twins, she reached the peak.

"Wow." The twins nodded as all three looked out, still a little breathless. Lost in the depths of the canyon, they could still follow Snake River by the gouge it cut into the basalt rock over millennia while a hundred miles away the Seven Devils, reaching nine thousand feet and a bit more, stood watching summer advance over the high prairie. The tallest peaks had snow on their flanks in August.

A welcome summer breeze ruffled their hair and clothes, tickling and cooling before floating on to rustle the grasses and small, low bushes. Callie could feel the sun, brighter and hotter at this altitude, heating her shoulders. Callie took a fast drink from her water bottle, checking it to see how much she had left. A little more than half. Plenty.

She glanced at the others. "Ready?"—and bombed off the top of the hill first, leaning forward a bit to let gravity provide acceleration. She ran loosely, feeling the trail underfoot, using short, quick steps. Behind her, she could hear the twins scrambling down the trail.

There was the sound of a rock clattering down the trail and a muttered curse, a "Whoa"—probably Anna, she thought—as she continued to pick up speed. The sounds behind her faded a bit as she focused.

Just before the first switchback, she hit a technical section of trail, larger jagged rocks and loose pebbles scattered in front of her. She leaned back slightly, slowing, and shortened her stride even more, her feet hitting the ground only long enough to adjust for the next step, making split-second decisions, her eyes surveying the trail ahead as she instinctively planned. *That rock, left foot. Open space, looks firm, right foot, tuck left foot to clear the tip of that rock, shift balance left, use edge of trail, over to that boulder. . . .*

She cleared the rocky stretch and, using her arms and hips in perfect balance, powered into the high side of the right-handed switchback turn, leaning forward and in, catapulting through the turn and exploding out to the next stretch, the rush of speed exhilarating. Callie, grinning, stretched out her stride in the smooth trail beyond the turn, feeling the increased impact on her feet, ankles, knees. *Getting out of control, ease back, crashing would be bad.* She shifted her hips back, slowed slightly, flowing down to the next turn.

The next switchback was rocky and steep, cut through with a deep gully where the winter runoff had washed away the silty clay and sand, leaving behind the broken rock. Callie braked into the turn, leaning to her left, picking her way through the treacherous footing. In the middle of the turn, just as she transferred her weight to a large chunk of granite, it broke loose, skidding into the gully and starting a small cascade of pebbles and stones clicking and shuffling as it tried to drag her in with it.

Callie felt the rock slide out as soon as her toes landed, and went airborne. Pirouetting in midair, she threw her arms out as she struggled to get her right foot down on solid ground. She landed, knee flexed, taking off again, less twisting on the second leap, clearing the end of the switchback. Still leaning, she was three steps into the flatter straight before she completely recovered her balance. She loped the final two hundred meters of the tapering slope, gliding to a stop in the clearing below.

Callie felt her heart thumping—partly from the effort, partly from the near disaster in the turn—and her legs were quivering a bit as she sucked in air. She turned back to check on the twins, surprised to see Anna and Hanna just clearing the last switchback, walking the turn, then trotting down to the clearing. She chugged a couple of gulps of water while she waited for them to reach her.

"You okay?" Hanna said as she eased to a stop near Callie. The younger twin looked anxious, mirroring her sister.

"Yeah. Why?"

"You were blasting down the hill and we could see you go flying into the turn there. One second you were running, then you were jumping and spinning."

Hanna took over. "Looked like you were jumping off a cliff, then you landed, looked like your knee collapsed, you jumped again, and we couldn't see you around the turn."

"Scared us," said Anna.

"We thought you fell."

The twins stared at her.

"I'm fine. A loose rock just knocked me off-balance a bit."

The twins kept staring. Callie looked back and forth from Anna to Hanna. Their stares, like she was a strange creature they found in the woods, were making her uncomfortable, .

"What?"

"How did you do that?" said Anna.

"I felt the rock slip, so—"

"No, no, not that," interrupted Hanna.

"The other part."

Callie swung her head to face Anna. "What other part?"

"I told you she wouldn't know," said Hanna as Callie looked at her, bewildered.

"Wouldn't know what? What are you talking about?"

"You ran away from us," Anna said.

"Oh." Callie paused. "Sorry."

"Not sorry," said Hanna.

"You never run away from us," said Anna, peering at her.

"We tried to keep up," said Hanna.

"But you were flying."

Callie shrugged. "I was just running, having fun. I like downhills."

"We noticed," said Hanna. She was starting to sound frustrated. Her sister tried again.

"What we want to know is how did you do that?" Anna made a patting motion with her hands, sideways, both flat in front of her, alternating up and down with each hand. "Happy feet."

"Happy feet?"

Both twins looked at her expectantly. Callie relived pushing off onto the downhill stretch, the sense of speed, picking her steps, high-stepping, sidestepping, as she went.

"I call it running."

"Okay," said Hanna, "but how?"

"I don't know," Callie said with another shrug. It didn't seem that complicated. "I just take what the trail gives me, try not to fight it."

It was the twins' turn to look confused.

Callie thought for a minute. "It's like I pretend I'm water. I let the trail guide me into the easiest path to the bottom. Sometimes that means a long step, sometimes a short one, so I have to keep my feet moving quick and stay in balance or I fall off the easy path."

Hanna looked skeptical but Anna started to nod. "Run like water. Just flow."

"Right. Flow. I try to flow down the hill."

Anna gazed at her skeptically. "Can you teach us?" She made the pitter-pat motion with her hands again. "Happy feet?"

"I guess so." Callie looked back up the hill. "Maybe another run, though? I don't want to run back up the hill."

"Okay," said Anna, sounding a bit disappointed, and the three girls broke into a trot. They left the flowers and meadow, reentering the dim forest. Even at midday, the sun could not penetrate the layers of vegetation. The single-track trail widened out to an old snowmobile trail and the girls ran side by side, the twins talking to each other across Callie. As they chattered away, Callie realized why they never saw any wildlife in Alaska. Anything bigger than a squirrel would hear them coming for miles and run.

"—and what really scares me are—" said Hanna.

"Long silences?" suggested Callie.

Hanna gave Callie a hurt look as she finished. "—rattlesnakes." She gave a little shudder with her shoulders.

"Snakes aren't too bad. It's cougars, they're the scary ones. They sneak up from behind."

"Good thing there aren't a whole lot of them around here," said Anna.

"More than you think. There were a couple of sightings close to town a couple of weeks ago. Fish and Game was out."

"Seriously? They find any?" said the younger twin. "What else did we miss while we were gone?"

"Not much," said Callie. "It's been kind of quiet." Her voice trailed off.

"Hear anything from Mark?" said Anna. On the other side

of Callie, Hanna was furiously shaking her head, silently chastising Anna.

Callie ran without speaking, her jaw set. Mark was sending her text messages every couple of days, short little updates.

The twins stayed right next to her. They swept down the trail, Callie gaining a few steps on a short downhill, the twins catching back up on the next uphill.

Anna was the first to break the silence. "Sorry."

Callie looked at her and a small grin broke out on her face. "Long silences."

It took the twins a second to realize what she was talking about. Hanna spoke first.

"You know, she can be bit of a brat." she said to her sister.

"Yeah, but she's our running buddy so we're stuck with her."

"Unless there's cougars," said Hanna

"Right. Then it's every woman for herself," confirmed Anna. She glanced slyly at Callie. "I take it you haven't heard anything?"

"He's been texting me." Callie didn't add any more.

The girls waited for Callie to continue. When it was obvious she needed more prodding, both twins made the same exasperated sound.

"And?"

"And what? He's still alive, as of Thursday."

"That's good," said Hanna.

"The 'he's still alive' part, that is," added her sister. "So how's California?"

Callie grunted. She hadn't returned any of his texts so she only knew the little bit he shared and only understood a bit of that. He had tried calling once but she hadn't answered and he didn't leave a message.

"I know that look." Anna was staring at her as they ran. Ignoring her, Callie wondered if the blond girl was going to catch a toe on a tree root. *Ought to be watching where she's going,* she thought.

"You're still mad."

Of course she was still mad, she thought. The knucklehead blows up the school and then writes her a goofy letter. She felt ready to burst. Without realizing it, she picked up the pace.

"He nearly gives that lady from Olympia a heart attack then runs away to join the circus. Why should I be mad?" she forced out.

Anna and Hanna paced her. They listened to her words but they had been her friends for too many years not to hear what Callie wasn't saying. Staring ahead without seeing, Callie didn't notice the emphatic hand gestures as the twins talked to each other in their own sign language.

"You have to admit, the zombie was funny," said Anna.

Hanna nodded as she ran. "It was pretty awesome, and, besides, the lady was okay."

"And he's not joining the circus."

"He'd make a good clown."

"I know what you're doing." Callie kept up the pace, losing herself a little bit into the motion, hearing the twins breathing, the antiseptic piney smell of the trees mixed with the earthy smell of the dead logs.

"We know what you're doing too," said Anna.

"Pouting," supplied her sister.

Callie ignored them. The trail was narrowing a bit as huckleberry bushes filled in the spaces between the trees.

Anna leaned forward at the hips enough to see her sister past Callie.

"Hanna, did Mark say good-bye to you?"

"Why, no, Anna, he didn't. Didn't even get a letter."

"How did you know that I got a letter?" A stride later, "Never mind. Jen blabbed."

"We like your little sister," said Hanna. "She's funny."

"Want to adopt her?"

"Not much," said Anna. "She's funnier when she's your sister."

Callie shook her head and slowed down, gliding to a stop in a little clearing where another trail joined in from the right. They were about a half mile from the graveled lot where Callie had parked, surrounded by green on all sides and a canopy of boughs above. Caught by surprise, the twins turned around to rejoin Callie.

"No, she's not funnier when she's my sister. She's a pain in the butt."

"Little sisters always are," said Anna. Hanna looked indignantly at her older twin. Anna continued. "That doesn't matter now. We were talking about Mark."

"I wasn't talking about him." Callie tried to keep the defensive tone from creeping into her voice.

"No, you were avoiding the subject." Anna paused to consider her words. "Avoiding it isn't going to change it. So admit it—yeah, it's crazy to drop a blow-up zombie, but that's not why you're moping. You're upset because he's not here and you miss him."

Callie frowned at Anna. "He never asked me out or anything."

"Right, he just made eyes at you and showed off around you for nothing. He was always a bigger goof"—Callie bristled—"when you were around."

Hanna jumped in. "Boys are dumb. But the letter means something."

"And you guys are texting."

Callie looked from one to the other. "I haven't texted back," she admitted, transferring her gaze to the ground.

Both twins stared at her. Anna was the first to speak.

"Girlfriend, you need to make up your mind. Either you start talking to him or cut him loose."

Hanna was nodding agreement. "Definitely."

"Since when are you two experts?"

The twins stared at each other, then turned to Callie and shrugged.

Anna tilted her head and looked at Callie. "We're not. We're just your best friends."

"That gives us special privileges like butting in and offering advice on boyfriends. Also, on hairstyles, clothes, and shoes. Pretty much all the important stuff," Hanna explained.

"You two are crazy." Callie was starting to smile—not much, but a little.

"Plus, long-distance romances are so . . . romantic," offered Hanna in an upbeat, hopeful voice.

"I'm not in a relationship."

"Uh-huh, we'll see," said the younger twin.

Her parents were in the backyard when Callie drove up, her dad firing up the grill. She shouted hello to them and walked into the house using the back door. She stripped out of her shoes and socks, releasing little puffs of dust into the air. Her feet around the toes and at the ankle above the line from her socks were black with the dirt from the trail. Sophie wandered in and began to snuffle the socks and shoes, her tail wagging.

She made her way upstairs to get into the shower to knock the sweat and dirt off but stopped at Jen's room and knocked.

"Yo," came a reply from inside.

"It's me," Callie said, swinging the door open and leaning her upper body through the gap.

Jen sat on her bed, propped up on a mountain of stuffed animals, reading. She was dressed in run shorts and a T-shirt.

"You go for a run?" Callie asked, surprised.

"Yeah. A short one."

"Cool." Callie hesitated. "If someone hacked my account—allegedly hacked," she amended as Jen started to protest, "and invited the twins—allegedly invited the twins—on a run, I might be inclined to say thank you to the hacker—alleged hacker."

Jen looked pleased with herself. "If I knew the alleged hacker, she might say you're welcome. Allegedly, of course."

"Of course. Allegedly. Got it." Another hesitation. "I'm changing my passwords."

Jen nodded.

"And if someone hacks it again, I'm going to pound them."

"Allegedly."

Callie stared at her little sister. "No allegedly."

Jen shrugged and met Callie's stare. "Gotcha."

Callie went across the hall to her room and unpacked her gear bag from the run. She put her phone on the dresser and stared at it.

"Crud."

She grabbed it and typed a fast text, then, gathering clean clothes, headed for the shower.

Chapter 28

"Mark?" asked Doc, standing with a clipboard, trying to get the runner's attention. He waved his arms a bit and addressed Mark in a louder voice. "Yo, chuckles!"

The teenage boy looked startled. "Huh?"

"Summer mileage. How much?" It was the first day of cross-country practice and Doc always charted how much base mileage his runners had banked for the upcoming season.

"One thousand thirteen," said the boys' team captain, and someone muttered *wow*. "It's prime. I wanted to be in prime shape and I was at a thousand and eleven but that's divisible by three so I did two more. . . ." His voice trailed off as he saw the incredulous expressions on the runners around him. "It's prime," he finished, sounding apologetic.

"I don't care if it's choice. A thousand thirteen for the summer is excellent. Good job." Doc moved down the list of boys. Nate was the only other boy to break five hundred miles for the summer, getting to just under seven hundred miles. The two freshman boys hadn't run at all. They were staring wide-eyed at Mark and Nate, the numbers seeming incomprehensible. He turned to the girls, starting with Callie.

"How many for you, Callie?"

"Eight hundred and sixteen point six," she said.

Doc peered over the clipboard.

"You sure about that point six?" he asked. "I mean, if it was point seven, I wouldn't want to cheat you." The team snickered and Callie felt her face flush. She stuck her tongue out at Doc.

"Point six is good enough."

"Okie-dokie. Eight hundred sixteen point six for Callie. Jenessa? How did we do?"

The other senior girl was stretching, right leg folded in as she worked her left hamstring. "About five eighty."

Doc notched an eyebrow. This was about double the brunette's normal summer running. *Something to be said for competition,* Callie thought.

"Twins."

"About four fifty," Anna answered for both.

"Mattie?" The redhead stood a little apart from the other girls, leaning one shoulder onto a tree.

"About six hundred."

Jenessa looked up from her stretch, startled. Callie saw the look, the intensity in Jenessa's narrowed eyes, and filed it away to discuss with Doc later. She wasn't going to have a repeat of the track season. Cross-country was a team sport and everybody had to pull together. Callie glanced at Mark; he'd seen it, too. Callie frowned. If it were anybody but Mattie, she'd ask his advice.

Doc peered at her. "That's really good, Mattie," he said cautiously, "but it's a lot for someone starting out. How are your legs?"

She shrugged. "I'm fine." She met his gaze with steady eyes of her own and he looked away.

Doc moved on. "Jen?"

"I'm the slacker. I only did about three seventy-five. Some bossy person told me to not get in a big hurry."

"Some bossy person was right." He finished with the last girl, Lily, a freshman who, like the freshman boys, hadn't done any running over the summer.

Doc looked at the kids scattered in a loose circle on the park grass, shaded by the large trees. Doc was already sweating despite the shade.

"Okay, most of you have been here before and have heard the speech. For you guys that are new, welcome to cross-country.

"The rules are simple. First, you need to be here on time—practice starts at three fifteen p.m. sharp, be here early—ready to run. Plan ahead and have all your run gear ready, a water bottle, and a snack. If you can't be here, let someone know, preferably the captains. That's Mark for the boys, Callie for the girls. Everybody got it?" Doc looked around the group, getting quick nods from the older runners, vigorous yeses from the youngsters in the group.

"Second, you're not doing anybody any good if you're running hurt. If you tweaked something, let me or your captains know. For the freshmen, you can expect to be sore for the first week or so. I promise it will pass and by the end of the season, you'll be amazed at how far you can run and how fast. I'm not talking about general soreness. But if you have an injury, a pulled muscle, problems with your shins, I want to know, and we'll decide whether you need some rest or maybe to just back off for a day or two.

"Last rule. I love running and I know some of the folks here do too. It comes second to school." Doc looked over the edge of the clipboard he still held. "I'm deadly serious about this rule." With his head he indicated a stack of paper on a nearby picnic table. "One of the pieces of paper over in those packets that you'll take home tonight has a contract in it, a contract between you and your team that says you agree to maintain at least a C average in all your classes. It also has a permission form for your teachers to share your grades with me." He scanned the group again. "Anything less than a C in any class, you don't run until we get it fixed. Understood?" Again, quick nods from the older runners. The freshmen were more subdued but nodding.

"Good. We've got three weeks before our first meet, down in the valley. The course is a little shorter, a nice way to ease into the season." Doc paused. "I have pretty high hopes for this year. On the boys' side, we return one of the better runners in the state, and Nate isn't all that far behind. You youngsters can learn a lot from them. We need one more runner to make a team, so if you know anybody that would like to join, let me know. I'll call them and see if we can talk them into having some fun."

Another pause. "The girls' team has a chance to be special." He moved his eyes from girl to girl. "Last year we got close to the podium, only missed by one point. That won't happen this year. I think that you girls," he acknowledged, "took it seriously. Your summer training tells me that.

"You are also adding some good runners. This year's team has the potential to be really good, competitive with anybody if we work hard and we get a little lucky. The hard work we can control. The great thing about running," Doc looked at the whole group, including the boys into the conversation, "is you get back everything you put in. There's no substitute for putting in the miles and that's what we'll do. Put in the miles, run our intervals, train our bodies and our minds. Then we trust our luck."

Doc paused to let it sink in. This was the first time Doc had ever predicted the results of the season, and Callie felt the extra weight that Doc had just added but goosebumps at the possibilities. Across the other side of the circle, Mark caught her eye and gave her a quick smile. *Fine for you,* she thought.

Doc put the clipboard down on the table.

"Okay. Let's run."

"Callie!"

She turned at Mark's shout. The run had been short, with everybody staying together in one big group, Doc running alongside encouraging the freshmen and watching his more experienced runners. The three miles were just enough, since she had run ten that morning knowing that Doc would keep it short to start.

"Hey." He was still dripping sweat but he had put his shirt back on. As he came running up, she could see Mattie hanging back. Mark was her ride again.

She studied him. The months away hadn't changed him much on the outside. He still had the mop of brown hair, quick smile, and mischievous eyes. He was sporting a better tan, courtesy of the California summer, and had put on some muscle—ocean swimming, he told Nate, was great cross-training once you were okay with getting eaten by sharks. The biggest change that showed was the way he held himself, a little taller, chin up, his gaze more direct and probing.

"I wanted to talk to you but I got in too late Saturday, and yesterday was crazy trying to get settled back in and spending time with my mom."

"What did you want to talk about?" She tried to keep her voice even but to her ears it came out cool.

"I, uh, well, I didn't have a chance to say . . . it was a little crazy . . . before I left . . ." He ran his right hand through his hair and looked off to the ground. "I'm sorry I didn't say good-bye," he blurted out, staring into her eyes.

Callie tilted her head to one side. "No problem. You were busy, what with the police and everybody asking you questions."

Mark stayed fixated on the base of the nearby tree. "Yeah." He was rocking his head back and forth, a small motion, releasing tension. "It got crazy."

"It didn't 'get crazy,' " Callie admonished. "You made it crazy. You've inspired a whole new generation of idiots."

"They never proved it was me." Still staring.

"No, they didn't." Callie paused. "And you never denied it, at least to me."

Mark stood there and Callie watched his shoulders twitch like he wanted to flee, the slight rocking of his head signaling his indecision.

"It was you, wasn't it?" Callie pressed. *If he lied to her . . .*

Mark tore his gaze from the tree he had been fixated on and met Callie's eyes. His face was nearly blank but his eyes reflected his inner misery. He sighed.

"No," he started and Callie started to frown. "It was me," he finished in a contradictory confession. Callie felt her knees get weak with relief.

"Are you going to tell anybody?" Mark was standing rigidly now, still meeting her gaze, the head movement arrested.

Callie considered it. "Probably," she said, and he looked alarmed, "but not until the statute of limitations runs out." She smiled at him. "I've got to get home. I'll see you at practice to-morrow."

She turned and started to walk to her car, where Jen was

waiting, scrutinizing them from a distance. Callie would be playing twenty questions all the way home.

Mark stood, watching her walk away.

"Callie," he called again.

She stopped again, turned at the hips to see him.

"Thanks for texting and calling," he said. "You were about the only one who did."

A puppy. That's what he looked like, she thought, one that was expecting a spanking. She nodded to him. "No problem."

"What was that all about?" Jen asked when Callie reached the vehicle.

"None of your business."

"Did he ask you out?" the younger girl pressured.

"Do you want to walk?" Callie retorted, short-circuiting the inquisition.

Jen grimaced. "No."

"Then get inside and let's go." Callie flung her gear bag onto the backseat and slid behind the wheel. As she did, she watched Mattie climb into Mark's Jeep, and scowled.

Chapter 29

With the hot, dry air sucking moisture out of her with every breath, Callie bore down in the last turn. The twins were right beside her, and ahead Mattie and Jenessa were well down the straightaway, the harsh summer sunlight broken up by pockets of shade under the trees. One more interval to go and then cool down—as much as was possible in near-hundred-degree weather.

Callie saw Doc standing at the chestnut tree that marked the finish line and checked her watch. Right on time. Doc met her eyes and was nodding. She nodded back and the twins jogged slowly to catch up to the girls in front. A few seconds later, Jenifer and Lily caught up, too. They jogged, resting as they made their way back to the start. Everybody was huffing, but the twins and Jen picked up the thread of their argument over who was the hotter actor. Callie checked Mattie and Jenessa. No change, as both studiously ignored the other.

The boys went by, Mark gliding, dried streaks of salt lining his face as he pushed through on his last one, Nate close behind, followed by the freshmen, stretched out in a line. Mark and Nate were breathing deeply but in good rhythm while the freshmen were gasping, loud in the still air.

The girls jogged back to the start and turned to face the last lap on the grass loop they were using for a course. Callie put her forefinger on the stopwatch button on her watch as Doc counted down to start the team.

"Ready, ladies? Three, two, one, off we go . . ."

They all surged out, Mattie and Jenessa leading as they had the entire workout, Callie and the twins running as one group, and Jen and Lily forming the last one. The grass was uneven and she could feel her ankles rolling a bit to compensate. Mattie and Jenessa were pushing hard. Callie had been watching them since practice started two weeks ago in case there was a repeat of the fight during the track season. *So far, so good,* she thought.

She was starting to pant and could feel the heaviness starting in her legs. Next to her, Anna and Hanna seemed to be handling the speed a bit better, twin blond ponytails streaming out behind them as they ran beside her, their strides synchronized. They hit the halfway point and without saying a word, all three girls accelerated another notch. The last interval was usually their fastest, as they ran for home.

One hundred yards from the finish, Callie heard the hard gasps of a runner struggling to catch them. Anna heard it as well. She glanced over her shoulder and grinned.

"Hi there, Jen," she said.

Hanna looked back too. "Having fun yet?"

Jen couldn't answer. She was struggling with the pace and the effort to catch the three older runners. Sweat was plastering her brown hair to her forehead. A distant fifty yards back, Lily was doggedly fighting through the workout. *That was me three years ago,* thought Callie, and felt a surge of sympathy for her. *Keep digging,* she thought, *you can do this.*

Callie crossed the line a half step behind her friends and just a few steps ahead of Jen, who dropped to grab her knees, trying to regain her breath. Callie was breathing hard but under control. *The extra miles,* she thought. *I couldn't have done this last year.* Lily was coming into the finish and she turned to cheer her on.

"Good job, Lily! Just a little more, good job, way to finish strong." Callie was clapping and the twins joined in; Jenessa and Mattie looked on with sweat-streaked faces, both of them bright red as they walked with their hands on their hips.

"Good job, ladies." Doc pointed to the back of his truck, where all the boys had congregated. "Go grab some water then let's get an easy cooldown in. Don't drink too much," he warned.

"—that our first meet is this Saturday. We're not taking the van down so you'll need to get rides from someone on the team or your parents. Do not wait until Friday to figure this out. Ask tonight if you're riding with your folks." Doc looked over the sweaty kids eating watermelon. "Be at the course by eight thirty so we have time to walk it. Everybody understand?" They got it. "Good. See you tomorrow."

"Callie, Mark, could you two stick around for a few minutes?"

After the other runners had finished, rinsed off the juices of the watermelon, and left, Doc leaned into the side of his minivan. Doc had two vehicles, a beat-up pickup that he usually drove, and a minivan. Jen waited, chatting with Mattie in the other parking lot, where Callie had parked.

"Okay, reports. How are the kids doing?" Doc looked at Mark. "You first."

"They're doing okay. The new freshman kid that Jake and Sam dragged in is the best of the bunch. The other two try hard but Will might be pretty good once he gets this figured out. Nate is solid but you knew that. Nobody seems to have tweaked anything. I think Nate is running extra in the morning." He looked to Doc for confirmation. "He seems a little dead-legged on the easy days and amped up for stuff like today."

"He checked with me," Doc said. "For now, it's okay, just like you two and the girls." He turned to Callie. "How are they doing?"

"Pretty good, Coach." She paused, trying to be careful in her phrasing. "Mattie and Jenessa seem to be feeding off each other a bit and I wouldn't say it's friendly, but they're not causing problems either. The twins are the twins. Jen is looking really strong and Lily—" She paused again. "Lily is a hard worker. She's never going to be a Jenessa but she's got a lot of heart. She's overworking a little bit trying to keep up."

"Vee kant all be stars," Doc said in an atrociously bad German accent. "She seems like a good kid. Every team needs them. Back to Mattie—no signs of that temper?" Mark shifted nervously as Doc questioned Callie.

Callie shook her head. "No."

He frowned. "Good. I don't mind the two of them battling it out on the course but it needs to stay out there. Two peas in a pod, those two are."

Callie blinked in surprise. "Excuse me?"

Mark seemed taken aback as well.

Doc looked at her. "Watch them. You'll see it."

Callie was shaking her head again. "I don't get it, Coach. See what?"

"They both run with their egos." He squinted at her. "Think

of it like this. You're a runner. It's something you do, a part of you. Follow?" Both kids nodded.

"They don't run, they race, and they're only as good as they finish. For them, it defines them as much as being a runner defines you, but if they lose, it's not just a run or a race, it's a disaster."

Callie looked at him dubiously, though Mark had a glimmer in his eye that showed that maybe he was getting it.

Doc looked at his watch. "Enough. I have to get. I'll see you two tomorrow. Easy day. We'll do a tempo run Thursday to get ready for the meet, then easy on Friday." He looked hard at Callie. "I got a call from the race director. Fairchild is going to be there."

Callie met his gaze, eyes narrowing. "Good."

They broke up, Doc climbing into his vehicle while Mark and Callie walked away. Jen and Mattie saw them coming and broke off their conversation as the two seniors approached.

"So?" asked Jen, Mattie standing beside her. Mattie looked from her to Mark, arching an eyebrow.

"None of your business, sis. Just team stuff." Callie reconsidered. "One thing. Fairchild is going to be there."

"Oh goody, we get to get stomped." Jen was frowning.

Mattie looked at her, puzzled. "Why?"

Mark intervened. "Those girls can really run."

"They've won State the last five years in a row. They're a private school and can recruit students who just *happen* to be great runners." She scrunched her face up at the memory of the Fairchild girls on the winners' podium. "Not very nice people, though. Everybody expects them to win again this year."

Mattie processed it, then smiled, not from humor but from anticipation. "We'll just have to fix that."

On Saturday, Mattie tried to do exactly that. Callie saw it in her eyes when they lined up for the waterfall start, each team in their lanes. The tension in the redhead was palpable and she kept looking down the line to the Fairchild crew, dressed in red racing uniforms with a diagonal white flash from the right shoulder to the left hip. The Fairchild girls were laughing, relaxed but ready.

The team did the last stride-out and settled into position, Jenessa and Mattie in front, the twins behind them, then Callie and Jen with Lily crowding up. Callie peeked around Anna to see the starter. The starter, also the coach of one of the local schools, gave the race directions, explaining the course. He brought them to a set position and fired the gun, starting the race.

The mass of girls surged and Callie waited that split second while the girls in front got moving then accelerated quickly to race speed, taking the jostling from the girls around her in stride. The first part of the course was on an asphalt road, wide enough for everybody. The course didn't narrow for a half mile, which was plenty of time for the field to thin. Jen stayed glued to her hip, lost in the excitement and out too fast. As Callie settled into the race, she counted. Five Fairchild runners ahead of her, two of them close. The twins were right behind the third Fairchild runner.

As they topped a small rise and started down a very shallow grade, Callie could see over the taller runners. At the very front, Mattie and Jenessa were dueling with the lead runner from Fairchild. Callie gave a little shake of her head. *Too fast, won't last.* She focused on her own race.

The teams cycled through the first loop and started the second, longer, dirt loop. The total course was under the 5K race distance for championship meets but was a good tune-up for the season. Callie dropped Jen at the big hill on the backside of the second loop, putting in a mini-surge as she crested the top that her sister couldn't match. Ahead, the Fairchild girls were running away from her on the downhill and she focused on making up ground.

She entered the last stretch, one hundred meters of open flat ground, ten seconds behind the red-clad racers, and pushed with a final kick, only to watch them surge away, gaining precious seconds. Callie passed one more girl, a local from the valley, a senior like her, as the spectators cheered.

Her chest was heaving as she walked through the finishing chute, the flags standing limp in the still air, a volunteer grabbing her tag as she passed and pulling it free with a quick tug. The tag was placed on a hook while another volunteer kept her moving down the chute, clearing it for the runners behind her. She exited to the right, heading to the picnic bench loaded with water, little paper cups two-thirds full.

The twins were there at the table, sipping water, faces flushed and sweaty.

"Good job," said Anna.

Callie grabbed a cup. "Thanks." She looked around. Jenessa was slouching, leaning on the picnic table in the shelter where the team threw their gear when they arrived. None of the boys were around. Warming up, she thought, glad that the girls raced first, before it got too hot.

"Where's Mattie?" She looked around, searching for her. She spotted her reclined against a tree, Doc kneeling next to her.

"She went out a little fast," said Anna.

"Kind of way too fast," said Hanna.

"She was on the ground when we finished."

"I think she puked."

"Be back in a second." Callie tipped her head to the twins and reached to snag another cup of water. Jen was coming out of the chute as she passed.

"Good job, little sis." She checked Jen as she went by. Her sister looked tired but okay, sweaty and red-faced like the rest of them. "Water over there." She half-turned, pointing with one of the cups in her hand. Jen steered toward the water, taking a cup gratefully from Anna. Satisfied, Callie proceeded to where Doc was tending to Mattie.

"Hey," she said, "need some water?" She held out the cup. She inspected Mattie as Doc stood up. The girl had a grass stain on the purple of her singlet and both knees were scuffed. Her face was a stark white with two rosy blooms high on her cheeks. Mattie took the proffered cup, taking just a tiny sip.

"Looks like you'll be okay," said Doc. "As soon as you're ready, you need to get on your feet and get walking, okay?" He didn't wait for an answer; the boys were starting in ten minutes.

Callie squatted down. "You need a hand up?"

Mattie shook her head. "No. Here, hold this." She passed the cup back to Callie as she struggled to her feet.

"Thanks." Mattie set herself and began to move. She glanced at Callie. "I'd rather take a charge," she said irrelevantly.

Callie laughed when she got it. Basketball. "Yeah, the pain doesn't last as long."

Together, they walked slowly back to the shelter. Jen was sitting next to Jenessa, chocolate-chip cookie in hand and wearing a broad smile.

Jen reached out and grabbed a handful of extra-cheesy Goldfish. "I love this part."

"Yeah, scooch over."

Jen obligingly shifted and Mattie sat down again, sipping her water. Jen held out a handful of Goldfish. "Want some?"

A queasy look crossed Mattie's face. "Uh-uh."

Callie glanced at Jenessa. "You okay?"

Jenessa looked up. "Yeah." She paused, then added pointedly, "Went out too fast." She didn't look at Mattie but the girl's shoulders stiffened.

Callie looked from Mattie to Jenessa, and Doc's advice to leave well enough alone echoed in her mind.

"First race of the season. It happens," she said, her tone conciliatory.

Neither girl responded. Jen munched happily on another cookie, oatmeal this time, oblivious to the tension from the other girls. The gun fired, starting the boys' race, and Callie left the three of them to go cheer on her teammates.

Fairchild won, just as they always did, but it was closer than expected. Roxanne, their lead runner, had taken first, a few seconds ahead of Jenessa, a pattern three years in the making. Mattie had taken fifth in her first race, a fantastic finish, as Mark pointed out.

The color was just then starting to return to Mattie's face but she had plenty of energy to glare at him. The twins had both finished in the top ten, Hanna at nine, Anna at ten, the volunteers not bothering to decide who actually finished in front but pulling the first tag that came by.

Callie saw the Fairchild coach huddled with Doc after the team results were announced and ribbons handed out. Cloverland was second, eight points behind the winners. Callie meandered over, curious, just as the two separated.

"What was that about?" she asked.

Doc was still looking at the retreating coach, eyes hidden behind sunglasses. In a quiet voice, he said, "He said he'd see us at State."

"Well, yeah."

The lenses turned her way.

"Byron"—that was the Fairchild coach—"said we put a scare into his girls." He hesitated, focusing back on the team in red and white, and his words took on a heated intensity. "I would truly like to do more than scare them the next time."

Callie stood there mutely. She looked at the Fairchild girls as they gathered their stuff to make the long trip back to Seattle. They expected to win and they had; they always won. They were number one in the state again just as they had been for years. The girls on the current Fairchild team never lost. They thought no one could even challenge them.

She felt something hard form inside, built from determination and desire.

We'll see you at State.

Chapter 30

Yep, she was definitely limping a bit on her right leg, observed Callie, as she jogged back to meet Lily. Today was an easy day and the girls were just covering miles, chatting and sometimes singing. Mattie, surprisingly, had a sweet, clear contralto and a weakness for old Patsy Cline songs. Anna and Hanna, on the other hand, could not have carried a tune if it were placed in their hands and only guessed at the lyrics, sometimes making them up as they sang.

"How you doing?" Callie asked as she turned back around to run with the young girl. Lily was a little larger than the rest of them, a softball player using cross-country to maintain some fitness.

"I'm okay." Lily made an effort to minimize the slight rocking motion that had caught Callie's attention. Laughter from the group ahead drifted back to them on the light breeze.

"No fibbing to the captain. Is it your shin or your knee?"

"Shin," admitted the girl. She hobbled a few more steps. "Feels like the whole front of my leg is on fire."

"Okay. You want to walk it in—we're only a half mile out."

"I can make it."

Callie could see little creases at the corners of her eyes narrowing every time her right leg impacted the asphalt of the path.

Lily looked at Callie. "You can go on. I don't want to slow you up."

"No worries. It's called an easy day for a reason. Did you know that Bill Rodgers used to run ten-minute miles—slower than we're going—on recovery days?"

Lily glanced at her captain. "Who's Bill Rodgers?"

Callie let loose an exasperated sigh but didn't answer. She paced the freshman back to the grassy lot adjacent to the parking lot where the van was. As they reached the end of the path, they heard whooping behind them. The boys were finishing, Mark in front, sprinting away, Nate just behind them. All the boys were wearing their T-shirts on their heads, draped down their backs like Indian headdresses.

Lily watched them running toward them. "Boys are weird."

Callie laughed. "Yep. But it could be worse. At least it's their shirts on their heads."

"What else would they . . ." Her voice trailed off into an embarrassed silence as a picture painted itself in her mind and under her already rosy cheeks, she blushed.

"Come on, let's go get some ice for your leg." Callie guided the freshman over to the van, popping the tailgate and pulling a premade ice bag from the cooler. "Here, run this along your shin."

Doc, standing near the van, came over when Callie broke out the ice. He checked Lily's shin, agreeing that shin splints were the likeliest cause.

"We're shutting you down for a day," he told the hobbled girl. "You can race this weekend if it isn't hurting too bad and we'll check it again on Monday. If we need more time off, we'll do it."

He called the boys over to join them. Except for Mark, the boys, glistening with sweat, were taking the shirts off their heads and using them to wipe down.

Mark, still wearing the shirt on his head, led them over. The sweat on Mark's chest highlighted the extra muscle, and he had runner's abs, not the bulky six-pack of a linebacker but the trim, tight core of the distance runner. While still slender, he was no longer a scrawny teenager.

Callie, staring at him, jumped a little bit when Jen snickered beside her.

"Too funny," whispered her younger sister.

"He looks ridiculous," Callie whispered back in agreement.

"I wasn't talking about him," teased Jen.

"Cute," observed Doc, glancing quickly at shirt adorning Mark's head. "Maybe you could braid it."

The team chuckled and Mark wore a wide grin. Doc checked to make sure all the runners were present. Satisfied, he started to discuss the race coming up on Saturday.

"Okay, easy tomorrow—really easy, no more than three miles for anybody. That includes all you mileage beasts." He looked at Callie, Jenessa, and Mattie, then at Mark and Nate.

Seeing them all nodding, he continued. "This weekend's race is loaded. Some of the best schools in our division in the state will be there and there'll be some schools from Idaho as well. Big meet, good competition. We were there two years ago so some of you know the course. It's fast—a lot like the state course except maybe a little flatter. Don't be surprised if your times are a bit better than what you've been running over the last couple of weeks."

"Is Fairchild going to be there?" asked Jenessa.

"Nope, they're headed to Oregon for a big meet there."

Jenessa looked relieved. Mattie saw it and frowned but didn't say anything.

"What time do we leave?" Callie asked.

"Need you here at six fifteen, bus pulls out at six thirty. We have the big bus so if your folks want to ride up, we have room. I also have directions to the meet if they need them."

Callie looked at Jen. Their parents would be driving. Hank had suffered through one ride Callie's freshman year and stated that he'd trade the fuel for time and a little quiet. On longer trips, the bus always stopped for food and the kids could spend an hour ordering a meal that they would devour in six minutes.

Doc looked at Lily, who was seated on the grass, still icing her shin, then to the rest of the runners. "I'm not at practice tomorrow. I've got some stuff that I need to get done at work. Meet Mark and Callie at the usual time. Stretch, run, some striders, and call it good tomorrow. Everybody got it? Okay, go load up."

"We have dates to Homecoming," announced Anna as they followed the outline Doc had laid out with the runners getting in the easy day as prescribed. Lily showed up even though she wasn't allowed to run, stretching with them and watching their piles of stuff while they ran. As usual, the boys' and girls' teams headed out in the same general direction before separating, the boys diverting into the woods on single track, the girls staying in a pack.

"Anybody else going?" Hanna twisted as she ran, trying to see the girls in back. By habit, Callie stayed toward the back of the pack, watching her teammates. Jenessa and Mattie ran in front, maintaining a buffer between each other, a neutral zone that neither encroached while the twins jabbered behind them.

"I'm going with some of my girlfriends." Jen tended to float up and down the pack like a butterfly flitting across a meadow. It wasn't a random dance. The butterfly always knew where it was headed. Right now, the butterfly was wedging herself between Mattie and Jenessa.

"So, are you both like, this serious, all the time?"

Jenessa glanced at Jen, then half-turned to yell back to Callie. "Is this what you get at home?"

Callie laughed. "No. She's way more pushy there."

"Be nice, big sis!"

"You two just leave Jen alone." Hanna was smiling as she came to the girl's defense.

"Jen, you can run with us. We'll watch as those meanies run each other into the ground."

The smiles vanished from the two leading girls as the jibe hit close to home. Mattie had closed the gap on Jenessa, staying with her a little longer each race, only to have Jenessa run away as they headed to the finish line, Mattie with too little in reserve to match the final move. All three races this year had followed that pattern, and the frustration was beginning to show with Mattie.

Ahead, a runner was coming at them and Jen dropped behind the two leaders, sliding to the side to make room. Jenessa moved to the right, running shoulder-to-shoulder with Mattie until the man, a local businessman, passed. Like two magnets repelling, Jenessa moved away from Mattie as soon as he cleared.

Callie redirected the conversation. "I'm skipping Homecoming. Seems like every time I go, I get a cold and then I run like crud for a month. Plus it's always cold at the game and crowded at the dance."

Jenessa turned around and ran backward so she could face the twins. "I'm going." She kept pace, feet making little scuffing sounds as she pushed off. "Who's taking you guys?" she asked Hanna.

Anna looked at her. "Other way around. We invited them." The older twin dropped back a half step to avoid stepping on Jenessa's toes.

"We met a couple of boys down in the valley. They're coming up to meet us at the game." Hanna dropped back next to her sister, opening more space to Mattie, who stayed focused on the path ahead. Callie knew Mattie was listening—she had twitched a bit when Callie said she wasn't going to the game or dance.

The butterfly drifted back to the twins, next to Hanna. "Anybody we'd know?"

"Probably not. They're not runners." Hanna smiled. "We met them on the river this summer at the beach at Hell's Gate. They were showing off waterskiing. Alex kept biffing it and Jordan, his friend, would try something even goofier and wipe out worse. It was hysterical."

As Anna and Hanna recounted the misadventures of their dates, the girls finished up the run. Callie had them do a set of accelerations, short ones just to open up their legs and work on form. Jen beat her on all four. At some point soon, Jen was going to be faster, thought Callie, watching her sister striding away. In front, Mattie and Jenessa floated over the ground gracefully.

The boys came back, Will, the newest freshman, leading, red-faced and puffing with the effort of pushing Nate on a broken-down bike while the others cheered him on. They rattled to a stop—the front wheel of the bike looked ready to fall off and both tires were flat. Nate was laughing as he nearly fell off the bike.

"Treasure!" Nate declared, smiling as he came over to the girls, his eyes lingering on Mattie. Mark beamed, proud that the boys' team was rounding into form. With him leading, most of the easy runs turned into adventure runs. Doc had drawn the line when they came back with a dog and asked if they could keep it. No live plunder and don't get arrested, he told them. And make sure they clean up after themselves.

Jenessa's face bunched up into a frown as she looked at the rickety bike. "Only a boy would consider that treasure." She looked back to the girls. Mattie was leaning against a tree, stretching her calves. Her gaze sharpened. Tucking her head, she worked on her left hamstring. "So are you going to Homecoming, Mattie?" Her tone was nonchalantly cheerful and she didn't look up but Callie could sense the undercurrents in Jenessa words.

Callie could also see anger in Mattie's eyes but caution as well. Mattie switched from calves to quads, using the tree for balance as she worked her way up her body.

"No." The answer came out flat.

"Oh." The senior runner looked at Mattie. "I just thought that you'd be going. You ride all the time with Mark and I just figured you two for a couple." She smirked.

There was a sharp intake of breath from the twins and Jen's head snapped up but she had the sense to squelch her tongue. Callie could feel the blood rushing to her face and her jaws clenched. With an effort, she took a deep breath and eased into a hip stretch, one leg flung over the other.

"Leave it alone, Jenessa." Callie hoped her voice sounded cool and controlled. *No cat fights now.* Callie fixed her eyes on a branch of the walnut tree overhead. From the corner of her eye, she could see Lily, standing confused as she looked from Mattie to Jenessa. The boys, oblivious to the tension twenty feet away, were finishing their accelerations.

"I was just curious. Everybody else is going except you. Even Mattie got asked out."

Mattie's face was as flushed as Callie's. She looked with narrowed eyes at Jenessa. "He gives me rides because he's my neighbor and I don't have a car." She dropped her head for a second, took a breath and, looking up with eyes glinting, continued. "And what happens in my life is my business, not yours. Feel free to butt the hell out."

Jenessa's smirk grew tighter and her eyes glittered as she realized that she had found an opening under Mattie's armor. "I just heard a rumor, that's all. Someone said you'd been asked out. She must have been wrong."

Mattie sat there, glowering. Callie could see her clenching and unclenching her fists, saw her open her mouth to reply, then close it again, knots growing on her slender face at the base of her jaw. Briefly, she closed her eyes. When she reopened them, the glint had sparked to flame.

The twins were signaling each other while Jen and Lily stood there slack-jawed in shock. Callie finished her stretch and was rolling back to a sitting position. She made eye contact with the younger runners. *Wait,* her eyes said, *trust me.*

Jenessa languidly stood, arching her torso to her left, hands pulled overhead, pulling her shirt up on the right to reveal a tanned, taut abdomen. "Sorry if I embarrassed you." Again, she dug with that nonchalant tone. "I just thought that you could get a date."

Callie watched Mattie go white-faced and her nostrils flared as Jenessa stood up in front of her, a pleased smile on her face. With a growl, Callie spun on her hip, planted her hands and swung her feet under her, then stood up smoothly face-to-face with Jenessa, two steps away from Mattie.

"That's enough!" She could hear the anger in her voice and saw shock spread on Jenessa's face. Callie struggled with the anger and lost.

"You're a great runner but a lousy teammate, you know that?" Behind her, she could hear a gasp. In the distance, Mark had the boys doing push-ups and was calling the count. In front of her, Jenessa blanched, but the shock changed to defiance. Before she could reply, Callie started the next avalanche of words, all the pent-up frustration boiling out.

"This isn't track where we run our own races. You can be the best runner in the state but it doesn't mean anything if the team doesn't work together and win together. In case you hadn't noticed, it isn't all about Jenessa."

"Who the hell are you to get up in my face?" Jenessa was shouting, unaccustomed to being challenged. The shout brought sudden silence to the park. The boys, finished with their push-ups, were gaping toward the girls. Out of the corner of her eye, she saw Nate step away from the other boys, concern on his face, stopping when Jen held up a hand. *Good girl. We handle this ourselves.*

"The team captain. And from where I stand," she glared at Jenessa, "the team is more important than a single runner, I don't care how good. It's like being the best basketball player on a losing team." Mattie, who had been hanging her head, avoiding the confrontation in front of her, looked up. "Who wants to say, 'Yeah, the team sucked but I was great.' " Callie leaned in toward Jenessa and softened her voice. "You're better than that."

Jenessa broke eye contact with Callie, staring out past her shoulder toward open space in the park.

"This team has the potential to be really good but only if we run as a team. You and Mattie will make the podium as individuals. You're in the best shape I've ever seen you—hell, we all are. We're all healthy, except for Lily, and we can fix her. The only chance the rest of us have to get on the podium is for the team to win."

Jenessa looked scornful. "So this is about Callie getting on the podium, is that it?"

The anger built, fueled by Jenessa's contempt. "It's about this team. You might have missed it but this team can run. We've won every meet this year except," she added over the rising objection from Jenessa, "yeah, against Fairchild. We lost to the best team in the state. Do you know how close we were to them?"

Jenessa looked at her. "Eight points."

Callie was surprised—she didn't realize that Jenessa kept up with team results. "Right. Eight points." Callie chanced a look at the other girls. "I went back and looked it up. No one's been that close to them in three years. No *team*," she added emphasis to the word, "has been able to challenge them. There's always some runners faster than the Fairchild ladies but not a whole team full. Fairchild wins because they have great runners at each position. Top to bottom they're strong." Callie leaned into Jenessa. "We're that kind of strong this year—if we run as a *team*."

Jenessa snorted, disbelief spreading over her face. "You think we can challenge Fairchild? No way."

She could feel the twins' and freshmen's eyes boring into her back. *Now. We're either a team or just a bunch of runners.*

Deep breath. She looked into Jenessa's eyes.

"Challenge Fairchild?" She fixed Jenessa with a stare, locking eyes, and shook her head. "We're not going to challenge them." Around her, she could hear the disappointed sighs of the girls.

One act of courage, a willingness to commit completely to a goal, can create memories that last lifetimes. The words came out more intense than she had meant even as fear spiked in her stomach, knotting it.

"We're going to run them down and beat them into the ground!"

Chapter 31

Callie waited, and she felt her awareness expand. In front of her, Jenessa's disbelief gave way to shock, a slow wave of change rippling on her face. Behind her, she knew where each girl was without looking, Mattie still seated on the grass, the twins, Jen, Lily. She felt the late-autumn sun filtering through the trees and the slow-motion rustle of the leaves on the breeze. She knew where the boys were, knew that Mark was staring. There was no doubt, no fear, just harmony between her and this moment. She waited, and then it was gone.

"You're serious." Jenessa didn't say it as much as whisper it, her eyes searching Callie's. Behind her, someone—Mattie?—muttered "cool" under their breath.

"I am." Callie and Jenessa were suddenly surrounded by the rest of the girls, all of them talking at once, the twins babbling, her sister asking questions, while poor Lily just wanted to know what was going on. The only voice missing was Mattie's. She had stood up, coming next to Callie. She was nodding, a slow acceptance.

Jenessa started shaking her head and the voices quieted. Callie waited for Jenessa to speak.

"You're crazy." Her voice had strengthened. "Fairchild . . ."

She stopped to think, plainly unsure how to phrase her objections. "Fairchild chews up other teams. They keep coming and they don't quit. And they get the best talent."

"Not all the best talent. You run here, not there," Callie reminded Jenessa. "You know how close you were to Roxanne?"

"Five seconds." Jenessa's face lost expression, only her eyes reflecting her thoughts.

"You can make up five seconds." Jenessa continued to look stubborn, so Callie added, "It's five seconds. Less than two seconds per mile and you've already gotten faster on the year."

"They've gotten faster too."

Callie ignored her. "You and Mattie took second and third to Fairchild's first and fourth. Nearly a tie, and you can beat Roxanne." She looked over to Mattie, who nodded. "The twins were just behind their number-three runner." She smiled. "The twins can take her."

Jenessa laughed in Callie's face. "You're dreaming."

"Hey!" The twins, in stereo voices, sounded offended. "Give us a little credit."

Callie barged ahead. "It's the last spot where we have work to do. For us to win, our number-five runner—me—needs to beat both their number-four and -five runners. It's the only way the math works out."

Jenessa kept shaking her head, and Callie fought to make sure her temper didn't erupt again. She forced her jaw to relax—she didn't realize how tense she was—and squared her shoulders.

"You're not going to tell me I can't, are you?"

Jenessa laughed again. "No, you go for it, girl." Another head shake. "Just . . . go for it."

"I will," she said, her voice low and intense. "The question is, will you?"

Jenessa's head jerked back as if Callie had smacked her. She started to say something, stumbled over it, and before she could start again, Callie rushed in.

"You really are a great runner but there are a lot of great runners out there and only one gets to be fastest. None of us are that one, the kind that gets touched by fate and goes to the Olympics. That's a whole 'nother kind of special." Callie tried to catch her breath but the words tumbled out and picked up more speed. "But we have a chance to do something special as a team and you're the one who has to lead the way. No one else can do that. You've got that gift, even if you don't believe it. Mattie can't do it—not yet—and the twins and I can't do it. We've got to do our jobs, score well at the back, but you've got the job of beating them all, Roxanne Kingsbury included. We need you to believe or it all goes to waste."

Abruptly, Callie stopped talking and stared at Jenessa with fervent eyes, searching for some sign that she had connected with her. Around her, the team hovered while Jenessa stood white-faced in front of them, her eyes darting from one to the next, looking for support.

"You really want to believe we can beat them?" There was skepticism there but a touch of hope, a faint echo.

Callie didn't answer except with one sharp, decisive nod of her head, never breaking eye contact, willing Jenessa to step up to her challenge. *You can do this. . . .*

"I think," Jenessa enunciated each word carefully, "that you are nuts." She stared at Callie, who tried to hide her disappointment. "But," she continued after a slight pause, her lips twisted into a wry grin, "all cross-country runners are nuts." She looked around at her teammates. "What do we have to lose?"

The team broke up and headed for home. Jenessa didn't even say good-bye, just heaved her bag on her shoulder and walked away. Callie watched her go, and then, turning, frowned, seeing her sister head-to-head with the twins. *I don't have the time,* thought Callie, *to deal with Jen's antics.*

She looked around for Mark. She needed someone to talk to. The boys had split up before the girls had finished, chased off by Mark. The only two left were Nate and Mark. Mattie had cornered Nate, who was shaking his head in denial while Mattie talked animatedly, her hands making little jerking movements. She saw Nate shake his head a final time and Mattie stalked off, making a beeline for Mark.

Callie sighed. She'd talk to Doc tomorrow at the meet.

"Hey, sis."

Callie turned to see Jen walking toward her, listing to the left as her heavy blue backpack, loaded with books, dragged her shoulder down. Callie hoisted her own bag—lighter because she had already put her books in her car.

"Ready to go?"

"Yep." Jen fell in beside her. Callie looked over to her, getting ready to ask about the twins and her conversation, but stopped, mildly surprised. Without Callie realizing it, Jen had grown and was now the same height as she was.

"You've grown again," she said.

Something in her voice caught Jen off guard and she shot a hard glance at Callie, squinting in surprise. She hefted her bag to keep it from sliding off her shoulder.

"Some, I guess. My knees were hurting again." Jen was at that stage where every growth spurt seemed to come with a bout of sore knees and klutziness. "Why?"

"No reason, just . . ." Callie didn't know how to put it into words. "No reason."

Jen looked over again. "You okay?"

Callie thought about it for a second. "I think so." She walked off the grass and onto the asphalt pavement. She screwed up her courage and asked, "How do you think they took it?"

"Anna and Hanna are excited. Don't know about Mattie. She's hard to figure. I think you scared the crap outta Lily."

"How did I scare Lily? I wasn't even talking to her."

"No, you were ripping into Jenessa. You're scary when you're mad. I don't think anybody else has really seen you like that." Jen chuckled. "That was a great 'mom' speech, all *I'm disappointed in you, you can do better.* Impressed the twins, too."

Callie got out her keys, the ring jingling as she sorted them to get the car key. "We can win this thing." She unlocked her door, flung her bag into the backseat, and hit the button to unlock the passenger door for Jen. They settled into the cloth-covered seats and buckled up, and Callie started the car, reaching to turn on the radio.

Seated to her right, Jen was staring out the window past Callie and back into the park. "I wonder what that's all about?"

Callie followed her gaze. Mark was standing under a maple, shoulders hunched and hands up in front of him, warding off Mattie. Even from a distance Callie could see the anger radiating from the girl to Mark.

Chapter 32

Scowling, Callie spat on the ground, careful to avoid the feet of other runners. A throng of sweaty girls milled, headed in the general direction of the far end of the finishing corral toward waiting coaches, family, and friends. Immediately in front of her, Jen was bent over, hanging on her knees as she tried to recover from her final kick, a scene repeated by other girls as they finished.

"Come on, kid sis," Callie advised her, still huffing herself, putting an arm on her sister's waist, feeling her and Jen's sweat merging. "You'll feel better if you keep moving."

Jen nodded and stood up, crunched in the middle still but not drawing whooping breaths anymore. As the pair walked slowly to the edge of the corral, the younger girl began to straighten. Callie twisted to see if Lily had finished yet. She couldn't see her.

Callie deposited Jen with the twins on the far side of the fluttering flags. "She's fine, needs water."

"We got her," said Hanna.

"I'm going to go meet Lily when she's done," Callie said, craning her neck in an attempt to see the finish line. She turned, leaving her sister in their care. She waded back, walking against the tide headed the opposite direction, heading for the clock that marked the finish. Girls, sweating and flushed, flowed past her. She caught snippets of conversations. The leanest, fastest girls were gone as the back of the pack—a little taller, a little heavier, just as dedicated—raced in.

The weather had turned chillier in the last week as fall set in, signaled by the ubiquitous black compression shirts under the racing singlets. Almost all of the competitors, if their hair was longer than shoulder length, wore a ponytail.

Callie got back to the finish just as Lily came across the line. She was limping again. Callie sighed and added it to the list of things to talk to Doc about.

"Good job," Callie told her. Lily looked at her gratefully. Callie gathered the freshman and, as she had done with her sister, guided her away. One of Doc's rules was that the team arrived at the start line together and left the finish line the same way, as a team. The other girls were waiting off to the right for Lily and Callie as they pushed past out of the stream of finishers. There was a little distance between where the twins stood with Jen and where Jenessa stood. Mattie, bundled up against the cool breeze, was hidden behind Anna, using the taller blond as a windbreak. Callie frowned again. Jen was avoiding looking directly at her. She caught Jen sneaking a glance but her sister looked away quickly.

Doc, dispatching the boys on a warm-up run to get them ready for their race, wormed his way through the crowd. Past him, forming a loose ring, stood the parents. Callie saw her folks chatting with Anna and Hanna's folks while Jenessa's dad positively beamed over his girl's performance. He turned to make a comment to Jenessa's mother, gesturing animatedly, while she stood quietly next to him. Mattie's father stood apart, at the end of the ring. He didn't seem to blink much, nor talk.

Doc stepped past two runners from an Idaho team with a quick turn of the shoulders to avoid contact.

"Great job, ladies!" He looked them over. His eyes seemed to absorb the bright sunlight, making the glacial blue glow. He focused on Lily. "How's the shin?"

"It's okay," the freshman answered.

"Take it easy back to camp and get some water in you, all of you, then do a cooldown run." Doc looked over the crowd to the colorful pennants lining the course, floating on the slight breeze. "Get out and cheer the boys while they race. Could use a couple of you on the far side, cheer them on. Figure thirty minutes or so."

"We'll go," Anna volunteered.

Doc was distracted, his eyes straying to the boys, who were loping in from their short warm-up.

"We'll sort it out, Coach." Callie scanned the girls. She'd get Lily to stay close to the finish and camp. She frowned as Jen slid behind Mattie, still trying to hide.

"Good. No cookies for you, Jen, until after the cooldown," he said, the sudden cheerful grin softening the jab. Jen had earnestly declared after the second meet that the best part of racing was the cookies afterwards. She had eaten nearly a dozen immediately after the race and, when they went out on the short, slow run to finish the day's work, her stomach had rebelled. Jen peeked around Mattie and nodded. Callie saw him pause, eyes speculative. Callie caught his attention with a quick wag of her head. Doc took the hint.

"Nice and easy," he reminded them as he slipped away. The girls followed him away from the finishing corral, everybody a little stiff-legged from the race.

The parents had a feel for the rhythms of race day, the early anticipation and nervous energy, the focus as runners went to the line, and the strained faces and semi-exhaustion at the finish. They gave the girls space. In an hour, the energy would return.

They walked along the rows of canopies that lined the chain-link fence that separated the golf course the meet was at from the nearby luxury homes, reaching the canopy that covered their gear bags and blankets. Callie walked over to her stuff and rooted around for her jacket. A few feet away, Anna and Hanna were doing the same while Jenessa flopped to the ground, pulling off her spikes and swapping them out for her beat-up training shoes before throwing on her newest running jacket, a bright neon pink with reflective stripes that clashed with the purple of the uniform.

Callie dropped to a cross-legged sit to exchange her own shoes. Jen, goose bumps on her thighs, was chatting with the twins, ignoring her own gear.

"Hey, you're going to freeze." Callie motioned to the mound of clothes that Jen had packed. "Put something on." She tried not to let the annoyance she felt color her words.

Jen looked over her shoulder, and there were still conflicting emotions in her sister's eyes. Callie slipped on her shoes, quickly tying the laces, cinching them tight at her ankles. Jen stood with her back turned. Anna had caught on and flashed Callie a quick glance and a subtle head bob, pointing at the shivering freshman with her eyes.

Callie stood, exasperated, and went over to Jen's clothes, selecting a warm jacket for her sister.

"Here," she said, thrusting the clothes into Jen's hands. "We need to talk." She gave a gentle tug on Jen's waistband and motioned with her head toward the fence behind them. "Come on." She turned, Jen reluctantly following. They still had about twenty minutes until the boys ran. This wouldn't take that long.

Callie led her sister around a small evergreen shrub, one in a line that the golf course planted to hide the fence. She turned to face Jen, fixing her with a stare. "What's your problem?" Her voice was frank but not unfriendly.

Jen crossed her arms, dressed now in the jacket, and didn't answer. The apologetic expression on her face changed and hardened. Sounds from the teams getting ready for the next race drifted over and there was a buzz from the tent line as runners came and went. A burst of laughter sounded loud, echoing across the verge of grass from a group of runners playing Frisbee. Jen turned her head, searching for the source of the laughter.

Callie kept looking at Jen, out-waiting her. Jen looked back to Callie and shrugged, dropping her eyes as she said, "Sorry."

"Sorry for what?" Callie demanded. Jen looked up, a fleeting glance, and then looked at her shoes again, shuffling a bit. Callie could see Jen wrestling with a mixture of guilt and pride.

"I . . ." Jen's eyes drifted up and looked side to side, looking for the answer that would deflect Callie. "For . . ."

"For beating me?" Callie supplied. Her sister gave a hesitant nod, and her shoulders slumped. Callie laughed, a sharp dismissive sound, and Jen looked at her with surprise. "You beat me. It was bound to happen, I just didn't expect it this soon." Her voice got hard, matched by her eyes. "But you don't ever apologize for that again." She glared at her sister, making sure she had Jen's attention. "You ran a great race. If it were anybody but me, you'd be jumping up and down and bragging. True?"

Jen nodded.

"Fair enough." Callie paused and her voice softened again. "Don't disrespect yourself like that. Not in running, not in anything. If you do great, celebrate." She held Jen's gaze steady with her own. "Got it?"

"Uh-huh." Jen still sounded unsure of herself.

"You know what you do next, right?"

Her sister looked lost.

"You get back to work, because the girl you beat today sure will." Callie smiled as she turned. "Now let's go cheer on the boys."

As they strode back to camp, Callie was already planning her workout for the next day. The course for Saturday was a grinder, hilly and dusty. She looked over and gave Jen another smile.

Jen, looking relieved, smiled back.

Next race, thought Callie. *'Cuz for sure,* she thought, *the girl you beat is already back to work.*

Chapter 33

Callie could feel the pressure of every eye in the universe turned on her, focused like lasers, squeezing the air out of her. The hallway, noisy as ever on this Tuesday morning until a second ago, seemed oddly hushed as though everyone was holding their breath. She was holding hers, she realized, letting it go. Her head cleared with the outrushing air.

"What?" she asked, and knew she sounded dumb. Her face still felt wooden as she stared up at Mark. He was red-faced under the brown hair—brushed for a change—and his eyes were flicking side to side then would fix on hers long enough to make contact before skittering back to the floor and down the hall.

He looked up again.

"I was, uh, wondering," he stammered, "if, uh, you were going to Homecoming?" He stood there, poised to retreat—or to flee. He was beginning to hyperventilate.

Callie could still feel the eyes on her but sounds returned, the banging of locker doors, the chatter of the kids in the hall as they shouted to each other over the others.

"I wasn't planning on . . ." Callie stopped as she realized what he was really asking. "Are you . . . asking me out?"

Mark bobbed his head, jerking a bit as he tried to control

the nervous energy. "Um, yeah. I heard, I mean, well, someone said, that you weren't going, that you didn't have a date, so they suggested, I thought maybe . . ." He seemed at a loss at how to continue and his voice tailed away.

Callie started to talk, and then shut her mouth. She could see the sweat beading up on his forehead. She was close enough to gather his scent. He had used aftershave this morning, a clean masculine smell, but nothing overpowering.

Then his words penetrated. He was not asking her out, he was being pushed into it.

"*They suggested*?" Callie kept her voice quiet, stepping in closer to him.

Mark got very still. He didn't answer.

"Who suggested?" She waited for him to answer but he stood there, glued to the floor, confusion on his face. Below the surface, she was tight with anger. She could feel it simmering but maintained her composure, face and body under control. She forced her breathing back to a near-normal level.

She resumed talking. "For your information, I wasn't going to Homecoming because I didn't want to go, not because I couldn't get a date," she said, voice still quiet and under rigid control. She could still feel the eyes, all those eyes, burning on the back of her neck.

"I wasn't going to Homecoming because every time I do, I get a cold and run like crap at State. And right now, that's more important than a stupid dance with—" She caught herself before she added "stupid boys." "You might think it's funny—and your buddies who put you up to this might think it's funny—to offer to go out with me out of pity." Her hair swung across her face as she shook her head and the anger finally overwhelmed her and bled into her words. "Too bad.

Go find some other 'needy' girl, see if she'll go out with you. I don't need any pity. Not from you, not from anyone."

Mark stood, a stunned and hurt look on his face. "It wasn't like that, she said—"

Callie's eyes flamed. "She said?" Her mind raced. *Jen!* Followed by, *I'll kill her.*

The first bell rang for classes, and locker doors closed as classmates shuffled to their rooms. Mark's eyes had begun to dance again, clearly seeking the nearest route to safety.

"I, uh," he fumbled, "got to get to, uh, class." Hands palm down in front of him, he cautiously stepped back away from Callie, turning when she was out of arm's reach and taking fast strides away, almost running in the fast-emptying hallway. He was a dozen feet away when he whirled around, face flushed, and spoke.

"It wasn't pity." His voice was low, just loud enough to reach her, and sounded miserably sincere. He met her look and she could see the distress in his eyes before he turned and fled.

Crap, she thought. She looked at her open locker and, reaching out, slammed the door shut, the sound reverberating off the walls. She turned to go the opposite direction of Mark to her classes when she saw her.

Mattie was standing by her locker, staring at her, disgust on her face. Callie realized the feeling of the eyes on her neck had not been her imagination. It wasn't the whole universe, just Mattie. Mattie had watched the whole fiasco.

Callie gathered her backpack and steeled herself to walk past the other girl. She kept her eyes locked on the far end of the hallway and her chin up as they crossed paths.

Double crap!

The twins looked confused. Everybody could feel the tension and they took turns glancing over to Callie. Doc noticed as well and also saw Mark avoiding even looking at the girls. He had been coaching teenagers long enough that he had a pretty good idea of what was going on even if he didn't have all the details. Every year, he swore he was done with drama. He was consistently wrong.

Anna had tried to talk to Callie but she had shut her down with a terse "none of your business." Jen had wilted under the glare she received from Callie when she joined the team for warm-ups. Jenessa looked interested. She smirked a little bit at Callie's anger and returned the stare she got from Mattie, arching an eyebrow.

Doc looked at the workout he had attached to his clipboard and the note attached above it from the school. With a deep disgruntled sound, he decided to change the workout. Today was a day for intervals, hard quarters. The team would still have time to recover before the race on Saturday. He called them over.

"Okay you all. Here's the plan," he started. "We're doing hard intervals with a bit of a twist." At this, the team perked up a bit. Intervals were fine but boring.

"We're going to do four hundreds on the track, minimum of eight for everybody, no maximum. You want to do extra, go for it." He paused to make sure they were paying attention. "Here's the other twist. I'm not giving you a pace to aim for. I want you to run to feel. No watches; leave them in your locker or with your gear. If it feels too hard, it probably is. Don't take it so easy that you're not working. The reps should be somewhere just faster than race pace. Listen to your bodies, really dial it in. Remember that you have to run at least eight so don't blow it up too soon. Recovers are a two-hundred-meter jog in between. Go as slow as you need to—you freshmen, if you need to, walk that recovery." The freshmen looked a little confused but nodded.

"No watch?" asked Mark, looking at the multi-sport, multi-lap watch that he always wore. He looked worried.

"Nope. Deal with it." Doc looked back to the rest of the runners. "Okay, girls, you start at the two-hundred-meter mark, boys take off from the start line. Mile warm-up before you begin your intervals, eight-hundred-meter cooldown and stretching when you're done."

He stopped to make sure everybody understood. Seeing agreement, he jogged them over to the track and sent them out on their warm-up. He settled onto one of the aluminum football benches to watch, the chill of the metal quickly penetrating the thin shorts he wore. He glanced at his watch. They had an hour. Cross-country practice would be over before the football team finished their film session of the previous game.

Mark and Callie took charge as the two teams finished the warm-up and got everybody on the line. Mark sent his group off first, charging ahead of the other boys as he tore into the first turn. Callie looked to the other girls and said tersely, "Let's go" and threw herself down the track.

Doc stood up and meandered over to the edge of the track just as the boys rumbled past.

"Good job, Mark. . . . Nice, Nate. . . listen to your body. Will, you're pushing a bit. . . ." Doc kept up the patter as the runners went by, and then focused on the girls. Jenessa and Mattie were out in front as expected, followed by Callie, the twins, and Jen and Lily, gamely hanging on.

"Good job, ladies," he said to the first two. He was silent as Callie, scowling, flashed by.

"Looking good, Anna, Hanna. Nice job, Jen." He encouraged Lily as she came by, looking for a sign that her shins were hurting. No limps today. *Good,* he thought. He looked around the track, seeing the boys cruise into the first rest interval, slowing to a jog as they completed the half-turn to the next start. Moments later, the girls finished the first hard lap. Unlike the boys, they didn't group up for the jog, though Jen and the twins slowed up for Lily.

Callie caught up to Jenessa and Mattie, starting the next interval slightly ahead of them. Reacting in surprise, both bolted after her, catching her in the turn and pulling away, each of them pushing the other. Doc smiled, pleased with the healthy competition. As the other girls came by, he shouted more encouragement. A few seconds later, he repeated it for the boys.

Six laps later, the teams were intermingled as the faster runners separated themselves from the others. The five boys were strung out, Nate having given up on trying to hang with Mark. As he came by Doc, he was focused on the track and seemed not to hear Doc's shouts. The younger runner's breathing had settled and his stride had smoothed out. He was running taller, too, Doc noted with interest. He jotted a quick observation on the clipboard and checked the time—he might have told the kids they couldn't have watches but that didn't stop him from tracking them with his—Nate was running slightly faster than usual, too.

On the far side of the track, he saw Mattie and Jenessa start their last lap. They were evenly matched, Mattie with a bit more speed, Jenessa better endurance. Behind them, Callie jogged into the next interval, slowing for a second next to Lily to talk to the younger girl. Lily was struggling with the intervals. She had started too fast, trying to stay close to the other girls, and was paying the price for it on the last couple as the lactic acid made each extra lap more painful and slow.

Callie ratcheted up the speed again. Her form was beginning to get ragged but she continued to attack the intervals, the scowl having been replaced by determination.

"Tighten up your form," he advised her as she approached. She glanced at him and gave an abrupt nod to acknowledge that she had heard him. Without slowing, she tweaked her arms into line and corrected the slight wobble of her head. Better balanced, she continued into the next turn.

Doc checked her time. *Still running too fast,* he thought. Her early laps had been nearly ten seconds ahead of her normal pace. Her legs were sound and would handle one day of too much speed without injury but she was pushing well beyond her race pace. He shrugged and focused his attention on the other runners. Anna, Hanna, and Jen had caught the last of the boys, and the group ran the final interval together.

Behind them and closing fast, Mark was into his ninth rep, running smoothly and powerfully. Nate was done with his eighth and was jogging very slowly clockwise around the track in the outside lane to join Jenessa and Mattie as they finished. Together, the three of them began a slow cooldown, shouting encouragement to their teammates as they passed. As each runner finished, they joined the group until only Mark and Callie were left. Doc strode across the infield to join his runners as they flopped on the freshly cut grass to stretch. A quick glance at his watch showed that they had about fifteen minutes until the football team showed up. The runners, especially the girls, didn't like working out around the football players. Mark and

Callie kept up the pace, chasing each other around the track, Mark closing in on each interval. He had already lapped her once.

Nate, one leg bent and thrown over the other as he loosened his hips, looked up as the coach joined them. "I liked that workout."

"How do you feel?"

"Pretty good." He hesitated and added, "I think maybe I ran too slow though. Seemed too easy at the end."

"You did fine," the coach reassured the sophomore. "How about the rest of you? Like the workout?"

A chorus of voices answered affirmatively.

"It's a little weird without a watch," said Hanna.

"At least we can count to eight," replied her sister, looking to the track, where Callie was wobbling down the straightaway. "What's up with her?" She looked to Jen as she asked the question.

"I don't know," Callie's sister answered, sitting up, little bits of cut grass attached to her T-shirt, her expression quizzical. "I haven't seen her this mad since I—" Jen stopped to rephrase it. "I haven't seen her this mad in a long time."

Doc stepped over to the side of the track as Callie came by. "Shut it down. You're done." He looked up. He raised his voice to be heard by Mark. "You too, boyo, shut it down," he said.

Mark heard him and started to accelerate, beginning a kick that would put him ahead of Callie at the line.

"Behave!" Pale blue eyes and bristling white eyebrows glared at the youth as Mark ran by. Mark shot him a startled glance but settled back, slowing to a normal pace and finishing ten meters behind Callie. The two of them started their cooldowns, running opposite directions around the track.

"That's interesting," murmured Jenessa. Callie's sister

squinted, studying the senior runner with a frown on her face.

Doc saw Jen's reaction and changed the subject. "Okay, everybody, that's it. You don't need to wait for them to finish today," he said, dismissing the team. "Grab your gear and skedaddle. You all did a good job today. Get some food and something to drink in you and I'll see you tomorrow afternoon."

They collected themselves from the ground, unwinding out of various stretches, the boys starting to banter between themselves. Doc looked over to Mattie.

"Mattie, could I talk to you for a minute, please?"

She turned to face him and he watched her shoulders slump a little bit. The others looked at her curiously, stopping to wait for her.

Doc shooed them away. "You guys go on. This is private."

When they left, Doc turned to Mattie. He wanted to have this done before Callie and Mark came over. She stood there waiting for him to speak, amber eyes glistening. He hadn't realized how tiny she was. He felt a deep sorrow filling him as he began to quietly speak.

"Mattie, I got a note from the school today about your grades."

She was very still and held his eyes but the muscles at the edge of her jaw were tight.

"At the beginning of the season, we talked about keeping grades up. The school district will let you run with a D, but the team policy is that everybody needs to maintain at least a C in all subjects."

Mattie kept staring at him, stone-faced. Doc was sure that she heard and understood, but she didn't give him any indication of what she was feeling. He reached out a tentative hand to touch her shoulder, but she shrugged his hand off. He let it drop.

"I'm sorry, Mattie," he said. "Until you get your grades up in algebra, you're suspended." He paused while it sank in. "You can't run."

Chapter 34

Callie snatched open the rear door to her car and threw her gear on top of her books, spare clothes, and the pile of accumulated debris as Jen climbed in the passenger side. Callie climbed in and slammed the driver's door shut. Out of the corner of her eye, she could see Jen looking at her. She could feel the anger building again. She thought she had burned through it on the track but the embers still glowed, waiting for fuel.

She gave her head a quick shake to clear it and put the key in the ignition, started the car, and began to back out. She quickly drove out of town and made the right onto the forest road that led home. Her knuckles were white on the wheel, and she consciously relaxed them.

Jen saw the motion. "If you want to talk—"

"I don't," she said, sharp and cold. Jen jerked back as if Callie had slapped at her.

The rest of the twenty-minute drive was made in brittle silence, Callie stewing. Her sister had the nerve to sit there like she was clueless and pull that *"Oh, if you want to talk . . . "* after trying to set her up with Mark or set Mark up with her or whatever it was that she was trying to do. Callie went into one of the winding turns too quickly and, gravel popping under her tires, swerved hard to get back in her lane.

It was bad enough when Jen played her games, but this time she wasn't just messing with Callie but scheming with Mark and messing with him, she thought with a frown. Callie kept seeing Mark's face just before he turned around the last time. *It wasn't pity.* She felt a sinking sensation in her stomach again. She had been surprised and happy that he was asking, before she realized he was asking because Jen put him up to it. *I would have said yes,* she thought. A worrisome nag drifted up from her subconscious—*You could have said yes anyway.* She hastily squelched that thought.

She cut into a turn, the right-side wheels drifting onto the gravel of the narrow shoulder. Callie added power, using the turn to catapult her car out of the turn. Beside her, Jen exhaled with an anxious sigh. Callie looked at her, eyes angry and accusatory, her mouth set in a grim line. Jen looked surprised, then angry. Callie looked back to the road just in time to see a coyote slinking across the blacktop, a quick gray shadow in the fading light. It was far enough away that she didn't need to dodge it. Still, she slowed down and scanned the woods to either side for other animals. With each scan to the right, she got a glimpse of Jen, sitting with her arms across her chest.

A few minutes later, they pulled into the driveway at the house and Callie swung around and parked on the far edge of the gravel. Almost before Callie set the brake, Jen was unbelted and out of the car, slamming the car door behind her.

"Don't slam my door!" Callie was opening her door while simultaneously trying to extricate herself from her seat belt, the belt catching her shoulder and pulling her sideways as she tried to hurry.

Jen glared and stomped across the gravel and up onto the porch. She shoved open the kitchen door and, with another quick glare at her sister, slammed the door.

As Callie stormed across the gravel lugging her books, she could hear voices inside, Jen shouting something, but the words were muffled by the logs and distance. Through the kitchen window, she saw her mom crossing the kitchen. The anger that had simmered all day began to boil over. Jen was acting like she was the one that had been hurt. Callie could see her mom buying it—Jen was convincing. Callie banged through the door and, as Jen had, slammed it behind her.

"While you're trying to get Mom to help you, make sure you tell her what you did!"

In front of her, Jen was standing tense and flushed while her mother stood at the end of the kitchen island with hands stretched out toward Jen in a calming gesture. At the table, her father was looking up from his computer, puzzlement in his eyes. The kitchen was already well lit with the reddish orange glow of the fading sun tinting the logs.

Jen turned away from their mother. "I didn't do anything!"

Callie snorted. "Yeah, right." Her chest was tight even while she felt light-headed and reckless. "You just made a fool out of me in front of the whole school. You set it all up and Mark falls for it and the next thing I know I'm yelling at him and you're, you're—"

"I don't know what you're talking about. I didn't do anything." Jen turned to her mother. "See, she's not making any sense," she appealed.

Their mother started to talk but Callie interrupted, nearly shouting. "You connived to get Mark to ask me out to Homecoming. He as much as admitted it."

"Bull! I never did. And if Mark said I did, he's a liar." Jen stood facing her sister, chin stuck out defiantly, eyes angry.

Callie lunged forward, colliding with her mother, who stepped deftly into her path. Callie rocked back a step, staring eye to eye with her mother. Callie, the green in her eyes glittering, met the cool, more serene green of her mother's. "She—"

"Stop." Sarah's voice was quiet but firm. "Stop right now."

"I didn't do anything," Jen insisted from behind her mother. At the table, her father was shaking his head and closing the lid on the laptop.

Her mother looked over her shoulder. "You, too. Stop."

"But she's—"

"Zip it," said her dad from the table. "Both of you, over here." He looked to his wife. "You want to handle this or shall I just knock their heads together?"

Both girls stood fixed in place, exchanging nasty looks.

"Dad, she keeps butting into my life. I told her I wasn't going to Homecoming and she decided—I don't know why—that I couldn't get a date so she tried to get Mark to ask me out—"

"Did not."

"Did too."

Their father looked from one daughter to the other. "This is about boys?" Neither girl answered him. He sighed and looked to Sarah. "You get to deal with it. Let me know if I need to kill somebody." To Callie, he said, "You, sit down on that end." He was pointing to his right. "You sit on that end," directing Jen to the seat at the far end of the table. As they grudgingly obeyed, he got up and leaned against the countertop.

Both girls sat slumped in the chairs, arms crossed and looking sulky. Their mother came and sat between them. She paused for a second and then dove in. "Callie, you first. What the heck is going on? Why are we screaming at each other?" She kept the same firm tone she had used earlier.

Callie felt the acute onset of embarrassment. "I, uh, I mean, she is interfering with me and—"

"Am not!"

Sarah glanced at her youngest daughter. "Quiet. You'll get your chance." She turned back to Callie. "Interfering how?"

Callie's face flushed. "She talked Mark into asking me out."

Jenifer started to speak but was silenced by a quick shake of her father's head. She slumped lower in the chair and her chin settled closer to her crossed arms.

"And Mark asking you out is a bad thing?" This elicited a snort from Hank at the counter, earning a reproving look from his wife. Sarah turned back to Callie.

"No, it— I mean . . ." Callie's voice trailed off. Sarah sat waiting patiently and the silence grew.

Callie stared at the table, noticing the grain of the oak running the length of the wood with its tiny imperfections in the surface, indentations and small scratches from years of family use. She gave a little shake of her head. She couldn't think any single thought through to the end. Before one thought was complete, it splattered against another thought or burst of anger or touch of regret. She focused on another grain line in the wood, following it with her eyes while each gust of new emotion played out on her face.

Sarah turned her attention to Jen. "Okay," Sarah said, "what's your side of this? Did you ask Mark to ask Callie—"

"No." Jen stared at her sister at the far end of the table, eyes and mouth folded and pressed.

"Let me finish," her mom remonstrated. Jen transferred her stare to her mother.

"Or did you induce, incite, influence, or otherwise indirectly but deliberately provoke Mark into asking Callie out?"

Jen uncrossed her arms to push against the table, sitting completely upright in the chair. "Why are you interrogating *me*?" she said, hands moving as she defended herself. "I'm not the one stomping around all day acting all pissed off then driving home like a maniac. You should have—"

"Watch your language," her mother warned, "and your tone." She and Jen stared at each other until Jen broke the contact, looking down to Callie.

"I don't know why she's mad at me. I didn't do anything."

Callie started to lift her head up and Jen could see the anger still there. Her hands moved faster. "Word went around the school that Mark had asked her out and she said no"—their mother shot a fast look at Callie's slumping shoulders and a flash of sympathy crossed her face—"and everybody was laughing at Mark because of it. But I didn't have anything to do with it."

"He said you did!" Callie was radiating anger toward Jen but the younger girl didn't back down.

"What," interceded their mother, "exactly did he say, Callie?"

"He said that Jen said, that she said—"

"Was it 'Jen said' or 'she said'?" her mother interrupted. "It's an important difference."

Callie paused and, in a subdued voice, said, "She said."

Jen looked triumphant, vindicated in her own mind against the charge. "I told you so."

"Knock it off!" Her dad, still leaning against the counter, gave his youngest daughter a penetrating look. She returned it with an aggrieved air, clearly suggesting that she was the injured party—but she looked away first.

Callie was back to tracing lines in the wood grain as Jen's told-you-so echoed in her ears. Jen had a lot of faults, probably more than the average little sister, she thought. She meddled and instigated and got everybody into trouble. When confronted, she dodged and evaded. She might even fib on occasion, but it was always with a wink, part of a setup to a joke or a prank and she was letting you in on it. Allegedly this, supposedly that. Callie stopped looking at the table and looked at her sister.

"You don't lie."

"I don't lie," confirmed her sister.

"You didn't put Mark up to it, asking me out?"

"I wouldn't do that to Mark."

Callie went back to staring. Her parents exchanged a glance and waited. Callie looked up again, made eye contact with Jen.

"You wouldn't do that to Mark," Callie repeated. She sat there looking at Jen. "So who did?"

Chapter 35

"I knew she'd be a problem," said Jenessa, her tone self-righteously injured and contemptuous at the same time.

"We knew she was having trouble in math," said Anna.

"We would have helped." Hanna glanced up toward the sky as she said it. Math wasn't their best subject either. "But we didn't know she was flunking."

"Shut it down, ladies," said Doc. "We're not going to waste energy on gossip. True, she's not quite meeting the standards that we have set for the team, but she's only a little ways from where she needs to be."

"Right, she's sitting at home while we're at practice, that's a little ways away," said Jenessa. "Well, that explains why she was avoiding everybody in school today."

Callie watched as Doc led the team through the shock of Mattie's suspension from the team. Jenessa was starting to annoy her, though. She was a hypocrite, she thought, remembering the hours that Callie had helped her with algebra and geometry and now precalc. It was the deal they made freshman year. Callie helped with math, Jenessa helped with English and, later, Spanish.

Telling the team not to gossip wasn't going to work, but it might divert Jenessa's attention from her and Mark. Callie had caught her in the halls laughing with another small group of girls as she recounted the debacle the day before. As Callie approached, they had fallen silent, whispering after she had passed. A burst of laughter caught up with her as someone in the group made a joke. Callie had grimly maintained her course, doing her best to ignore them.

In Brit Lit, Jenessa sought to invent more drama. "It's probably a good thing you told him to beat it," she said. "Word is that he's spent all morning in the lab." Her voice dropped to a whisper, adding with a conspiratorial flourish, "Mr. Poulson is watching him."

Callie had rolled her eyes and focused on the novel they were studying. Mark had been working on experiments in the labs for weeks, with the encouragement of Poulson, completing an independent study project.

She had tried to talk to Mark but he kept disappearing. She staked out his locker before first period but he never showed up and, when the bell rang, she made her way to class feeling slightly guilty. She had seen him briefly as the boys' team gathered but they took off on their run before she had a chance to catch him. He still looked angry, turning his back when she had gazed his way.

Now this. Mattie's suspension caught everyone by surprise and Callie felt a twinge of guilt for not knowing that her teammate needed help. She sighed.

"What's the workout, Coach?" she asked.

Doc quickly ran down the details. "Go out easy, twenty minutes, then Lily turns back, followed by you and Jen two minutes later, the twins thirty seconds after that, Jenessa chasing one minute later. Your goal on the way back is to not get passed by anyone with a later turnaround. Step it up, tempo run." The girls looked confused until they got the splits settled.

"So we turn around at twenty-two thirty?" clarified Anna.

"Exactly," replied Doc. "Then you try to catch Jen and Callie, who are trying to catch Lily. Stay ahead of Jenessa." When everybody was clear on what was expected, Doc sent the group off. The girls started their watches and ran. By an unspoken agreement, they avoided the topic of Mattie.

At exactly twenty minutes, Lily turned around and began speeding back to the start. Callie and Jen started their countdown. As the two sisters made the break to chase Lily, Jenessa eased over to run next to Callie. Callie made the turn and, as she did, she heard Jenessa's voice, mocking.

"Still think we can win State?"

That evening the depression settled in. The practice had ended with everyone feeling disjointed. Callie had caught Lily, hammering past her with more than a quarter mile to the end. Jen had stayed right with her. The twins weren't far behind and Jenessa was last in, leaving her in a foul mood.

Now, sitting cross-legged on her bed, wedged into the corner where the slope of the roof met the wall, she wondered if the week could get worse. Strewn across the bed were her schoolbooks and papers, homework completed. Downstairs she could hear her folks and Jen talking, the voices indistinct as they drifted through her closed door. She looked at the book on her nightstand, a recent bestseller on running. She wasn't in the mood.

Mattie's absence was a hole sucking all the energy from the team. It was doing the same to her. Everybody had bought into the idea that they had a chance—except, maybe, Jenessa. Callie frowned. She hadn't figured Jenessa out yet.

She realized she hadn't figured Mattie out either. Mattie wasn't just the perpetually angry girl she saw in the hallway at school. Callie watched her at the practices. She was the one who shouted encouragement to the others, egged the twins on when they were goofing—heck, a lot of the time, she instigated the antics—and even took Jen and Lily under her wing. The anger was still there but it erupted at races now. Mattie raced angry.

A couple of times at practice Mattie had been about to say something to Callie but changed her mind. The first time it had happened was early in the season after a hard workout in the valley. As a reward for working hard in the nearly triple-digit heat, Doc had let them frolic in the icy water of the river. In the midst of a water fight with the twins, after soaking Hanna with a sudden deluge, Mattie had turned to speak to Callie. The tawny gold eyes were sparkling with pleasure but Callie watched as a screen came down and the familiar Mattie returned.

It had happened at least twice since then.

The door to her room, closed but not latched, banged open as the dog thrust herself into Callie's room, sashaying over with her tail wagging.

"Nice manners, Sophie," Callie chided the dog. Sophie put her head on the edge of the bed, big brown-yellow eyes looking up.

"Fine," said Callie, bending forward at the waist to reach down and give the dog a scratch. Sophie sighed.

"So the whole pack isn't together and you had to go looking for the missing one?" she asked the dog. Sophie's tail wagged faster as Callie talked to her, though the teenager was pretty sure that the dog's vocabulary was limited to "out," "sit," and "food."

Callie rearranged the bed, moving the books and papers to the floor, and swung her legs over the edge of the bed.

"Move."

Sophie obligingly shifted to let the girl off the bed. As Callie passed by her dresser, she grabbed her phone, leaving it connected to the charger. She quickly went through her contact list and found the name she was looking for. Thumbs flashing, she sent a text.

`Let me know if I can help`

She put the phone down and went out, turning off the light behind her, going downstairs to join the rest of the family. At eleven when she went to bed, there was still no reply.

The girls nearly lost the race on Saturday. It took a last-second surge by an exhausted Jen to gain the one extra place they needed. Jenessa and the twins had bad races. The twins, out late the night before at the Homecoming football game, looked tired when they boarded the bus and, once on the course, had run like they had army boots on, finishing in a workmanlike but uninspired manner. Callie had them in sight the entire race.

Jen was tired too, but it hadn't affected her race. Confident from her race the previous week, she had charged out, challenging Callie from the start. The two of them charged the first hill and Callie briefly accelerated. Jen matched her and, when Callie slowed, surged on the hill, opening a lead.

Callie knew this course, a hilly beast with lousy footing, and she almost smiled as Jen took the lead. Jen crested the hill with a twelve-yard lead and was already breathing hard. Callie reeled her in on the downhill and, at the base of the next hill, surged to run next to Jen. Jen accelerated again, and Callie let her go.

It was the fourth hill, a little over two miles into the three-mile course, when Callie attacked. She caught Jen on the downhill as she had previously, but instead of surging at the base and backing off, she held her pace for the first quarter of the hill, listening to Jen's heaving gasps. As Jen sucked wind in, Callie surged again, keeping her arms in tight and driving with them to help her up the hill. Jen could only watch as Callie, passing two more runners on the way to the top, surged again, flowing over and around the ruts, aggressively attacking downhill.

Jen finished with a tremendous kick, nearly falling after she passed the banner for the finish, and grabbing at her knees as she tried to get precious air into her lungs. She came through the finishing chute to find Callie there, paper cup half full of a pink watery sports drink extended in her hand.

"Thanks," Jen managed, draining the cup in one long swig. She grimaced. "I don't know what flavor that's supposed to be but it's nasty."

"You okay?"

Jen eyed her. "You're evil." Her breathing was almost normal again but she was dripping with sweat even in the cool air. Last night had been the first real frost of the year and it lingered into the day.

They heard Anna and Hanna cheering for Lily and went back to the line to join them. At the canopy, she could see Doc and Jenessa talking, Jenessa gesturing, emphatically shaking her head no as she did so. Puzzled, Callie turned back to the race and cheered for her teammate, who was trying to outsprint two other finishers. She'd worry about Jenessa later. The team still had one more runner to bring home.

"That's the way, Lily—come on, you're almost there!"

Lily surged to the line, winning a battle against two

other runners that did nothing to affect the standings. Callie had always—until last week at least—scored points for the team, but that was more because they didn't have enough runners than any great talent of hers. Occasionally she wondered if she would have run cross-country at a large school where thirty or forty runners came out but only seven counted for varsity.

Callie went looking for Doc and found him at the start line getting the boys ready to start their race. Not a good time to talk to him. She spied the twins on the other side of the starting line and held up an arm, pointing to her watch. Anna nodded; after the boys started, the girls would start their cooldown.

Doc had his team set with Mark, towering over him, in front to lead the team out. Nate was right beside him, with Will stationed next. The boys' team was quietly improving and had a slim chance to go to State as a team. They had to earn one of two open slots.

The girls had only one allotment. It was winner-takes-all at Districts to get to State. With Mattie, the girls were the favorites to win the district. Without . . .

Callie had tried texting and then calling Mattie every night. No answer, nobody home, nobody knew if or when she would be back except Mattie.

And Mattie wasn't telling.

Chapter 36

Jen couldn't make up her mind. She pulled a dress from her closet. Tried it on. Took it off. Jen tried on six different dresses before pulling a raid on Callie's wardrobe and liberating a salmon-colored number from the back of the closet. Tried it on. Took it off. Tried on another dress wangled from her mom. Took that one off. Finally decided on the salmon dress again, modeling it barefoot for her parents down in the kitchen, doing a little ballerina pirouette on the tile, plenty of deeply tanned skin visible under the spaghetti straps.

"How do I look?" she asked, settling down from her toes. Callie nodded. The dress fit, clung really, accenting her figure. When Callie had worn it three years ago, she was pretty sure she didn't have those types of curves.

"I think," her dad started, then paused to make sure he had Jen's attention, "that it will be awfully cold tonight and you really ought to consider a snowsuit."

"Daddy!"

"Don't mind your father, sweetie, he's in shock. The dress looks just fine." Her mother walked around, tweaking the seams at the sides to get them straight. "There."

Jen looked at her feet, white skin to the ankle where the sharp line of her tan started. "I'm going to need some shoes." She glanced at her mom. "I was thinking of the white heels?"

"Which white heels?" Her mom eyed her with suspicion. "*My* white heels? My stilettos?"

"Yes," said Jen, dragging out the sound as she folded in her shoulders in an imitation of timidity. "And some stockings," she added. "I have runs in mine."

Her mom stepped back, judging sizes. "The shoes will fit, but you might want to get stockings from Callie." She looked to Callie. "Do you have any or are we going to have to make an emergency stop on the way in to town?"

"I've got a pair," Callie said. She smiled as she said it, looking not at her sister but her father, who had alternating pained and proud expressions creasing his features as he puttered around the kitchen, pouring himself some iced tea.

"Okay, youngest daughter, I think you're set. Honestly, it would be easier if you planned this ahead of time." She looked her over one more time. "You're going to look very nice tonight."

Jen looked down at her feet, swinging the tip of her right foot in a small loop.

"What?" Her mother sounded exasperated.

"I was thinking—"

Callie heard her dad mutter a very quiet "uh-oh."

Jen ignored him as she looked at her mother, doe-eyed, her brown eyes pleading. "—that Dad was right. It's going to be cold tonight—I checked the forecast—"

"You did, huh?" her mother asked with a touch of sarcasm.

Jen nodded solemnly. "I was thinking," she restarted, "that maybe I could, uh, borrow a jacket?"

"Which jacket?"

"The long leather one?"

"No way, young lady." Sarah's tone was uncompromising.

"But," argued Jen, "the jacket is fantastic and with the dress, would look really hot—" She was interrupted by a bout of coughing from her father as he inhaled a sip of his iced tea. He looked at her, shaking his head, eyes bulging as he attempted to recover.

"Absolutely not. I am not letting you take my nicest jacket to a school dance and have it ruined." Her mother's voice was adamant. "And don't do that to your father, it isn't nice."

Jen tried arguing unsuccessfully a few more minutes. With a sigh, she capitulated and headed upstairs with Callie to get the stockings. As they went up the stairs, Callie could hear her parents talking quietly, then the soft laughter of her mom.

"You didn't really think that you could talk her out of that coat, did you?"

"Nope, but it was worth a try." Jen smiled to herself. "Did you see Dad's face?" She laughed. "Totally worth a try."

Callie watched from the front door as they loaded into the car—once the obligatory pictures were taken, of course. Jen had stumbled on the way to the car, tall heels sinking into the gravel of the drive, as she walked precariously from the added height. Newborn colts were more stable than her sister, Callie thought.

She closed the door and turned, nearly tripping over the dog.

"Move, goofball," she said to Sophie. Sophie obligingly moved, tail wagging, and followed Callie into the well-lit kitchen. She looked at the remnants of dinner and decided to do the dishes later. The house, normally full of sounds, felt empty. Callie thought about Jen headed to Homecoming. A spasm of regret clutched at her belly and she pushed back against it before it could spread.

You are not going to Homecoming so you don't get sick so you don't suck at State again this year, she reminded herself as she meandered upstairs, not sure what she was looking for. She turned into her room, flicking the light switch on as she entered.

She had added a new poster to her wall to join Pre. There were no words of wisdom on the poster, just an image of a woman running free through the woods, lake and sunlight in the background, the trees forming long shadows across the leafy trail. Where Pre forever forced his will onto the track, the young woman simply communed with the woods.

Sophie breathed heavily behind her, waiting for Callie to settle down so she could find a comfy place near the girl to lie down. She yawned.

Callie looked to her phone and picked it up. *Time for the nightly exercise in futility,* she thought. She started thumbing in a message, the same one that she had sent the night before and the night before that. And stopped, staring at the letters backlit on the screen. What was that Mark had quoted? Einstein? Doing the same thing over and over and expecting a different result was the definition of insanity. Or something like that, she thought, not certain of the memory though she was pretty sure she got the general idea right.

Impulsively, she cleared the message and tucked the phone into a pocket.

Time to try something new, she thought. The decision triggered fear, a twitchy feeling along her nerves, and she noticed that she was taking short, shallow breaths.

Before she had a chance to change her mind, Callie went

downstairs and gathered her keys and a jacket—her dad was right, the night was cooling rapidly now that the sun had dropped—and, with a "mind the house" command to the dog, went to her car.

As she drove, all the reasons she was being an idiot flashed through her mind. It was an impressively long list. The fear broadened and Callie had to consciously control her breathing. Belatedly, she realized she hadn't left a note for her folks. One more thing to worry about—she would have to make sure she beat them home.

It was a twenty-minute drive, but she spied the gravel drive on the left in the beams of her headlights before she lost her courage, and she made the turn, following it as it weaved through the trees before emptying out into an open space in front of the house. Callie parked to one side and sat there with the engine running. *This is dumb,* she thought. *They already know I'm here.* As if in confirmation, a curtain moved at one of the windows. Callie sighed and killed the lights and engine.

There were no outside lights on and she almost tripped on a loose board on the steps. She crossed the porch and reached to knock on the door. She could see tiny tremors in her hand. Callie took a deep breath and rapped firmly on the door three times. Inside she could hear movement and voices, then someone coming to the door.

The outside light blazed on as the front door opened.

"What do you want?"

Chapter 37

Callie stood trapped the stark glare of the porch light while Mattie stood in the open doorway waiting. She tried to formulate an answer, opening her mouth to speak and then closing it again. Now that she was here, she didn't know how to answer the question. She was not sure what she wanted.

From the dim interior of the home, she heard Mattie's father say, "You're letting the heat out, Matilda. Send whoever it is away and close the door."

Matilda? thought Callie.

There was a flash of emotion on Mattie's face, gone too quickly for Callie to identify it. She opened the door further and waved at Callie. "Get in before you freeze."

Callie entered, and found herself standing in a medium-sized family room. The lighting was dim and blue-tinged from the multiple flat screens arrayed around a large flat table that held several computers and dominated the far end of the room. The furnishings were sparse. The room opened to the breakfast nook and she could see a dining room table with two chairs beside a kitchen that had nothing on the countertops. Reflections of light gleamed off the surfaces and a faint hint of acrid heat from the computers tainted the air.

Mattie's father looked up from the monitors and Callie felt an uncomfortable sensation as though she were being broken down into bits and put back together again.

"I know you," he said.

"Yes, sir, Mr. Rede," replied Callie. She was finding it hard to meet his eyes. Her impression at meets had been that he didn't blink, but he did—not much and with none of the warmth in his eyes that she was accustomed to from others. There wasn't coldness either, just a sense of being impersonal and distant. "I go to school with," she hesitated, "Matilda and we run together."

He considered this new data. To his daughter, he said, "She can stay." With that, he turned back to a keyboard and began typing.

Mattie grabbed her by the arm and dragged her down a hallway, looking over her shoulder. They came to the second door on the right and Mattie led her into a bedroom, closing the door firmly. The light here was warmer, though not much more abundant. A single bed dressed in a light pink comforter was set in the middle of the wall opposite the window, a single small dresser against the wall by the door, a single perfume bottle resting on a silver tray on top. A small desk with schoolbooks stacked on the surface, and a chair, Mattie's book bag hanging from the back, were the most disorganized features of the room.

Mattie turned to her. "Don't call me Matilda," she said.

Callie nodded. "Right."

Mattie let out a breath. "Thanks." She peered at Callie. "So what did you want? You didn't drive all this way for no reason."

Callie felt awkward and covered it by shrugging her shoulders. "I've been texting you and I tried calling but you didn't answer."

"My phone—" Mattie paused, correcting her statement. "My *use* of a phone has been suspended indefinitely." She wore a blank expression as she said it but her voice carried undercurrents of tension. "I never got the texts."

"Oh."

Again emotions flickered across Mattie's face. She asked again, "What did you want?"

Callie controlled her hands; she could feel them getting fidgety. "I guess, I wanted to help."

"With what? I don't need help." Mattie stood there motionless, eyes hooded.

Callie's fingers began interlacing and twisting slightly. "Yeah, with math, I think you do. I think you want help but don't want to ask anybody or owe anybody."

"Well, you can think anything you want but go mess with someone else's life and leave me alone.

"That's not very fair," said Callie. "And algebra is kicking your butt and you know it."

"I can figure it out!"

"Sure, but Doc's not going to let you run until—"

Mattie interrupted. "So this is about Callie's little dream of winning State? Let's get Mattie back running before it's too late. No, I don't think I need that kind of help."

"Dang it." Callie's voice started to get loud and she could hear the anger building. "Why do you have to be so—"

Mattie shot a panicked look at the closed door. "Don't shout at me!" Her voice wasn't much above a loud whisper but as intense as a sharp slap. "Just leave me alone." For an unguarded second, her eyes were touched by despair.

Callie lowered her voice, making the effort to relax her hands, which had balled into fists. "You say I want you back because I want to win State. I do, more than you know, but that's not why I'm here. You're right, we can't win State without you. Heck, our district is so tough we might not even *get* to State if you're not there.

"Here's the weird thing. Do you realize the only time you smile is when you're running? The rest of the time, you're either mad as hell or just don't give a crap, but when you run with the twins or Jen or Lily, it's like there's a whole other Mattie, and I like that Mattie. She laughs and jokes and sings. She's one of us, part of our family." Callie paused to catch her breath while Mattie stared at her, wide-eyed in disbelief.

"But when you race . . ." Callie shook her head. "The Mattie that shows up at races is scary. She races with demons and I can't do anything to help that and I don't know if I even understand it." She stared at Mattie. "I'm not sure you understand it either. But I can help get you back to the team, to the people that make you smile and laugh and actually like you, but only if you're willing to accept the help." Callie couldn't hold the stare any longer and, eyes moist and blurry, looked away.

The entire house was quiet. Not the serene quiet of a mountain lake or the pastoral quiet of new wheat fields or even the quiet of sitting beside a close friend, the kind of quiet that soothed and healed. This quiet shouted you down, swallowed sounds and joys and hope.

Staring at the perfume bottle, Callie thought of her kitchen at home, the warmth of the light and the wood. There was always some sound in their house even if it was just the dog snoring. Jen abhorred silence. If Jen was home, she was talking and joking. Her mom talked—no, Callie realized, she asked questions then listened. Her dad joked and laughed or would read them bits of the book he was reading, sections at random that struck his fancy.

"It smells like her."

It took Callie a moment to realize that Mattie was talking about the bottle. "It's your mom's perfume?"

"It was the only thing he let me keep." Mattie's voice got very soft and far away. "She wrote me a letter once. It was at the post office when I got the mail." Mattie looked behind her and sat, back upright, on the edge of her bed, gazing at a spot low on the wall. "I don't know what it said and I'm not allowed to get the mail anymore," she finished more firmly.

"How long has it been since you've seen your mom?" Whether it was due to the prying nature of the question or the slightly morbid curiosity, Callie suddenly felt embarrassed.

"The night she left."

Callie counted silently and then tried to see herself without her mother for four years. She couldn't do it.

Mattie looked into a far distance and her voice was so low that Callie could barely hear her. "I'm going to find her."

"How?"

"I've got the boy genius working on it." Mattie smiled as she said it, and glanced at Callie. The smile faded as she saw the expression on Callie's face. "It's good for him to work on something other than blowing up the school."

Callie said nothing. Mattie glanced at her again and let out a huff of exasperated breath.

"You really are an idiot."

Callie rocked back, shocked at the sudden attack. "Excuse me?" she said defensively.

"You both are."

"What are you talking about?"

"You and boy genius. Mark."

Mattie's gaze was steady and Callie couldn't see any anger in her, but the whole change of direction in the conversation was disconcerting.

"It's Saturday night, the dude asked you to Homecoming, and you're here with a loser like me," said Mattie. "Like I said, you're an idiot."

"You're not a loser," Callie said, automatically deflecting away from the subject. "And I wasn't going to Homecoming anyway."

"Whatever. You know you fidget with your hands when you get nervous? It's very distracting."

Callie glanced down and quickly untwined her fingers.

"Sorry."

"Why didn't you just say yes?"

The question caught Callie off-balance. "To Mark? Because someone pushed him into—" Awareness flooded into Callie. "You . . ." She struggled to form the words, get them in the right order.

"Yeah, guilty."

"But . . . why?"

"Because he's an idiot. Or at least, he's an idiot every time you're around. Most of the time he makes sense and he's got this super brain, but he starts talking to you and he goes all stupid. It's actually pretty hilarious."

"But I thought you . . . him . . . you're together all the time." Callie knew she sounded like a blithering airhead but was having trouble getting her thoughts organized. Convinced Jen was innocent—for once!—she had settled on Jenessa as the most likely culprit.

"We're not together all the time," Mattie explained. "He worked out a deal with my father"—she glanced at the closed door again—"to drive me to and from school when he got his license. He used to try to come over but . . ." She shrugged. "It was uncomfortable."

Callie could picture Mark in the room with all the computers. He'd understand the computers and maybe even Mattie's father, probably better than most.

"I just thought that you . . ." Callie swallowed and pushed forward. "You were always around. I thought that maybe you, you know, were interested in him."

"Oh hell no!" Mattie's eyes were huge. "No way. Boy genius is way too smart and too stubborn to be my type. And who else am I going to hang with?"

Callie digested this and looked at Mattie. "Nate?"

Mattie took in a deep breath and inclined her head. "You can't tell." Her eyes dropped back to the spot on the wall. "Please?"

"No problem," said Callie. "But I don't get why you kept giving me the evil eye when I was around Mark. What did I do?"

Mattie glanced up from the spot. "Say Jen comes home with a boyfriend. How would you feel?"

"Oh." Callie processed the idea of Jen dating, flashing back to the pirouette in the kitchen. "Dude better be a good guy."

"Yeah," agreed Mattie. "It's more like that."

They sat there on the bed, each in their own thoughts and, for a little while, their quiet created a little bubble that fended off the quiet of the house. Callie was the first to stir. She looked at Mattie.

"You're right, I feel like an idiot."

"Boy genius will keep you company. Besides, was a boy involved?"

Callie looked at her, puzzled. "Yeah?"

"Then that's all the defense you need." Mattie smiled for the second time that evening. "You're forgiven, sister." She wavered then added, "And if the offer of help is still there, I'll take it."

Callie started her car, giving it a minute to warm up before she left. They had agreed to meet after practice Monday to study—Mattie had a test Tuesday and if she did well enough, might have her eligibility back. Following Mattie out of the bedroom, Callie had watched the other girl's body language change, chin dropping as the already slender frame collapsed in on itself.

Callie put the car into reverse to swing around and leave. As she did, through the window she saw Mattie in her room, door closed, pick up the bottle of perfume and unstopper it. The last image Callie had before she left was of Mattie, standing with the flask held close to her heart and her eyes closed.

Chapter 38

"Forget Saturday," Doc told the girls.

"We had a bad race as a team. It happens," he continued, "and usually around Homecoming. The best thing we can do with a bad race is learn from it and move on. You ladies have been running really well and you'll do just fine on Thursday."

Callie looked around the park where the team was gathered. The first leaves were starting to fall from the trees. Mattie was back at practice, wearing a sweatshirt even though the daytime temperatures were still moderate and the sky was clear and bright. The younger runners had welcomed Mattie back to the pack with enthusiasm. Callie was keeping her eye on Jenessa. If there was trouble with Mattie, it would come from the other senior, but Jenessa was acting odd, subdued. She had been that way in class, too, and when Callie probed, just brushed her off.

Doc started talking again. "Easy day today. I want you ladies running at conversational pace. Relax, chat, cover some miles. Mattie," Doc said, looking right at the girl. "I want you running with Lily."

Mattie glanced over to Lily, who was stretching, bright orange tape on her shins. Running up and down the hills had triggered more pain and Callie had taped her up before practice to help support the muscles.

"How far do you want us to go?" Mattie asked.

"Keep it short, no more than three, and keep it flat," the coach replied. "Lily, if it gets too bad, I want you to shut it down—it's okay to walk it in."

Lily started to protest but Doc talked over her. To Mattie, he said, "Keep an eye on her."

He turned to the twins. "You two get Jen. Make it five or so, but easy." Jen struggled to her feet and walked over to Anna and Hanna gingerly. Her feet were still tender from the abuse of the high heels she'd worn to the dance two nights ago.

Callie looked at Jenessa. "That leaves you and me."

Jenessa shrugged and looked to Doc. "How far?"

"As far as you need to go," he responded.

Callie raised an eyebrow. Jenessa only glanced at Doc then gathered her legs under her and stood, shaking her shoulders to loosen them.

"You ready?" she asked as Callie walked over.

"Yeah," Callie replied as she slipped her sunglasses down. "You lead."

The two girls eased out while the others were getting organized. From behind them, they heard Doc shout, "Everybody check in with me when you're done." Callie waved an arm to let him know they had heard, and kept going. Jenessa led her out onto the highway, running along the shoulder facing traffic for a half mile before leaving the pavement for a graveled road that led west. Callie knew the route. They would be making a couple of more turns onto smaller and smaller roads, first gravel, then bare dirt, before coming back on a piece of single track that wound across some forestry land on the other side of town. There were a series of gentle rolling hills but it was an easy course and mostly untraveled once they left the highway.

Callie loped next to Jenessa as they made the first turn. They were settled into a nice rhythm and Callie could feel herself shifting to that happy place where the effort matched the mood. A light sweat built on her skin, cooled quickly by the light breeze, and Callie realized that she was smiling.

"I don't want to go to Great Falls," Jenessa said, breaking the silence.

Privately, Callie agreed with her. "What's in Great Falls?"

"I got offered a scholarship."

"That's kind of cool," said Callie.

"The school's in Great Falls."

"Yeah, well," offered Callie in sympathy. She had visited Great Falls in Montana a couple of years ago. It had snowed in June and it was always windy.

"You got a couple of other schools looking, don't you?" asked Callie. "Maybe you'll get an offer closer to home."

"I don't care about closer to home. I'd rather get the heck away from here," said Jenessa with a little toss of hair. "But I want someplace warm."

Callie grunted. She liked the small towns and open fields and forests, but at least half of the kids at school couldn't wait to get to the big cities, Portland or Seattle, places more hip, more exciting, than the farm country they grew up in.

"You applied to schools yet?" Callie asked her.

"Mostly on the west side," confirmed Jenessa. "Not U-Dub, though. Smaller schools."

"Hawaii is warmer," joked Callie.

Jenessa flashed a smile. "I can put it on my list." She ran a few steps in silence. "My dad would have a heart attack."

"Too far away for his little girl?"

"Too many dollars," said Jenessa, her voice sharp. "He wants me to take the scholarship before they pull it and give it to somebody else."

"Oh." Callie was planning on working her way through, keeping costs down as she went. She wasn't getting any running scholarships, though she had applied for some academic ones. Her folks had warned her against going too far into debt for school. The numbers were scary.

They made the next turn and the gravel fell away to dirt, the road surface dusty from a summer of no rain. They hit a section of washboard ruts in the road and Callie changed her stride to avoid jarring her legs on the uneven surface. She was starting to pant and realized that Jenessa had ratcheted up the pace.

"Hey, you're killing me here a little bit," she said to Jenessa.

The other girl glanced over. "Sorry," she said, and slowed.

"Have you talked with Doc?" Callie asked. "He's pretty good at trying to get help, sends out race results to the college coaches."

Jenessa frowned as she ran. "Yeah, he's done that. One of them was there Saturday."

"Where from?"

"Spokane."

"It's not any warmer there," observed Callie.

Jenessa grunted. "It doesn't matter," she said. "I won't be getting an offer. I ran like crap."

"Well, maybe," admitted Callie, "but that doesn't mean you won't get an offer. You're like top three or four in the state."

"It's a small school division. Lots of fast girls at the big schools," argued Jenessa.

"You're really a negative Nelly today, aren't you," said Callie. "They wouldn't be looking if they didn't think you might fit. Other than that chick from up north, it's you and Roxanne from Fairchild."

Jenessa grunted but Callie knew she was right—the info was online and she had been tracking Fairchild and a couple of other top teams.

They powered on without talking, the whisper of their footsteps triggering small scurrying sounds from the underbrush that lined each side of the road. Callie loved the scent of the woods and soil, just minutes from the smelly highway.

"Doc yelled at me," said Jenessa.

Callie mulled over Jenessa's words, and then responded, "Yeah, I saw." Not prying, but willing to listen.

Another grunt from Jenessa. "Of course you did. You see everything," she said.

They were quiet for another hundred yards when Jenessa spoke again. "How do you do it?"

"Do what?"

Jenessa took her time in answering. "You have it all mostly together."

Callie glanced at Jenessa in surprise, scuffing the bottom of her shoe on the top of a rut as she did. "I do?"

Juggling the team and school and Mark sure didn't feel like having it all together. She looked at Jenessa again.

"Not really," she said, and laughed. "Mostly I'm faking."

"Yeah, I get that," said Jenessa. Little twitches around the eyes, a quick downturn of the mouth hinted that more was going through her mind. "I can't fit into all the boxes."

Callie nodded and kept running, wordless.

"Everybody keeps trying to shove me in a different direction," Jenessa continued, breaking the silence. "I mean, everything was going fine and all but now . . ." She lapsed back into her thoughts.

"I was supposed to be a doctor," said Jenessa.

"Lot of science," said Callie.

"Yeah, that's why I said 'supposed,' " said Jenessa, "but now I don't know what I'm going into. You know where you're going at least, right?" Jenessa still had her eyes on the ground in front of her and didn't wait for an answer. "We graduate this year and I have no idea what I'm supposed to do next."

Callie thought about it. "Maybe just go 'undecided' for your major and figure it out when you get to wherever?"

"Yeah," said Jenessa, "I guess." She glanced over to Callie and flashed a quick smile. "I could go into winemaking."

"Where do you get a degree in that?"

"Cornell." Jenessa laughed. "My dad would flip. Big bucks and booze."

Callie laughed with her. "Yeah, but it sounds pretty cool. Do you have to be twenty-one?"

"I have no idea."

Callie could see the opening in the tree line signaling the turnoff for the single track back through the forest. Impulsively, she sped up.

"Race you," she challenged Jenessa with a grin as she began to run away.

"Hey, hold up a sec."

Something in Jenessa's voice made Callie turn back, dropping back to the slow jog they had been holding.

"What?" Callie asked.

Jenessa was walking.

"You okay?"

Jenessa stood there, a light sheen of sweat on her skin, the buzz of insects louder than their breathing. Her eyes were troubled again and she searched Callie's face.

"Doc says we have a chance," she said. "To win, like you said."

Callie detected undercurrents of doubt and hope combined in the other girl's voice. She nodded and said with more confidence than she felt, "We do."

"That's what Doc said," the other girl said, "on Saturday."

"I thought you said he yelled at you."

"That, too." A grimace flashed briefly, and then disappeared. "He got on me because I ran really bad."

"That's not like Doc."

Jenessa looked off into the woods. "He said that I've been racing all season not to lose instead of trying to win."

"Except you've won everything except against Fairchild," said Callie.

Jenessa shook her head. "He's right." She peered at Callie. "You got Mattie to come back."

Callie shrugged. "The team needs her," she said. In her mind, she could picture the perfume bottle on the dresser. Private things and not to be shared. Callie matched Jenessa's gaze. "We need everybody."

"That's what Doc said, said he needed me to run to win instead of just trying to beat Mattie." She paused and said with another small grimace, "He said I was letting the team down and letting myself down." Callie couldn't see Jenessa's eyes under her sunglasses but couldn't remember ever seeing Jenessa lose composure like this. It sounded like she was close to crying.

"Ouch," said Callie. "That's why you weren't going after Mattie today?"

"You thought I'd act snotty?"

Callie hesitated. "Pretty much."

"Do you like her?"

Callie started to answer and then stopped to really think about the question. Slowly, she said, "Yes, I think I do." She heard the surprise in her own voice. "I think she has boxes of her own."

Jenessa frowned. "I don't think I want to." She began walking toward the trail. Callie fell in next to her. "It doesn't matter, though, does it?"

"You know, Doc is putting you into another box."

"You should know, it's the same box you shoved me into."

"Me?"

"The 'lead the team to State' box," said Jenessa, glancing at her. "Was it your idea or Doc's that we were going to win State?"

Callie thought it over. "I don't know. It was just one of those—bam!—kind of things. Maybe both of us."

Jenessa stopped and turned to face Callie. "How close are we really?"

"Close enough that we can take them, not so close we're going to blow them away. We're going to need to be a little lucky, no injuries and everybody races out of their minds." Mentally, Callie crossed her fingers.

"At least you're honest."

Callie considered her soberly. "Yeah," she said. Lightly, she added, "Wanna know a secret about boxes?"

Callie could see squint marks around the sunglasses as Jenessa looked at her, like she wasn't sure that Callie wasn't poking fun at her.

"What secret?"

Callie pointed around to the empty dirt road and surrounding trees. "Listen. Just squirrels and birds and bugs. No boxes. Out here, nobody can take anything from us or force us to do anything we don't want. You just come out here and run like heck, forget everything else."

Jenessa looked around as Callie talked.

"It'll be waiting when we get back."

"Yeah, but it's not here now."

Jenessa smirked, a quick flitter on the lips. "That's pretty corny."

Callie opened her mouth to reply but, as she watched, Jenessa's smirk tranformed into a smile.

"Corny, but you're right," said Jenessa. She glanced from Callie to the woods and laughed as she bolted for the trail. "Race you!"

Her laugh hung in the air and it took a second before Callie had a chance to process what Jenessa said. It hit her and she bolted off after the other girl.

"CHEATER!"

Another laugh floated back as Callie plunged onto the shady trail behind Jenessa.

Chapter 39

"Hey, you going to hog the bathroom all morning?"

Callie checked herself in the mirror one more time, gave herself a smile of approval, and opened the bathroom door.

"You can have it," she told Jen. Her sister brushed past her, in a hurry to shower. Callie crossed the hall to her room, where she had already laid out her clothes on the bed. She dropped her bathrobe and stepped out of her slippers. She quickly wriggled on her nicest jeans and slipped into a frilly green blouse, leaving the top button open and fluffing her loose hair over the collar to get it to drop across her shoulders.

"Hurry it up, you two. You're going to be late," her mom yelled from downstairs.

"Be down in a minute," Callie shouted back. She heard the shower shut off.

She looked at her beat-up running shoes. Nope, not today. She skipped over them and picked up a pair of low black heels, grabbing them by the straps along with a pair of knee-highs. She hefted her school bag onto her other shoulder and snagged her run gear with her free hand. Bags protruding from both sides, she made her way down to the kitchen.

Her mom glanced at Callie. "Breakfast is ready."

She studied her daughter as Callie slid on the tan-colored knee-highs. A minute later, she began to dish scrambled eggs and sausage onto a plate.

"If you want toast, you'll have to make it," her mother said. She took a step toward the stairs. "Jen!" she shouted.

"Coming!" Jen replied, and Callie could hear her banging her closet door shut. A moment later, Jen was skipping down the steps. On the last step, her foot slipped off the tread and she landed flatfooted and hard, arms flailing as she barely maintained her balance.

"Owww," she said as a grimace crossed her face.

"No breaking ankles before State," Callie admonished without looking up as she snagged a sausage with her fork.

"Oh, thank you for the sympathy," Jen retorted as she leaned on the bannister and shook the ankle. "No, really, I'm quite all right."

"I'm going to be home late tonight, Mom," Callie said. "I'm studying with Mattie after practice."

"What about me? You're my ride home." Jen sat down and her mom handed her a plate. She took a sip of orange juice, giving Callie an appraising look. "And how come you're all dressed up?"

"You can wait for me or maybe get Dad to swing by and pick you up," Callie said.

"I'll ride with Dad," Jen decided. "So why are you dressed up?"

Callie's mom intervened. "Eat, Jen. The two of you are already running late."

"Just curious," said Jen.

"Just eat."

Ten minutes later, they were almost ready to go. Callie fished out her keys from her purse and tossed them over to Jen.

"Hey, can you start the car?"

Jen snagged the keys and, hauling book and gear bags, went outside. Callie bent over to slip on her shoes. When she sat up, she saw her mother scrutinizing her. Callie gave a little shrug that elicited a small laugh from her mom.

"You look very nice." Reaching out, Sarah gave her eldest daughter a hug. "Have a good day, okay?"

Callie stood off to one side to avoid the stream of mostly groggy teenagers flowing into the school. The fall morning was cold but she had left her jacket in her locker. She watched the parking lot and saw Mark pull in. As usual, he had Mattie with him, and she saw Callie first as the pair crossed the asphalt lot to the walkway in front of the school. Her alert eyes gave Callie a quick once-over, top to bottom. Subtly, she started to open space between her and Mark.

Mark saw her three seconds later and she watched his body language change from easygoing and relaxed to hostile in the space of two steps. He forged ahead, pretending not to look at her, but every other step he would snatch a glance at her. He turned to say something to Mattie but discovered that, while he had been distracted, she had veered off completely and was walking away.

"Mark."

Callie left her voice noncommittal, but even so, several students glanced at her, then at Mark, and at least two eyebrows were raised. Callie ignored them while resigning herself to the fact that she and Mark, fodder for much conversation last week, were again going to be a hot topic of gossip.

He made eye contact briefly but showed no indication of slowing so she stepped away from the side and moved in front of him. A step and a half away from her, he slowed and, without looking at her, sidestepped to go around. She stepped with him, closing the gap, and reached out with her right forefinger, placing it in the crease between the muscles of his chest. Her touch was light, close to a caress, but powerful enough to bring Mark to a full stop.

Callie had spent the entire previous day rehearsing speeches, discarding them one after the other as mushy or maudlin or dumb and frequently all three at the same time. She had finally settled on a mature speech and practiced it until she had it perfect, the tone reasonable and the words sounding just right, just like it should when you want to start a serious relationship.

What came out was, "Hey."

She was staring into his eyes and she could see the hostility fading, his features softening but confused and very cautious. His eyes roamed, looking down at her—even with her in heels, he was six inches taller than she was. After a quick embarrassed glance, he avoided the one open button on her blouse. She realized how close they were standing to each other but didn't move away and she didn't move her finger. Unseen and unheard, the majority of students went around them, joking and chuckling with their friends.

"Want to talk?" she asked him.

Mark shook his head. "I'm not good with words," he said, diverting his gaze.

"Then just look at me," Callie said, pausing while she waited for him to do so, "and I'll do the talking for now."

He nodded.

"I was an idiot," she said, and his eyes narrowed slightly at the word, "and I would love to go to Homecoming with you. I'm sorry."

Her finger was making tiny circles on his chest as she spoke. Through the thin shirt he wore, she could feel the heat of his body.

"Instead, we'll have to start somewhere else, not Homecoming. Just so you know, if you ask me out to a movie, I'll say yes. If you ask me out to dinner, I'll say yes. And, as of right now, I'm still available for Prom."

She looked up at him. "This is where you ask me out on a date."

He met her eyes, face flushed. "A . . . date?"

"A date. You. Me. Dinner. Or a movie. Or just a walk."

She waited.

"Walk?" Mark repeated, confused.

"I would love to," said Callie. "We don't have a race this weekend, so how about Saturday afternoon."

Mark nodded his head, eyes slightly glazed, as the first bell rang.

"Lean down a little bit."

"Huh?"

"Lean down," she said, showing him by almost laying her head against his chest, then lifting it back up. As he did what she asked, she went to the tips of her toes and gave him a peck of a kiss on his right cheek.

"Have a good day and I'll see you at practice," she breathed softly into his ear.

He was standing stock-still as she sashayed away.

"She's a little slow," Anna said.

"Definitely," agreed Hanna, "but dang, when she figures it out, she doesn't waste any time."

Callie looked at her friends with a sour expression.

Alerted by Jen, they had been waiting for her just inside the main doors.

"The boy didn't stand a chance," said Anna.

"Were you taking notes?" Hanna asked her sister.

"I was too busy watching. Did you see Mark's face when she kissed him? He looked like he had been hit by a truck."

"I liked the finger in the chest thing," said Hanna. She looked at Callie. "Did you plan that or was it just a 'it happened' thing?"

"You two are going to harass me about this forever, aren't you?" asked Callie.

The twins looked at each other and shrugged.

"Yes," they replied in synchronized voices.

"I'm waiting until we get home," offered Jen with a mischievous smile. "Dad's going to freak."

"I have to get to class," Callie said, ignoring her sister and moving toward the sanctuary of the school. Over her shoulder, she heard the twins talking as they made their way in the opposite direction down the hall.

"Practice is going to be a hoot," said Anna. Hanna's reply was lost but Callie could hear them both laughing.

Chapter 40

Saturday they went for a walk.

Mark picked her up from her house—coming in to greet Callie's parents—early in the afternoon. Callie heard him driving in and came downstairs, frowning at her dad, who was feigning intense concentration on his gun-cleaning supplies and the 9mm parts sitting in front of him. To one side of the table, he had placed a shotgun.

"Really, Dad?" Callie said as she went to the door to meet Mark. "Isn't that a little obvious?"

Hank looked up. "Obvious?" He wagged his head side to side, a slight motion though his eyes held steady. "I was aiming for clarity." Across the kitchen, her mother, helping Jen bake a batch of cookies, snagged her youngest daughter by the collar of her shirt as Jen tried to beat Callie to the door.

"Here," she said, passing Jen the bowl, "stir this while I add the raisins . . ."

Callie tried to rush Mark back out of the house but it was twenty minutes later before they actually left.

As Mark promised, he brought her home in time for dinner. Callie watched Mark's Jeep until it left the driveway. She was softly humming as she came in.

Jen, nearly bursting with curiosity, pestered her for details but Callie just smiled at her and refused to discuss it.

It was a nice day. A walk with Mark—and driving Jen nuts.

The team crushed the competition at the next race and the one after that. Mattie was back and running better than ever. Whatever doubts Jenessa had, she was using as motivation, and she was asserting herself out on the racecourse. The whole team was loose and relaxed and exuded confidence. Looking down the line at her team, Callie was reminded of the Fairchild squad, lean and fast and focused.

The fiercest battles were taking place far from the front. Jen was still improving and Callie was running out of tricks. Twice in a row Jen beat her, sticking to her like glue for as long as she could and using her faster kick at the finish to blaze past Callie when the chance presented itself.

The last race before districts had been another hilly one with long, slow upgrades that Callie ground out using her superior strength, then, released from gravity, flying down the hills, "flowing like water" as she called it. Even then, the gap had been much closer than anybody expected. Jen was carving out a niche as the best freshman in the district.

She also wasn't apologizing anymore when she beat Callie.

Only Lily wasn't getting faster and stronger. Before each practice, Callie wrapped her shins to try to help with the pain, but it was clear that the younger girl was struggling. Doc held her out of the last race to protect her legs from the hills.

Lily had stood there with her arms crossed, and glared at him. "I can run."

"Not today," said Doc. The deeper into the season they got, the testier he was.

She had dressed out anyway and accompanied the team to the meet, hobbling from point to point to cheer the girls as they ran past, then did the same again with the rest of the team to cheer the boys. After the meet, Callie had made her sit with bags of ice strapped to her shins until it was time to get back on the bus for the two-hour drive back home.

By districts, Doc was uncharacteristically snappy. The weather had turned the day before the meet and the cool and clear days of fall had devolved into driving rain, achingly cold water sluicing diagonally across the course. And Jenessa was sick.

Doc hovered. "How are you doing, Jenessa?"

Jenessa was curled in a sleeping bag, shivering from the lingering fever.

"I'm running," she told Doc. "Deal."

He went to get the race numbers from the coach's packet and kept looking over to her doubtfully. He checked the weather again. It was still lousy. He checked Lily's taped legs. He glanced at his star runner quaking. He peeked from under the canopy at the gray above and checked his watch.

Turning back, he found the twins situated in front of him.

"Coach," said Anna.

"You're kinda—" said Hanna.

"—freaking us out."

Doc looked to the identical faces. "What?"

"You're pacing . . ."

". . . and growling . . ."

". . . but not the funny growling . . ."

They swapped a look and Hanna shrugged. *Might as well,* the shrug said.

"... but kind of ..."

"... worried ..."

"... like, way stressed."

Callie watched from the corner of her eye and felt a little sympathy for Doc. He didn't stand a chance against Anna and Hanna. They were steamrolling him.

"I am, am I?" said Doc, the white eyebrows squeezing down over glinting eyes.

"Uh-hunh," said Anna.

Doc started to speak but was plowed under by Hanna.

"So breathe," she said.

Anna: "In ..."

"But—" Doc tried to slip in.

    Hanna: "... out ..."

        Anna: "... in ..."

            Hanna: "... out ..."

"Besides, we already got this," finished Anna. She smiled at Doc, teeth gleaming in the gloom.

"You never 'got this,' " said Doc.

"We got a plan," said Anna.

Doc looked confused. "Who has a plan?" Doc usually had a talk with the team before races to cover race strategy and tactics but had held off today, still not certain that Jenessa could actually race and hoping for the weather to change. It was still forty-five minutes to the start of the race and a few minutes before they would even start warming up. Plenty of time ...

"Cap't Callie," said Anna, pointing over to where Callie sat next to Jen, sharing a heavy quilt. Doc followed Anna's finger to Callie, but she had studiously averted her gaze, looking out over the golf course to a foursome finishing up in the pouring rain. By the time the runners were on the course, all the golfers would be done.

Doc looked back to the twins. "So what's the plan?"

"Run like hell, win this thing, and get back on the bus," said Hanna, beaming at him.

Doc's lips twitched and he said, "That's the plan?"

"Uh-hunh," they both agreed.

Doc's lined face broke into a roguish grin. "I can live with that." He suddenly looked stern, though his eyes gave him away. "Run like heck, ladies—this rain stinks!"

From the sleeping bag, Jenessa stuck out her hand, right thumb up.

The race itself was the most miserable that Callie ever ran. Temperatures were stuck just above freezing and, once the race started, it seemed as though the wind was taking a perverse pleasure in lashing them with hard, stinging droplets. They had left a mountain of warm-ups at the start line when they stripped down to race, and the starter wasted no time in getting them onto the course.

Jenessa struggled but Mattie stayed beside her. Jenessa later told Callie, "She never shut up, talked the whole way around the course." Jenessa seemed almost embarrassed by it. Callie and Jen paced each other for the first half of the race, but on the mostly flat course, Jen gradually pulled into the lead and, as she had before, put it away on the kick, finishing four seconds ahead of her older sister. The only runner not in the top ten was Lily.

They watched the boys qualify for State from the bus.

Chapter 41

"Welcome to State."

Doc stood in front of the team as they finished their dinner in a small meeting room at the hotel. Earlier that day, the runners had walked the championship course with Doc pointing out particular hills, slow spots, and, at the back portion of the course, the loneliness away from the crowd where focus was crucial. Now, Doc presented the race plans, dispatching the boys first before briefing the girls.

"Once we get warmed up and we're on the line, I want Jenessa and Mattie at the front, the twins right behind them. Callie and Jen," he looked at the sisters, "you're right behind them. Lily, park right behind Callie.

"Make sure you get out in good order—no running each other over. At least one girl from some team goes down every year, let's make sure it isn't us. Everybody charges that first hill so be careful not to go out too fast, especially you, Jen."

Jen bobbed her head.

"I want you to stick with Callie." He focused on Callie. "Push the pace a bit and, if the Fairchild girls take off, you're going to have to go with them. That pretty much applies to everybody except you, Mattie." He looked apologetically toward the girl seated at the end of the table, her plate of pasta wiped spotless with garlic bread.

"You're going to be stuck on an island. None of the Fairchild girls except Roxanne can run with you."

Mattie looked at him impassively.

"The important thing for you is going to be holding position. We can't have another team slip a runner between us and cost us points. That applies pretty much to all of you. Don't get so focused on the Fairchild girls that you lose track of the other runners.

"That last little hill before the long fairway is where we're going to make our move. I want you to close up on them right before that hill, make up a little ground on the roller-coaster section," he said, referring to the series of small ups and downs that ran around the green for hole 14. "Close on them and then take them on the last uphill. After that, it's all downhill to the finish. Kick it in with everything you got. If we can catch them flatfooted on the hill, we can build a bit of momentum that they won't be able to recover from."

Doc looked at his team.

"All of you have had a great season. I just want to tell you before tomorrow, no matter what happens, I'm proud as heck for everything you've put into the season and proud as heck to be your coach.

"Now get out of here. Go enjoy the mall." He looked at the boys. "And stay out of trouble," he added.

The lights adorning the large tree reflected in Mattie's eyes as she studied the ficus that stretched two stories into the air, nearly touching the skylight of the mall. The shoppers—many of them young and trim and wearing running shoes and walking in groups of seven or eight—dodged around the Cloverland girls.

"*Crazy,*" Mattie said. She continued to gawk at the tree, planted in the indoor courtyard of the mall.

Hanna laughed. "We come here every time we make State."

"That's once," clarified Anna.

"The malls in Seattle are better," said Jenessa. "They have way more stores."

Callie smiled as Mattie looked at Jenessa with suspicion.

"She's right, but this beats anything in town for us," she said. "Come on, let's go. Doc only gave us an hour and then we have to get back to the hotel."

Together the girls ambled off, Mattie still swiveling her head to take in all the sound and color and confusion. The air was perfumed with a mix of scents from the profusion of stores. Jenessa smirked at the look on Lily's face as a girl, pale-faced with bright red lipstick and dressed entirely in black, slouched past with her boyfriend, who sported a tall, jet-black Mohawk.

"Hey, whoa!" said Jen, making a beeline to the other side of the broad concourse.

Callie looked to the store that Jen was headed for and sighed.

"Doc said to stay out of trouble," she said, calling after her.

"I don't think she can hear you," said Anna.

"I don't think she wants to hear you," said Hanna with a grin. The two of them started across, joining Jen under the Victoria's Secret sign. Jen stood in front of the plate glass with her head cocked over to one side, studying a bra and panties set adorning a mannequin in the window. The rest of the girls followed.

"I was expecting more."

Hanna looked at the display. "I think they keep the good stuff inside."

Jen glanced wistfully at the door. "Yeah," she said as the others joined them. She studied the mannequin critically. "I don't think that would fit."

Mattie laughed at her. "If it did, you wouldn't be able to run." The expression on her face changed and her eyes became unfocused.

"Cinnamon buns," she said.

As soon as she said it, the others could detect the sweet aroma. Callie felt a pleasant rumble in her belly as the scent became stronger. She scanned the concourse, gaze skipping past the beauty supply and clothing stores on the ground floor, then shifted to the upper story.

"Up there, I think," she said, pointing to a bakery above them. "Next to the jewelry store."

Mattie nibbled on her bottom lip. "I'm hungry," she said, staring up.

"I wouldn't mind a smoothie," said Jenessa with a shrug.

As the girls sauntered toward the escalators, Callie saw the Fairchild team at the end of the long walkway, dressed in their team warm-ups, stopping to loiter in front of one of the shops.

The bakery was situated at the outside edge of the food court. With so many options—more than in their entire town— the girls split up, Callie and Mattie opting for the cinnamon rolls while Jenessa got her smoothie. Lily tagged along with Jenessa and ended up with a tropical fruit concoction. She took a tentative taste and surprise lit up her face as the flavor hit her tongue. The twins and Jen picked up iced lattes with double shots of espresso.

They reassembled at the railing overlooking the mall, scouting the terrain. At the far end was a bookseller, but Callie knew better than to suggest that they visit. As she looked around, she saw the boys chasing each other, sprinting up on the down escalator, Mark in the lead.

"Uh-oh," said Jen. She pointed. Mall security had spotted the ruckus and the guard was stalking toward the miscreants that had interrupted his dinner.

"MARK!" Mattie bellowed, her voice cutting through the hubbub of the shoppers. She pointed to the guard approaching the top of the escalator.

Mark shot a startled glance to where she pointed. He burst into a big smile, and with a wave, he reversed direction, charging at his teammates, to get them moving in the right direction. They all got turned around and managed to avoid landing in a muddled heap at the bottom. With another wave, they took off at a brisk jog toward the exits. The security guard *hrumphed* at the top of the escalator and hitched his belt up as he watched them disappear.

On the far side of the promenade that encircled the upper floor, the Fairchild team had watched with amusement. As Callie made eye contact with them, Roxanne, the team's best runner, held up her right hand, two fingers extended in a peace sign. Roxanne turned to her team and said something that got them all laughing and, as Callie watched, Roxanne folded down her middle finger and extended her thumb, forming an L. Callie flushed with anger as the Fairchild girl turned and pointed the forefinger right at Jenessa. The Fairchild team turned, laughter reaching across the intervening gap.

The sudden intake of breath beside her let her know that Jenessa had seen the same thing. As Jenessa started to raise her own hand to respond, Callie saw Mattie's hand grasp their teammate's forearm.

"Not here," she said.

Jenessa, face red with anger and eyes bulging, turned on her. "That's bull!"

Mattie released Jenessa's arm. "Don't let her do it, don't let her get into your head." Her eyes reflected the same anger the other two felt, but there was a purposeful calmness there too.

"But—"

"Don't let her in," said Mattie in a quiet voice. "She wants you to think she owns you, but she wouldn't have done that if she wasn't a bit worried too." She looked at the backs of the Fairchild runners as they walked away. She stared right into Jenessa's eyes. "We get even tomorrow," she said. She still hadn't raised her voice, but the intensity in her tone interrupted the conversation between the twins and Jen. None of them had seen the gesture.

Quickly Jenessa explained, her hands slashing through the hand signs that Roxanne had used.

"How rude!" said Anna, her forehead furrowing as her eyes narrowed.

Callie kept her voice matter-of-fact though she was seething inside. "Mattie's right," she said with a dismissive toss of her head toward the other team. "Save it for tomorrow." She looked at her watch. "We have enough time to hit the bookstore."

"I want to . . ." Jen's voice petered out and she shrugged. "Jerks."

"We might as well head back to the hotel," said Anna, sounding dejected.

"Or we could go find them," offered Hanna. For once, she wasn't smiling.

Anna looked sharply at her twin. "Not a good idea."

"I got some ideas on what we could say," said Jen. "And I bet you ten bucks I can get it all out without a single four-letter word."

"How about a five-letter word?" asked Hanna.

"Chill, people," said Callie. "We're not going to go looking for trouble . . . yet. Let's just get out of here and go watch a movie or something tonight." She glanced down the concourse and popped the last of the sweet roll into her mouth. "I want a good night's sleep. We have some butt to kick tomorrow."

That got a little laugh from Lily but there was some grumbling from the other girls. They finished their snacks and headed out.

The boys were waiting just outside the doors when they emerged into the bright lights. Callie shook her head as they took turns throwing pieces of bark at each other. Mark was the first to notice the mood of the girls and slid over to stand next to Callie.

"What's up?" He sounded puzzled.

"Ran into the Fairchild team inside," Callie said, "and they were their usual charming selves." She quickly recounted the events.

"Wow," Mark replied, and then ducked quickly as a chunk of bark flew by. "Hey, no throwing stuff at the pretty girls!" He turned back to face Callie. "Not very classy."

Will hollered back, "I was aiming at you."

Callie glanced at Mark. "Nope. Even the twins are mad," she said before correcting herself as the twins started to gather bits of the landscaping, "—were mad." She shouted over to the girls, "Watch out for Nate, he's sneaking around the bush."

"We can take care of ourselves," said Mattie, timing her release perfectly to catch Nate on the shoulder as he emerged from hiding.

Jenessa retreated to stand next to Mark and the three of them watched as the twins and Jen ganged up on the freshmen boys while Lily joined forces with Mattie, pelting Nate. It wasn't really fair, thought Callie. The twins and Jen, normally hyper anyway, were stoked on the caffeine from the double shots in the lattes. The result was a nearly continuous bombardment from the girls.

Jenessa looked at the two team captains. "Not exactly staying out of trouble, are they?"

Callie smiled. "Not exactly getting into it either."

"It only counts if you get caught," added Mark.

"Like the escalator?" asked Jenessa. "What if the guard had been at the bottom?"

Mark laughed. "We'd have had to run faster and get to the top."

A group of older ladies entering the mall gave the cavorting teenagers sour looks as an errant wood chip sailed past them.

"Sorry about that," Mark said to them, and then shouted to the team. "Yo, ya'll! Time to pack it in and get back to our rooms before Doc has a conniption."

Mattie threw one last chunk of bark at Nate, just missing, and said, "No problem."

The other kids slowly wound down, unloading the last of their ammunition at any handy target.

"Let's get this cleaned up," said Callie, pointing to the mess of the sidewalk.

"Yes, Mom," said Jen, but she began to scuff bits of the landscaping back into the planters. In short order, the walkway was cleared. Straggling out, the team headed into the parking lot, toward the brightly lit hotel that sat on a short hillside overlooking the mall and, in the distance, the Columbia River. The last twilight had faded a half hour ago and the sodium lights cast a yellow glow to the parked cars. Used to stars sparkling in crystal air, Callie found the lighting disorienting. She leaned in toward Mark and he put an arm over her shoulder. It felt right and she snugged in a bit closer.

At the front of the pack, Jen and Will walked next to each other as everybody stayed to the right of the driving lane and close to the parked vehicles. The twins jabbered at each other a few yards behind them. Jenessa walked alone, immersed in thought. Worrying, Callie knew.

Callie saw Will reach into the pocket of his windbreaker with his right hand, saying something to Jen. Callie could hear her infectious giggle. Will's hand came out of his pocket, holding a wood chip for inspection, and Jen's giggle turned to a laugh. He slowed a half step and playfully cocked his arm to lob it at Jen, saying something to her.

"No way," Jen taunted Will. She sprinted away, looking over her left shoulder as he brought his arm back.

Callie's laugh choked in her throat as she watched the backup lights on a large pickup truck flash on just in front of Jen on her blind side. Beside her, Mark stiffened, and his grip on her shoulder tightened as he watched and did the same calculations.

"JEN!"

Her sister was nearly to a stop when the driver of the truck punched the accelerator. Jen heard the throaty roar of the diesel engine of the truck and Callie could see Jen's eyes get huge as she whirled to face the sound of the truck rolling at her. She stood there, frozen in place, and then, in slow motion, began to lean away from the threat.

As Callie watched, the truck hurtled toward her sister, the brake lights coming on too late. She knew it was too late and she heard the sound of the bumper hitting Jen's leg. Jen emitted a surprisingly quiet "oomph" as she crumpled. The truck came to rest partially over her sister's limp body.

Chapter 42

"JEN!"

Before the truck had rocked to a stop, Callie had shrugged out of Mark's arm and was running toward Jen, weaving past the other runners. She heard Mark running behind her and the slamming of the truck door.

"Oh, sweet Jesus," said the driver of the truck as he cleared the tailgate, "a little girl." He was an older man, dressed in jeans and a well-worn flannel jacket.

Jen was lying there with her eyes open and unfocused. Callie stopped next to her and knelt. She took a deep breath and a calm dropped over her, the panic shoved back as she focused on the first-aid training she had gotten at the hospital over the summer. The rest of the team surrounded her, smothering.

"Don't move, okay," she said to her sister. Jen focused on her face and nodded. Her eyes were still huge, and she was breathing fast.

"Is she okay?" asked the man, distress plain on his face.

Callie turned to Mark. "Keep them back. We need to block cars."

She fumbled in her pocket, found her phone, and pulled it out. "Somebody call Doc and my folks." She looked at the shocked faces around her. She fumbled for her phone and lobbed it to Jenessa. "Call."

She turned back to Jen. Her sister stared up at her.

"Did I wet my pants?" she asked.

Callie rocked back a little and looked under the bumper.

"I don't think so."

"Good. I was worried about that."

"Is she okay?" asked the man again. He stood at the corner of the truck by the tailgate, shifting from foot to foot, unwilling to come closer.

Callie looked up and the hot exhaust from the diesel engine hit her in the face. "Turn off your truck!" A little of her anger bled into her voice.

The man winced and nodded. "I'll call my insurance company," he said as a flash of light lit the scene, startling both of them. Callie glanced up—Jenessa was taking pictures with her phone.

"Documentation," Jenessa explained. "Your folks are on their way."

"I've got insurance," muttered the driver as he fumbled with the ignition key. The rumble of the engine died. "What were you kids doing out here anyway?"

The kids, spread out by Mark to direct traffic around the downed girl, muttered. Shock and fear were progressing quckly to anger. A small crowd was beginning to gather, peering intently around each other to get teh best view.

Callie ignored him. "Jen," she said, "do you have any back pain? Can you feel all your fingers and toes?"

"I can pull the truck up," suggested the man.

Callie shot him a harsh look. "Don't move the truck. We'll wait for help. It won't be long."

He withered in her gaze and nodded. "I'll call my insurance."

Jen looked up at her. "Thanks. I didn't want to get run over again tonight."

Callie felt some of the tension relax. "What hurts?" she asked.

"Mostly just my leg," said Jen, "it hurts." She tried to move it and a grimace twisted her face.

"Don't move it yet," advised Callie. "I don't see any bleeding. Once help gets here, we'll get you out of there and find out what's up, okay?" She tried to keep her voice calm and professional but she could hear some of the brittleness of worry in the words.

"I'm sorry, sis," said Jen, so low that only Callie could hear.

Callie put a reassuring hand on Jen's shoulder.

The security guard from the mall was the first to arrive, huffing as he shoved his way past the kids and scowling at Mark, who still had a phone to his ear.

"She hurt?" he demanded. He glanced around the circle of kids, and then at the position of the truck. "You're blocking the lane. Folks got to get by."

The focus of anger shifted from the pickup driver to the mall cop. The kids forming the semicircle closed more tightly around the pickup. Jen very quietly began grumbling. Callie caught a couple of words that would have gotten her in trouble if their mother had heard. Callie looked up from where she was kneeling, half-turning to glare at the mall cop. "We're trying to make sure that no one else gets hurt."

"Don't know why you should be screwing around out here in the first place."

The driver, sensing an ally, said, "I was just backing up and this kid ran right behind me." He offered his insurance card to the guard. "I got insurance."

Mark switched his gaze from the guard to the driver, glaring at him with a hint of contempt as he put away his phone. "Yeah, don't walk in the mall parking lot and you won't get hit by idiots backing out at a hundred miles per hour." He turned and faced Callie. "The cops say that they won't send anybody out unless it's a major injury or alcohol was involved."

"That's right, this is private property," said the guard, hitching up his belt where the oversized flashlight, holstered, was dragging it down. "They don't come out unless I tell them to, mostly." He stared sharply at Mark. "You're the kid on the escalator."

Mark was interrupted before he could reply.

"Easy, son," said Doc as he slipped past, giving him a squeeze on the shoulder as he did. He looked at Callie.

"She okay?" he said to Callie.

Callie nodded. "I think so; at least, I don't think there's anything major wrong. No bleeding and she's being a smart-aleck."

"Good." He faced the guard. "Thank you for organizing the kids to set up a security perimeter," he said. "That was most helpful."

The man looked uncomfortable. "Wouldn't need it if they were where they should be," he said, his face looking as though he were sucking lemons.

Doc transferred his attention to the driver. "The parents will be here shortly," he said, flashing a fast glance at Mark. Mark inclined his head toward Jenessa.

"They're coming," she said. "I called them while Mark called you and the police."

"Good," said Doc. He looked back to the driver. "When they get here, we'll get information swapped and get you on your way."

"Okay, fine," said the driver, "but she ran behind me, it's not my fault."

"Excuse me!" said an indignant Jen from under the truck. "Since when do pedestrians not have right of way?" She started to lift herself onto her elbows. "*Ouch.*"

Callie put a hand back on her shoulder and Jenifer settled back to the ground.

"He's not allowed to run people over just because he has a big ol' wannabe cowboy truck," Jen said. As she spoke, Sarah and Hank were stepping through the perimeter. Both went immediately to Jen's side, Sarah dropping down next to Callie, Hank leaning over them all.

"You okay, baby?"

"Mostly," replied Jen. "I feel kind of dumb lying here."

Hank, grim-faced, went over to Doc and the pickup driver. "Howdy, Doc," he said. He held out his hand to the driver. "I'm Hank Reardon."

The older man stood a little taller, exposing a rotund midsection as the flannel jacket pulled open. He glared at Callie's dad before taking the proffered hand, shaking once and releasing it quickly. Unconsciously, he wiped his hands on his pants.

"Jeff Anderson," said the driver. "Your girl ran right behind me. I didn't have a chance to stop or nothing."

Hank gave Anderson a withering look. "We'll worry about that later. I'll have you give your information to my wife. She can take it back to the office and discuss it with the other lawyers Monday morning."

Anderson blanched. "She's a lawyer?"

"She works at McSorely and Harms," said Hank with a hard edge to his smile. "She's used to handling this sort of case, knows the paperwork."

He turned to Doc. "If Jen's not hurt too bad, we should get her out from under the truck. We need to get her to a doctor."

"I can pull up the truck," Anderson said, repeating his earlier offer.

"No. Give us two minutes and we'll have her out," said Hank. He looked at the insurance card that Anderson was crushing in his fist. "You might want to get your license and registration out. I'll ask my wife to come over." Again, he used that hard smile but his eyes stayed grim.

Together with Doc and Mark, the three of them got positioned to ease Jen out. Hank and Doc were on either side of Jen's hips, reaching under the chrome bumper, and Mark was stabilizing her shoulders. On the count of three, they all lifted. Jen gave a little cry of pain as her hips left the ground, and then they had her out, standing on one leg.

Hank brought the car over and loaded Jen into the backseat, helping her stretch her injured leg on the seat. Sarah, finished with Anderson, walked over. Meanwhile, Doc had gathered the rest of the team. They were waiting for Callie before heading back to the hotel.

"We'll call you when we know what's happening," Sarah said to Callie. "Try not to worry," she added uselessly. Sympathy filled her eyes and she gave her daughter a hug before climbing into the car.

Callie waited for the call in the lobby of the hotel. She sat in one of the armchairs, nursing a cup of hot chocolate and nibbling a cookie, more for something to do than because she was hungry. Jenessa, Mattie, and Lily were in a separate connecting room while Jen and Callie shared their room with the twins, but they flocked into Callie's room while they waited for news. The constant chatter and speculation drove Callie out.

She was staring at the fake fire, oblivious to the other guests wandering past—many of them fellow competitors—when Mattie appeared at the end of the hallway. Mattie looked around as though she was wavering, until she saw Callie and strode into the lobby toward her. She flopped into the chair next to Callie.

"Anything?"

"Not yet."

The fake fire flickered but added nothing to the brightly lit lobby except the distraction of its dance. Mattie was the first to speak again.

"What do you think of Doc's plan for tomorrow?"

Callie pulled her eyes away from the fire. "What about it?"

"I was thinking . . ." Mattie said, and suddenly looked uncertain. She squared up her shoulders and a wry smile flashed across her face. "Dangerous habit," she said with a derisive snort but continued. "Anyway, I was thinking that Roxanne is like me."

"In what way?" asked Callie. "You'd never have acted like that at the mall." Her eyes showed her anger.

"Not like that," said Mattie. "The way we run." She paused. "Why has Jenessa never beaten her?"

Callie thought about it for a few seconds. "Well, for starters, I've never seen them racing. They're always way out in front of me so I'm guessing some." She thought, taking a deep breath as she did. "From what I can see and what Jenessa and Doc have said, Roxanne keeps edging her at the finish. Jenessa has gotten closer since we were freshmen but Roxanne is just a little bit faster."

It was Mattie's turn to stare at the fire. Callie waited, giving her time to think. Mattie was bouncing her head side to side lightly as if she was arguing with herself.

"Yeah, she did that to me in the eight hundred," Mattie said. "She sat just off my shoulder into the last two hundred and out-kicked me." Her face contorted. "That pissed me off."

Callie waited for Mattie to come to the point. She glanced surreptitiously at her phone—still nothing from her folks.

"Roxanne's a big kicker, bigger than me, maybe—but Jenessa's been kicking my butt all season, right?"

Callie nodded and said, "Yeah."

"How?"

Callie paused, not wanting to hurt Mattie's feelings. She sounded almost apologetic when she answered. "She's fitter than you." Callie met Mattie's eyes. "She's fitter and she lets you set the pace until you run yourself out. She lets you kill yourself so that you can't out-kick her and then she grinds past you in the last mile." She shrugged. "You let her."

Mattie stared back. "That's what Doc said, too."

"Then why are you asking me?"

"What if we did that to Roxanne?"

Callie mulled it over. "You mean Jenessa forces the pace?" She shook her head. "She won't do it. Roxanne's psyched her out so many times that Jenessa twitches when you mention her name."

"No, I mean, what if I go out after her. Jenessa will follow me out, right?"

Callie shook her head again. "You go out with Roxanne and she'll chew you up," she said.

Mattie frowned impatiently. "I know that . . . but will Jenessa follow me out? Can we burn out Roxanne's kick if I hammer her early?"

"It could work, I suppose," said Callie as she grasped what Mattie was proposing. "If you act like a rabbit for Jenessa, Roxanne might go out too fast to cover you and Jenessa's used to the pattern. . . ." Callie's phone buzzed in her hand, interrupting her. She looked at it. Her folks had texted.

Jen's okay. We're on our way back.

Callie suddenly felt light-headed.

Mattie saw her expression change. "What's the word?"

"She's okay."

Jen entered the hotel room on a crutch, her dad holding the door for her while she navigated her way in. Doc showed up in the hallway and quietly began to talk to her mom.

"Howdy, everybody!" Jen half-shouted as she leaned on the crutch.

Anna and Hanna sprang off the nearest of the queen-size beds while the rest of the girls, some on the bed, Jenessa in the only chair, turned to face the door.

"Jen—" said Anna as she stopped short. Hanna plowed into the back of her, wiggled around, and also stopped. They both eyed the crutch.

Jen saw their looks and laughed. "Pretty cool, huh," she said. She waggled the tip in their direction, rocking unstably as she did. Hanna reached out and steadied her shoulder. "Don't need it but the doc—not Doc but the doc, the doctor said it was a good idea." She giggled.

Anna looked at her suspiciously. "She sounds loopy."

"Whacked," agreed her sister.

Callie looked at her dad. "They give her something?"

Her dad nodded as her mom and Doc entered the already crowded room. "He said it was going to hurt later so he gave her some painkillers," he said. He added, as an afterthought, "Jen's a bit of a lightweight."

The twins managed to steer Jen into the armchair in the room, shoving the little table aside to make room for her. Jen flopped back into the cushions, right leg extended out, and dropped the crutch.

"I'm thirsty," she said, and started to struggle back to her feet.

Mattie slid off the second bed in a supple motion. "You stay put," she said and slipped past the clutch of people by the door to get some water for Jen.

The boys, attracted by the commotion, wedged their way into the connecting door.

"She okay?" asked Will.

"I'm sure we're violating some sort of occupancy rule," said Doc. He turned to Hank and Sarah. "Okay if I tell them?"

Sarah nodded.

Jen shouted from the chair, "Just a big old bruise." Her words were slurring a bit and "bruise" sounded more like "brush." She took the water that Mattie held out. "Thanks." She looked at the roomful of people. "Doc said . . ." She looked at her coach and leaned her head to one side. "*Other* doc said nothing serious, gonna hurt, nothing broke." She giggled again. "He was wrong, doesn't hurt a bit."

"That must be some good stuff," said Jenessa.

"Yesh," said Jen. She looked around the room and put on a comic-looking scowl. "Why you all up . . . we got a race tomorrow."

Chapter 43

Callie woke to the sound of the shower running, the thrumming sound of the massage setting vibrating through the thin walls of the hotel. The twins were practicing synchronized snoring in the other bed. Next to her was an empty spot where Jen had crashed the night before, insisting even as she dropped off to sleep that she was going to race.

Callie struggled out of bed, head feeling mushy, and headed for the bathroom. She walked into a bank of steam. The ventilation fan whirred trying to keep up with the shower.

"Hey, it's me," said Callie as she walked in.

"Hey," replied Jen, sounding tired from behind the shower curtain. The water shut off and Jen's tanned arm snaked out to grab one of the oversized towels. She rattled the curtain back and hobbled out, towel wrapped around her. She amintained a firm grip on the towel rack. The outside of her right thigh was a mass of purple bruising where the truck bumper had clipped her.

"Holy crud," said Callie, staring at the contusion.

"Yeah, well," said Jcn. "Could have been a lot worse." She started to towel off her wet hair with practiced, vigorous effort. She finished, bending over to shake her hair loose before standing back up and flinging it back, wincing as she shifted her weight. She quickly smoothed her face. Callie watched her with concern.

"I need you to tape me up," said Jen. Her face expressed her determination.

Callie stared at Jen's leg. "Have you talked to Doc?"

"I specifically asked the doctor last night and he said that running wouldn't cause any more damage," she said, wrapping the towel around her body. She crossed her arms. "You can ask Mom."

"That wasn't all he said, I bet," said Callie.

"He also said it was going to hurt and I was an idiot," Jen said. She smiled suddenly, transforming her face. "He was half right. It hurts."

Callie stared doubtfully at the leg. "It can maybe control some swelling—they've got some wrapping techniques for it—but that's about all it's going to do."

"That will have to be good enough."

Doc strode into the dining area where the hotel hosted the continental breakfast and spotted them immediately, weaving among the tables to where the girls were sharing a couple of tables. Jen sat with her leg stretched out straight.

"Boys not here?" he asked.

Callie shook her head and said around a bite of syrupy waffle, "Not yet."

He peered at Jen. "How's the leg?"

"Hurts a bit," she admitted, "but I'll be running." She met his gaze with steady and confident eyes.

Doc gave a little shrug. "We'll see."

Jen started to object but Callie interrupted first. "I'll need some tape for her and Lily. Can I get the med bag after breakfast?"

323

Jen took Callie's cue and put her head down, focused on eating.

"Yeah," said Doc. "Everybody else doing okay?" His gaze sharpened on Mattie and Jenessa. Mattie had a huge plate of food in front of her and was steadily shoveling it in. Neither had looked up when he came to the table, and both bobbed their heads in answer to his question without looking at him. His eyes narrowed.

"We're okay," said Anna. Her voice was quiet and her face calm but Callie could see tension just below the surface.

Doc switched his attention to the twins.

"Ready to roll," said Hanna, staring at him as she took a sip of her orange juice. "Except for one thing."

"What?" said Doc.

"Breathe," said Anna.

"In," said Hanna.

"Out," finished Doc for the other twin, "I know." He looked at his watch. "I'm going to get the boys moving. Bus leaves in forty-five minutes." He looked around the tables before settling on the twins.

"Smart alecks," he said with a wry smile.

Lily frowned as her eyes tracked Mattie and Jenessa. Both girls were gesturing as they carried on a quiet conversation, their heads next to each other. Callie saw the look.

Callie stopped walking and turned to face the younger runner. "Leave it," she advised.

Lily looked at Callie in confusion and asked, "They were weird all night. What's going on?"

Callie watched as Mattie's right hand described a circling motion around her left as Jenessa nodded. She was pretty sure she could decode the gist of the conversation. "I think some people are about to get surprised."

They piled off the bus, carrying their gear bags and blankets, leaving their personal stuff on board. Doc checked the team in and picked up the race packet with their numbers and the course map, and together they went to the site they had set up the day before.

The morning was chill, but not cold, with some clouds floating eastward, high and bright over the course. There was barely any breeze to flutter the triangular pendants on the race ropes.

Most of the camps, arranged in parallel lines facing each other, were empty. The smaller schools raced first. Callie's race was literally the first of the day, and the bigger schools would not arrive until a couple of hours before their own race. By noon, all the spots would be teeming with nervous runners and the open spaces between would become filled with Frisbees and footballs as the guys burned off excess energy while they waited.

The kids staked out their spots under the canopy, the twins huddling together in a blanket. Mattie, swathed in several layers of clothing, wrapped an old sleeping bag around her, trying to stay warm. Jen paced, keeping her muscles loose. Under her sweats, she wore an intricate weave of tape on her right thigh that Callie had put on for her. Doc had checked the work and given his approval, though he was still skeptical that Jen would be able to race.

Hank and Sarah were the first parents to show up, closely followed by the parents of the twins. The area around their encampment gradually grew crowded with family and a few friends that had made the two-hour trip to watch the race.

Callie's parents stayed off to the side, talking quietly with Anna and Hanna's folks. Every few minutes, Sarah's worried eyes would drift to Jen's leg. Callie stopped watching them. She could feel their stress and steadied her breath. *In. Out.* She felt the tension flow out.

Jenessa was with her parents, more listening than talking, as her dad, looking more portly than usual in a red down jacket, spoke with urgency. Callie watched as Jenessa gave an abrupt shake of her head and walked away. Her father looked surprised.

Callie raised an eyebrow at Jenessa as she rejoined the team, climbing back under her own blanket.

"It's all good," Jenessa said.

"Time to warm up, ladies," said Doc.

Callie looked up at Lily. "How does that feel?"

Lily rotated her ankles and flexed her leg. "Good."

The rest of the team was getting up and shedding excess clothing. Doc led them out toward the start line before veering off the golf course and onto the nearby streets. The girls ran on the edge of the road, avoiding the influx of spectators headed for the course. They kept the pace down, not much more than a slow jog as their muscles warmed up and their breathing evened out.

Callie watched Jen but her younger sister, after the first minute of running, showed no signs that she was hurting. Doc was watching too, and seemed relieved.

"If you see someone flying away from you, don't be afraid to take a chance and go with them. Let them pull you," he said, part of the steady stream of advice that he was giving.

They looped back to the entrance, dodging more people as they went through the athletes' gate. Two minutes later, they arrived back at camp and Doc got the race packet with their numbers. He started handing them out and the girls pinned them to their uniforms, with a matching number affixed to their left hip.

The twins were winding bright pink pre-wrap into headbands to keep their bangs from hanging in their face. All the girls had their hair pulled back into ponytails, held in place with simple elastic hair bands.

Callie checked each of the girls for jewelry. None. Good. It was a disqualifier.

Jen was still pacing. The twins watched her, and Anna leaned over to say something to Hanna, who nodded in agreement. Jenessa had her eyes closed but Callie could see her eyes moving below the lids, visualizing the upcoming race, getting herself ready. Callie looked at Mattie, who met her eyes with a steady stare, the wildness sitting just below the surface, waiting. Lily just looked scared.

"Relax," Callie said to the freshman.

Lily gulped and nodded but her eyes were still jerking side to side and she was breathing too fast.

She jerked again when Doc spoke.

"Time to spike up, ladies."

Callie waited for the twins to clear, and then did an acceleration with Jen and Lily right beside her. Jen struggled for a second before finding her footing. They looped back to the start line as the other teams sent flares of runners out onto the course.

Doc was waiting for them when they arrived back at the start.

"Good luck, ladies," he said. He glanced down the line to where the Fairchild team was positioned. "I'll see you out on the course. Remember to stay close—"

An air horn bleated into the still air, interrupting him. Four minutes to race time, and time for Doc to leave the team. He offered a final "good luck" and left the starting area.

"Everybody ready?" asked Callie. A quiet chorus of yeses answered her. She leaned into Jen and said softly, "Just hang tight on me."

Jen glanced at her.

Two minutes to go. The referee started giving the runners directions, the same ones that they had heard all season long. He finished and, looking up and down the line of taut runners, turned to walk out to start the race.

"Time to race, ladies," Callie said under her breath to her team. Peering forward between the twins, she caught Jenessa reaching out and giving Mattie's hand a quick squeeze.

The referee put up his right arm.

"Set!"

The gun shattered the morning.

Chapter 44

As the gun sounded, Callie leaned into Anna's back, heart already racing, and felt Lily's hand in the small of her back. She watched while Jenessa and Mattie sprinted out, Mattie slightly in front and angling to the left for the crest of the first hill to set up for the first turn. It took a full precious second before Anna accelerated into the space left by the front two, and Callie followed her. On her left—where Jen could use Callie to shield her leg from contact from the other runners crushing away from the start line, all of them headed for the same spot on the hill—Jen grunted as she got under way.

Callie kept her hand out toward Anna until the twins picked up speed and started to pull away.

"Stay tight," she said to Jen as she took a slightly wider line to the top of the hill, avoiding the congestion as girls flowed to the left toward the rope line that kept the cheering spectators from pressing onto the course. Soon, they were running on the right edge of the pack with open ground at the foot of the hill in front of them.

Ahead, she could see the leader, a runner from a tiny town by the Canadian border, already with a sizable lead. Mattie led the next rank of runners, a group of about a dozen girls. Jenessa ran at the back of the pack. As she relaxed into race pace, Callie sneaked a glance to her left, picking out the Fairchild runners that she and Jen would be stalking. . . .

Doc watched, shoulders tight, as the race started and the team surged out. No stumbles. He watched carefully as the field spread, and saw Jenessa and Mattie rocket toward the front, efficiently clearing the pack. The twins were close behind.

He let loose a small sigh of relief as he watched Jen run with no apparent distress. He estimated the line that Callie was drawing and nodded. *Smart girl,* he thought, understanding that she was trading a small amount of distance for clean running room and protecting Jen at the same time.

He checked back to the rear of the field. Lily was doing fine, fighting her way through the crowd.

Doc looked back to the leaders and a quick frown crossed his face. The whole front pack was surging, opening up a ten-meter gap, trying to keep up with Mattie. . . .

Mattie crossed the top of the hill, a gradual downhill ahead of her that banked to the left. Behind her, she could hear the breathing of the other runners. She could feel the tightness across her chest from charging the hill and she backed off the pace slightly, just enough to ease the tightness as she focused on the leader. As she eased up, the noise of the pack closed in on her. She kept waiting to see a runner come up next to her.

Come on, she thought, *where the heck are you?*

Callie picked up the pace slightly as they hit the downhill. Ahead, some of the girls were struggling with the pace, going out too fast in the excitement. Anna and Hanna, loping with those long legs, were sweeping past an entire pack as they dialed into their race. They reached clear space and sped up, building on their gap as they chased the pack in front of them.

Callie did a quick check. She was breathing hard, but that was expected—she knew it would be worse later. Legs felt good, lively, shoulders and arms loose. That would change too, but so far so good.

Jen was sticking right next to her, the cadence of her steps in rhythm with Callie's. Once she gave a little grunt as they traversed a particularly uneven patch of turf. Callie glanced over but Jen was focused on the backs of the red-clad runners twenty yards in front of them, a slight furrow on her brow.

"Relax . . ." Callie said, using the push-out of air to vocalize.

Jen's shoulders dropped a bit and the frown went away as she bobbed her head once. . . .

Doc outran the mob of people leaving the start line. Mark and Nate trailed him as they dodged around the entrance to the gated community built facing the golf course. The girls were running along the backside of the houses now and the leader would be clearing the far edge in just a couple of minutes. Jenessa would be just behind her.

Doc looked at his watch—he started it out of habit when the gun fired—and commented to the boys, "We have about a minute."

They all looked up the course. Doc kept checking his watch every few seconds. The digits changed so slowly. . . .

Mattie saw her out of the corner of her eye, a flash of an arm, as she headed for a copse of trees. She increased her pace slightly again and heard the girl match her. They flashed through the trees and back into sunshine. She could feel the sweat building up above her eyes.

"Way to go, Mattie!"

Mark's voice carried down the course and she lifted her eyes from the ground briefly, seeing Doc and Nate and the boy genius at the left edge of the course, leaning into the rope. She heard Doc and Nate chime in, urging her on.

She caught a glimpse of a bright red singlet. While she had been looking at Doc, Roxanne had pulled up next to her on the right, breathing hard.

Gotcha, thought Mattie with grim satisfaction and buckled down, focusing on the turn ahead and setting up her line.

"Good job, Jenessa!" Doc shouted as his lead runner came by six seconds behind Mattie. "Pick it up and hang with Mattie." He clapped his hands. "Looking great . . ." She gave him a thumbs-up sign as she glided past.

He looked at his watch as Mattie reached the first mile marker at a dogleg in the course. "Too fast," he muttered as more cheering for the runners broke out farther down the course. He did the quick math in his head. Jenessa was on pace.

The twins had caught the pack in front of them and were efficiently moving through it. They were running with a small gap between them and, as Doc watched, they passed another runner, one on each side in an easy swerve out and around. The girl they passed, already struggling, deflated and Doc watched her slow. They took advantage of the gradual downhill to break free of the other runners and close onto the next one. They were right where they were supposed to be, perfectly positioned at the first mile.

Callie and Jen rolled into view. They were running in open space, the runners spread out. The coaches around Doc were shouting to their runners to *"go get that girl, that one, you can do it."* Next to him, Mark was cheering for the girls as they went by.

Jen had a small hitch in her stride. Doc saw it.

"I shouldn't have let her run," he said, the words nearly swallowed in the noise of the crowd.

"Good luck with that," came a deep voice from behind him with a snort.

Doc turned and saw that Hank Reardon was standing right behind him, regarding him with a wry expression. Doc nodded.

Callie cocked her head over, listening. She could hear the change in Jen's stride, the hitch that Doc saw.

Callie shot a look to her freshman sister. " 'Kay . . . ?"

"Yeah," Jen replied as she exhaled.

Callie could feel the burning starting in her chest, a deep fire as her lungs desperately pulled in air. The strain of breathing was making her tense her shoulders and she consciously relaxed them, flexing her hands as she did.

The cool air couldn't keep up with the heat she was generating, and her shirt was already soaking through with sweat. One of the girls up ahead was running with a black undershirt and looked like she was already overheated.

Callie leaned into the downhill without thinking about it, picking up speed and leaving Jen temporarily a step behind. Jen, imitating Callie, caught up. They rounded the hairpin, the finish line to their left, and headed out in the opposite direction toward the silence of the backside of the course where races were won or lost, far from the eyes of the crowds. Callie's stare flicked back and forth from the ground ahead to the Fairchild runners.

"Stay close," said Callie. She wasn't sure if she was talking to Jen or herself. . . .

Mattie hit the first set of rolling hills, a mile and a half from the start, a bit more to the finish, and charged them. Roxanne lagged up the hill and tried to take control of the pace and pass on the first downhill. Mattie stepped with her and Roxanne started to back off, the strain clear on her face.

Mattie shot her a look of contempt and Roxanne, anger filling her eyes, bore down, breathing hard.

Mattie knew that her face looked the same way but she kept hammering at the other girl. They circled around a building, some sort of maintenance building. The girl in front was out of sight, hidden by the next hill and some trees.

How the heck does she run that fast? thought Mattie, feeling her legs getting heavier. Her breath was coming in ragged gasps but Roxanne was suffering just as much. *Just a little longer. . . .*

Doc watched as Mattie and Roxanne battled for second place, their figures shrinking as they headed away. Jenessa, running strong, had worked her way to the front of her pack. She looked comfortable, working hard but right where she should be. Still, she was forty yards behind the other two as they disappeared behind the maintenance shed.

He watched as each of his runners made the same journey out and around the backside of the course, and he worried and he checked his watch.

Two long minutes later, he saw Roxanne lead Mattie onto the long straightaway that paralleled the fence that separated the golf course from the roadway. Doc shook his head. Even from here, he could see that Mattie's form was falling apart, arms and legs not quite in line and her head flopping side to side in small arcs with every step.

Jenessa popped into view, flowing smoothly over the ground. Doc peered at her and the gap to the group of runners behind her. With a start, he realized that Jenessa had closed nearly ten yards on Mattie and Roxanne.

He looked more closely at Roxanne. Mattie was falling apart faster but the Fairchild runner was having problems of her own.

Son of a gun, he thought. *It's a heck of a gamble.*

He spun to Mark. "Did you know about this?"

Mark threw up his hands, shaking his head. "Nope."

Nate just looked at the two of them, confused.

Jen's right foot landed in a divot, and she felt the jolt all the way up her ankle, through the knee, and into her badly bruised thigh. She stumbled slightly, delivering a small hip check to Callie before recovering. Callie just slid with the impact, absorbed it, steady as ever.

"Sorry . . ."

Callie glanced at her and nodded. "Keep . . . running . . ."

I'm trying, Big Sis, I'm trying, Jen thought, *but it hurts.* She locked onto Callie. Just stay with Callie until it's time to kick. That was the plan.

Mattie could feel the desperation building up along with the pain as she passed the two-mile mark by the first of the two ponds that lined this fairway. Roxanne was three strides in front now. Mattie could feel her muscles burning with lactic acid and knew that she was getting slower with every step, her legs getting heavy. She fought to keep her head from wobbling side to side, and she had lost control of her breathing. She tried to surge to catch Roxanne, press her again.

"I got this," said a soft voice over her left shoulder, shocking her. Mattie hadn't heard Jenessa coming.

Relief flooding through her body, she shot a look of thanks to Jenessa as her teammate flowed by.

She watched as Roxanne tried to accelerate away from Jenessa, pumping her arms, but Jenessa stuck with her, slowly reeling her in. Roxanne couldn't drop her.

She focused on her race as the other two girls curled off the turn on the second lake. One mile to go. She was in no-man's-land with nobody to run with. All she had to do was hang on.

Jen and Callie rounded the turn along the fairway, passing the first lake. Jen felt her thigh spasm, a quick flash as they turned slightly to the left. The pain was sharp and gone but it sparked doubt, a fear that grew and gnawed at her. Jen notched up the pace. The Fairchild runners had opened up a thirty-yard gap.

Callie, already breathing hard, stepped up with her. "Patience . . ." One word per gasp was all Callie could get out. ". . . Roller . . . coaster . . ."

Jenifer just grunted. She could feel the thigh spasm again and feel her stride shift from the smooth steady rhythm she had been trying to force to something akin to a flat tire.

Not now, she thought, *please not now.*

Callie felt the change in Jen's stride and heard her sister's breathing start to take on panicky overtones. They were somewhere between two miles and forever, and the fire in Callie's chest was burning hotter and hotter. The sweat was dripping into her eyes, burning them with the salt, and her throat was raw. Her legs still felt shockingly good and she felt a deep appreciation for the extra miles she had run.

A detached part of her mind was calculating distances and angles and the other runners. She factored in Jen's deteriorating condition and realized that Doc's plan was never going to work. Jen had all the guts in the world but she wasn't going to be able to kick on that leg.

She measured the distance to the Fairchild girls. Twenty-five yards. They had closed some.

They cleared the turn and Callie could see the course, a short straight, a turn, the hill where they would again hear the crowds cheering. In front of her at the end of the straight, the twins were chasing down the stragglers as runners continued to fade. Her eyes tracked around the path she would be taking and she saw Jenessa trailing Roxanne by a step. There was no sign of Mattie—she must be hidden by the trees.

Another quick calculation and she stepped up the pace a fraction, eyes locking in on the next set of runners. Jen went with her.

The race leader flashed past Doc as she started up the hill that led to the rolling hills the team nicknamed the roller coasters. The girl looked strong and in control. Doc felt a bit sorry for her. She deserved better competition. She would get it at the national meets.

He watched as Roxanne led Jenessa up, then back down the hill as the course turned back toward the finish. Mattie was a full thirty yards behind them. The twins peeled around the corner and attacked the bottom of the hill as Jenessa passed.

"Great job!" Doc shouted at her, and received another thumbs-up signal. She looked good, better than Roxanne. "Take her early," he shouted at her receding back but she didn't give any clue that she had heard.

Mattie was next, grimacing at the shouts from Nate and Mark. Each muscle in her arms and shoulders and legs stood out, overstressed as she kept running, focused on reaching the finish.

As she went past where he stood at the far point of the spectator zone, Doc made eye contact and, in a gentle voice that only she would hear, said, "Good girl."

Gratitude replaced pain in her eyes for a moment and then she was gone.

The twins flew by, flashing smiles as they did.

In the far distance, Doc saw Lily, running far into the back half of the race but still competing as she passed another runner.

Jenessa was on her way back from the second hairpin turn, racing across the roller coasters, side by side now with Roxanne. Jenessa powered around the verge of the green and opened a small gap on her rival as they headed for the last dip before the uphill that overlooked the finish line.

He was so focused on Jenessa that he almost missed Callie and Jen as they ran by. He looked at the misery on Jen's face and a sinking sensation filled his chest.

Jen started up the next shallow grade. The ups were easier on her thigh than the downs were. A bit more than a half mile to go, about four more minutes of pain. *Roger Bannister ran a mile in less time,* Jen thought randomly, distracting herself from her leg.

They approached the last hairpin, twenty yards in front of them, and Callie swung wide to go around a runner. Jen didn't recognize the uniform, had no idea where the girl was from.

She never heard the girl coming back around her. It was the same girl, unwilling to concede any ground. The girl bumped her, just the tiniest of nudges on her shoulder but that was enough to twist Jen's hips, punishing the banged-up thigh once more. The pain shot through the rest of her leg as it spasmed and buckled, driving her sideways. She stumbled, recovered from a near fall, and staggered as it seized again, and stumbled to a complete stop.

As soon as she saw her sister start to topple, Callie slowed, trying to turn back to check on Jen.

"KEEP RUNNING!" Jenifer shouted at Callie, bent over, holding her right leg, fingers splayed across the tape that Callie had put on that morning. The sisters' eyes locked.

"GO!" Jenifer screamed.

Doc was headed to the finish line when he heard Jen yelling. He skidded to a stop and started back when Hank Reardon waved him away.

"We've got her!" His voice carried over the cheering.

Doc nodded and turned to race back toward the finish. Jenessa and Roxanne were just climbing over the hill. Jenessa had a small lead and Doc watched as she kicked first, before she got off the hill, trying to gain some ground on Roxanne.

Jen watched her sister accelerate again but it was hopeless. Two seconds, maybe three, but the Fairchild girls hadn't slowed. They added another ten yards onto their lead, running with determination, closing on the point of no return, the final kick.

Jenifer saw Callie measure the distance to the other girls. Then Callie kicked from six hundred meters out. Shocked, Jen watched her sister attack on the downhill before the roller coasters, a full three hundred meters earlier than planned.

What's she doing . . . ? Jenifer thought, dismayed, and then realized that Callie wasn't going to quit. *Too far, way too far to kick . . .*

Jen set her jaw and started limping her way to the finish, keeping to the outside of the course to let the other runners get by.

"Get them, Sis!" she yelled.

Callie was already too far gone to hear.

Callie focused on the Fairchild runners. The look on Jen's face had scared her and the fear had sent a shot of adrenaline into her system. She barreled down one of the little rollers and saw that she had closed the gap again. The Fairchild girls were saving for their kick.

The heat in her chest started to change to constriction and she was starting to struggle to keep her lungs full enough.

She fixed her eyes on the red uniforms. She was gaining. *How long can you run without air?* she wondered.

Mattie reached the peak of the hill and looked down to the finish line. The flags on the course looked fuzzy but she could see the line.

She watched as Jenessa dueled with Roxanne. The Fairchild girl was not breaking. Mattie felt a touch of despair. It didn't work. She watched as Roxanne crept closer. It looked like she was right on Jenessa's shoulder with fifty yards left.

Doc was watching the same duel ten yards away from the digital timer, the numbers turning over inexorably. He waited, watching as they sprinted for the line. When they were fifty yards out, he shouted, "Now, Jenessa, everything you got!"

Jenessa lifted up, gained a foot of ground on Roxanne, and Roxanne cover the move, closing again on her shoulder.

The noise from the crowd was deafening as they cheered the girls. The winner, already sipping water, watched.

There was nothing more Doc could do, but he stood there, hands clenched, willing Jenessa on. He was shouting, his voice drowned out by the rest of the cheering crowd. Midway up the hill, he could see Mark and Nate and the rest of the boys urging the girls on.

With twenty yards left, Roxanne finally broke, a small fumble in her stride, then another.

Mattie got caught watching the finish and didn't realize that someone was going past her until they were already a step ahead.

Oh hell no! she thought and, using the last of her reserves, launched her own kick.

Callie caught the two Fairchild runners as they came off the loop around the green, blazing past in full stride. She could see the last hill in front of her and she focused on it. Her legs were starting to tighten up and her calves were threatening to cramp. Everything across her back was tense and her shoulders hurt. Her chest and jaw were masses of pain. With effort, she relaxed her jaw, but there was no relief for the pain in her chest. The fire was searing in her lungs and her heart was trying to pound its way through her rib cage.

Behind her, she heard the Fairchild girls accelerating, but she already had a five-step lead and they were trying to speed up on the uphill.

Callie tucked in her elbows and drove up the hill.

Doc saw Anna and Hanna blow over the top and head his way as Mattie crossed the finish line two steps ahead of the other runner. She staggered as she ground to a rough halt and dropped down to her knees.

The finish line workers, most of them experienced volunteers, helped her to her feet and moved her down the line, one at her elbow, until she was safely in the chute and in the right order. Another took her race tag as she moved in the narrowing line.

Doc turned to face the course in time to watch the twins kick. The two blondes glanced at each other two hundred yards out—and smiled as they opened up their long legs and closed on runners.

They passed four runners, including one from Fairchild, as they charged down the fairway, twin blond ponytails streaming out behind them. Thirty yards from the finish, they passed the last one and continued into the chute, Hanna a half step ahead of her sister.

Mattie was fighting her stomach, trying not to dry heave anymore, when a pair of shoes stepped into her range of vision.

"Here," said Jenessa, holding a cup of water down to Mattie and helping support her with a hand on Mattie's waist. Mattie looked up with gratitude before another paroxysm of heaves bent her completely over again.

Callie's legs relaxed as she cleared the last uphill and she started the descent to the finish. Just like last year, she could see the flags—brighter this year, and sharper in the clear air. Without thinking, she pushed her hips forward to fall down the hill faster.

She lost track of the other girls—something was wrong with her hearing. They had to be there but she couldn't tell how close so she focused on the clock. The numbers were clear and sharp but they made no sense and she discovered she didn't care.

The fire had spread. Not content in her chest, she could feel it moving into her muscles, the big ones like her quads and little ones that she didn't know existed until they joined the pain.

It was a downhill, she thought. *Flow like water. . . .*

Everything was so clear. She could see Doc at the finish line. He was shouting but he wasn't making any sounds. Mark was shouting at her, too, from farther up the course.

Her fingers were tingling and she tried to relax them, to put the effort into running faster.

She felt the other girl invading her bubble before she saw her. She didn't dare turn her head but it had to be one of the Fairchild runners, catching her on the way to the finish. Gradually, she saw her slipping into her vision on the left, the pumping arms first, then the head and torso.

The other girl's form was sloppy, Callie decided, and focused on her own form, running taller, lengthening the fire but getting a little more air in her lungs at the same time. As gradually as the girl came up, she drifted back.

Callie saw Mark sprinting parallel to her, dodging spectators, to get to the finish line. The crowds were still doing their soundless cheering and Callie saw some of them pointing behind her.

The grass seemed as smooth as the surface of a still lake. Seventy-five yards of it in front of the finish line.

As she got closer, the flags to either side faded as her focus narrowed to the line. Callie felt suspended in time, her body and mind in perfect union, both sharing the pain and driving her forward.

She saw the tape that they had put out at the finish line and knew that it was hers to break. She needed to be first to the tape and she lost sight of the finish except for the tape, almost glowing.

From the right side, she saw the next runner challenge her, sneaking up, trying to keep her from the tape. She willed herself forward but the other girl wouldn't go away.

Callie stared at the tape—*her tape,* she thought, fifteen yards away, as a blackness eased into her mind. First it swallowed the crowds. Then, the girl next to her disappeared as the darkness encroached—but not really. A part of Callie knew she was still there. Finally, it started on the tape, at either end, but Callie could still see the middle, the spot that she was going to break.

As it ate the tape, Callie leaned in with her chest, catching the tape, feeling it break underneath the pressure of her body and, as she did, she thought, *That's what it's like.*

She had a smile on her face as she hit the ground.

Chapter 45

The finish line erupted in pandemonium as Callie skidded across the grass and the Fairchild runner sprinted into the chute past her.

"A tie!" called the nearest volunteer, and the crowd buzzed. Ties were almost unheard of, though the rules were specific; if the first five runners tied, you added in the sixth runner.

Doc knew all this and instinctively looked up the course. Fairchild already had six runners in and number seven was nearly at the line. Callie had been trying to hold off— No, Doc corrected himself. Callie had been intent on winning and she had needed to beat both the number four and five runners.

Callie had beaten one cleanly but the second one had caught her at the line.

Lily appeared at the top of the hill and started her way down to finish out her race, the team's number-six runner this year. A few seconds later, Jen appeared, hobbling while her dad walked next to her in the spectator zone.

"That's crap!" said Mark. "Callie won that." He sounded defensive. "She leaned in at the finish, just like she's done it a thousand times. The other girl tried to get a shoulder in but Callie leaned." He looked over to the awards area, anger plain.

The Fairchild runners were beginning a tentative celebration on the news it was a tie, though their coach was quietly chastising them. Doc could read the expressions but he didn't know if the other coach was cautioning the kids against a premature victory dance—or for letting it get this close.

Doc turned to Mark and said, "Maybe, maybe not. But you and the other boys have a race to run, too."

"But it's still—"

"You need to get your team together and start getting warmed up," Doc said. His stare was piercing, eyes glowing as they reflected the blue skies and bright sun. "I can guarantee you this won't be over before your race."

Mark looked stubborn and got ready to protest more.

"Callie did her part," Doc said to him. "It's time for you to do yours."

Mark met Doc's eyes and nodded. "We'll do that," he said. He gave out a sharp whistle to signal the other boys. He turned back before he left. "It wasn't a tie."

Doc hoped he was right.

The camera would tell.

It took almost three hours to get the results.

The team milled about as rumors circulated. It was a tie, the Fairchild girl won, the camera was inconclusive. The longer the race officials put off the announcements, the more time the kids had to invent new scenarios, each a bit more ludicrous than the previous.

The only calm one was Callie, though it had taken the whole team to convince her that there wasn't a tape at the finish line.

"But I saw it," insisted Callie. "Clear as day."

"You were the only one that did," said Anna.

"I know the EMTs checked you out," said Hanna, "but you

sure you didn't hit your head?"

"Hush, speedy," said Anna. "She's fine—plus she saw it before the big crash."

"I said I was sorry!" Hanna glared at her sister as Callie glanced down at the grass stain on the front of her shirt.

"I can't believe you let your little sister beat you," Callie teased.

"Hey, Hanna," hollered Jen from the other side of the tent where she was lying with a large bag of ice pressed against her leg, "you don't have to take that from big sisters. Trust me, I know. Give 'em half a chance and they get awfully bossy."

Callie threw a towel at her.

The individual awards were first and held no surprises. Jenessa had placed second overall while Mattie had held on for fourth overall. It was the first time in school history that Cloverland had two girls on the podium at the same time.

The announcer rattled through the first series of finishers, eighth place to fifth, almost in a single breath while the spectators shifted around, anxious for the real winner. A spark of anger lit in Callie at the disrespect shown to the other teams.

The fourth-place team was announced, a team from western Washington, hurried onto the stand and back off. Likewise for the third-place team from Spokane. That left them and Fairchild. Callie found herself holding her breath. It made her chest hurt again so she let it out and steadied herself. In. Out.

She smiled and nudged Anna with an elbow. "In. Out."

Anna laughed. "Yeah, harder than it sounds."

After a pause, the announcer started to talk again, his voice tinny from the microphone.

"Ladies and gentlemen, this was the closest finish we have ever had here at the State Championship meet. We would like to assure all the participating teams that we have done everything in our power to determine the champion. We apologize for the delay.

"We have had five separate judges review the photographic evidence for the proper placement of the fifth runner for Cloverland High School and the fifth and sixth runners for Fairchild Academy.

"Also, because a single point separates these two teams, we have reviewed the placement of each runner up to and including those finishers, to ensure that each gets correctly assigned.

"A final word from—"

The announcer was interrupted by a brash voice from the crowd, "All right, already!"

The speakers emitted a sound suspiciously like "harrumph" and the announcer began again.

"A *final* word from the athletic association and the sponsors of the race. This was a tremendous race and we would like to point out that, with results this close, we have very nearly co-champions. Neither team should be disappointed in their performance this morning."

Callie sighed. She didn't want to be a co-champion.

Mark saw the expression on her face. "Hang in there. You got this," he said with a wink. "I was there even if you weren't."

"In second place, with a total score of twenty-eight points . . ." The announcer paused and Callie forgot all about "in, out"—"in second place, Fairchild Academy—"

Whatever else the announcer said about the second-place team was drowned out by the cheers that exploded around Callie. Mark, babbling excitedly, picked Callie up.

"I told you," he shouted as he spun her.

Epilogue

Callie got up quietly and dressed quickly in the chill air. The sun was just starting to break over the horizon, and a fast peek out the window at the new snow told her that she should put on some warmer gear.

Sophie heard her stealthy movements and wandered in, cocking her head at her, the tail slowly picking up speed.

Callie reached for her gloves on top of the dresser next to the picture from State. The photo, signed around the edges by the whole team, showed them up on the podium. Jen was standing on the bottom platform, her leg wrapped in ice, Doc next to her, propping her up. The rest of the team followed, stair-stepping up the blocks on alternating sides. They had worn team warm-ups and their best smiles.

Callie had tried to get them in the order that they finished, but the other girls had pushed her until she stood on the top platform, the number one blazoned below her. Below the team, a sign read STATE CHAMPIONS.

The school had held a rally to celebrate and the local paper had run an article on them, mostly focusing on Jenessa and Mattie and the duel with Roxanne. Jen got a little write-up as the girl that wouldn't quit and finished the race on one leg. Callie and the twins had been mentioned briefly in the third paragraph. It was better than nothing.

She grinned at Sophie. "Ready?" She grabbed the leash and headed out the door.

Callie laughed at Sophie cavorting in the snow before she eased into her morning run. Sophie calmed down and settled into a trot next to her as they left paw and foot prints in the virgin snow along the trail, joyful tracks glittering in the glow of the dawn.

<u>Thank you . . .</u>

. . . for buying *Finishing Kick*. I hope that you enjoyed reading it. Writers don't say that often enough.

<u>And another thank you . . .</u>

In agreement with my publishers—I had to arm wrestle them into agreeing, but agree they did—10 percent of the proceeds from *Finishing Kick* will be donated to high school cross-country teams. To see details, visit <u>www.paulduffau.com/sharing</u>

Run gently, friends.

Paul Duffau

A high-octane adventure on a wild Montana mountain as one girl finds herself racing for her life against a malignant fire.

It should have been the highlight of the summer, a training camp for elite runners in the mountains of Montana. Coached by her father, and frustrated by his efforts to hold her back, Becca Hawthorne dreams of competing in the Olympics. She earned her chance to test herself against the best runners in the Pacific Northwest. But now she faces a tougher opponent than even the fastest girl.

An action-filled roller coaster ride that keeps you turning the pages as the fire creeps closer.

About the Author

Paul Duffau lives in Eastern Washington, along the Snake River. An avid runner and former ultramarathoner, his running novels and stories touch on the human side of this most individualistic event.

He also writes crime fiction, humorous short stories, and, with his wife, stories benefiting the animal welfare community.

For even more information, and to follow current projects, he can be found at http://paulduffau.com

Made in the USA
Lexington, KY
23 June 2014